All the Days of Our Lives

ANNIE MURRAY was born in Berkshire and read English at St John's College, Oxford. Her first 'Birmingham' novel, *Birmingham Rose*, hit *The Times* bestseller list when it was published in 1995. She has subsequently written fourteen other successful novels. Annie Murray has four children and lives in Reading. You can visit her website at www.anniemurray.co.uk.

ALSO BY ANNIE MURRAY

Birmingham Rose

Birmingham Friends

Birmingham Blitz

Orphan of Angel Street

The Narrowboat Girl

Poppy Day

Chocolate Girls

Water Gypsies

Miss Purdy's Class

Family of Women

Where Earth Meets Sky

The Bells of Bournville Green

A Hopscotch Summer

Soldier Girl

My Daughter, My Mother

The Women of Lilac Street

Meet Me Under the Clock

War Babies

ANNIE MURRAY

*All the Days of
Our Lives*

PAN BOOKS

First published in Great Britain 2011 by Macmillan

This edition published 2011 by Pan Books
an imprint of Pan Macmillan
20 New Wharf Road, London N1 9RR
Associated companies throughout the world
www.panmacmillan.com

ISBN 978-0-330-45821-4

7 9 8 6

A CIP catalogue record for this book is available from
the British Library.

Typeset by SetSystems Ltd, Saffron Walden, Essex
Printed in the UK by CPI Group (UK) Ltd, Croydon, CR0 4YY

Visit **www.panmacmillan.com** to read more about all our books
and to buy them. You will also find features, author interviews and
news of any author events, and you can sign up for e-newsletters
so that you're always first to hear about our new releases.

For Liz Downer,

with thanks for her friendship

Acknowledgements

I drew on a great many sources in preparing this story, but particular thanks are owed to the following:

The Birmingham History Forum, and especially to the Heartlands Local History Society for their welcome and help.

Jane Freebairn at the WRAC Association.

A number of Poles have told me their stories over the years and some, I know, would prefer not to be named. But my particular thanks go to Lubek and Ewa Wruszczak for their friendship and generous gift of their time.

The website describing many of the Polish Resettlement Camps in the UK (www.polishresettlementcampsintheuk.co.uk) was very helpful, as were a number of excellent books, especially *Heart of Europe: A Short History of Poland* by Norman Davies, *Keeping the Faith: The Polish Community in Britain* by Tim Smith and Michelle Winslow, and *Worlds Apart* by Henry Pavlovich.

1945

'Mom, Mom!' Robbie threw himself, sobbing, against his mother's legs. 'Wanna come with you!'

'Oh, *Robbie*.' Em, in the middle of buttoning up her cardigan, bent over, upset and exasperated. Her son's head was clamped to her thighs and she stroked his hair, hating to see him cry. 'Don't do this, babby. Come on, let go now. Mommy's got to go out for a bit, that's all.'

Her mother, Cynthia, swooped down. 'Robbie, stop that now.' She managed to wrestle him up into her arms. 'That's right, come to Nanna. Your mom's not going to be out for long. It's just like when she goes to work. You've got to stop going on like this. That's it – let's sit you at the table and I'll get you some nice bread and a scrape of jam, if there's any left!'

'Thanks, Mom.' Em picked up her bag. Though a mother herself, she still looked young enough to be a schoolgirl. 'I dunno what's come over him.'

'Oh, he'll grow out of it. But I've told you, haven't I? You need to be firmer with him.' She stood behind Robbie, who was still grizzling, and gave Em one of her looks. 'You sure you want to go over there? Seems a bit morbid to me.'

Em hesitated. 'I've told Mr Perry I'm going – he gave

me a couple of hours off. And I know Bert was . . . well, everyone knows how horrible he was, but I'm going for Molly. I just feel I should.'

Cynthia nodded. 'I s'pose you're right, love. And however vile he is – was – you have to feel some pity for the lad, with that family behind him.'

On her way out, Em glanced in the mirror by the front door and patted her straight, mousy hair. She almost despaired of keeping anything in the way of a curl or wave in it for long. The air in the street felt warmer than it had in the house, big white clouds sailing across the summer sky.

Em smiled to herself for a second, then adjusted her face. You're going to a hanging, she rebuked herself. Blimey, a *hanging*! Bert Fox, Molly's younger brother, whom Em had known all his life, was today due to be hanged by the neck until he was dead. Eight in the morning was the hangman's hour, and it was already a quarter past. Walking to the bus stop, she realized with a shudder that Bert must have met his end – deep in the bowels of the prison somewhere, hidden from the eyes of the crowd outside – while she was eating the last of her breakfast and getting her cardigan on. The finality of it seemed terrible.

She climbed onto the crowded bus and paid her fare in a daze. Why *was* she going, like a tripper to a seaside attraction, to see the notice of the hanging on the doors of the prison? Bert had been a nasty, rat-faced little boy living in a yard along the street, who had grown into a sadistic, criminal man. All through the war he'd done nothing for the country but cheat and steal, with his band of mates, running all sorts of black-market rackets while evading the call-up. But it wasn't that he'd been arrested for. The police only caught up with him after his latest hard-faced girlfriend had been found floating in the murky waters of the Cut – the Birmingham and Warwick Canal. She'd been strangled, and all evidence pointed to Bert Fox, then of Lupin Street, Vauxhall.

But Bert was the brother of one of Em's best friends, Molly. And Molly, still in Belgium with her ack-ack battery, was not in a position to be present even if she'd wanted to be, which Em doubted. It felt wrong that no one should be there. Bert and Molly had had a cruel, squalid childhood, and Bert had at least tried to keep their drunken mother, Iris Fox, in some sort of comfort out of his criminal profits.

As she left the bus and its perspiring passengers, Em saw that going to the prison was a way of trying to tie parts of her life together when everything felt as if it was scattered apart. Molly was so far away, but most of all, Em was worried about her own husband Norm. The war in Europe may have been over, there was a new Prime Minister, Mr Attlee, a fresh start, but who knew how long the war in the East might go on? Em was horrified by the thought that Norm might be re-posted. He had miraculously survived so far – that was how Em felt – but if he was sent out east, surely his luck would run out? She ached for him to be home, to see their three-year-old son whom he'd never yet set eyes on, and to be a family properly, instead of all this waiting. Then she could stop feeling so anxious all the time. If going to pay her respects to Bert, however much he deserved what he'd got, could make things feel more right, then that's what she'd do.

Walking across Cathedral Square to the next bus stop, she saw VOTE LABOUR flyers left over from the election, blown against the edge of the path. And she had voted Labour, though it did seem hard on old

3

Winnie. Em didn't dwell on politics much, but voting Labour seemed to mean that things would be fairer.

Shielding her eyes, she looked up at the grand edifice of St Philip's Cathedral and thought that one day she must go inside and look. She had never been in there in all her life.

'Oops – careful! You want to look where you're going!'

The woman scolded, but did not really seem very cross, more amused. Em was aware of a green suit, remarkably vivid in these drab days, on a slender figure, neat black court shoes and dark hair taken up into a stylish pleat.

'Oh – sorry!' Em said, then looked more closely. '*Katie?* Katie O'Neill?'

Even after all this time, and in these smart clothes, the long, pale face of the girl who had once been her best friend was immediately familiar. She saw Katie recognize her and a confusion of emotions flicker across her face, first amusement fading in her eyes, then what seemed like fear, and finally a wary politeness.

'I remember – you're Emma Brown, aren't you? You haven't changed a bit.'

Em thought back to Cromwell Street School, where she, Katie and Molly had been classmates. She and Katie had been top of the class and best friends, playing and giggling their way through life – until Em's family had run into troubles. After Cynthia had had Violet, Em's youngest sister, she'd fallen into a depression and had to be taken into the asylum. Katie had turned against Em and had been unkind and spiteful, refusing to be friends any more, in a way that had hurt Em dreadfully at the time. Then, within about two years, Katie and her mother had disappeared from the area and Katie didn't attend the school any longer.

These painful memories lay between them now, but Em wanted to forget the past; it seemed petty to dwell on things that happened when you were so young.

'How's your family?' Katie asked politely. Em noticed that she spoke very nicely, with hardly a trace of an accent.

'They're all very well, thanks,' Em said. She felt rather scruffy beside Katie, in her old frock and scuffed white shoes. 'And yours?'

'Yes, thanks. They are too.'

Another memory got in the way. Last year – it seemed another life, with the war still on. That was it, January 1944, that cold night, she knew she had seen Katie. That time Katie had almost run into her, rounding a corner not far from home. Em remembered it very clearly because she had seen such a look of wariness and desperation in Katie's eyes as she hurried past, swathed in a big coat. And Em was sure she had not been mistaken in noticing that Katie had been cradling a tiny infant in her arms. But she could hardly ask her about that now.

'That's good,' Em said. 'Well, our mom's much better these days.' She found herself rattling out information in the hope that Katie might offer some back. 'She's very well, and she's such a help to me because I've got a little boy, Robbie, he's three and his dad's away in the army. And our Sid – d'you remember him? He's about to get married to his girl, Connie – they've been courting a good while.'

She saw Katie arrange her face in a pleasant, polite expression. She'd grown into a looker, Em thought. Her face was slender, pleasing in shape, eyes still that pretty sea-blue. While not unfriendly, it was clear she was not going to give anything away about herself.

'Are you off to work?' Em asked.

'Yes.' Katie made a gesture in front of her with her hand, but didn't volunteer any more information. Perhaps her mom had made that suit, Em thought. They'd never seen much of Mrs O'Neill, who'd kept herself to herself, but hadn't there been some talk of her being a tailoress? 'Do you work in town too?'

'Oh no!' Em said. Again she found herself talking fast out of nerves. 'No, the thing is, I'm going up to the nick – it's . . . d'you remember Molly Fox, from over in the yard – and from Cromwell Street?'

A disgusted downturn of Katie's mouth indicated that she did. She smoothed her skirt as if wiping away specks of dirt. 'Oh my goodness, her. What a family!'

Em choked back the desire to snap: *Well, she was a better friend than you ever were, you with your spiteful, stuck-up ways!*

'They're hanging her brother today.' It came out abruptly and she kept her eyes on Katie's face, watching the shock register.

'No! I'd heard about it, but I hadn't made the connection – that brother, what was he called?'

'Albert. Bert.' Before she could ask, Em added, 'He strangled his girlfriend.'

Katie shuddered. 'They were always going to come to a bad end. Disgusting, the whole lot of them.'

'In fact Molly's doing very well,' Em said defiantly. 'She's in the army, in ack-ack – in Belgium. And they've promoted her to Lance Corporal. You'd be surprised if you saw her now.'

Katie raised her eyebrows. 'Goodness! Well, there's room for all sorts in the army, I s'pose.'

They both fell silent.

'Well,' Em said, hurt all over again. 'I'd better get on.'

To her surprise, Katie then gave a genuine smile, which lit up her face. This was more like the old Katie that Em remembered. 'It was nice to see you, Em. I'm glad everything's going all right for you.'

Em found herself smiling back, remembering what fun Katie had been at times. She longed for them to sit down somewhere, with an afternoon to while away with cups of tea, and tell each other everything about their lives. But she could see that wasn't going to happen.

'Thanks,' she said, surprised to find a sudden lump in her throat. 'Bye then. Don't make yourself late for work.'

She watched as Katie walked away, seeming so familiar, yet with a closed air of mystery about her. What had happened to her in all this time? Em saw, sadly, that she barely knew Katie O'Neill at all.

1931–1944

I

KATIE

One

1931

Katie crept up to the front door, biting her lower lip as she unfastened the latch, praying that the door wouldn't creak and give her away. She clicked it shut and stood behind it, screwing her eyes tightly shut. Please don't let Mother have heard her come in! If only she could have a few minutes – all she wanted to do was run up to her room, bury her face in her pillow after what she had just done, after what Mother had *made* her do.

But of course her mother's ears were sharp as a cat's.

'Katie, is that you down there?'

'Yes,' she called faintly. Sometimes it felt as if Mother knew everything that was going on in her head.

'Come up here – now, please. You've kept me waiting.'

Katie climbed the two flights of stairs, the first flight covered in brown linoleum, the attic stairs just bare boards. Her white ankle socks were the only bright thing in the gloom, left, right, left, right, her long black plaits swinging as she climbed, past the two rotten treads that groaned when you stepped on them. She felt like groaning too.

Her mother, Mrs Vera O'Neill, turned as she reached the attic, taking her brass thimble from her finger. Vera had been sitting working in the remaining light from the window. As she swivelled round, her face was in shadow so that Katie could only make out her outline. This made her even more forbidding than usual, the ramrod-straight back, the well-built body, simply but elegantly clad, her thick, golden brown hair swept up and piled on her head in the same style her own mother might have worn. There was nothing modern about Vera O'Neill. Katie could just see the gleam of pins that she had pushed for safekeeping through the collar of her green cardigan. On the work table behind her could be seen the black Singer machine, the glint of scissors, reels of thread and the length of grey serge on which she was working.

'And did you do as I asked?' Even though she couldn't see her mother's face, Katie knew it wore that look which always made her feel bad and guilty. How could she do anything to displease Mother, whose life was made up of Grief and Suffering? Vera's voice was smooth and well spoken, the Birmingham accent almost completely schooled out of her long ago, in a private establishment in Edgbaston. However much she had been reduced to living in poverty, Vera O'Neill made it clear with every ounce of her that this was not where she had started off in life, nor did she belong here.

'Yes,' Katie said again. She stood with her hands clasped in front of her, feet neatly together, as Mother – woe betide her if she ever called her Mom – liked her to do. Vera was like a puppet master: she liked to be in control.

'Good girl. I hope you made yourself quite plain. And you keep away from Emma Brown at school. I don't want you associating with people like that.'

'But,' Katie dared protest, 'isn't Mrs Brown just a bit poorly, a bit like Uncle Patrick is a bit poorly sometimes? Won't she get better?' *And she's my friend*, she wanted to cry.

Her mother seemed to swell in the gloom so that Katie would have taken a step backwards, had she dared. Vera O'Neill leaned forward.

'Now listen to me,' she hissed. 'You do not speak about your uncle and that Mrs Brown in the same breath, d'you hear? You're talking about your father's brother – it's not the same thing at all! Uncle Patrick has a troubled nature, it's true, but he's of sound mind and don't you ever, *ever* tell anyone otherwise. He's never been sent to the asylum, has he?' She sat back again, steely and imposing. 'Anyone who gets sent to the asylum is a different kettle of fish altogether, and they don't come out again in a hurry. We don't want anything else to do with people like that, do you understand?'

Katie nodded. Their superiority over everyone around had been drummed into her.

'Good.' Her mother's tone lightened for a moment. 'Now, you said you've found a new friend at school to play with – is it Lily?'

'Lily Davies. She's . . .' She's all right, Katie wanted to say. Not as much fun as Em, though. Sometimes she thought her mother didn't really want her to have friends at all – she wanted her all to herself, at her beck and call. 'Yes, she's nice.'

'And she sounds as if she comes from a good family – for round here anyway. There, so that's all settled. I know it seems harsh, dear, but it does count, who you associate with. It forms your character. We shan't be here forever – as soon as we can, we'll move somewhere much better. You'll thank me in the end, I promise you.'

Katie nodded, trying to swallow down her tears. She couldn't keep from her mind the mucky state of the Browns' house, and of Em herself. And the wretched sight of Em's face when Katie had handed over the cruel verdict: 'Mom says she doesn't want me having anything to do with you . . . She says it ain't right (why had she said "ain't", if not to defy her mother!) the way she's gone and left you. She says your mom's not right in the head . . . that I'm not to be friends with you.'

Worse even than the cruel words, the hurt they painted on Em's face, was the glimmer of enjoyment that Katie knew she'd had in saying them. In those moments she'd felt high above Em. *We're better than you* . . . And now she was sorry and she hated herself for it.

In a thick voice, she said, 'It ain't Em's fault, ar it?'

'I *beg* your pardon?' her mother said ominously.

'It's not,' she corrected. 'It's not Em's fault.'

'No, it's not,' Vera O'Neill agreed. 'Not directly. But what's bred in the bone comes out in the flesh. She'll be tarred with the same brush in the end. You keep away from them, do you hear? Now – I need to finish this before the light goes. As you know, I have to work very hard to keep us. Now off you go.' And she turned, bending her elegant head back over her work table.

Freed at last, Katie hurried down to the little room she shared with her mother and flung herself face down on her bed.

'See,' she muttered, as if Em was in front of her. 'Mom says your mom's a loony – that's why I had to do it. A mad, stinking loony, so there!' And then she burst into tears.

Kenilworth Street, in an old district just to the north-east of the centre of Birmingham, had only been their home for just over a year. Before that Katie had been to St Joseph's Roman Catholic School, near where they had lived off Thimble Mill Lane, about a mile away. So far as Katie was concerned, things had been happy enough there. She'd made friends and done well. But her mother had suddenly announced that they were moving, and before the school year was even finished she had been snatched away and landed up in Kenilworth Road, in a new class at an ordinary council school where there were no crucifixes or statues.

'Your uncle has found us a more suitable house,' her mother told her. 'We need to leave immediately.'

It was true that the house had an attic room, unlike the last one they'd been living in, but otherwise it didn't seem much better. To Vera's shame, it still backed onto a house that faced into a yard, which meant walking round and sharing the communal toilets. Vera, who hadn't seen the house before they moved, was furious.

'I told you – I want a house with its own privy!' she ranted at Uncle Patrick. 'How could you? You know how I feel about having to associate in this horribly intimate way!'

'I'm sorry, Vera,' Patrick said, in his usual gentle, sagging way. 'But it is a better house than before – there's a room for you to work in, and the rent's not much more, either.'

'Well, I suppose we'll just have to put up with it – for now,' Vera snapped.

17

Katie, then aged seven, didn't question anything. Her mother was not someone to argue with, and it just seemed the way things were. When she asked about seeing her friends from St Joseph's, since they weren't an impossible distance away, Vera said sharply, 'There's no need to keep up with those people. You'll soon make new friends. And pray to God we shan't be here long in any case.'

Vera O'Neill was always keen to remind Katie that she hadn't spent all of her eight years in such a poor place.

'When your father was still alive we lived in a much better neighbourhood,' she would say. The time *before* – that is, before her father, Michael O'Neill, contracted TB and died, when she was not yet two and a half years old – was always spoken of as a lost golden time, like the time in the Garden of Eden, before anyone had come across any talking snakes or apples. It sounded very nice to Katie. She had only the vaguest memories of her father, but they were good ones, warm ones of being held, and his death felt like the gateway into loneliness.

But for her now, this was home: the constant whiff of the gas works at Windsor Street, the whistle of trains going in and out of the shunting yard, the great chimneys of the power station looming behind the long skeins of sooty brick houses and the equally sooty brick edifice of Cromwell Street School. And going to school – because she lived at number six and the Browns lived at number eighteen – had always meant calling for Em on the way. But not any more.

Two

She woke the next morning from a broken night's sleep and a dream of seeing Em at the Browns' green front door, of them both smiling and linking hands and everything being all right. She woke with a terrible ache in her chest.

And now she was going to have to walk past Em's door on the way to school, without knocking for her.

But by the time she had dressed and tried to swallow down the porridge that her mother insisted on her having, she had worked herself up into a different mood. She was full of confusion – but she had to obey Mother. So she put on all her pride. Wasn't it true that Em's family was a bit rough? Some of the things her brother Sid came out with! And Bob, her dad there with his stubbly cheeks, coming home all covered in coal dust from the power station! But Katie ached to have a father, like all those other children who waited for them outside the pubs in ragged shorts and with grubby knees, knowing there was a dad in there who, in the end, would come out to them. And it had been lovely seeing Em's baby sister Violet – Katie had felt very jealous. If only she had a baby sister to play with! And a house with other brothers and sisters, and all sorts going on. But then, as Mother had pointed out, some people round here bred like rabbits, having all these children they couldn't afford to feed. Maybe she and

Em shouldn't have been friends after all, she told herself. It had only been because there was nobody better. Now Lily Davies had come along – and she only had one older sister – Katie could have a friend who was more like her.

She set out along Kenilworth Street in the chilly morning with her head held high. As she approached the Browns' house she saw that the lady across the road, Jenny Button, who ran her little bakery from her front room, was out cleaning her step. Jenny was a very corpulent lady and knelt down with a grunt, took her scrubbing brush from her pail of water and called out, 'Morning, bab!'

'Good morning!' Katie called softly, not wanting her voice to carry as far as Em's house. She kept facing away from number eighteen, her whole body tingling with dread in case the door opened and Em should come out on the way to school.

But Em did not come out. Em had first stopped coming to Girls' Life Brigade, which they'd done together before, and lately she'd been absent from school a lot. When Katie had called for her, Em would say miserably, 'I'm stopping at home today.'

As she passed by, out of the corner of her eye Katie saw Molly Fox come out of the entry to the yard near Jenny Button's shop. She could tell it was Molly from her thick, blonde hair. The Foxes lived on one of the back yards, where five or six jerry-built houses would be constructed facing inwards, sharing three or four toilets at the end, a communal wash-house with a copper and a mangle for laundry and usually a stinking pile of ash and refuse. Molly's house was not that different from the one Katie was living in, which had one room and a scullery downstairs, two small rooms on the first floor and an attic. But while the O'Neills' house faced the street and backed onto another house, the Foxes' was built hard up against the wall of a factory. And like the other houses in that particular yard, it was in a wretched condition.

Katie saw Molly hesitate on spotting her, and she didn't call out to ask if she could walk with her. Molly shrank back until Katie had gone right past. Katie gave a smirk. She knew Molly was frightened of her, of her popularity and her sharp tongue. It made her feel powerful, making Molly cringe. She knew Em thought her rather unkind to Molly. Em was softer-hearted, even though she found Molly annoying as well.

Sitting in the classroom at the little double desk with its attached seat that she had used to share with Em, Katie sat in dread for the first few minutes of seeing Em come in through the door.

A couple of weeks ago, when Em had been absent a number of times, Miss Lineham had tutted and said, 'Again! This is too much. Now – Lily Davies!' Lily, as the new girl, had been put in the empty seat alongside Molly Fox. She had kept complaining to Katie about the smell. Molly always had a powerful reek of urine about her. 'Lily – come and sit next to Katie O'Neill – quickly, please.'

Katie saw Molly controlling her face so as not to show how much she minded. She always seemed to end up on her own, but she really was dreadfully smelly – even the teachers noticed. And Miss Lineham wasn't known for her kindness. Though quite young, she was harsh and spiteful.

Now Lily had taken over Em's place, it was Em who had to sit next to Molly, if she ever turned up. Seeing her empty seat, Katie remembered with a sudden pang all their games with Ella and Princess Lucy. Em had a rag doll, Princess Lucy, with patched pink cheeks and yellow wool hair and her eyelashes stitched on. Katie's doll, Ella, had a white china face with tinted cheeks and a rather flat cloth body. They had had hours of fun with them. Even Princess Lucy and Ella couldn't be friends now! The thought brought tears to Katie's eyes, which she quickly wiped away so that Lily didn't see and ask what was wrong.

Miss Lineham called the register. Once again, Em was absent.

It was a great relief that Em wasn't at school that particular day. Katie found Lily rather dull in comparison, but she was eager enough to be bossed around, which Katie found flattering, and she didn't have to spend the day trying to keep out of Em's way, or sit next to her and see how unhappy she was. Em had looked so pale lately and, when she did come to school, Miss Lineham had caned her for not paying attention. Em never got the cane as a rule and it had come as a terrible shock.

Katie didn't really understand what was going on in the Browns' house even now. First there was the baby – Em's mom had given birth to the youngest in the family, Violet – then Em had gone all distant and subdued. She no longer looked clean and nice, like she used to. Then she more or less disappeared from school, and now there was this talk about Mrs Brown going to the asylum. Katie tried to shrug it all off. She was not to know or have anything to do with people like the Browns, Mother said. And she always had to do what Mother said.

*

Over the following weeks Katie lived in dread of running into Em. To her relief, Em was still staying off school a lot. But one evening, when Katie was playing jackstones out on the street with some other girls from school, Em came out of the house. Katie lowered her head immediately, pretending she hadn't seen her.

'Oi, Em! You coming out to play?' one of them called. There was no reply at first, so the girl tried again. 'Em?'

'Can't – I got to go somewhere.'

Katie kept her head down, hearing Em's feet hurrying past. She hoped Em hadn't seen her there in the group. She felt so ashamed, and so unsure what to think. Should she trust her mother's version of things or her own – that Em was her friend? But it was too late now anyway.

But as winter set in, one day Em started coming back to school. One bright, crisp day Katie nearly ran into her going through the school gate. Her heart started thudding with panic. This was so horrible! If only Em would go away, just leave the school so that Katie didn't have to face all this, and the way she had been so mean and nasty to Em! As their eyes met, Katie turned her lips up into a quick, darting smile. She didn't dare do more, but she didn't want to turn away without doing something that said: *I didn't really mean it. I want to be your friend really, only I'm not allowed.*

She couldn't stop thinking about it all morning, and all the more so because Lily Davies was absent that day, leaving the space next to her empty. What if she made it up with Em? Would her mother ever know? But with a plunge of dread she knew that she would, somehow. Mother always found out everything. On the other hand, if they made it up for a bit, at least they could be friends again for a while and Em might not think so badly of her.

After playtime Miss Lineham ordered them all out into the playground for PT. She produced a pile of wooden hoops and the children stood squinting in the bright sunlight, rubbing their hands together in the cold.

'Right, children,' Miss Lineham commanded, 'Line up in twos, please!'

Katie's heart started to beat very hard again. Dare she ask Em to be her partner? In the old days they would always have shared a hoop, no question. For a few seconds she dared to hurry towards Em, and thought she saw Em watching her hopefully and start moving towards her as well. But then Molly Fox was at Em's side. Molly Fox of all people! The thought of the Fox family made Katie's flesh creep. Katie was stung by the rejection. A sneer spread over her face. Well, if that was what Em wanted, Katie didn't want to be her partner, or her friend. She could keep rough, stinking Molly Fox, so there!

'Will you be my partner?' she asked a mousy girl called Gladys Day, who agreed eagerly, flattered to be asked.

At the end of the lesson, though, when they'd gathered up the hoops and were heading inside, Katie noticed that Em was near her in the line and she hung back so as not to get close to her. But to her discomfort, Em turned round, her cheeks blushing pink and said, 'Hello, Katie.' Her voice trembled a bit. 'Can you come and play out later? I haven't seen you for a long time.'

Katie looked down at her feet in their neat black pumps. She felt raw from what seemed like Em's rejection earlier. Fancy choosing Molly Fox as a partner over her! And Mother said . . . Against her better nature, she looked up at Em contemptuously.

'I told you, didn't I? How many more times?' She repeated all the reasons in a superior voice. She wasn't to have anything to do with someone whose mother was in the asylum, let alone anyone who played with Molly Fox. 'My mother says I should keep away from both of you. We thought you were from a nice family – but you're not.'

She turned, looking away so as not to see Em's face again this time, and ran after the others. She could see the last of the children in the playground eavesdropping on what had happened. Some of them were making faces at each other. Nosy parkers! But as Katie was going in through the school door, she glanced back. Em was standing in the playground where she had left her, all alone, as if she was rooted to the spot.

Three

All Katie knew was that her mother had married for love, a man who was an Irishman and a Catholic, and because of this Vera O'Neill's parents had cut her off like a diseased limb.

The one photograph of their wedding day – he dark, handsome, much taller than his stately bride with her old-fashioned hair and adoring smile – rested in its frame on the front mantelpiece.

When Katie thought about her father, she remembered a pair of well-polished black boots close to the brass fender by the fire, her sitting beside them, running a finger over the shiny surface and his voice, 'Can you see your face in there then, Katie-Kitten?'

She could recall the sound of him more than a face – a gentle, lilting voice. There was an overall shape, the memory of black hair, hands with black hairs on the fingers and neat half-moons in the nails, of being held in strong arms, a smell of tobacco, that voice which held a smile in it.

No certain memory of his illness had stayed in her mind at all. Her mother said he had been ailing for months, starting with the coughing, then worse, and heartbreaking to watch. Katie had been so young they had kept it all from her somehow. But she did remember being taken up to see him in bed once or twice.

'Why did Daddy pass away?' she asked, several times over the years, trying to make sense of it all.

'I told you, he was very poorly,' Vera O'Neill would say, putting on a soft, sing-song voice when she spoke of this, almost as if it were a tragic fairytale. 'He had a sickness in his lungs called tuberculosis. I nursed him for as long as I could. He suffered so much, my poor darling Michael, and he went into the hospital at the end. I felt I'd failed him, but it had to be. That's why you don't remember.'

Uncle Patrick had come home from Africa within months of his brother's death, but Katie didn't remember this either. It felt as if Patrick had always been there. Yet she had never once confused him with her father, despite the fact that what she recalled was often muddled and disjointed. There was another memory of being carried, this time by her mother who was wearing a green coat; Katie remembered curling her left index finger through one of the buttonholes, which had darker green stitching round it. They were outside a black, shiny door with a narrow window halfway up, below which was a brass knocker. Then the door was open: in a dark hallway a large man with a neat moustache, who stood up very straight. A woman, much smaller, was trying to see round him, just her head and shoulders showing and sandy brown hair. She knew now that these people had been her grandparents, but she had never seen them again after that day. Things were said, no voices raised, but a poisonous tone, eyes narrowed, frowns, then the door slammed in their faces. And on the way back her mother kept talking in sharp bursts, but not to her. There were enormous emotions somewhere. That was what her mother was like. Just under the surface, something

27

swelling, frightening, that Katie could never understand.

Very rarely, her mother's emotions did burst out, like
on those mornings with Uncle Patrick when Katie was
small.

Patrick was her father's elder brother by eight years,
but looked a good deal older. He was thin to the point
of emaciation, slightly stooped, with sunken cheeks
and stone-grey eyes. But his voice reminded Katie of
her father, and his eyes were like her own, a blue that
seemed to contain a vision of the sea. He was very
variable: sometimes full of endless, wiry energy, full of
songs and tales; at others, silenced, almost unable to
move.

'Your uncle has been in Africa,' her mother told her.
'The climate takes it out of people. It doesn't suit
everyone. He and your father were Cork men – that's a
very different sort of place, by the sea and full of mists
and cool greenness.'

Her mother seemed to be in love with the idea of
Ireland as much as she had been with the husband who
had come from there. It was all part of the fairytale.

Katie was used to Patrick as someone kind and gently
spoken, except when he was in his excited moods, when
he became loud and talked so fast that the words tripped
over one another and he began to seem alarming. To
her, he was never anything but kind. Information came
to her as torn rags, never a full cloth. Uncle Patrick
had come back from a country called Uganda, where
he had been with a Catholic missionary order of the
White Fathers. When he told Katie this, she imagined
everything about them ghostly white: skin, hair, long

28

white robes. Maybe that's why her uncle's hair was almost white, unlike her father's raven-black. They might not have let him join otherwise.

'I was never a Father,' he told her in his lilting voice. 'I was just one of the humble Lay Brothers, doing a bit of teaching and other jobs they found me. I was never anyone of importance, don't go thinking that.'

She did not know why he had come home to his brother's widow; perhaps because he had nowhere else to go and knew that she was alone and needed support. There was nothing for him in Ireland now, and he seemed to feel a duty to look after Vera.

'It's a terrible thing, your father going like that,' he would say to her sometimes, shaking his head sadly. 'God knows, a man in his prime like that, with a family.' The implication was always that it should have been he who died instead.

Though in Uganda he had at some time been teaching young children, he never looked for the same work in England. He could not have managed it. But he did work – at any job he could find. He looked after Vera, in his way, and she him. Katie had also come to take for granted the mysterious mixture of rage, shame, regard and tenderness with which her mother seemed to regard him.

But she remembered those mornings, once or twice, when she was still quite small, waking to hear her mother weeping hysterically next door, in the tiny bedroom that was Patrick's. They were living off Thimble Mill Lane by now, not in the first house they had when Daddy was alive, which was bigger and in a better area because Daddy was an engineer, who'd been through all his apprenticeship. They had come down in the world. Her mother had been left in poverty, that was all she knew, like Enid Thomas, their neighbour, who had lost both her husband and son in the Great War.

'Please,' Vera was shrieking desperately, 'Get up, for pity's sake.'

Katie crept to the door, her thumb in her mouth. Patrick slept on a mattress on the floorboards in the barest of rooms, insisting that he didn't need more. He was used to Africa, to having very little, and seemed to feel he deserved even less. He was lying curled tight on his side, and Vera had hold of his arm. She was down on one knee in a posture utterly unlike her usual reserved dignity, tugging frantically at him.

'You've *got* to. What's the matter with you, in heaven's name? Just lying here – get yourself up!' Another tug on his arm. 'You're already late – they'll sack you if you keep this up, and then where will we be? I'm hardly getting any work living in this slum – we'll end up in the gutter!' She stopped pulling at him and put her hands over her face, breaking into deep sobs. 'I can't do everything: I can't manage . . .'

Her tears seemed to get through to him and Katie saw Patrick sit up as if it pained him, as if a pile of lead weights had been heaped upon him. He dragged his hands down over his hollow face. He looked so sad, but all he said was, 'All right, all right, Vera. I'm up now. Don't be shouting. Just leave me be.'

But there were days, just a few, back then, when he couldn't get up at all. Katie didn't notice very often, especially once she was old enough to go to school. She hardly realized that jobs came and went. He worked in factories, on building sites, at the wharf, came home black for a time when he was a stoker in the retort house at the gas works. He would lose one job, find another.

But there were other days when he bounced about, as if he had more energy than anyone else. He would get very excited, talk loudly and endlessly, and there was always a plan for something big.

'I'm going to start my own little firm very soon,' he'd say. At first Vera had seemed to believe him, not knowing the pattern. In spite of everything, she looked up to him. He'd had an education. Patrick's schemes – for making umbrellas, then a new kind of wheelbarrow, a car even, then sweets another day – all sounded marvellous and almost plausible. He knew exactly how to do it: whatever it was, no one had ever done it this way before. He knew where to get money, he had his eye on some premises somewhere and he knew just the fella to help him and get the business up and running. They'd soon be out of here, living in a grand house in the suburbs with a vegetable garden and roses.

Patrick had a particular love of the psalms, and amid the stories from Irish folklore and the songs he sang to Katie in his tuneful voice as she stood at his knee, he often read her psalms. In what Vera came to call his 'quick moods', he saw very particular significance in them – some lines shining out, intended specially for him.

'Come here now, Katie,' he'd say, his ocean eyes aflame with excitement. Scooping her onto his knee, he'd hold the scripture in front of her – his worn old Douay Bible, one of the few possessions that he'd carried back with him from Uganda. She could feel his scrawny legs under her and see how shiny thin his trousers were, so old that the black had faded to grey

31

and smelled unwashed. His shirtsleeves were frayed at the ends and his jacket patched repeatedly by Vera. Around her, Katie would feel his body thrumming and twitching, never still. His breath smelt of tea, or sometimes of camomile or rosemary. He had a great belief in herbs as being good for him in some way

'See here now – this is it: "For thou shalt eat the labours of thy hands: blessed art thou, and it shall be well with thee." D'you see now? That shows for certain we're going to prosper – it's all going to happen, see? *See?* And look here . . .' Flick, flick. ' "Thou hast understood my thoughts afar off: my path and my line thou hast searched out." It's all God speaking, loud and clear: "The Lord is my helper, I will not fear what man can do unto me." ' Phrases were flung out, using the Bible like a fairground lady with a crystal ball. ' "Thou openest thy hand, and fillest with blessing every living creature." Oh yes – the tide's turning, girls, you can be sure of that.'

In his slow moods, he would never ever have addressed Vera as a 'girl'.

Katie came to know and love the words and rhythms of the psalms through these strange conversations, while Patrick's dry fingers flicked the pages restlessly back and forth. And for his kindness and attention to her, she came to love him too.

Sometimes Patrick disappeared for several days and came back even more whippet-thin. He told them he spent the days walking, out to the Lickeys, the Clent Hills, or wandering the roads, as far as he and his shoe leather could last, while the burning desperation had taken hold of him. Katie remembered him coming back looking completely spent, having inexplicably lost all the buttons from his coat, the flaps held round him with a piece of farmer's twine, his socks gone and the shoe leather splitting away from the soles.

'Dear God, look at you!' Vera breathed when she saw him come in the door. Her voice held anger and pity, and a desperation of her own. 'What will people think? And look at your shoes!' She seized the coat and sewed on more buttons.

Katie was used to the fact that while this was normal for her, the reality of their home life was to be a secret from everyone else. People were not invited in, and none of her friends from school ever came to the house. Vera held herself apart from her neighbours: no one was to see Patrick any more than was necessary. No one was to know – not even Enid, Vera's one friend in the district. She kept up the pretence that no one noticed.

'One of the boys at school said Uncle Patrick is a loony,' Katie told Vera once, while she was still at St Joseph's. 'He said that's why the Fathers sent him home.'

Vera's face tightened. Again there was one of those inner storms that didn't break out, but you could feel its vibrations.

'Now look . . .' She gripped Katie's hand so tight that she squealed. 'If anyone says anything to you about your uncle, you say to them, "I don't know what you mean. My uncle has been in Africa. He's suffering from a tropical complaint." Don't get angry – just pass it off casually. Say you don't know any more.' Once more she gripped hard. 'Look at me . . .'

Katie raised her eyes to her mother's intense gaze. Mother was far more frightening that Uncle Patrick. She didn't understand what was the matter with him, only that he struggled heroically day after day.

'There is no one in this house who is fit to be called

a "loony". It's a spiteful lie and we're not having it – d'you understand?'

'Yes.' She was trembling. 'Mother.'

One of the best things about Uncle Patrick was that he lived a very austere life. He was not a drinker or smoker, so had a few pennies to spare. Above anything else, he loved being in water.

'I learned to swim by jumping in the waves,' he told Katie. 'We'd spend hours down on the strand. Nothing like it. I'll teach you one day.'

Neither of their poor little houses had a bathroom, and Vera flatly refused to use the tin bath that hung on a nail in the yard at the back.

'I'm not going back and forth round there with buckets of water,' she said with a shudder. Even if Patrick offered to carry the water, she wasn't having it. 'I shall wash myself in privacy – heaven knows, there's little enough of it round here as it is.'

Once every week or ten days they walked up to Nechells Park Road to the huge, ornate building that contained the Public Baths. Vera and Katie would pay their pennies for a hot bath and a towel and join the queue waiting on the benches for the bath cubicles. The soap the baths provided was a yellow carbolic, hard as a stone, so Vera brought their own soap, a cake of Lifebuoy sliced in half so that each of them could take it in with them.

You were not expected to spend much time in the bath. The attendants who came in, in overalls with their big scrubbing brushes to clean the bath after each customer, were banging on the door if you'd been in there ten minutes.

Katie loved the baths, and lying in the warm water, especially on cold winter days when you'd gone in with freezing feet, was a real treat. Sometimes they stung as she got into the luxurious, shimmering water and her chilblains would ache and itch. She would ease her long, slender body down into the warmth, pick up the soap and wash away any tide marks as fast as possible so that she could lie there, the tiles of the steamy cubicle dewy with condensation, wallowing until the banging started;

'Hurry up in there. Time's up – there's plenty more waiting out 'ere!'

Katie and her mother took baths, but Uncle Patrick went as often as he could afford to the main swimming baths in the same building. He plunged his bony frame into the water and, with a jerky, awkward style, ploughed up and down, one length breaststroke, one length crawl, alternating. Whatever state he was in before he left the house, he always returned looking a bit better.

'The water's grand,' he told Katie. 'Nothing like getting in there for a good bathe.' And occasionally, on the way back, he brought home fish and chips and pease pudding, all of which Vera seemed to think was vulgar, but she ate it anyway and Katie thought it the most delicious food you could ever have.

Every so often Patrick would promise, 'When you're a bit bigger I'll take you along with me.'

Katie grew up used to her double life, the secrecy of home. But then Em's mother Cynthia was taken away and everything was confusing. Even then, she understood dimly that what had happened was too close to home, and that it made her and her mother cruel in their fear of disgrace. Who was mad? What did that mean? How was any of this to be understood when no one ever talked about it properly? All she knew was that it was frightening and that no one wanted to be near it. It led to disaster. So she in her turn had been cruel to Em. Had *had* to be.

Four

Shortly before Christmas when Katie was nine, some-thing happened that changed their lives. Vera O'Neill got a job in the millinery department of Lewis's Depart-ment Store. She was employed to help with the Christmas rush, but when she had been there only a few days, she was asked if she would like to take on a permanent job, working Tuesday to Saturday. With her knowledge of sewing and her old-fashioned, lady-like ways, she was well equipped to work there and she jumped at the chance. It seemed to be exactly what she needed to restore her lost confidence.

'I'll be able to take on some of my tailoring still,' she said, flushed in the face as she told Patrick and Katie that evening. 'And you're old enough for me to take on a job outside the house now, Katie. You'll have to be very grown-up and responsible.' There was a note of warning in her voice as she paced up and down the room, as if to say: *Don't think I shan't be watching your every move, even if I'm not here!* 'Now, I have a feeling we're on the way up. Everything's going to change.'

Patrick was having one of his calm days. He smiled, looking up from his paper and said, 'That's good, Vera. That's very good now.'

The transformation in her mother was startling. Vera seemed younger, lighter in herself. Katie had not known, until then, what life had sucked out of her. In celebration, after school had broken up, she took Katie out for a treat, dressed in her Sunday best, a dark-red dress. They had been in Lewis's before, of course, but then it had always been a case of: look, but don't touch.

'I'll take you in to see Father Christmas,' Vera said. She was excited herself. Katie had never before seen her in such an indulgent mood. 'And while we're at it, it's high time you had your hair cut.'

Lewis's, with its grand building in Corporation Street, was always exciting to go into, as if you were entering the world of wealth and glamour. When you walked in, there were those lovely smells, of soap and scent wafting from the perfume and make-up department on the ground floor. Then all those stairs up, up the high building, and the floors full of clothes and gloves and shoes, and soft, lacy undergarments and silk stockings – things that they could never afford, but that it was achingly fun to admire.

'Can we go and see the pets?' Katie asked, clutching her mother's hand as they climbed up the stairs to see Father Christmas. '*Please?*' The very fact that she felt she could ask showed that this was a day unlike any other.

Vera hesitated, as if calculating in her head, then the most wholehearted smile Katie had seen in a very long time spread across her face.

'All right then – just this once.'

It was a day Katie would never forget. First of all they queued to get into Santa's grotto, where she stared amazed at Santa's long, white beard as he lifted her onto his lap.

'Well, you're tall, but you're a very light little girl,' he said. Katie put her hand up to her ear. His voice was so loud and booming! 'How old are you then, my dear?'

'I'm nine,' Katie whispered.

'My, my,' he said. 'Who would have thought it? Now – what would you like Santa to bring you for Christmas?'

My daddy, was the plea that welled up in her, but she knew that was silly, so she said, 'A nice dolly.'

She came away not with a doll, but with a colouring book, but she was pleased with that too. Then they visited the millinery department where Vera worked, behind one of the long wooden counters with brass tape measures screwed into them, and all the big bolts of cloth behind. Katie took everything in, thinking it was lovely. Her mother looked around as if claiming it in some way.

From there, they went to Pets' Corner, where you could stroke the rabbits and guinea-pigs, and there were even chimpanzees like old men with sad, brown eyes. She loved the way the rabbits kept nibbling and watching her at the same time, as she stroked their smooth, soft backs.

'In the summer they take them out on the roof,' one of the ladies who worked there told her. 'But it's too cold for them at this time of year.'

'Can we come in the summer?' She looked up at her mother eagerly.

'We'll see,' Vera said. It was so strange, suddenly having her mother say 'yes' to things or even 'perhaps', instead of 'no' as it had always been, so that Katie had given up asking.

Next they went to the children's hairdressers. Katie gasped with excitement as she went inside. She had never seen anything like it before! The children having their hair cut were seated on horses rather like the ones she had once seen on a carousel at the fair! It was nothing like the little barbers' shops she saw in the streets near where they lived.

'Oh!' she cried. 'Can I go on one of those?'

'Yes – just wait your turn,' Vera said, with a polite nod to one of the hairdressers as they took their place in the queue. It felt almost as if they were play-acting at a life they didn't really have.

She loved sitting on the horse, pretending she was out for a ride, and a number of inches were shorn off her hair so that it only reached just below her shoulders.

'That did need a tidy-up, didn't it?' the woman said. Then she tied it back with a pink ribbon, which looked lovely against her dark, wavy locks. Katie was ecstatic and bounced happily back to her mother.

To finish this extraordinary afternoon, Vera took them both to Lewis's tea room. Katie sat at the table, aware of her shorter hair, which also smelled envelopingly nice because the lady had sprayed something on it. Every so often she put her hand up and felt the ends of it, and the ribbon. She gazed round the tea room with its little tables with white cloths and comfortable chairs, at the waitresses in their neat black-and-white uniforms, offering cakes to the customers on three-tiered stands. Katie's mouth was watering before the cakes got anywhere near them. There was piano music in the background, and there was nothing ugly or dirty to be seen. It was like being in heaven. If only things could always be like this!

'I want to be a waitress when I grow up,' she said passionately.

Vera glanced at her with distaste, then away, trying

to attract one of the waitresses' attention. 'Oh, I don't think so.' Her voice was acid and forbidding. Katie shrank inside. Mother was back, the usual Mother who could turn on you in a second.

But she did not feel crushed for long because one of these heavenly beings came to take their order, smiling prettily as they requested tea and a cake. The choice of cake was very difficult, but she picked a delicious pink sponge with cream in the middle and cherries on the top. Vera had a scone with jam and a tiny pot of whipped cream, and showed Katie how to eat daintily with a little cake fork, and they each wiped their mouths on the starched napkins.

'I shan't need any dinner,' Katie said, scraping the last trace of cream from her plate with a sigh of satisfaction. She looked across the table at her mother and saw with a new shock how she looked as if she was in the right place, in a way she never did in their poor little house.

'Mom?' Vera didn't correct her this time for not saying 'Mother'. 'Are we rich now?'

A bitter expression passed across her mother's face for a second. 'No, dear. Not rich. But things will get better. We shan't have to live in that slummy place for much longer.'

After Christmas they moved house. Katie could feel her mother's grim relief as they left Kenilworth Street behind. Patrick hired a van to take their belongings and got a friend to help him.

'Are we going too?' Katie asked. 'Can I ride on top?'

'No, you certainly can't,' Vera said sharply. 'There's

not the room, and I'm not having us perched up with our chattels for all the neighbourhood to see. I'll take you on the tram. Your uncle will go ahead of us.

The only sad part was saying goodbye to Mrs Thomas, but both women promised that they would remain friends and visit each other. Mrs Thomas kissed Katie on the cheek and said, 'Bye-bye, love. I'm hoping we'll see something of you. Don't forget your Auntie Enid, will you?'

She stood on the step waving her hankie when Katie, with tears in her eyes, waved back until they couldn't see Mrs Thomas in her pinny any more.

They moved to a nice little house in Sparkhill, not far from the park with its lovely green space and bandstand, where Vera said there would be music on warmer days. The house had a back and a front room, three bedrooms including an attic and, best of all, a scullery at the back with a copper to heat up for laundry, and a strip of garden with their own private privy behind the house.

As they walked along from the tram stop on the Stratford Road, the van was still outside. The street was cleaner and much nicer than the one they had left, and when Vera stepped inside the new place where their belongings, including her sewing machine, were being unloaded, she put her face in her hands and burst into tears.

'Oh, at last,' she sobbed. 'A halfway decent home – after all this time.'

Katie was excited by the move. She had a room of her own now, up in the attic.

'It's no good putting your uncle up there,' Vera said.

She didn't need to say more. Sometimes Patrick

paced the floor for parts of the night. It would have driven them to distraction trying to sleep underneath.

Very soon after they moved in, Patrick disappeared for several days. Vera seemed calm about it.

'He'll be back,' she said. 'He likes it here really – he'll be able to go to Mass in Evelyn Road. He just doesn't take very well to things changing. It sets him off. Like when he came back from Africa.' That was her explanation for things. Africa. She always blamed it on things outside him, like the weather, or Africa. She was never, ever able to acknowledge that Patrick himself had anything wrong with him.

Over the next weeks Vera O'Neill set to work with her Singer, making pretty curtains to give them privacy and turning the bare house into a home. Gradually she saved up for some pieces of furniture – not new, but in reasonable condition. She found a table and chairs for the back room and a comfortable couch for the front, with a curved wooden frame and upholstered in deep-blue velvet. She bought some rugs to go by each of the fires.

Moving house also meant a new school for Katie. She was glad in a way. Cromwell Street School was all right, but ever since what had happened with Em all those months ago, they had been avoiding each other and had scarcely spoken a word, even when Em came back to school. Katie had wanted to explain – it wasn't my fault, it was Mother – but when she saw Em playing with that Molly Fox, of all people, and looking through Katie as if she didn't exist, it had hurt Katie's pride. She had expected Em to be less self-sufficient and strong, to beg her to be friends. She made do with Lily Davies and a few others, but it had never been the same. Even though she would be starting at Clifton Road School when the term had already begun, she looked forward to a new start. And though it was hard at first, some of the girls were friendly and she soon settled in.

Five

Summer 1937

'Disgraceful – absolutely disgraceful.' Katie heard her mother's voice as she slipped in from school and the sunny afternoon. 'And she's so common. I don't know why they've allowed it. Is that you, Katie?'

'Yes,' she called, putting her worn old satchel down in the front room.

'There's tea in the pot.'

She knew what she would find, going through to the back room. It was Monday, washday, the day Vera didn't work at Lewis's. Once the morning toil of a copper full of water and the mangle was over, often Vera got together with Enid Thomas – usually in Sparkhill, because although Enid had to go to the trouble of making the journey once or twice a month, she liked coming.

'You've got your house so nice, Vera,' she'd say. 'It's a pleasure to visit.'

Vera was still working four days in the week and did not have much time for any social life. She had joined the Townswomen's Guild and very occasionally went to their meetings, and was on civil terms with her neighbours, but she was so closed and aloof in her dealings with people that Enid was still her only real

45

friend. Enid's role, Katie could see, was to listen a great deal to Vera's opinions and feel honoured to be her friend.

They were sitting at the table with the brown teapot in a crocheted cosy and their cups, and a plate with the remains of a cherry Madeira cake. The back door was open, giving them a view of the narrow strip of green garden along which the full line of whites hung, puffed out gently by the breeze.

'Hello, bab,' Enid greeted her, peering up at Katie through her wire spectacles. 'Oh, my word, I think you get prettier every time I see you! Isn't she lovely, Vera? Not long now, eh – and then it'll be all over. Out in the working world.'

'Yes.' Katie smiled, pouring herself a cup of tea and hungrily cutting a slice of cake.

'Your mom says you're going to the Commercial School?'

'Umm.' Katie nodded, through a mouthful.

It was her last term at school. If anyone had asked her how she would like to spend her future days once her education was over, she might well have said, 'Reading.' But no one did ask, and sitting with your nose in a book was obviously no way to earn a living. Vera had decreed that Katie should apply to the Commercial School on the Stratford Road to learn shorthand and office skills, and Katie had agreed, having no idea what else she might do apart from work in a factory or shop.

'And what about that friend of yours – Amy, is it?'

Katie swallowed. 'She wants to work in Woolies – like her mom.'

She saw Vera frown.

'I think I'll go outside,' Katie said. 'Leave you to it.'

There was an old tree stump a little way down the

garden and she sat down, holding the remains of her cake in one hand while she pulled off her socks with the other. The cool stalks of grass felt lovely between her slender toes. There was a little apple tree at the end of the garden, which already had tiny, hard fruits on it. She breathed in, enjoying the peace, hearing the rise and fall of the women's voices inside. No doubt Mother had resumed her enthusiastic demolition of the character of Wallis Simpson –*Twice divorced! And American!* – who had been the reason for the King's abdication.

'*Disgraceful!*' Katie mimicked. '*Absolutely disgusting!*' She giggled to herself. They had all celebrated the coronation of the new King, Edward's brother George VI, last month, and there was still bunting left fluttering across some of the streets to remind them. But even all that excitement had not given them as much to chew over as Edward's marriage to *her* – that dreadful woman. Promises were made to be kept; it was disgusting. Katie could see her mother swell with outrage whenever she talked about it. She couldn't really see why her mother got so het up about it all. Being the King and Queen didn't sound much fun anyway.

She sat, dreamily enjoying the feel of the sun on her face and eating her cake. Voices could be heard in other gardens and, somewhere in the distance, a dog barked on and off. Sitting there, Katie realized that she couldn't now remember the last time she had heard the sound of her mother's weeping coming from the bedroom next door.

Over the past years while they had been in Sparkhill, things had settled down in the O'Neill household, or so it seemed.

This was what made what came later such a shock.

Vera O'Neill had turned her little terraced house into what appeared to be a haven of genteel peace. She had made curtains and covers for the beds. She had persuaded Uncle Patrick that he did deserve to sleep in a bed and not just on the floor, and had made peg rugs to cover some of the bare boards of his room. Scattered round the house, and especially in the front room, were delicate lacy mats she had crocheted, and on a larger one, placed on a side table in the front room, she kept a glass vase of flowers that she replenished every week, buying fresh ones from the lady in the Bull Ring on Friday afternoon, when she was selling them off. In front of the vase rested a picture of Katie, taken in a photographer's studio when she was just thirteen. She had had her dark hair arranged loose over one shoulder and her head turned very slightly to her left, so that she was looking round at the camera, half smiling. Katie was quite surprised by how nicely it had turned out. After all these years of teeth dropping out and being replaced and feeling awkward, she suddenly looked more grown-up.

'It's a lovely picture,' Amy had said wistfully. She was a good-natured, easy-going girl who lived the other side of the Ladypool Road, where they did a lot of their shopping. She had a gaunt face with dark rings under her eyes, a beaky nose and slightly protruding teeth. No one could have called her a looker, but she was good company.

The other picture, in pride of place, was the wedding photograph. Vera in an ivory-coloured dress, her smile frozen forever, stood with her arm slipped through that of her tall, dashing new husband Michael O'Neill, looking up at him with his glossy black hair and that smile, which would win any heart. The adoration was clear in her face.

As Katie grew older, more and more she saw her own features in her father's smile. But what would he have been like? It was terrible not knowing. Would he have resembled Uncle Patrick at all, have been kindly but unstable? When she asked her mother that question, she got a scornful snort in reply.

'Of course not! D'you think I'd have chosen someone like *him*!' She rolled her eyes to the ceiling, indicating Patrick's room. They were completely different – you only have to look at them.'

And it was true. How did Michael's winning smile and handsome features in any way resemble Patrick's ascetic, haunted ones? All that you could see in common was the shape of their hairline, a marked curve, dipping to a point in the middle and arching back – no receding hair in their family.

'If your father had lived, he'd have been a successful engineer, not a navvy like Patrick, humping coal around.'

'But he looks after us,' Katie argued. 'Doesn't he? And he can't help it.'

'Huh,' Vera acknowledged, but she couldn't argue.

Katie didn't like it when he mother was unkind about Patrick, even when he couldn't hear it. Every day he came faithfully home, turning down the entry and in through the back door.

'Don't bring all that muck and mess in through the front,' Vera ordered him. But Katie knew that Vera didn't want people to see him coming in the front. She made him wash in the scullery sink before he came through into the house.

But even Patrick had settled, at least into a pattern

that they could more or less predict. His moods came and went in waves, fast and slow, as Vera called them, with brief periods of calm in between, when he was almost like a normal person, before it all began again.

His involvement with things ebbed and flowed. You could tell how he was by his comings and goings in his parish, the English Martyrs in Evelyn Road. For some weeks he'd stay away, sometimes not even going to Mass on a Sunday. At first, when they moved to Spark-hill, the parish priest, Father Daly, called round when Patrick disappeared. He soon gave up, recognizing the pattern himself. Within a few weeks Patrick would start going back to Mass, his thin hair carefully combed back. He'd gravitate, by gradual stages, from slipping in at the back of the congregation to moving forward to the front. Katie went with him sometimes, so she saw the way it went. Soon after that he would rejoin the choir. Patrick had a lovely baritone voice and it was a joy to hear him sing his heart out. He would help with the St Vincent de Paul Society, giving support to the poor, and anything he could – while he was in the right frame of mind. This would last a while and then he'd be off again, not to be seen for weeks. The choir got used to it too. That was the thing about Patrick; he was so polite and gentle, and basically lovable, that in the end he found people who tolerated him. As she grew up, Katie realized that the White Fathers must also have tolerated him for a long time before he became too much of a handful and was despatched home.

It had been similar with jobs. He'd worked in factories at first, but – having no skills – had done menial jobs, packing, fetching and carrying, which also suited his restlessness better than standing still. Among other smaller firms he'd been at Cannings and Co. in Great

Hampton Street, and at Wilmot Breedon at Hay Mills. He preferred being outdoors and for a while was with Midland County Dairies. But his disappearing for three days once, without a word, did for that job.

Then he had a stroke of luck. After they'd moved to Sparkhill, he met the Lawler brothers. They were twins, though not identical, and Catholics from the neighbouring parish in Balsall Heath. They ran their own business, Lawler's Coal and Coke Deliveries.

'I think Father Daly must have put in a word,' Patrick said when he'd been with them for a time. 'They've been very good to me, God love them.'

The work suited him: it was outdoors and physical, and Seamus and Johnny Lawler were able to tolerate his occasional absences. They had a younger brother, Dougal, who was the 'special' one and not quite all there. He didn't have a proper job, but helped out a bit when Patrick didn't turn up. So he had been working for the Lawlers now for several years and would drag himself along there, however bad he was feeling now, to repay their kindness to him.

It was in his 'fast' moods that he was more likely to disappear. Katie liked it best when a 'fast' mood was building up, because Uncle Patrick would be full of energy. He would fill the house with noise coming from his room, pacing and talking, and now and then a muffled shriek, as if he was letting it all out into his pillow. There'd be endless talking and recounting of stories, tales of his childhood in Ireland and anecdotes about Uganda. Katie learned about some of the children he remembered and about miraculous healings, like the woman who had a gigantic growth in her body. To cure it she decided to carry her rosary beads everywhere with her, praying to them and kissing them morning, noon

51

and night, and within a few weeks the growth shrank and withered right away. There were all sorts of stories about animals and snake bites, and then his money-making schemes, and after a time Katie would stop enjoying the mood because the twitching and talking and pacing increased until he was like a loose wheel that was about to spin off. And that was when he would disappear, for two days, three – even a week once – and come home bony, dishevelled and exhausted, his chin stubbly as a doormat, his shoes in need of a cobbler. And already he would have begun to sink.

Even in all this, his wild moods, she had scarcely ever felt afraid of him. Katie had spent quite a lot of time with Patrick during her childhood. Almost every Saturday, unless he really couldn't manage it, they went swimming.

They had gone to the baths in Nechells, and now to the big brick building on the Moseley Road. Katie had taken to the water like a fish and was now a strong swimmer, so that Patrick didn't have to tow her along by her hands, telling her to 'Kick your legs now, Katie – that's right, nice and strong.' She liked going into the echoey old baths with their little cubicles for changing along the side, and it always felt like a treat. Uncle Patrick had an ancient costume, or 'togs' as he called it, which covered him top and bottom, its baggy blackness only highlighting the scrawny whiteness of his arms and legs. Katie's costume was a dark-red knitted thing, which got so heavy when wet that it felt more of a hindrance than a help. But they both got in eagerly and swam up and down as best they could, amid the other earnest swimmers and dive-bombing lads. To anyone who gave them funny looks, she'd give one right back: she felt protective towards Uncle Patrick.

When they got outside, their wet hair slicked back over their heads, as often as not Patrick would say, 'Let's just go in next door for a few minutes, shall we?'

It was he who had introduced her to the library, and the hushed, brown atmosphere of the books lining shelves and the newspapers, heads bowed over desks.

'Here now – why don't you give this one a try?' he'd say, on every visit, pulling out old cloth-bound copies of *David Copperfield* or Walter Scott or Robert Louis Stevenson. 'These are some grand books.' Katie read some of them, and for herself picked girls' school stories: *Queen of the Dormitory* and *The School by the Sea* by Angela Brazil, *What Katy Did* by Susan Coolidge and *Little Women* by Louisa M. Alcott.

She discovered other worlds, and how she could travel off into a book, into a place so different from these streets, which were the only scenes she had known; places where she didn't have to tiptoe around Mother, and where the sudden stark silence of the house when Uncle Patrick crashed into his black, slow times were lost to her. She was far away in America with the sisters Meg, Beth and Amy, and best of all Jo, who wanted to be a writer. Or she was gasping with horror as Katy fell off her swing and was confined to bed for months and months. Or laughing at the pranks of Angela Brazil's schoolgirls.

'You've always got your nose in a book,' Vera would say, half grateful at getting some peace and half resentful that Katie's attention was diverted away. 'You could be helping me, not just sitting about. When do I ever have a chance to read?'

The truth was that Vera was not a reader at all. She thought reading was all right for men, but that Katie ought to be perfecting her sewing.

'It'll stand you in good stead for life. Look at me – I was in desperate straits when your father died. If I hadn't been able to sew, where would we have been?'

Reluctantly Katie learned hand stitching, cross-stitch and blanket stitch, running stitch and back stitch, open seams and French seams, pin tucks and collars, button-holes and zips. In fact her fingers were nimble and, like most things, she took to it quite easily. But she was always more than happy the moment she could escape from sewing and bury herself in a book again.

She knew, when she stopped to think about it, that most of the things she liked best she had been taught by her uncle.

Six

'One more week,' Amy said, through a liquorice lace she was chewing, 'and we're free forever! Here, d'you want some?' She dug down and brought out a coil of liquorice, dusted with bits from her pocket, but Katie wasn't fussy. After all, sweets were sweets.

'Oh, yeah – ta.' Soon she was chewing away too. Amy had sweets far more often than Katie, because of her mom working at Woolies. Because of her sticking-out teeth, she always looked rabbitty when she was eating.

'Cept you're not going to be free, are yer?' Amy said pityingly. She saw the working world as a heaven of grown-up freedom after the classroom. 'Going to the Commercial School and that. D'yer want to go – really and truly?'

Katie shrugged. 'Dunno. Mom says it's the right thing. I've gotta do summat.'

As soon as she stepped outside the house into the school world, Katie changed the way she talked and became much broader Brummie.

Amy shook her head, her ponytail swinging. 'Stuck back in classrooms again, with teachers bossing yer – I'd *hate* it!'

They were walking along the Stratford Road amid the bustle of traffic, trams and cars and horses and carts. It was a hot day and the smellier for it, the fumes from the buses, sweating horses and people, and piles of manure with shiny-green flies buzzing round.

'Shall us go to the park for a bit?' Amy said.

'I can't be bothered to walk all down there,' Katie said. 'My feet hurt. I want to get home and get my shoes off.'

'Oh . . .' Amy's face fell. 'I don't want to go home yet. Mom's out – there's only Granddad there. I mean, you can come to ours if yer want . . .'

Katie did go to Amy's house sometimes, but today it wasn't an inviting thought. It was a beautiful afternoon and at the back of Amy's house there was only a little yard, which at this time of day was full of blue shade. Amy knew by now never to ask to go to Katie's, but a plan was forming in Katie's mind. She thought of their sunny strip of garden, she and Amy lazing on the grass with a drink of lime cordial and a biscuit. Her mother and Uncle Patrick were both at work . . . The idea grew. She'd never thought of defying her mother before. Fear of her ran too deep, and she and Amy usually went to the park or said their goodbyes and went home after school. But there was already an end-of-term feeling.

'Why don't you come to ours instead?' she blurted out, before she could change her mind.

Amy stared at her. 'What – your house? I thought you weren't allowed?'

'I ain't – but just for once, who's gonna know?'

'You sure your mom won't be there?'

'Nah – she's at work.'

'All right then.' Amy linked her arm through Katie's. 'Come on – skip with me.'

'No!' Katie moaned. 'My foot hurts!'

Giggling, they approached the house. There was no

warning. Everything seemed quiet and just like normal from the outside.

Katie fumbled with the key in the lock at the front and the two of them got the titters again.

'Sshhh!' Katie said urgently.

'Hurry up,' Amy said, crossing her legs. 'I don't half need the lav.'

Both giggling, they burst into the hall. Then froze.

Through the open door of the front room, Katie saw a large, pink-faced young man sitting in the chair opposite the door. It took her another second to realize that he was a policeman. He had taken his helmet off and was holding it on his lap, as if for reassurance.

'Katherine?' Her mother's voice came from somewhere else in the room.

Frantic, Katie turned to Amy and mouthed, 'Go home! Quick!'

Amy didn't need telling twice and shot back out through the front door.

'Yes?' Wondering if her mother had heard Amy, Katie moved into the front-room doorway, but soon forgot all about that. There was even more of a shock. The sun was shining brightly through the nets onto two figures sitting by the window, who were thrown into silhouette. One was her mother and the other she recognized, squinting, as Father Daly, the assistant parish priest. She couldn't see either of their faces properly, but the atmosphere in the room was very solemn.

Before she could speak, Vera O'Neill said, 'Go up to your room, dear. I'll come to you shortly.'

Katie couldn't think what to do. She sat on her bed, tracing the lines of the pink candlewick with her finger. Nothing made sense. Why was that policeman in the house, and the parish priest? Was it Uncle Patrick? Had they come to arrest him? What could he have done?

From downstairs came the sound of them talking quietly, just the men's voices. Eventually she heard movements, voices in the hall, the front door closing. This was followed by a silence so long that Katie wondered if her mother had gone with them. Then at last she heard her mother slowly climbing the stairs.

'Katie?' Her voice sounded strangely weak, as if she'd had the air knocked out of her, but Katie could tell nothing from her face. Vera came and sat beside her on the bed, taking very deep breaths, seeming unable to speak. Katie's insides were knotted tight. She was filled with a sense of utter dread.

'Why were they here?' she whispered.

Her mother suddenly put her hands over her face. 'Oh my Lord. Oh God in heaven!' She began to shake.

After a moment she yanked her hands down to her lap, forcing them to be still and swallowing hard, determined not to give way to her emotion. The words jolted out of her.

'Prepare yourself for a shock. It's your uncle. They ... I was at work ... He ... The police came ... He's been found – in the canal. Last night, when he didn't come home – well, it was one of those nights. There've been so many, when he just goes off, walks himself into exhaustion.' She stared in a haunted way towards the window. 'I didn't think ... He wasn't – I mean, so many times, when he's been—'

Abruptly she sat up, gathering herself and turning to Katie, her eyes full of a terrible intensity. She put her hands on Katie's shoulders, gripping painfully hard.

'It was an accident, that's what it was. A tragic accident that no one could have prevented. D'you understand, Katie? No one else knows how he went about at night, and no one needs to. We don't know anything, except that he set out full of life, and now he's gone.'

Katie burst into tears. 'What d'you mean, he's gone? Did he jump in the canal?'

'No!' her mother cried furiously, shaking her.

'Ow! Mom! Don't – you're hurting.'

'Don't you *ever* say that. Don't you even think it, d'you hear? It was an accident. That's all.'

Katie was sobbing. 'Is Uncle Patrick dead? Isn't he coming back?'

Her mother stopped shaking her and let go, as if she had gone limp.

'No,' she said bleakly. 'He's not coming back.'

The coffin was moved into the house the next day, while Katie was at school.

'What happened?' Amy said as soon as she got there. 'Why was there a policeman at your house?'

'It's my uncle,' Katie said, her eyes filling with tears. 'He's died in an accident.' All day she was close to tears.

'I think you'd better come in and pay your respects,' Vera said when Katie came home. She seemed to be holding herself in very tight. 'Come along now – let's get it over with.'

It was strange and terrible seeing the coffin taking up most of the front room. There was a candle burning on the side table, in front of the wedding portrait. But the lid of the coffin was already nailed down. Vera had laid a string of rosary beads on the top, and a small posy of flowers.

'They said they thought it better that we didn't see him,' Vera explained. 'What with him drowning. He'll be changed. But you can say goodbye to him anyway.'

Katie stood by the long box with its brass handles. She reached out a finger and ran it along the smooth wood. It didn't seem to have anything to do with Uncle Patrick. She wondered what it meant, him being changed, and the thought made her uneasy. Then she thought about him when he was alive, and that made her feel very sad. Soon she turned to go out. She tried to forget that the coffin was there, but she kept seeing it in her mind.

That evening, there was a knock at the door. Vera opened it to find Patrick's employers, the Lawler brothers.

'We've heard the news,' Seamus Lawler said, taking off his cap. Johnny Lawler followed his example. 'We've come to pay our respects.'

'You'd better come in,' Vera said quickly. To Katie's surprise, she seemed glad to see them. There was no one else to share their loss, to come and see them, apart from Enid Thomas.

The men went into the front room, there was a pause, and then they came through to the back. They were both dark-haired men with stubbly faces that always seemed cast in shadow, not helped by being constantly dusted with coal.

'Well,' Seamus said awkwardly. He usually did the talking. 'We'll be on our way then, Mrs O'Neill.'

'Would you like a cup of tea?' Vera offered.

'Oh well, no – but thanks,' he said. 'We'll be going.' There was a pause. 'Will you be having a wake for him?'

Vera looked confused, anguished. She didn't know what to do, was too English, not instinctively Catholic and too much in shock. 'Well, I don't know – I hadn't thought.'

'Well, you know, we could put on a bit of a wake for him, Mrs O'Neill. If you want us to.'

Her eyes filled with tears. 'I'd . . .' She struggled to control herself. 'I'd be most grateful.'

'Right then – that's settled.'

There was a Mass at the English Martyrs parish. It was one of the very few times Katie could remember seeing her mother at Mass, though Patrick had told her that Vera had converted to marry his brother, and had attended Mass devoutly when he was alive.

'I think she lost her faith when he died,' Patrick said once. 'It's never easy, that sort of thing, losing someone so young.'

She would not have brought Katie up as a Catholic – it was Patrick who had done that, as best he could, talking her through her catechism and making sure she made her First Holy Communion in a white dress.

Father Daly said Mass for Patrick O'Neill, as he had been the priest who knew him best. He said some kind words about him, about his work as a Brother, his faithfulness to the parish. His death was treated compassionately, in no other way than as an accident.

Standing in the dark church and seeing his coffin up near the altar, now looking small, though it had looked quite big in their front room, started to bring home to Katie that he was never coming back again. All the kind things Patrick had done for her passed through her mind: the way he had been there steadily through her life, like a father although he wasn't one; the way he had encouraged her at school, introducing her to the library and the world of books; the swimming. She thought she might burst with grief as the coffin was carried in slow procession from the church. She would miss her kind, tormented uncle. She knew, more clearly in those moments than she had ever known before, that his life had been a constant battle with suffering, which he had borne with a quiet, heroic bravery; and she knew instinctively that that day, for no reason they would ever fathom, it had become too much for him. There had been no accident; he had lost the battle. The tears ran down her cheeks and, as she looked up at her mother, she saw that her face was wet as well, with grief for a man whom she had not loved as a husband, but who had won her gratitude and an odd kind of respect.

Seven

1942

'Well, I might have a job for you,' the lady in the Labour Exchange said. She had a miserable, whining voice and seemed to begrudge handing out jobs, as if they were her personal property. 'There's a position for a shorthand typist...' She eyed Katie over her horn-rimmed spectacles, then peered down at Katie's references. 'They're probably looking for someone with more experience, but,' she added dismally, 'you look as if you might stand a chance.'

She told Katie that the firm off Bradford Street, which made carburettors, urgently needed a secretary for one of their quite-senior staff.

'Shall I tell them you're interested? They're offering four pounds a week.'

'Yes, please!' Katie said.

She left the office daunted, but excited. Four pounds! That was a hell of a step up from her present wage of fourteen and six in the typing pool. And to think she started as a filing clerk only five years ago on nine shillings! But she was bright and good at her work: she knew she stood out. Serck Radiators, where she was working now, would give her good references, and her looks didn't do her any harm, either.

As usual, she was very smartly dressed. Katie had inherited her mother's elegance along with her father's dark looks. Ann and Pat, friends with whom she'd shared the two years of evening classes – shorthand, typing and bookkeeping – at the Commercial School in Sparkhill, always said she looked dressed fit to kill. And thanks to Vera's sewing lessons, Katie could make almost anything. She browsed round the Rag Market for second-hand clothes made of nice materials and remade them into garments to fit her.

'I wish I could sew like you and your mom,' Ann would grumble, pulling her badly fitting skirt down as it ruckled up over her plump hips. 'I always look like a bag of muck tied up in the middle, compared with you!'

Today Katie was wearing a well-tailored suit in an attractive navy twill that Vera had made for her before the war. It always ironed up nicely and looked good as new, and under the jacket she wore a cream blouse with a Peter Pan collar and small pearl buttons. She had had her hair cut recently, level with her shoulders, which brought out its natural wave, and she wore it fashionably rolled and pinned back from her face at the front and sides. Her face had matured and filled out a little; she looked a little older than her years and had turned into a beauty, with her dark-haired Irish looks needing no make-up to improve them. Even the woman at the Labour Exchange looked at her with reluctant admiration.

She made her way across to Bradford Street and climbed the hill, pleased to see the imposing, blackened red-brick frontage of St Anne's Church up on the right. The sight of it comforted her. She still went to Mass quite regularly. She had missed her uncle such a lot after he died, and still there was an ache in her heart whenever she thought of him. Going to Mass seemed to bring her closer to both him and her father. She had a Mass said for each of them every year, though she didn't tell her mother about that. In fact, Vera was so nervy these days that Katie didn't tell her about very much.

A few minutes later she was looking up at an imposing factory building with a row of arched windows on the second floor, below which ran a white banner on which was painted in dark-blue letters: ARTHUR COLLINGE.

Oh well, she thought. Here goes.

'Well?' Vera asked when she got home.

'I've got it – a new job at Collinge's! Shorthand typist for a Mr Graham!'

She saw her mother's face relax. 'Who's Mr Graham?'

'He's the head of the something-or-other . . . Process Department, that was it. I could hardly take it all in. I haven't met him yet – it was just the Labour Manager that I saw, who does all your cards and everything. Shall I put the kettle on?' she offered. 'I'm dying for a cuppa.'

They continued talking in the kitchen as the kettle hissed on the gas.

'But as they were showing me out – it was one of the younger typists was told to take me – we passed this old lady with her specs on a chain round her neck. She looked ever so old to me, but the girl nudged me and said, "D'you know who that is?" Course I said no, and she said, "That's Mr Collinge's secretary, Miss Hurley. Ooh, she's a tartar!" So I said, which I shouldn't have really, "The sort who can strike you dead with a look!" I mean it was bad of me, but we just got the titters then. It's a good job I was on my way out!'

To Katie's relief, Vera smiled faintly. Her mimicry could often raise a smile from her mother. It seemed to bring out something irreverent in her.

'I'll be keeping out of her way.' She turned from laying out the cups. Carefully she said, 'Are you all right, Mother?'

'Oh – yes, just a bit tired,' Vera said. 'I could do with a cup of tea. I've only just got in. So when do you start?'

'Tomorrow. I hope I can do the job: I don't know if he realized I'm only nineteen, but he never said anything. It'll keep me on my toes all right – and I haven't met Himself yet, either. That'll be the acid test.'

As they drank tea she sneaked glances at her mother when Vera was not aware of being watched. Since Patrick had died, Mother had become even more anxious, worrying about the slightest thing, especially since the war had begun. The worst months of the Blitz had taken their toll on everyone's nerves, but it seemed to have affected Vera particularly badly. She had kept on her job at Lewis's and had helped out in the first-aid post in the store's basement when times were at their worst, until her nerves got the better of her and she had had to stop. She had suffered with a lot of sickness, bouts of gastroenteritis that she was sure were brought on by nerves. Unlike the very tight, controlled mother Katie had always known, Vera had begun having fits of weeping and shaking, which Katie found frightening. If she tried to comfort her, Vera would turn against her and tell her to go away and leave her alone.

'Go on – go!' she screamed at Katie once during a particularly bad outburst. 'What use has anyone ever been to me?'

She had visibly aged, her hair almost completely grey now, her face haggard, though still handsome in its way. Katie felt she always had to be strong and positive, to keep her mother's spirits up and spare her worry. She did feel sorry for her, and it made her own life easier too if she kept the peace.

In the winter of 1940, after the worst of the bombing of Coventry, Katie had moved to her new job with Serck Radiators, as it was nearer home. She didn't have to travel so far to work, which was easier for her, and she knew that Vera worried constantly about her, especially in her previous job, at a firm in Oldbury, which was quite a journey away. A few times the air-raid siren had gone off before she had got off the bus and they had crawled into Birmingham or even abandoned the journey, making all the passengers pile off into the nearest shelter they could find. There was one night in November when Katie hadn't got home and had spent a cold, cramped night with strangers in a factory cellar, listening to the thump-thump of bombs falling around them. She had had to go straight back to work the next morning, knowing that her mother would be beside herself with worry.

For a short time she had been out with a lad she met at a dance that Pat had talked her into going to, at the Moseley Road Baths. They would lay boards over the pool and use it as a dance floor. Katie was shy of young men and scarcely knew how to dance, or what to talk to them about. The only man she'd ever really known was Uncle Patrick! But her pretty looks soon drew the attention of a slim, dark-eyed young man who said, over the noise of the music and shuffling feet, that his name was Terence Flowers.

'D'you want to dance?' he asked politely, then added disarmingly, 'I'm not much good at it, I'm afraid.'

'Me neither,' Katie confessed. There'd never been a chance to learn to dance, but she wished she could. It looked fun whirling round the dance floor. Was it really that difficult?

'Well, shall we just have a go?' Terence suggested. 'Everyone just seems to move their feet somehow – I don't think it matters.'

'So long as we don't trample on each other too much,' Katie laughed. She felt fluttery and nervous. She didn't know many lads, having no brothers, and had never been out on a date. They were just starting up with 'Java Jive' by the Ink Spots.

'I like this one.' Katie smiled.

Terence held out his thin arms and gingerly they linked hands, shuffling round the floor. They instinctively liked each other and ended up laughing at one another's attempts to dance. Terence clowned around, joining in with the lyrics, and he had an impish smile that Katie liked, even though she couldn't hear much of what he was saying to her. After a couple of dances he leaned close to her ear and said, 'Shall we sit the next one out?'

They stood at the side, looking across at the changing cubicles, and tried to talk, though it was difficult over the noise. Katie kept seeing her friend Pat's blonde head in the crowd, dancing with a huge, stocky bloke she'd met that evening. Once they danced past quite close, and Pat gave Katie a cheeky grin and a wink.

Terence told her he worked at the Austin. They got

on well that evening, and as they were leaving, he asked if Katie would like to go out with him again. Shyly she agreed, though with misgivings as to how she was going to explain this to her mother. Vera was so fiercely over-protective that she didn't like Katie doing anything.

'Who was he?' Pat asked as they left the dance hall. 'He looked nice – all puppy-eyes!'

'He's called Terence Flowers,' Katie said.

Pat snorted. 'Good job his first name's not Colin – Collie Flowers, get it?'

'Ha-ha,' Katie said. 'Anyway, what about that hulk you were dancing with?'

'Oh . . .' Pat wrinkled her nose. 'I shan't see him again – he smelt terrible.'

Katie laughed. 'Well, I s'pose that's as good a reason as any!'

It was difficult going about in the blackout, but she did see Terence a couple more times. One evening they went out to the Alhambra Cinema on the Moseley Road. Katie loved going to the pictures and the Alhambra was very exotic, with a big glass bowl lit up against a blue ceiling to look like the sun, and pretty-coloured tiles. They watched a funny film called *The Man Who Came to Dinner* and she found herself laughing as much at Terence's infectious chuckles as at the film itself. She came out of the Alhambra feeling very fond of him.

Another night they even went over to Selly Oak and met his mom, a nice, welcoming lady from whom Terence had clearly inherited his brown eyes and dark arched brows. They sat and drank cocoa together and chatted, until Katie was horrified to realize how late it was.

'Oh, my word!' she leapt to her feet, heart thudding. 'I must get home. My mom'll be having a fit!'

'Don't worry,' Terence said, seeming puzzled. 'It's only just gone nine. I'll see you home.'

It took them quite a while to get from Selly Oak to Sparkhill. The bus across from the Bristol Road was running late and, standing in the dark Edgbaston street, Katie found she was getting more and more wound up. She could never relax, where Vera was concerned.

'I'm not half going to get it in the neck when I get home,' she said miserably.

'It can't be that bad, surely,' Terence said. 'Here, I'll come in and explain that we were at mine and we forgot the time.'

'Don't you think I can manage to explain that for myself?' Katie snapped sharply. She was immediately ashamed. 'I'm sorry, Terence – but the last thing you must do is come in. You don't know my mother. She gets herself in a right state.'

'Don't you want me to meet her then?' He sounded hurt.

'Course I do – but not tonight. She's bound to be all mithered about me being late and she's just as likely to snap your head off as anything.'

She and Terence said goodbye at the bus stop.

'It was really nice of you to come all this way,' she said. 'I hope the buses behave for you, going back.'

'That's all right,' Terence said easily. 'See you soon, eh, Katie?'

She wondered if he would try and kiss her or anything, but he didn't. He was a nice, friendly person and she enjoyed his company. But perhaps he walked out with a lot of girls on just a friendly basis? She was so ignorant about how it all worked – men and women, courting and all that went with it – that she didn't know what might be normal at all.

The house was quiet, and dark. As she crept along the hall, Katie realized with surprised relief that her mother had gone to bed. Thinking she might as well go straight up herself, she didn't bother to turn on the light in the hall and felt her way along the wall to the stairs. She had stepped onto the first stair when the voice came from the dark back room.

'And where, pray, have you been?'

'Oh!' Katie jumped violently. 'Mother! What on earth are you doing there, sitting in the dark?'

Stepping down, she felt around for the switch in the back and turned on the light. As soon as she did so, she wished she hadn't.

Vera was sitting bolt upright in her chair beside the fire, which had almost gone out. The room was very chilly. She stared across the room at the wall, not meeting Katie's eyes.

'Mother?' Katie faltered, shrinking inside. Nothing was said, but she felt as if she was in a room full of gas. If she were to strike a flame, however small, the whole house would blow up.

Vera got up and, ignoring Katie as if she wasn't there, went upstairs and shut herself in her room.

Eight

Katie found her first weeks working at Collinge's rather lonely.

After that night she had not seen Terence again. He had left a couple of notes for her, but she didn't reply, and he gave up. Vera had gone up to bed that night and, afterwards, had not spoken one word to Katie for two days. Mealtimes were silent, the two of them at the table, avoiding each other's eyes.

At first Katie was resentful. All I did was go and see a friend for one evening, she thought. But as her mother's thunderous silence began to work on her, she felt first deflated, then guilty. Her mother was expert at tugging on the reins of her emotions, and especially at making her feel guilty. She knew Vera worried. And she had had such bad shocks in her life: first her husband dying, then Patrick. She was always afraid of something terrible happening to Katie, who was the only person she had in the world. By the time the silence had gone on for the third day, Katie came home from a tough day at Collinge's feeling close to tears and ready to eat humble pie. She just couldn't stand another evening in, with Vera giving her the silent treatment, the only human sounds coming from an occasional muffled voice from outside, beyond the swathing blackout curtains. She might as well give in. Vera always had to be in the right.

Before either of them had even begun cooking tea,

Katie went to her mother in the kitchen. Vera was standing at the sink in the scullery, her hands in water.

'I'm very sorry if I've upset you,' she said. 'I never meant to. I was just out with someone I met. I wasn't doing anything wrong, I promise.'

Vera turned her head, and for a second her eyes wore a harsh expression as if she was about to speak angrily. Then she looked down at her hands in the water.

'You must . . .' She swallowed. 'You must consider my feelings. Here I am, all alone . . . You go off, and I've got no idea where you are, whether you're with some man.'

'But—' Katie tried to interrupt. She hardly ever went out! Her mother was making her sound like a wild and uncontrolled man-eater!

Vera silenced her again with a look. She lifted her hands out of the sink and reached for the towel on its nearby hook.

'I think it would be better if you didn't go out of an evening.' She dried her hands and put the towel back. 'I mean, look what happened to your uncle . . .' She covered her eyes with a hand for a moment. Katie realized they both knew that Uncle Patrick's death had not been an accident, but never could this be admitted out loud. 'At least until the war's over.'

'Until the war's over?' Katie was outraged 'But that could be years – we don't know when it's going to end, do we?'

'Of course not – but did you hear what I said? I'm not having it. You'll stay in.'

Katie had not had much of a social life before, but she had at least seen some of her girlfriends. She'd more or less lost touch with her old school friend Amy, who had worked on the Woolworth's counters after leaving school, had married a boy called Dickie when she was seventeen and moved over to Northfield. So far as Katie knew, Amy was looking after their little boy while Dickie was away in the army. And with her mother's curfew on her, which she was sitting out, hoping that she would soon change her mind, Katie only managed to see Ann or Pat on a Saturday.

The nice friendly typist she met when she went to the firm for the first time must have left by the time she got there, as she never saw her again. One or two of the other girls in the pool were nice enough, but the other shorthand typists at Collinge's were older than her, and though none were as old and fearsome-looking as Miss Hurley, they were more like mothers to her than friends. There was an especially kind one called Maureen, who sometimes stopped by and asked how she was getting on.

At first she found the work daunting. There was the walk into the factory, being eyed up by the young men with their loud, saucy banter and admiring remarks thrown in her direction. She tried to ignore it, but she dreaded ever being sent down into the works and having to walk past lines of the gawping, greasy-handed young men. And there was her boss, Mr Graham, a crusty, heavy-featured man in his forties, who came to work in a shiny, badly fitting suit. He smoked almost constantly and sent her out in the dinner break to buy him Capstan Navy Cut tobacco to feed his hungry pipe. She came home with her clothes stinking of it at the end of each day. He was pleasant enough, but was under pressure and curt with her, especially at first when she made mistakes and misunderstood things about the work schedules that she was hammering out on her big Remington typewriter.

'Good God, woman!' he exploded sometimes. 'Are you trying to thwart the war effort single-handedly? Type this again – it's a shambles. The place'll be chaos!'

But most of the time he did acknowledge that she was really quite good at her job, for a beginner. And that he was prone to exaggeration. One morning, soon after she arrived, he stopped in the middle of dictating a letter that she was hurriedly recording in her fast Pitman shorthand and stared at her from under his bushy eyebrows as if seeing her for the first time.

'Miss O'Neill – may I ask how old you are?'

'Nineteen, Mr Graham.' Katie looked up, to her annoyance feeling a blush spread through her cheeks.

He stared a bit longer and then said, 'Good heavens. Nineteen. Is that *all*? They'll be sending us tots in napkins soon . . . Now – where was I?'

They soon came to an understanding. The firm was at full stretch producing carburettors and other parts for military vehicles, for which firms like Standards in Coventry had converted their manufacturing for the duration of the war. There was a job to be done and everyone was expected to get on and do it. The works beneath them was going at full tilt, the place humming with activity.

The air raids had petered out completely for the moment, it seemed. Nothing had happened since July, and one day Mr Graham remarked, 'At least we can get on with our job these days, instead of having to dive down into the flaming cellar all the time. To tell you the truth, Miss O'Neill, we often didn't *go* down into the shelter. I used to say to my typist then, "Come on, let's stick it out and get on with it, or we'll never get through it." '

'And did she?' Katie asked, since he seemed to expect a response.

'Course she flaming did! And none of the Hun have hit this building, I'm glad to say. But if they tried it again, I'd expect you to do the same!'

Occasionally she caught glimpses of the Old Man, as everyone called him, Mr Arthur Collinge, who was not so very old – in fact probably younger than his secretary Miss Hurley, and not nearly as intimidating. Sometimes she would pass him in the corridor, often holding an armful of papers, a grey-haired man with a sagging but kindly looking face, and he would half smile and murmur 'Good morning' whether or not it was the afternoon.

Katie joined everyone in the works canteen for her breaks, and gradually became accepted among the other women and shared the works gossip and jokes. Now and then a group from ENSA came to entertain them and there was a sing-song. She came to enjoy Collinge's over the first few months there, and was so tired by the end of the day that, for the time being, not being able to go out at night didn't seem too much of a hardship.

Nine

'Katie – here, coo-ee!'

Katie stood by Lewis's, looking round through the Christmas crowds, and only after a minute worked out where the voice was coming from. Ann's plump figure was skipping up and down and waving, over by the air-raid shelter.

'Oh, there you are!' Katie hurried over to her. 'Sorry – couldn't see you for looking!'

'You had your head in the clouds as usual, I s'pose,' Ann tutted, but she smiled fondly. Ever since they had been at the Commercial School together, Ann had cast Katie in the role of the clever one, while she was the one with the down-to-earth common sense. Katie knew that neither was quite true, but she played along with it.

'Where d'you want to go: Lewis's? We could go and see all the decorations.'

'No,' Katie said quickly. Vera was working there today and she wanted to keep well out of her way. She kept the peace at home, but at a price. All the time she was tiptoeing round. 'Let's go over to Lyons's.'

Ann looked a bit disappointed, but didn't argue. 'She's a bit of a tartar, your mom, isn't she?'

Katie put on a bright smile. 'Oh yes – a bit.' She didn't say any more. She never told anyone what it was really like. She smiled, looking round. It was a nice day, she'd had a good read on the bus coming in, her book tucked in her bag now, and it felt very nice to be out amid the bustle with someone of her own age.

The cafe was warm and steamy and, as they took their coats off, Ann said, 'Ooh, look at you all dressed up as usual. Did your mom make that frock?'

'No – I did,' Katie said, looking down at her dress. 'You must've seen it before? I've had it ages.' It was a pretty, soft pink dress with buttons down the front and a white collar.

'No, I don't think so.' Ann sighed, sitting down. 'You always look so nice.'

It was true, Katie did feel rather elegant compared to Ann, who today was wearing a rather hectic green-and-brown checked skirt and a tight jumper the colour of broad beans. Nothing ever seemed to fit right on her, but none of this made any difference to her social life. With her blonde, buxom good looks and big smile, she was never without invitations. Where do my nice clothes ever get me? Katie thought rather wistfully as she sat down. Even without her difficulties at home, she was so shy of men.

The girls settled with their drinks and had a good natter about their friends. Pat was engaged to a lad in the navy. Ann chatted on in a torrent about her big family, in which there was always some drama going on; about how her mom's two sisters had had a years-long feud and then Iris, the oldest, was killed when a bomb hit the factory she was working in, and how the other one couldn't get over it and her nerves had gone; and a gruesome story about a lad in the factory who'd got his index finger snapped off in one of the machines; and finally about the new lad she'd met called Gordon, who was a fireman. Katie was always amazed by the sheer number of Ann's boyfriends, who seemed to come and go like buses.

'Gordon says he's going to take me out somewhere really nice for New Year's,' Ann said. She sat forward with her ample breasts resting with a resigned air on the table, and swinging a teaspoon between her finger and thumb. 'Dancing and that.' She gave one of her big grins. 'You ought to find a nice bloke and come along with us, Katie – make up a foursome. You got anyone in the running?'

'No, not at the moment,' Katie said, thinking regretfully of Terence. It was months now since she'd even been out with him. She felt badly about ignoring him and had hoped she might run into him again somewhere, so that she could explain, but it had never happened. 'What's Gordon like?' she asked, hoping to hear about romance and flowers and sentimental things – about all that she was missing.

'Oh, he's all right, I s'pose, Ann said. 'A bit boring really, but he'll do for now. He's on the shop floor.' Ann had also found work in a parts factory. 'Is there any talent at yours?'

Katie made a face. 'No – not really.'

'Oh, there must be *someone*, surely?'

'No. I spend most of my time stuck up there with smelly old Mr Graham, who's about a hundred and ten. He stands there like this . . .' Katie leaned back and did an imitation of Mr Graham stroking his portly tummy as he thought what to say next. She wanted to get Ann off the subject of New Year, her lack of a boyfriend, not to mention the impossibility of leaving her mother to see in the New Year alone. 'Then he strokes his chin and sighs, and there's a great big waft of tobacco breath, and then he says, "Right, Miss O'Neill, are you ready?"

when I've been sitting there ready for him to stop puffing and blowing and get on with it!'

Ann giggled at Katie's imitation. 'You should've stayed in the pool – at least there's the other girls.'

'Pays better, though. We're s'posed to be getting the boss's son in our office after Christmas. All the women keep going on about him,' and she mimicked Maureen's reverential tones: "Young Mr Collinge – he's been *to the University* . . ." So goodness knows what that'll be like.'

'Oh, blimey.' Ann was not impressed. ''E'll be a boring so-and-so, I'll bet. He'll think 'e's God Almighty an' all.' But then she let out her infectious chuckle. 'That's blokes for yer in the main, isn'it!'

They parted in New Street afterwards, wishing each other a happy Christmas.

'Have a good New Year's!' Katie said cheerfully, as if she wasn't bothered. 'Don't do anything I wouldn't do!'

'Oh, I s'pect I'll see you before then,' Ann said. 'I'd better get off and get a couple of presents for my sister's kids, the little buggers! Tara, Katie!'

Fondly, Katie watched her walk away. Ann's busy, highly populated life made her feel very lonely.

Katie was dreading Christmas. It had been bad enough before, but since Uncle Patrick had died, everything seemed far bleaker. At least when he was alive she knew they would always go to Midnight Mass, and sometimes her mother even came too. And Patrick had got them playing games – cards and dominoes and guessing games. He had been used to jollying children along and had ideas up his sleeve. But each year since seemed to have become more difficult, and a few days ago Katie had had an idea. Why hadn't she thought of it before?

'Mother, shall we ask Enid over to share Christmas dinner with us this year? Otherwise she'll be all on her own, won't she?'

'Yes, all right,' Vera agreed. 'And knowing Enid, she'll bring some of her rations over too.'

On Christmas Eve Katie said, 'I think I'd like to go to Mass this year. Will you come with me?'

'You do know I'm not a Catholic, don't you?' Vera replied harshly.

'But you . . .'

'Yes – I was one all right. A lot of good it did me too!'

But she did go, in the end. They stood side by side, warmed on this cold night by the congregation packed in side by side. Katie listened to the Latin words and watched the priest and altar boys at the front, remembering how Uncle Patrick had always stood beside her like a thin shadow, his head humbly bowed and hands clasped. Tears slid down her cheeks and she quietly wiped them away. That night, more than any other she could remember, she felt her lack of family. All the questions that she knew never to ask began to surface in her mind. Where are my grandparents? And what about aunts and uncles and cousins? Why are we so alone in the world? She had asked questions when she was a little girl, and had been palmed off with answers that she had had to make do with. Her Irish grandparents were dead, she was told, and her other grandparents had moved far away. Even her one set of English cousins was abroad.

Her mother seemed stonily calm, yet forbidding, and as they walked home in the darkness, Katie knew that this was not the time to raise the subject.

Thanks to Enid, they got through Christmas quite enjoyably. Enid had made a little cake with dried egg and a few bits of fruit she'd saved up, and she brought a few of her rations to share – tea and butter. They had a very small beef joint and, later in the afternoon, they went out for a nice airing round Sparkhill.

'Thanks ever so much for inviting me, Vee,' Enid said as they put the kettle on, on their return home. 'It would've been a long, slow day on my own.'

'Oh, it's good to have you,' Vera said, setting out cups. 'Isn't it, Katie?'

But on New Year's Eve they were on their own, and it felt as if the evening would never end. Vera was going down with a cold and was feeling tired and sorry for herself. Katie thought about Ann, out dancing with Gordon, and her resentment built up. Was she going to be shut in here with her mother's moods for the rest of her life, while everyone else her age had a jolly time and met men and got married?

Once they'd had a bit of supper she settled down by the fire and, as usual, hid her nose in a book: *Gone With the Wind*. She had read it before and it was an old favourite. Her mother had started off some knitting with a few balls of pretty cherry-coloured wool that Katie had managed to get hold of as a Christmas present. Vera had made her a little blouse. The room was cosy with the blackout curtains drawn, the fire well stoked and the lamps on. For a time they listened to the wireless.

82

After a while Vera reached across and clicked it off, without saying anything, and went back to her knitting. A horrible tension grew in the room.

Katie got up and made them each a cup of tea, then sat down, tucking her feet under her, and tried to lose herself in Scarlett and Rhett, enjoying the feel of the heavy book in her hands, the smell of yellowed paper, but it was no good. Unable to bear her mother's mood any longer, she dared to break into the silence.

'Mother?'

Vera looked across at her with a strange, almost hostile look, and Katie nearly lost her courage. But she forced herself on.

Gently, as if talking to a child, she said, 'You've never really told me much about Daddy ... You see, I can't really remember anything. And I'd like to know a bit more, if you don't mind.'

Vera flinched visibly, but as Katie went on speaking her face changed and a soft smile appeared on her lips. When she spoke it was in the sing-song tone that she sometimes put on when talking about the past.

'You know, Katie, it's strange that you should bring that up now, because every day you look more like him. Oh! He was a handsome man – and from a good family, never think otherwise. People can be so rude about the Irish, but he was no navvy, your father. You know he was an engineer. When I met him he was just coming to the end of his apprenticeship at the Wolseley works, all set for a really top working life.'

'The first thing I noticed about him when we met was how tall he was, and his eyes – those deep-blue eyes that seemed only for me, twinkling with laughter. I'd never met anyone like him. Of course my own family were very prim and were not keen on the Irish, and Catholics of course – oh!' She made a gesture which implied that, for her parents and their ilk, this was beyond anything. 'He completely changed my mind about all that. He was so intelligent – like your Uncle Patrick was, of course – and so lively. We laughed all evening, and by the end I knew I'd fallen in love with him and he with me. It was as sudden and magical as that. Oh, I hope you have that feeling one day, Katie, that you meet a man who you can look up to, who just sweeps you away! My Michael, I used to call him . . .'

She reached for her cup and saucer and took a few sips, holding it up close to her chest. Katie realized how much she loved hearing this story, only a little of which she'd heard before. It made her feel that she had been conceived in love, and that such a perfect marriage was possible.

'Whatever obstacles my family put in the way, I would have done anything then to be with Michael. His mother had died when he was quite young, and his father had passed away just before we met. So he only had Patrick, who was away on the missions, and a sister, your Auntie Mary, who was already married – she was the eldest. We never heard a word out of her. I think she has a good many children. So our wedding was a very quiet affair – just Michael and me and a few friends. And then you came along. We had our lovely little house and life was a dream . . . We were devoted to one another. And then . . .' She leaned round to put her cup down, face darkening. 'Then he was taken from me, in the very cruellest way . . .'

Her face started to crumple.

Oh heavens, I should never have asked, Katie thought. Now Vera was going to go off into one of her weeping fits. The grief never seemed to be far away, waiting to jump out.

Hoping to distract her back to the good memories, Katie asked childishly, 'So where did you meet my daddy?'

Vera was visibly trying to control herself, but barely succeeding.

'It was at a party in Hall Green. Exactly twenty-one years ago. Nineteen twenty-one. By the time we parted that night – it was so hard to let him go, let him out of my sight – it was nineteen twenty-two.' Her tears started coming then. 'It was a New Year's Eve party. The happiest day of my life.'

Ten

1943

Katie wished desperately that she'd never mentioned her father that night. It had set Vera off into a fit of tears, and in her distress she had taken to bed without ever seeing the New Year in, leaving Katie sitting up with only Rhett and Scarlett for company, trying to block out the sound of her mother's inconsolable weeping through the floor. The next day Vera had reverted to the silent, stony manner that she had quite often adopted when Katie was young, as if nothing and no one could get through to her or make any difference. Katie knew there was nothing she could do or say that would help, and she spent the day tiptoeing round her mother.

So going back to work at Collinge's, amid the bustle of production schedules and letters to be typed, with the busy works humming away beneath them, felt like going back into life. She found herself looking forward to seeing the other typists, just to have a normal, friendly conversation with someone.

I've got to get out of home, she thought, as she sat on the bus the first day back. I can't just stay walled up there forever. For the first time she was furiously angry with her mother, without feeling guilty about it. Yes,

Vera carried a terrible grief, but why should she, Katie, give up her whole life over something that wasn't her fault, and all of which had happened before she could even remember?

'Talk about a face as long as Livery Street,' Maureen said when she walked into the works to clock in. 'You all right, Katie?'

'Oh, sorry, yes!' Katie said, pushing her lips into a smile. She hadn't realized she was walking around with a frown on her face.

'That's better,' Maureen said. She was always rather motherly towards Katie. 'By the way,' she leaned closer, 'today's the day *he* starts, isn't it?'

Katie had forgotten about the arrival of Mr Collinge junior, but when she got upstairs to Mr Graham's office, it was to find that things had already changed. Pushing open the door, she saw Mr Graham and another slender, athletically powerful man, both with their backs to her, bent over the table under the window. At another desk opposite hers, she noticed that a second shorthand typist had been ensconced in the office as well. They certainly hadn't wasted any time.

In those seconds she felt the eyes of the typist boring into her, and took in that she was a thin person with honey-blonde, wavy hair and sharp features. Her gaze did not look in the least friendly. Then the two men straightened up and turned round. Mr Graham was looking his usual unkempt self, and made the young man beside him stand out even more in contrast. Katie took in that, as the other women in the factory had said, young Simon Collinge was the image of his father. He was tall with dark-brown hair and a healthy-looking face, which would one day fall into lines resembling those of Mr Collinge senior, attractively shaped lips and grey eyes that had a quizzical light in them, as if he found life in general rather amusing. Though he was smartly dressed, his tie was already slightly adrift, which made him look appealingly absent-minded, rather like an artist who forgets about his clothes.

'Oh,' Mr Graham said in his usual unexcited tone. 'This is Miss O'Neill, who works for me.'

'Morning!' Simon Collinge greeted her cheerfully, but then, seeming unsure what to do next, held out his hand. Katie, blushing, reached forward to take it. Her hand was held in a surprisingly strong grip. 'How d'you do?'

'As you can see, Mr Collinge has joined our department,' Mr Graham said. Katie could tell he was not best pleased about this, though it was always rather hard to tell when Mr Graham *was* pleased about anything. 'He's been at Herbert's in Coventry after leaving the *University* . . . ' This last word was uttered with barely disguised contempt. 'And now he's come back to join those of us who've been scholars at the University of Life and Hard Knocks.'

Simon Collinge laughed at this, which was the only thing to do, even though the words had been laced with sarcasm, and Katie joined in, enjoying his infectious chuckle. Mr Graham didn't laugh, instead looking even more fed up, as if the arrival of Collinge junior was the cross he had to bear. He waved his hand towards the other typist.

'And this is Mrs Crosby.'

The blonde woman nodded, turning her lips up insincerely.

What the hell's eating her? Katie thought, as she slid

onto the chair behind her desk. She doesn't need to look so flaming mardy with me when she's never even met me before.

But Katie couldn't help noticing that Mrs Crosby must have been at least ten years older than her, and looked as if she didn't like coming up here to find that she was on a par with someone so young.

Oh dear, Katie thought, picking up her shorthand notebook amid all the bad humour of the room. This is going to be jolly. All she could do was keep her head down and get on with her work.

'You could cut the air with a knife in our office,' Katie said to Ann when they met up for a coffee that weekend. 'There's Lena Crosby looking daggers across at me all day, because I have the cheek to have a job in the department office when I'm younger than her. And then there's old grumpy Graham and that Mr Collinge – I mean, they're like a pair of those ... What d'you call them?' She made a gesture, fingers poking up from her head.

'Reindeer?' Ann suggested, and they both laughed.

'Something like that, yes! Both trying to make out they've got the biggest whatsits – antlers. It's been the same all week – especially Mr Graham. If you even mention that Mr Collinge has been to the university, he starts to swell up ... And I get home and Mom's not well and she's feeling sorry for herself. I can tell you, it's good to get out!'

'It sounds it,' Ann laughed.

But Katie's joking complaints were the nearest she ever got to telling the truth about things – especially about her mother. She had been so conditioned never to say anything about her home life that she would have felt disloyal even hinting at how things really were.

'What you need,' Ann said, 'is a good walk round the shops.'

Katie groaned. 'What, with a handful of coupons? And that's if there was anything decent to buy. I'm saving my coupons for a proper pair of shoes. I keep getting to work with my feet all wet!'

'I know,' Ann said gloomily, her hands curled round her cup of coffee to warm them. 'Still, at least you can make things for yourself. You always look nice, no matter what, Katie.'

'Thanks,' Katie said. She did take pride in her appearance and there was nothing she liked more than a new outfit, given the chance. 'But I've had most of these clothes for years. It's not as if we've got any spare curtains to cut up!'

'This flaming war's sucked the fun out of everything,' Ann said gloomily. Then her eyes began to twinkle. 'Well – maybe not everything.'

'Go on.' Katie grinned. 'Tell me.' Hearing about Ann's evenings of fun with Gordon was about the nearest she was going to get to a social life for the moment. She sat back and listened to Ann chatting about dancing and going to the pictures. But she found her mind wandering.

It was true that things were difficult at the works. Mr Graham's grudging working relationship with Simon Collinge, and Lena Crosby's obvious resentment of her, had made the week difficult. On the first dinner break Katie had wondered whether she and Lena would eat together and maybe get to know each other. It would have been nice to share chats and jokes about work with someone in their office. It wasn't looking very promising, but Katie lived in hope. Lena Crosby got straight up from her desk and walked out, without even acknowledging Katie's presence. She left a strong smell of stale cigarettes behind her. Only the men were allowed to smoke in the office. She was clearly desperate for a puff.

'Huh, be like that then,' Katie muttered under her breath.

She went down to the canteen and ate with the other women she already knew.

'Where's that new one who's working with you?' Maureen asked.

'I don't know – she must've gone out,' Katie said.

Maureen grimaced. 'Ooh – like that, is it?'

'Well, she's not very friendly so far,' Katie said, shrugging.

'And what's *he* like?' Maureen was full of curiosity.

'Seems nice enough. I don't really know.'

'Goodness . . .' Maureen eyed Katie's already empty plate. 'You must've needed that.'

'I've got to nip out,' Katie said. 'If I hurry, I can just make it to the Bull Ring – get a bit of fruit for my mom. She's going down with a nasty cold.'

'Aren't you a good girl!' Maureen's words followed her as she dashed out.

As the week went by, Lena Crosby did not get any less chilly and disappeared each dinnertime. When they were all eating one day, someone said, 'I heard she's got a husband who's a prisoner-of-war in Germany.'

Everyone looked a bit more sympathetic after that.

One afternoon, when they were all working away in the office, Katie was typing a great sheaf of correspondence that Mr Graham had dictated to her earlier, and he was busy at his desk. Simon Collinge was standing close to Mrs Crosby, giving her dictation in a low voice so as not to disturb the others. Miss Crosby sat very correctly at her desk, her feet neatly together, rapidly taking shorthand. Katie looked up, fingers pausing on the keys of the Remington, hardly realizing she had stopped work. She looked at Mr Collinge's tall figure, one long arm bent to rest a hand on his hip in his relaxed-looking manner, his expression one of intelligent concentration. A physical sensation went through her at the sight of him. It was the shape of him, the way he stood. And he looked so intelligent. Gosh, he's really nice, she thought. She didn't realize she was staring.

After a moment he must have felt her looking at him and turned. Their eyes met for a couple of seconds and she could see he was curious, meeting her gaze. She looked down, blushing in confusion. He'd caught her staring at him! But she kept thinking about it after-wards. Hadn't she, in that very brief look, seen the beginnings of a smile in his eyes?

Most of the time they had little reason to talk. She was not his typist, after all. But the next afternoon, when Mrs Crosby was sitting in her usual frigid silence and Mr Graham was at his desk muttering grumpily to himself about something, it was her turn to glance up and see Mr Collinge looking at her. To her extreme annoyance she blushed, thickly, and was about to turn away when he gave a mischievous glance round the office as if to communicate something to her, as if to say: *What a shower!*

Without thinking, before she could stop herself, Katie pulled her cross-eyed face that she and Em used to make at school when they wanted to be cheeky about the teacher. She saw Simon Collinge look bemused, before a grin broke over his face and he turned away so that Mr

Graham didn't see. Katie was mortified. What on earth did she go and do that for? But at least he had looked amused – she hoped to goodness he'd carry on seeing it that way.

That evening as she hurried home she kept thinking about it, about the way he had looked at her, worrying about how badly she had put her foot in it. She had plenty of other things to be thinking about, like seeing to the tea because her mother's cold was obviously turning into something worse and she was becoming more and more feverish, and about stoking the fire and washing up. But it was his face that kept coming back to her. That wide smile. She couldn't seem to stop thinking about it.

Eleven

Vera O'Neill's cold turned into a nasty bout of the flu. She took to bed in her little room with the pale-blue walls and white window frames, the pretty flowered coverlet flung to the bottom of the bed when she was too hot to bear it, then pulled up again as she grew cold and shivery. Katie, attending to her every need, lit a fire in the grate and made drinks and refilled the hot-water bottle from time to time. There was a wicker chair by the bed with a cushion made of floral material that matched the coverlet, and Katie sat with her mother and kept her company.

'It's a good job it's the weekend,' she said. 'Otherwise I'd be worried about leaving you to go to work.'

Vera smiled glassily and said in a rasping, martyred voice, 'I expect I'd have managed. But I'm glad you're here. Could I have another sip of water, dear?'

Katie reached over for the glass of water on the bedside table and helped her mother take a mouthful. She saw the muscles in Vera's neck strain as she lifted her head, and the crinkly look of the skin of her neck and chest, which made her see once again that her mother had aged. Lying there, she looked vulnerable. It was a rare thing for Vera to be ill as she was usually a very healthy woman, but Katie realized she also seemed to be enjoying it, lying back and being looked after, almost like a child.

Vera slept fitfully on and off. Katie sat reading *Dombey and Son*. As the day passed into evening, she turned the lamp on so that she could see her book. The room was cold, so she rebuilt the fire, but Vera grew more and more feverish, tossing and turning, delirious. Katie thought she should not leave her for too long. Should she call a doctor? she wondered. But she didn't like the idea of walking the dark streets and calling on Dr Radnor, who was a rather sour man.

She cut herself some bread and cheese and ate it sitting upstairs on the little Turkey rug by the fire. The room was softly lit and the only sounds were the coals hissing and Vera's restless murmurs from the bed. It all felt rather stifling and, to escape, Katie lapsed into a dream: in the flames she kept seeing Simon Collinge as she'd seen him that first day, so different from the bantering lads downstairs, long-limbed, energetic, leaning over the work table, then turning with that energy of his, his handsome smile, which turned into the impish grin he had given her when she pulled that face. She found herself smiling back as if he was actually in front of her, then she caught herself. How stupid she was being! There was she, a little typist, and he not only the boss's son, but someone who'd been to the university, somewhere she couldn't even imagine! She really was going to have to pull herself together and stop mooning about like this.

A gasp came from the bed behind her. Vera was thrashing her head from side to side.

'Is that him . . . ?' she said in a slurred voice. 'Spots, Spots, come here!' A moment later, more loudly, she cried, 'Daddy! Is that you, Daddy?'

Katie got up and went over, alarmed. She sat down and reluctantly took her mother's hand. This felt awkward.

Being in any way close to Vera was not comfortable. But soon Vera had gone back to sleep.

Vera's throat was on fire. One minute she was sweating, the next shivering with aching cold. The glands in her neck throbbed, and if she opened her eyes the walls seemed to bulge in and out, so she mostly kept them closed, except when she was looking for Mummy. She seemed to have been gone for a long time. Where was she? And why was Spots barking, on and on, next door?

The little bedroom in Sparkhill seemed to have become her childhood room in Hall Green, with the watercolour picture of Jesus calming the storm on the wall by the bed, so that that was what she saw each time she looked up: Jesus in a halo of light amid the towering waves and bucking ship. He would always be there to make things right, that was what Mummy said – Mummy with her childlike beliefs.

They were Congregationalists, deeply involved in the Church and Bible Study, saying prayers before every meal. Vera had no brothers and sisters, so she was thrown into the company of her parents and of adults in general. Her father, Harold Porter, was a big man, imposing, with strong-featured good looks and dark-brown curly hair. He was a travelling salesman, and good at it – his looks must have helped, his air of knowing something that other people would benefit by learning from him – so they had a car. He was away for a night or two quite often.

When Vera was eight, he disappeared for two years, almost to the day.

Vera's mother, Jean Porter, a tiny, doll-like woman

with curling auburn hair and porcelain skin, told no one that he had gone – not even herself.

'I haven't seen your Harold for a while,' her friends might remark. Vera could remember them, in the parlour with the net curtains, drinking tea and eating dainty scones and cake.

'Oh, I know,' Jean would say in a vexed way. 'It's so naughty of him. He will take on these big jobs that keep him away from home. He was home earlier in the week, but you missed him, I'm afraid. He's had to go away again on urgent business *overseas.*'

At this, her voice would sink to an awed whisper and the other women would look suitably impressed. If they ever asked exactly what he was doing *overseas*, Jean would laugh in her girlish way, fiddling with a curling strand of her hair and say, 'Oh, you know – it's all to do with buying and selling. I don't interfere too much in his work, to tell you the truth. You know what the male of the species is like, don't you? They don't like to be interfered with!'

She would tell her friends that he was due home in a few days, and that then they would be away, taking a little holiday – perhaps by the seaside?

Vera, whose ninth birthday came and went without her seeing her father, did start to doubt things. When Mummy said to people that Daddy had been home for a few days last week, she started to think that yes, perhaps he had been? Hadn't he come in and kissed her goodnight? And when Mummy said in the holidays once or twice that they were not going to go out of the house for a few days, because so far as everyone knew they had gone on a little holiday to the seaside, hadn't she joined in when Mummy asked for this to be their game of pretend?

97

'You can tell your friends about the cliffs, and the rock pools – you know, going out with your net on a lovely sunny morning, and catching crabs and sea anemones and tiny fish, with the sand between your toes and the sound of the waves in your ears . . .' By the time she had spun her story, Vera almost felt as if she *had* been to the seaside. To confuse things further, on one of 'Daddy's' holidays by the sea, they had taken a train all the way down to Bournemouth and spent a few days with Jean's mother in a little boarding house looking over the sea. It was blissful for Vera, as her grandmother was a kindly woman, but there was still no sign of Daddy, even though Mummy told her to tell her friends that he had been there with them, but had now had to go on a long journey.

After a time this became close to normal, but now and again Vera would ask, 'When is Daddy *really* coming back?'

Her mother looked at her stony-faced. 'What do you mean, *really* coming back? You know perfectly well that your father is a very busy man, back and forth on business. He's with us as often as he can be. Now don't be demanding, Vera. We just have to accept that this is the way it is.'

'I don't believe you've got a dad,' one of her friends at school started on her once.

'What d'you mean – course I have!' she retorted.

'Where is he then? Is he a ghost or something?'

'He's just busy: he's away on business,' she said defiantly, making herself believe it as she said it.

'Huh – my mom says he's run off with a bit of stuff!'

Vera got caned that day, six raps on each hand, for slapping the other girl soundly round the face.

Just before her tenth birthday he did come back.

She saw him first, one afternoon when she came home from school. Even though it was threatening rain, she had stopped two doors up to play with Spots, the Jack Russell, leaning over the neighbour's fence, stroking him, and he kept jumping up to meet her hand and yapping with enthusiasm. Then she caught sight of someone just inside her own garden. There was a rose bush by the gate with pink blooms, straggly now and needing deadheading at the end of summer, and he was standing there next to it, just standing, as if in a dream.

Her heart gave an enormous leap. It was him. It *really was* him!

'Daddy!' She started to run, as fast as she could. 'Daddy, Daddy!'

He turned to look at her, bewildered, as if he couldn't remember who she was. They stood each side of the gate for a moment. There was a strong breeze and it was just beginning to drizzle.

'Vera,' he said, gently, 'little Vera. You've got so big.'

He came and opened the gate to let her in. He didn't lift her up into his arms, but took her hand and led her to the front door. She wanted to cry, but didn't let herself. She didn't know whether to trust that he was here.

'Are you coming home *really*?' she asked.

He looked down at her, his eyes affectionate but sad. 'Yes. I think so,' he said.

Vera had cried, 'Daddy, Daddy!' out loud in anguish as Katie sat on the bed beside her.

'Mom – Mother?' Katie said, taking her hand. 'What's the matter? Are you all right?'

Her mother's hand felt hot and dry. She gave a small

moan and opened her eyes, and for a few moments it seemed as if she was looking at a complete stranger. In a cracked voice she said, 'Is he still here?'

'Who?' Katie asked gently.

'Daddy – I mean . . .' She looked confused. 'Oh, I don't know,' she said, seeming to come back to herself. She gave a little sobbing sigh. 'They all go, all of them. They're always taken from you.' Her voice was desperately sad.

Katie felt for her. All she knew was that her grandparents didn't want anything to do with them, that Vera's husband had died so young. She had great sympathy for her mother. But it meant that she had never felt that she was enough, that there was anything adequate she could do to make up for all her mother's grief and pain. All she could do now was pat her hand.

'It's all right, Mother. You'll be better soon. Then things won't look so bad. D'you want another sip of water?'

But Vera ignored the question, squeezing Katie's hand with sudden ferocity. 'You won't go away and leave me, will you? Promise me?'

With a sinking heart, Katie looked back into her mother's intense, feverish gaze. What was she asking? Katie felt trapped, stifled, but what else could she say?

'I . . . No, of course I won't, Mother—'

Vera's head came off the pillow. '*Promise* me.'

'I promise.'

Twelve

Vera seemed less feverish the next morning. Katie had left her with plenty to drink and the reassurance that Mrs Hargreaves from next door would look in on her this morning, and that Enid was due to come over in the afternoon. It was a lovely day, bright and crisp, and even right here in the middle of town, hemmed in by factories, it lifted the spirits. Katie was so glad to be out of the house and breathed in deep, her lips turning up in a smile at the sense of freedom and of being away from her mother.

Her smile met that of Simon Collinge. Until then she had assumed that he came into work with his father, but no, there he was getting out of what seemed to be his own shiny Austin 10 tourer! The sight of the car removed him into a life of wealth and privilege very far from her own, and immediately she felt embarrassed and foolish about daydreaming over its owner. What on earth did she think she was playing at! She lowered her gaze and was hurrying past, but he jumped energetically from the sporty little car to land in front of her, and perched his hat lightly on his head in time to tip it off again for her benefit, in a way that was gentlemanly and self-mocking at the same time.

'Morning!' he called cheerfully. 'Lovely day.'

'Yes,' she agreed, her heart speeding like a motor that had been turned up. 'Lovely car as well.'

He smiled. 'Oh, she is, isn't she? Goes like the clappers.'

Katie could feel the eyes of the stream of workers coming into the factory all watching this exchange and tried to walk on again. But Simon Collinge slammed shut the door of the car and fell into step beside her as they made their way into the works. You could hear the racket of the machines from behind the closed doors. He was carrying his coat over his arm and held his trilby resting on top of it. His hair had a slightly rumpled look, as if he had brushed it, but it wouldn't lie flat. Katie had to restrain herself from reaching up and smoothing it down as if he was a child.

'Have you been here long?' He spoke in a relaxed way that put her at her ease a little.

'Oh, no – only a few months.'

'Really?' He sounded impressed and turned to look directly at her, which brought an embarrassed flush to her face. 'Where were you before?'

'I was at Serck,' she told him, trying to sound casual.

'Oh, marvellous – that's good . . .'

She wasn't quite sure why this was so good, and it dawned on her that he was rather nervous of her, which somehow put her more at ease.

'And you were working at Herbert's?'

'Yes, that's right. I thought I'd go somewhere and do some time in a place that wasn't the family firm – just for a while anyway. All good experience . . .'

He began to peel off as they got inside.

'I'm going onto the floor for a bit.' He turned, walking backwards as he spoke to her, moving towards the shop floor. See you up in the lions' den!'

Katie laughed at this unexpected comment and heard his laughter too as he disappeared through the swing doors. She liked the way he was so light-hearted and ready for a joke.

She had to calm herself down as she climbed the stairs, because her face was all pink and she had a broad grin stretched across it. If only she didn't blush so easily and give herself away. She stopped on the stairs and took some deep breaths.

'Stop being so silly,' she ticked herself off. 'He was only making polite conversation with you – it doesn't mean anything!'

But as she went into the office she could feel Lena Crosby staring curiously at her and felt herself blush even more. Even after she'd sat down at her desk, it was a long time before her heartbeat slowed to something approaching normal.

Over the next few days, whenever Simon Collinge came into the office, Katie always looked down and busily got on with her work. But sooner or later she would raise her head and become aware of his eyes fixed on her, though he was at his desk, seemingly wrapped in deep thought about a technical problem. She was astonished at his effect on her. She had never really believed all those romantic stories about women going weak at the knees, melting inside – or however they put it. Not until now. The very look of him, the curve of his long back, the lift of his hair in a boyish wave from his forehead, the way he sat hunched with his head in his hands, thinking hard, tapping his toes and sometimes drumming his fingers on the desk, the air of confidence he gave off – everything about his sheer masculine presence did make her feel, yes, soft and melting inside! And she was very embarrassed about it, because surely he was not looking at her on purpose, and she didn't want to make a silly little fool of herself.

But he seemed to glance across at her often. Sometimes he would just raise an eyebrow in a humorous way, or pull up one side of his mouth in an uncertain smile. Soon he seemed to keep finding excuses to talk to her, passing her on the stairs up to the offices or on her way in and out of the building. They were only polite fragments of conversation. She had mentioned in the office that her mother had had the flu, and he asked if she was better. Or it was something about the weather, or the war. That was what everyone talked about – all the moans about rationing and shortages. But even this amount of attention felt very flattering to her and made her even more aware of him.

Katie, who had always made sure she was turned out well for work, found herself making an extra-special effort with her appearance. She always kept her clothes clean and well pressed, and her favourite was the navy suit and cream blouse that she mostly wore, knowing the outfit flattered her. Sometimes, instead of the jacket, she wore the skirt with a soft, cherry-coloured cardigan, which looked very striking against her dark hair. She made sure she kept her hair nicely trimmed, and it waved prettily along her shoulders. She rolled a piece of it and pinned it back from her face and knew it suited her. She knew she looked the best she could, under wartime restrictions.

Most of the day they were all in the office working flat out and there wasn't much opportunity for conversation. Then one day, when Mr Graham was out of the office talking to a supplier, Simon Collinge finished dictating a letter to his shorthand typist and then, still in a businesslike voice, said, 'Now, Mrs Crosby – I'd like you to pop out and see if you can find me some cigarettes, please.' He fished in his pocket for money. 'Here are my coupons – anything smokable will do.'

To Katie's amazement, Mrs Crosby, who was a good few years older than both Katie and Mr Collinge, looked across at him with thinly veiled insolence and, tilting her head towards Katie, said, 'Why can't she go? She's the office junior. And anyway, there won't be any – I'll have to go miles.'

Katie was shocked. What a way to talk to your boss! And she didn't like the way Lena Crosby had tried to put her down.

If Simon Collinge was put out, he didn't show it. He leaned on the edge of Mrs Crosby's desk and, showing that he was not prepared to be contradicted, said, 'Miss O'Neill works for Mr Graham, not for me. There's no need to go far out of your way – just see what can be had round here. Now, if it's not too much trouble, Miss Crosby . . .'

Lena Crosby got up, bristling with resentment and, with a nasty look from one to the other of them, went to get her coat.

'Thank you,' Mr Collinge called after her.

As Mrs Crosby left the room, a faint 'Huh!' from her emerged from behind the closing door.

'I think I've just put my foot in it,' Simon chuckled, and his eyes were full of amusement.

'It's cold out there,' Katie said. 'And she'll have to queue – if there're any cigarettes to be had.' Although she couldn't help noticing his expectation that some-one would wait on him in this way, he *was* one of the bosses, however young, and she didn't feel sorry for Mrs Crosby. She was too mean-spirited and vinegary. 'I expect she just wanted to huddle up in here.'

'Well, she'll be back soon enough.' He shook his head. 'Not a great one for office banter, is she?'

'Her husband's a prisoner-of-war, apparently,' Katie said.

'Oh, is *that* the trouble? I hadn't realized. But all the same . . .'

He picked a slide-rule up from the work table and turned it round in his hands in his usual restless way, pacing around the office until he somehow ended up perched on the edge of Katie's desk. Finding him suddenly so close to her set her heart beating hard in self-conscious alarm. Don't be silly, she told herself. He's just being chatty.

'So – how're you liking it here?'

'It's nice. I like it better than my last job.' It felt like a silly answer, but what more was there to say?

'Why's that then? The stimulating company?' He threw the rule up in the air and caught it just above her head, making her jump, then laugh.

Should she tell the truth: *Because you're here, because the pay's better . . .* ?

'Well, it's more interesting,' she floundered.

He seemed to find this funny. She found that he was looking straight at her, interested, his grey eyes intent on her face as if he was looking right into her.

'Tell me a bit about yourself,' he said. 'About Katie O'Neill – and not about work, I mean.'

Katie froze. All her life she had been conditioned to not telling people things. 'There's nothing much to tell. I just live with my mother. It's all very boring, not like you, going to the university and everything.'

'Well, yes – that was all right. I know I was lucky – but I was a complete flaming disaster when I got there.' He started telling her jokes about things he'd done wrong or misunderstood; technical things. Katie didn't really know what he was talking about, but she enjoyed his infectious laughter and, above all, that he wanted to talk to her. 'Anyway, they let me stay on and finish, even though the war had started by then – I s'pose they thought we might all be useful for something when we came out the other end. I mean, going there was a privilege, I know that, but in the end it was lots of blokes and machine tools and engineering. Nothing glamorous about it – and no nice girls like you. Not in engineering.' He winked. 'And in the end I knew I'd be back here, family firm and all that. Lucky again, I s'pose most would say.'

'But isn't that what you want?' she asked, surprised. 'Being here, running the firm and that?'

'Oh – yes. I s'pose so,' he said carelessly. 'We've all got to do our bit. I'd have liked to join up really. Lads my age: it doesn't feel right not going, even though you know really that you're well out of it – well, if it's anything like the last lot, anyway. Dad survived because he was running the firm. My uncle was killed out there in France. So I know that if we've managed to dodge Mr Hitler's bombs, we're the lucky ones being here.'

It hadn't done him any harm, she thought. Good job, sporty car.

'The only thing is . . .' He was talking seriously now, with a boyish air of vulnerability. 'In the long run it just feels as if it's all been mapped out for me and I don't have any say in it.'

She was touched that he would admit such feelings to her. But, genuinely puzzled, she said, 'Isn't it like that for most people?'

Simon Collinge gave a slightly bitter laugh. 'Ah, I can see you're a realist, Miss O'Neill, not a romantic.'

'Am I?' she was saying, not sure if this was a compliment, when Lena Crosby pushed the door open, her nose pink with cold. Finding Simon Collinge on the edge of Katie's desk, her expression stiffened further into one of sour disapproval.

'Your cigarettes,' she said, holding them out with a martyred air as if they were something rather distasteful. 'Lucky they had some at that place in Digbeth.'

'Ah – thank you very much! Much obliged,' Simon Collinge said, taking them across to his own desk. As Lena went to take off her coat, he turned to Katie and winked, and she had to hide her smile.

That evening as she left the works, it was already dark as usual. She was walking along towards Bradford Street when the car drew up alongside her.

'Let me give you a lift home?' He had leaned across and wound down the window.

'Oh – no, it's all right. 'I've only got to go to Digbeth to get the bus. There's no need for you to go out of your way.'

'It's not out of my way, I don't think. Somewhere off the Stratford Road?'

'Yes, but . . .' She began to cave in. It would be so nice to get into a car instead of freezing at the bus stop. And did this mean . . . ? What did it mean? Was she being pursued, or was this just a more general friendliness? How were you supposed to tell?

He was jumping out and coming round to open the door for her. 'Come along – hop in.'

The car smelled nicely of leather inside. She realized just how comfortably off the Collinges were. She had heard through the firm's gossip that Simon did not live out in Solihull with his parents, but in a little house of his own, which his father had bought for him.

'It's lovely,' she said, settling into her seat. Just friendliness, she told herself firmly. She was so beneath him – why would he even look at her?

'Much better in the summer with the top down,' he said. 'Then you can really feel the wind in your hair! Right,' he went on, once they were both in their seats. 'Tell me where I need to go – we'll soon have you home. I get a few supplementary coupons to get me to and from work, and I'm sure they'll stretch to include your place.' They pulled away from the kerb. 'Not that I'm in any hurry to be out of your company ... In fact,' he looked each way as they crossed over into Cheapside, 'I'd say it was rather the opposite.'

So it *was* more than friendliness! Katie had a feeling of unreality. Here she was, sitting in Simon Collinge's car, and he was saying these things to her. She glanced at his profile in the gloom. He was so handsome. Had he really said he wanted to spend time with her? She was full of tremulous feelings. Was this love – could she be in love with this man already?

'Whereabouts do you live?' she asked, hoping that didn't sound too forward.

'Kings Heath. I've got my own little place. The old man bought it, more as an investment really, but he said he didn't think us living and working together for-ever was the best of ideas. Especially after my being at the university. They thought I ought to stand on my own feet. They've still got my brother living at home. My sister's married – with a couple of kids.' He peered out of the windscreen as they slowed down again. 'It's flaming dicey, this blackout driving ... What about you – your family, I mean?'

'Oh, there's only me and Mom. No brothers or sisters. My father died when I was very small.'

'That's sad. My goodness, I can't imagine that – growing up on your own. It must make you very independent.'

Katie thought back to her odd, secretive childhood. 'I suppose everyone's different,' she said carefully.

She enjoyed bowling along in the car, passing a couple of buses on the way, and the blacked-out cars and trams. All too soon they were pulling up outside the house. Simon cut off the engine.

'Well – thanks very much,' she said, reaching for the handle.

'Wait – just a minute.' He put his hand on her arm. She leapt inside.

'What is it?' She tried to keep her voice steady.

'Look, Katie – I know we work in the same office, and we all have to be careful of our behaviour and such like. But would you come out with me? For a drink or something? You're – well, I think you're a really nice girl and I'd like to get to know you better. I could call for you . . .'

She was so excited, her heart beating so fast, she could hardly think what to say. Simon Collinge, asking her out! But she wasn't allowed out: what would Mom say? Her mind was working very fast. All she could think of was that she must say yes, that seeing him again was the only thing that mattered, whatever else. She'd get round Mom somehow.

'I'd like that,' she said, thinking how weak that sounded compared to what she meant.

'Tomorrow? Go on: say yes!'

'All right – yes!'

'Good, tomorrow it is.' She saw that he had expected her to agree, assumed he would get what he wanted in

110

life, and for a second she felt a niggle of resistance to him. But she wanted it too, so much! And he looked so delighted she had agreed that it took away any doubt. He leaned quickly towards her, and for a dizzy moment she thought he was going to kiss her cheek, but instead he released the door and pushed it open.

'Well, good. Marvellous! I'll see you in the morning. Goodbye, Katie. Have a good evening.'

'Bye,' she said, still recovering from the non-kiss. 'Thanks for the lift.

'My pleasure.'

When he'd driven away, his hand just visible waving, she stood outside the house, hugging herself, not noticing the cold. Simon, she muttered. He'd asked her out with him just like that! Simon, Simon. Tomorrow!

Thirteen

Does it show, she wondered the next morning as she walked into the office. Can anyone see that I'm – well, that I can't stop thinking about him? That a smile keeps wanting to break out all over my face? She thought of her mother, of the way Vera had described falling in love with her father. Wasn't this how it was supposed to be?

Vera had commented on her early arrival home the night before, and Katie had told her that she had been lucky with the bus. The first of the lies. How easily it slipped out. What else could she do with a mother who wanted to control every aspect of her life? She compounded the lie by saying that she had been asked to work late the next evening, that there was a rush on. Vera looked put out, but she couldn't argue.

Simon Collinge was not there when she arrived, which was a relief and gave Katie time to compose herself. Mrs Crosby was the only one in the room, sitting behind her typewriter, with a compact open, putting her lipstick on, a hard pink that did not make her powder-dusted face look any more approachable.

'Morning,' Katie said. It seemed a good idea to try and keep Mrs Crosby as sweet as possible, though it was an uphill struggle.

The other typist snapped her compact shut and gave Katie a look of unveiled dislike. 'Morning,' she said sarcastically. 'Miss.'

Catty bitch, Katie thought to herself. She sat at her own desk and was looking through her notebook in the cold winter light from the long windows when Mr Graham came billowing in.

'Morning, ladies!'

Katie's heart, which had started turning somersaults when the door opened, steadied again.

'Now,' Mr Graham said, struggling out of his coat. 'Let's get going.'

A few minutes later the door opened again. Katie glanced up in confusion, her cheeks reddening, but Simon Collinge swept into the room in his normal way, cheerful and relaxed, rubbing his hands together.

'Morning, everyone! Flaming cold, isn't it?'

His smile washed over everyone. Katie smiled back, politely. Business as usual – no one must know.

But as she was about to go back to work, she saw Mrs Crosby staring at her across the room with a knowing, spiteful expression.

She met Simon Collinge as arranged, round the corner from the works. Katie was relieved to know that Lena Crosby had gone home: she had seen her go mincing out of the office before Katie left herself, without saying a word, her camel coat belted tightly round her thin waist. Katie wrinkled her nose rudely at the woman's departing back.

'Goodnight to you too,' she muttered, in Lena Crosby's whingeing voice.

Then, dithery with nerves, she gathered up her things and hurried to the place where Simon was to pick her up. That was what she called him in her mind already: Simon, Simon . . .

His car came cautiously along with its blacked-out lights and braked beside her. Once again, he jumped out and helped her in, and she liked the way he was so gentlemanly. Not that she had any other males to compare him with except Uncle Patrick.

'There,' he said when they were both settled inside. 'At last! I thought the day would never end. Now – I'm taking you out for dinner.'

'Dinner?' she said, startled, picturing her tea drying up in the oven at home.

'Well, what passes for dinner these days. I'd love to be able to wine and dine you properly, but as it is, there's a perfectly good British Restaurant in the parade, not far from my house – all right if we go there? Slumming it just a bit, I know, but I can't drive too far afield and the food's quite adequate. The main thing is, we can have a chat away from the ranch, as it were.'

Katie wasn't the least bothered about where they went, she was so amazed at actually being with him, in his car. And it was so dark outside that he could have taken her to Timbuktu and she wouldn't have known the difference. As they drove slowly away from the factory, to her relief he chatted away, telling her more about his family, his older sister Sue and her little boy Kevin.

'He's a smashing little kid,' Simon said and Katie was warmed to hear the fond tone in his voice. It seemed promising that a man should like children. She enjoyed looking at his profile as he drove, knowing that he could not turn to look at her for long. 'He's five now and already keen on football. Richard – that's my other brother – and I always play with him when we see them. They live out in Bromsgrove fortunately, away from the worst of it. You must have had it bad where you live?'

'Oh my goodness,' she said. 'Every night now it still seems like a miracle that you can get into bed and go to sleep without spending half of it shivering under the stairs!'

'Under the stairs? Didn't you have a shelter?'

'Well, no. The thing is, there's only Mom and me, and we didn't have anyone to help put up an Anderson. The understairs cupboard in our house is just about big enough for the two of us, so we made do.'

'What about those other ones: the cage type?'

'Morrison – no. We didn't like the idea of that taking up half the house. Anyway,' she said lightly, 'we survived, didn't we?'

He braked, ushered her out of the car and, taking her arm, led her towards a blacked-out place that she could only just make out in the darkness. As they approached, the door opened and closed again, and for those seconds she saw light inside and heard a burst of voices.

Inside, behind the steamed-up, blacked-out windows, a canteen had been set up and tables arranged round a large space. There were quite a few people eating and there was a fuggy atmosphere, damp and sweat-tinged, along with the smells of the food.

'Here we are,' Simon announced. 'Eating amid the people. Let's go and see what they've got tonight.'

He addressed the women serving the food in hearty tones and Katie wondered what they thought of him. He seemed so superior to them, and she could see that he knew it, but was trying not to show it. She felt proud to be standing here beside him. He's an engineer, she thought. Like Daddy was. That was really something.

'Grilled chops and veg and jam tart and custard,' one of the women informed him in a bored monotone.

'Lovely!' he said. 'Suit you, Katie?'

'Yes, of course,' she said.

They carried their plates – dark gravy pooled round mashed potato and cabbage on one plate, wafer-thin jam tart on the other – to a table that was dotted with the remains of other eaters' meals. A young woman hurried up and wiped the table with a grim grey cloth.

Simon Collinge sat down, unwinding his scarf from his neck and hooking it over the back of the chair. He looked around with what seemed to be a certain amusement, as at finding himself in such a place.

'You comfortable – got everything you need?' he asked, leaning towards her. 'Here, let me pour you some water. The Claret will have to wait for another time!'

Katie smiled, though she had only the dimmest idea what he meant. Wasn't it wine he was talking about? They started on their meal, eating from tinny-tasting forks. The food was not bad at all, Katie thought, realizing how hungry she was.

'So,' Simon said, while eating enthusiastically, 'tell me some more about yourself. What d'you like to do – in your spare time, I mean? Are you keen on sport, for instance?' He laid his knife and fork down for a moment. 'I'm a keen golfer myself. Nothing like it . . .'

'Oh, I've heard it's very enjoyable,' Katie said. She tried desperately to think of any sporting interest she might have or suddenly acquire, but nothing came to her. The last thing like that she had done was in her school gymslip, and then only under sufferance. *I like reading* was all she could think of. But she didn't need to say anything and sat back, relieved, as Simon chatted away amiably.

'My father's always been a golfing man. Never misses a weekend if he can help it. My mother's a golf widow. So he signed me up as soon as he could – got me some irons when I was hardly big enough to hold them! But that's the way: start young. It's fantastic – you should learn. Course at the moment it's no good – half the courses have got ack-ack batteries and such-like dumped in the middle of them . . .' He made a woeful face. 'Not so good that, but needs must! Just as I was really beginning to improve my handicap, though . . .' He talked on for a time about his favourite golf course, about putts and bunkers and something called 'teeing'. Katie found her mind straying a little and glanced at the couple closest to them, the woman in a brown pork-pie hat. She and her husband seemed to be arguing. She quickly brought her attention back from eavesdropping, relieved that Simon was still talking. She was warmed by his enthusiasm, but also afraid that he might expect her to ask questions and she didn't know what to ask. Mostly she didn't know what he was talking about.

'That sounds lovely,' she managed to interject brightly, on a couple of occasions.

'Oh, there's nothing like it,' he enthused, and then he was off again. She became desperate to change the subject.

'Your dinner'll get cold,' she said as he was drawing breath and he stopped, smiled and said, 'Goodness, yes – you shouldn't get me onto golf! It's a bit of a passion of mine. Better eat up.'

As soon as he'd taken a large mouthful she said, 'You worked in Coventry, didn't you? What was that like?'

'Cov?' he chewed, then swallowed. 'Oh, well – I missed the worst of the bombing of course. By the time I got there the place was – well, it was in a terrible state.

Had the guts blown out of it. I don't know if you know, but before the war, old man Herbert, who I was working for, had given a fortune: a hundred thousand pounds or thereabouts, to build a museum and gallery for the city. By good luck they'd only built the basement by the time the war got going, and they stopped for the duration – otherwise the place would have been matchwood, like most of the rest. I mean seeing all the cathedral down like that...' He shook his head. 'Anyway, course Herbert's is a grand old firm – good experience before I came back under the thumb of the Old Man! I had digs there with a strict old tartar called Mrs White – watched me like a hawk, she did. I'm damn glad to get back to my own place, I can tell you.' He picked up his spoon. 'Come on, let's get this pudding down us. It's already stone cold.'

Katie smiled and picked up her spoon. She rather liked cold custard. He leaned forward, watching her intently. 'You know, I think you're a bit of a witch, aren't you?'

'Pardon?' she asked, startled.

'Well, you've got me talking away, asking me all sorts of questions, and I'm keeping on and on about myself like a proper bore – and you've hardly said a word about you.'

'That's all right,' she said with a trace of dishonesty. She had had more than enough of golf. But she did want to hear about him and his family. 'There's not that much to say.'

He sipped his water, peering mischievously at her over the rim of his glass. She enjoyed looking into his face. 'I don't believe you. You're like the Dark Lady – full of mystery.'

'Oh, Shakespeare's Dark Lady?' she said, surprised.

Here was something they could talk about. Perhaps he loved reading too? 'D'you like Shakespeare?'

'Yes – well, I'd like it more if I had more time. To be honest, I had a . . . Well, a sort of girlfriend when I was at the university. She was doing a degree in English Literature and she told me about the Dark Lady. I don't really have time for that sort of thing.'

'No, well, I've never seen any of the plays or any-thing,' she said, 'except an amateur production of *Twelfth Night* in a village hall. Mom and I were invited. It was absolutely terrible!' She put her hand over her mouth, giggling at the memory. 'But I like reading the plays – and the sonnets.'

'You like reading? That's nice. You'll have to show me some of them.' She was fairly sure that he was not really interested, but appreciated his humouring her. She was surprised. She had thought that was what people did in universities. But of course, Katie told herself, Simon was a busy man, running an engineering com-pany, not footling about with poems. It was a shame, all the same.

'Not really my thing,' he went on. 'Any spare time I get, I'm out on the golf course – or cricket in the summer of course. Now that's another marvellous game . . .'

'I go to the library a lot,' she said quickly. 'My uncle . . .' But she ground to a halt. Why talk on about this when he wasn't interested in it?

'Go on?'

'Oh nothing – he's dead now. But I borrow a lot of books.'

Simon leaned forward, bringing his face as close to hers as he could. 'You don't make it easy to concentrate in the office.'

'Me? Why?' She felt like giggling, almost as if she'd been drinking something stronger than the tap water they were sipping. She was aware only of him now, not any of the other diners around.

'Oh, Katie – do you really have no idea how lovely looking you are? There's me trying to keep my mind on . . . on flaming drawings and motor parts, and there you are across the room looking absolutely ravishing!'

His use of this word made her laugh all the more. He reached across, saying, 'May I?', serious now, and took her hand. 'I really do want to know about you,' Simon said. 'I'm not just making conversation.'

So she told him, a little – the bare facts – drawing a veil over quite how poor they had been and Uncle Patrick's difficulties and how he died. She portrayed a gentle, sheltered upbringing. Out of her usual reserve, she did not talk for long. Soon afterwards he suggested they leave, and they put on their coats and went out into the freezing night.

'Ooh,' Katie said, her chest clenching with the cold. 'My, that's a shock.'

'Let me get the engine on – that'll warm us up . . . Come on – you get in and get warm.' He ushered her considerately into the car and she was warmed by this as much as being out of the frosty night.

They drove home, Simon talking a little more about his family. He pulled up just along the street from her house. Only now, Katie was suddenly seized with dread. What on earth was the time? Could she go in looking as if she'd been toiling away at the works all this time?

But a second later she realized angrily that she didn't care. Why shouldn't she have some life? She felt she was being swept along, as though in a fast-moving stream.

Nothing and nobody was going to stop her seeing Simon, if he wanted to see her. It felt exciting to be wanted by someone.

He turned and looked at her through the darkness. She couldn't see his expression.

'This has been the best night of my life,' he said.

'Really?' She was so amazed by this that she almost laughed. Her heart was pounding hard. He was having more and more of an effect on her. Was she really that special to him? Surely he couldn't mean that, not with all the busy life he had had . . . the other girls?

'Well,' she dared to say, 'it's certainly been the best *I've* had.'

There was a silence, during which they looked at each other across through the gloom.

'May I kiss you?' he asked.

Timid, but wanting the kiss more than anything, she moved towards him and felt herself taken into his arms. She wrapped hers round him, acutely aware of the weave of his jacket under her hands. It all felt astonishing, miraculous. Their lips found each other's gently, then passionately. She didn't know how long they sat there. All she could feel was the closeness of him, the warmth and slight roughness of his cheek, his searching lips, until they drew back for a moment. Katie felt dazed.

'It's so fast – all this,' he said. 'But my goodness, you're so beautiful. I do believe I'm in love with you, Katie.'

'I – I love you too,' she said, feeling astonished, crazed even, at bringing out these words for the first time ever, and so soon. Was it wrong to say such weighty things so easily? Or was this whole evening just in her imagination? But he was here, she could feel him. It was all real. 'I don't want to let you go ...' she whispered. 'And have to see you tomorrow and pretend I hardly know you.'

'I know.' He kissed her neck, her cheek. 'But at least we *shall* see each other tomorrow. That's good, isn't it? And tomorrow night? What about that? Please don't tell me you can't!'

'Yes,' she said, without hesitation. 'Of course I can.'

At last, reluctantly, they released each other and she stood and waved as he drove away, her heart full to overflowing.

Fourteen

'And where were you last night?'

Vera's voice was calm, but held a brooding coldness that Katie knew spelled trouble. She didn't know exactly what time she had finally slipped into the dark house, trying desperately not to let the door squeak, taking off her shoes to creep up the stairs. All the time, struggling through the darkness in which her own breathing sounded deafening, she expected Vera's voice to ring out accusingly. But there had been only silence. She had got away with it – for the moment.

And at that moment she didn't care what trouble she got into. She's not stopping me seeing *him*, that she isn't! She lay in the dense darkness, gradually growing warmer, and seeing again and again Simon's face as he had looked at her in the car: *'I think I love you . . .'* She was too excited and infatuated to sleep. Wasn't he everything she could have dreamed of? He was handsome, gentlemanly, educated and with good prospects, of course – even property of his own and a car! But though these things all added to her sense of wonder that he was interested in her, it was his sheer presence – the way he looked into her eyes as they talked, the slightly nervous way he rubbed one of his thumbs with the other as they were sitting at the table, the way his eyes crinkled at the corners when he smiled and his rumbling laugh. Of course it had been a bit of a struggle making conversation at first. They had different interests, and a man had to have his interests, would be dull without them. And they had yet to get to know each other properly. Over and over again she relived the moment when his lips had touched hers, the flicker of his tongue, her first time in the arms of a man, their first kiss. It took her a long time to fall asleep.

When Katie woke the next morning she dressed, humming happily to herself. Holding up one of her lisle stockings to check for holes, she wished she had something much more feminine to wear. She decided to treat herself to some new silk stockings. Her one pair had been mended so many times they were past it. She dressed smartly as usual, feeling different now, older, as if she was suddenly more a woman of the world.

Her mother's voice cut through her happy mood. She was looking up from the bottom of the stairs, holding a cup of tea. 'You may have thought I didn't hear you come sneaking in, young lady, but I did.'

'I told you . . .' Katie stood at the top of the stairs, glad that her face was in the shadows. 'We had to work late. There's a proper flap on.'

'Until nearly *midnight*?'

All she could do was keep heaping lie upon lie. 'Well – yes. There's a great big order come in. The factory's running all night, and sometimes it all just piles up.' She reached the bottom of the stairs, brazening it out. 'It's quite like to happen again, by the sound of things. I might be kept on late tonight.'

Vera examined her closely, eyes narrowed. Her face still showed the remains of her cold and Katie was struck again by how much older she looked. 'Are you telling me the truth, Miss?'

'*Yes*. Course I am! What else would I have been

doing? There is a war on, you know,' she added pertly, walking past her mother. Inside was a swelling sense of triumph. Why should Mother always have everything her way? I've got a heart that beats as well, she thought. 'I must get some breakfast – I'm famished.'

Katie could hardly wait to get into the office again to see him. She stood in the crowded bus, full of anticipation of what she would see in his eyes when she walked in. Of course they needed to be careful, absolutely discreet, but she knew how his eyes could flash her a sign of what he really felt. They had often made humorous faces across the office already.

But she was in for a shock. All day Simon Collinge behaved as though last night had never happened, as if he barely knew Katie and she was nothing more than his senior colleague's secretary. In fact when Mr Collinge senior came into the office during the morning while Lena Crosby happened to be out of the room fetching something, Simon sent Katie on an errand instead, speaking in a cool, clipped tone, which seemed designed only to put her in her place.

On her way along the corridor to fetch the drawings he had requested, she kept her head lowered, watching her neat black work shoes, stung almost to tears. How could he speak to her like that, and not even so much as look at her all morning, when last night . . . ? She felt hurt to the core. How could he switch like that and be so cold? But there were people around in the busy corridor and she couldn't just let her emotions out. By the time she had gone to perform her errand and returned to Mr Graham's office, she had pulled herself together. Of course her lovely Simon couldn't let his feelings spill into his working life. It would have been quite wrong and embarrassing, especially in front of his father. Professional men did not behave like that! It did seem hard, though, having to shut all her passionate feelings away all day and pretend. If only he would give her just one little look, one sign!

But she walked back into the office with her face composed, wearing a cool, workday expression.

'Here you are, Mr Collinge.'

'Thank you,' Simon said curtly. He stood bending over some other document and not even looking up. It was Mr Collinge senior who thanked her with a faint nod.

Though she had given herself a stern talking to, Katie still spent the afternoon feeling angry and rejected and didn't even so much as look in Simon Collinge's direction if she could help it. She left the office at the same time as Lena Crosby, with a curt 'Goodnight' to both the men. After Lena had gone up Bradford Street to catch her bus, Katie walked on through the cold, mizzling dark, her hands pushed down into her coat pockets, feeling very sorry for herself. Just one look, one little wink across the office when no one was looking, and she would have known everything was all right. Couldn't he even have managed that? And so much for wanting to see her again – he seemed to have forgotten she existed! Was he just playing with her? A lump came up in her throat and she was so lost in feeling sorry for herself that she didn't hear the footsteps hurrying to catch up, until his hand was on her shoulder, swinging her round.

'Hey – I thought we were going out for a drink!'

Who said? she thought crossly. When did we say that?

'Were we?' she said in a neutral tone. 'I wasn't sure. You seemed to be very busy still.'

A gaggle of workers from the shop floor was approaching, now that the shift had changed, and Simon took her arm and steered her round the corner.

'Never too busy for you, K-K-K-Katie. Come on, let's go somewhere warm and away from here.'

Still angry, wanting to punish him for the way he'd hurt her today, she felt like telling him she couldn't come. She looked away from him, along the factory walls.

'I can't just come out whenever I like, you know.'

'Whyever not?'

'It's my mother – she's sort of an invalid.' More lies tripped off her tongue, so easily. 'I have to be home quite a bit to look after her.'

'Oh, I see.' He sounded a bit put out. She could just make out his long, pale face in the gloom. 'You never said. Well, look – just one drink. Surely the old girl'll be all right while you have a quick one?' He put his hands on her shoulders. The blackout had its uses, she thought – they didn't need to worry about people seeing them. And he couldn't see those miserable tears in her eyes. 'I don't think I can stand it if you go off now. D'you have any idea of the agony of having you so close to me in the office all day? Wanting to come to you and put my arms around you?'

Katie felt her ruffled feathers being smoothed down. She began to relent, which of course was what she really longed to do.

'I just thought . . .' Those foolish tears welled up. 'I just thought you'd forgotten all about me.'

'Oh, Katie!' He laughed and reached out to stroke her cheek. 'What's this – not crying, are we? Look, I'm sorry.' Now he did really sound sorry. 'It's just, I knew that if I kept looking at you ... Well, I might not be able to control myself – and that sour-faced Crosby woman would be onto us and there'd be all sorts of gossip. I know it's awful, but it's better to keep this sort of thing quite separate, surely you must see that? It doesn't mean anything. There's you across the room, with your lovely face and those lips that I've been longing to kiss all day, and me having to sit on my hands and take a very serious' – he was clowning now, and all she could do was laugh – 'interest in the manu-facture of motors and the war effort, when all the time this delicious woman is sitting there just in my line of vision. Oh, the agony!'

He reached forward and pecked her on the cheek and she forgave him instantly. Of course he was right. They all had to keep their minds on what was important: winning the war! How childish she was being.

'Just one quick drink then . . .'

'Oh, thank goodness! The lady relents!' He took her arm in that way she loved and said, 'My car's just back round the corner.'

That night she was home by nine o'clock, to find her mother staring stonily at her and a plateful of greyish fish and potato congealing in the oven.

'Sorry, Mother,' she said, not feeling in the least sorry. Her heart was singing like a bird and her body tingling all over from being held tight in Simon's arms. They'd been to the Hare and Hounds in Kings Heath and they'd talked about some of the day-to-day things in the office, about some of the characters at the works, and had let off steam about the grimness of Lena Crosby.

'I think we ought to tell her she's got to smile for the war effort!' Simon joked. 'I've never seen anyone who can keep up a sour face such a percentage of the time. It must be a record!' His exaggerated bafflement made Katie giggle helplessly. Later she told him a little bit more about Vera, saying she was over-protective.

'Well, we'd better get you back a good bit earlier tonight, hadn't we?' he said, and she was warmed by his consideration.

But there'd been time for a brief stroll, arm in arm, and he'd taken her in his arms at the edge of the park.

'At last – I've got you to myself,' he said. And they kissed and cuddled. He stroked her hair and looked at her in the darkness. He ran a finger softly down her cheek. 'Oh God, you're so lovely.'

And she wanted to tell him how handsome he was, what the sight of him did to her, but she didn't know how to begin and ended up saying, 'You're lovely too', and it didn't feel quite enough.

'My house is not far from here,' he said after a time. 'I ... well, it would have seemed a bit forward to ask you back there straight away ...'

'Do you live on your own?' she asked, surprised.

'No, I've got two lodgers. They're both war workers – they've come here from Wales. Good lads. But it is a bit of a chaps' house – could do with a feminine touch. I'd like you to come and see it soon – so that I can have you all to myself.'

She felt a thrill go through her as he said these words. All to myself: what did he mean? What did he expect of her? She was so full of desire for him, feeling his lean, hard body pressed urgently against her. But all the while she scarcely knew anything, about desire and what it was supposed to mean. In the books she read, if they referred to it at all, there was always a rosy haze around everything and, after the first few kisses, no one ever seemed to go into any detail. All she knew was that she wanted something, wanted him, in a way that nice girls *didn't*. Anyway, that probably wasn't what he meant. He surely just meant that they could sit in private and share a drink.

As they sat in the car as he dropped her off that night, Simon reached across and gently touched her chin, turning her head towards him.

'Oh, Katie – I can't stop thinking about you, day and night. You will come out with me again, won't you?'

She smiled. 'Of course I will. And thank you – for the lift and the drink and everything.'

'Oh, that's a pleasure. One last kiss – please.'

The feel of his lips was very fresh on her, and no matter how grim her mother's face, she didn't care.

But as she put her plate of fish down in the place that her mother had left laid on the table, Vera's voice came to her, hard and angry. 'You're lying to me. I know you're going about with someone.'

Katie almost dropped the plate. 'What?' But the wretched blushes came, and she couldn't help it.

'See, look at you all telltale pink.' Vera sat up straighter, accusing. 'I saw you with him – with that fancy car.'

'What – when?' They had been so careful, parking along the street. It was so dark; how could she have seen, unless she was deliberately spying?

'Tonight. Just now.' She sat back in a nasty, satisfied way. 'You must think I'm a complete dupe, that I don't have eyes. Who is he?'

'All right.' Katie sat down, shaken at the lengths her mother was prepared to go to invade her life. 'He's . . .' She was about to tell the truth, but then thought: Why should I? Why should she know everything? 'He's a nice man, that's all. And yes, I went out for a drink with him.'

'Were you with him last night?' The question slammed at her.

'Yes, if you must know.'

'You were out shamefully late.'

There was a nasty, insinuating tone in her voice that roused Katie's temper. 'What are you saying? He took me out for dinner, that's why. And I'll go out with him again, if I please.' She stood up. 'I'm not just going to be your prisoner at your say-so all the time. I love him, and I'm twenty years of age – you can't stop me going out and seeing people, spying on me like some old gossip. And you can keep your nasty fish as well – I'm not hungry!'

She slid her plate across the table so hard it almost fell off the other side, and stormed up to her bedroom.

Fifteen

As the winter passed into spring, Katie grew more and more besotted with Simon. Any doubts were pushed aside. She was in love! It was all she could think about. It was the first time she had ever gone much against her mother's wishes. At first, Vera was furious.

'Is she still giving you the silent treatment?' Ann would ask, when Katie met up with her.

She hadn't told Ann exactly who Simon was. She was so used to keeping things secret that she only gave away a few bare details. She did not question his need to be discreet.

'It's like trying to get blood out of a stone with you,' Ann would say, exasperated. 'Go on – what does he look like? Is he a dish? What does he do?'

She bombarded Katie with questions, which she sometimes answered, but just as often didn't. But for the first time she had confided in Ann about her mother and what she was really like. Ann had been appalled.

'But now, after all this upset,' Katie told her, 'something's changed.'

She knew that she had more power on her side now, though she would not have said it quite like that. But Vera seemed to sense there was something in Katie's life that had a stronger pull on her than she, Vera, did, and she had begun to behave more moderately, as if afraid of pushing Katie further away.

'She's not easy,' Katie had said with a sigh. 'I suppose she's never really got over losing my father.'

'She doesn't *sound* easy,' Ann said. 'After all, she can't expect you to stay a child forever, can she?'

After several days of silence heavy with anger and resentment, after Vera found out that Katie had someone else in her life, one evening when Katie came home she found her mother in bed.

'Mother?' Katie walked through the silent house and realized that Vera must be upstairs. She knocked on the bedroom door and went in, to find her mother lying on her side, facing the bedroom wall. She stood looking at her for a moment, concern fighting with exasperation. 'What's the matter?' she said in the end, controlling her voice. 'Are you ill?'

There was silence, before a convulsive sob came from the bed.

'Mother?' She dared to go nearer. 'Has something happened?'

There was another sound of distress. Katie, full of dread, dared to go and sit beside her, and Vera began sobbing, emotion pouring out of her.

'I just can't bear it! You're not my little girl any more. You're deserting me! What's going to happen to me? I'm here all alone . . . I'll be alone, forever – I can't stand it . . .'

The sobbing went on and on, and Katie listened with a mixture of sorrow and bafflement. She could see that her mother got a bit lonely, but her reaction seemed so extreme. It was very hard to know what to say, but she knew she had to try.

'I shan't leave you alone,' she said soothingly. 'You know I shan't. But I do need to go out sometimes. It doesn't mean I won't come back. Why do you think it does?'

Her mother had quietened and was listening.

'The thing is, you should be pleased for me. D'you know why? You know you told me about when you met Daddy, and how it was and all that you felt? Well, I've met someone who . . .'

This seemed to bring on more sobbing, so she stopped.

'I know you lost Daddy, and it was very unfair and sad, but aren't you glad I've found someone whom I can love and who loves me?'

Vera sat up, her hair dishevelled and her eyes red from crying. Katie moved back, afraid of the wild look in her mother's eyes.

'And are you so ashamed of me that you can't bring him home to meet me? Or is it him you're ashamed of? Perhaps you'll think I'll look down on him, that he won't be good enough for you – some factory Jack you've decided to throw yourself at? Is that it?'

The direction of the conversation had shifted so fast that Katie could barely keep up.

'No . . .' she said unsteadily. 'Of course not. I'll bring him to meet you soon . . .'

A few days later, when Vera was calmer, she said to her, 'I'll bring him round to meet you. But let us just get to know one another a bit more first, eh? Otherwise I might find out it's not worth your trouble.'

'I thought you said he was the great love of your life,' Vera said sarcastically.

'Well, yes, but . . .'

'As you like.' She turned away. 'But you be careful. Men are fickle fools, and don't say I haven't warned you.'

Katie was astonished by this outburst, when her mother was usually so starry-eyed in her description of men. But she knew then that she'd been right to delay bringing Simon round. He had been cautious about coming to meet Vera and seemed reluctant to take her formally to meet his family. The fact that she already knew his father from the works seemed to complicate things as well.

'I don't know,' he said, when they were sitting in the car again, safe in the darkness, one evening when he dropped her off. 'Maybe we should just give it a bit of time. After all, what's the rush? As soon as you get all the families involved, it all gets very serious and . . .'

'Well, *I'm* serious,' Katie protested, a bit hurt. It felt important that things were on the right footing.

'Oh, love – I didn't mean that. But supposing your mother doesn't like me? And knowing my family – well, they're marvellous, but they tend to take over. They'd want us round there every week, and we shouldn't have any time to ourselves. I've seen it all with my sister. And if there's one thing I want more than anything, Katie . . .' He turned to her and shifted closer, leaning over to kiss her neck. 'It's to be alone with you. Really alone. Oh!' he breathed her in. 'You smell so lovely.'

His breath on her neck made her feel warm and full of desire. Though she wanted to feel as if their relationship was serious, and for him to feel proud and introduce her properly to his family, she had misgivings about it too. Supposing they didn't think she was good enough for him? After all, she was just a typist. Perhaps they had more ambitious plans for their son. And she also longed just to spend time alone with him away from all the busyness of the week. She turned and kissed him.

'All right,' she agreed. 'Mom's getting used to the

idea gradually.' She looked up at him, seeing him looking down longingly at her. 'And all I really want is to be with you.'

Soon she didn't question the way things were. She and Simon had some evenings together, but the best day was Sunday, or at least the Sundays when he wasn't expected to go and have lunch with his mom and dad. This happened every other week, and as Saturday was usually still busy at the factory, the free Sundays became very precious. As the weather warmed up a bit, they would drive a little way out of town and go for walks on the Lickeys or the Clent Hills, or even, if Simon had enough petrol coupons, as far as the Malvern Hills. They walked and talked. Katie relaxed more with him and found that she could make Simon laugh. They would stop wherever they could find a cosy place to have cups of tea, talking about dreams of the future, when the war was over, of going to the seaside, even to France.

If it was wet, they went to Simon's house in Kings Heath, and hoped Dai and Lewis, the two lodgers, would not be around. She had been impressed when she saw the house, a spacious terrace with a wide front window, furnished in a comfortable style with a big old settee in the front room. Though he had his own house, much of the furniture was obviously second-hand. Simon had a gramophone and a selection of records, nearly all jazz, and the two of them spent cosy winter afternoons curled up in his front room in front of the gas fire, with cups of tea and the gramophone playing Jelly Roll Morton or Duke Ellington while the rain poured down and the windows steamed up. Sometimes they read, or talked. The news had been full of the victory over the Germans at Stalingrad.

Last Sunday when she was there, and a March wind was blowing so hard outside that they had decided against walking, Simon stretched his long body languidly and smiled round at her. 'Marvellous, this music. It just sounds like freedom to me – and sunshine and all the good things.' He twisted round and sat sideways on, laying his hand on her breast, looking longingly at her. 'Good, good things.'

His touch had filled her with desire, making her arch her back a little, but she was afraid. Every time they were together now, Simon became more and more insistent. They kissed, and often progressed far further than that, up in his bedroom overlooking the back garden. At first he had begged her to let him see her breasts, and at last she had let him undress her, unbuttoning her blouse with a wondering, hungry expression on his face, which made her love him all the more, fumbling so that she had to help, then unfastening her brassiere, peeling it away to expose her breasts, white and neatly rounded.

'Oh,' he said. 'You're perfect.'

He'd knelt and licked her nipples as she sat on the side of the bed, and at first she was embarrassed to see a man on his knees in front of her like that. She took his head in her arms and held him as his tongue gave her lovely sensations that went right through her. Again she had the feeling of being swept along by him. He looked up longingly at her.

'I want to lie with you,' he said. 'You're my woman, and I want you. Say you'll be mine, Katie? Come here . . .' He got to his feet and started to lay her back on the bed, which had a soft, silky green eiderdown on it. She was drawn along by his desire. But then she baulked. In those seconds, confused misgivings swarmed in her head. Oh yes, he wanted her – but wasn't he just a spoilt boy who always made sure he got his own way? What about what she wanted and her feelings? But hadn't she led him on? Now they had got this far, it seemed wrong to refuse him what he needed. She would have to do it ...

But panic rose in her. 'I can't ... Not yet ...' She pulled away. 'I just – I don't know ... I'm not ready. What if – I mean, you know, a baby ... ?' Now they were talking again she felt exposed and chilly, and tried to cover herself with her free arm.

'You won't have a baby,' he said firmly. He came and held her, talking to her rather as if she were a child. 'It doesn't happen that quickly, and anyway I've got something to stop it. Please believe me, Katie darling, there's no harm – it's the most beautiful thing in the world.' She could sense his urgency. She looked up at him.

'You've done it before. I mean, you've been with someone?'

A muscle twitched in his face. 'No one like you. No one that I've really loved. I want to know what it's like with the woman I truly love.'

Moved, she reached up and stroked his face.

'Just give me a bit more time,' she said.

She knew, with every week that passed, that she must soon give in. Their time together now always ended up the same, with each of them naked to the waist, touching, arousing each other and then pulling away with a sense of things remaining unfinished, and though Simon was patient with her, she could tell he was frustrated.

She had some idea, also, from a chance remark Ann made, that it was bad for men not to have their desire satisfied. Ann, she imagined, must be satisfying Gordon's desires quite freely. And Katie had some idea that if men were kept from sexual release, it actually injured them.

This time, when Simon leaned round and looked at her with such a wretchedness of desire, she knew she couldn't say no. They had the house to themselves and she could not hold back from him any longer.

'I do want you,' she whispered. 'Really I do.'

He was working his fingers inside her blouse, his eyes glazing with desire.

'Will you let me this time, my darling? I'm just burning for you – I don't think I can wait much longer.'

She followed him upstairs, led by the hand, feeling her legs turn weak with anticipation of what was about to happen. She had never seen a naked man, or been naked herself in front of anyone, not even her mother, for many years now.

Inside the room there was an awkwardness of removing clothes, which seemed to go on for a long time. Stripped to the waist, Simon turned to her. His upper body was familiar, lovely to her, with the V of dark hair on his chest. Otherwise he was smooth to her touch.

'I've got some French letters. We don't want to get you into any trouble.'

When they were both naked, he held her close. Feeling him hard against her, his penis like a strange branch coming out from him, the smells of their bodies, she wanted reassurance.

'Do you love me?' she asked, looking up, round-eyed.

'Oh, my darling, of course I do!' He reached down

and kissed each of her breasts in turn. 'Oh, lie back for me, will you – quickly, there's a girl. I need you so much.'

The eiderdown was cold under her back. She waited as Simon sat with his back to her. She heard him curse quietly, and a horrible smell of rubber crept to her and she realized he was putting the French letter on. Then his warmth came down on top of her, his body thrusting hurriedly between her legs, and in those seconds before he managed to get inside her she thought: Oh my God, oh Jesus and Mary, what am I doing? And it was painful and intensely strange, and soon delicious as well and there was no going back. It was soon over, though. Simon seemed lost in his own feelings, and when he climaxed she held him, soothing him and stroking his back as he gasped and then was calm. That she could give someone such pleasure!

She lay looking at the ceiling, his face pressed to hers, loving him, yet feeling a little empty and thinking: I am not a virgin any more.

Sixteen

Does my face look different? Katie wondered several times over the next few days. Her mother didn't seem to have noticed anything. But she asked herself again on the Monday morning when she went into work. She and Simon had come to an arrangement now. She thought he enjoyed the secretive nature of their relationship.

'I'm sorry I can't pay you any attention like this in the office, Squeak,' he said, soon after they were together.

Their lovemaking had made everything more intimate between them. Katie felt, in a heady way, quite equal to him now. And this development had meant they were focused on each other physically, so that she could push away her doubts about how much they had in common, and how sometimes she could find her mind wandering when he was telling her things and how he didn't seem to listen properly when she was talking to him. Without difficulty that all slid to the side of her mind, now that she had begun to satisfy him in the bedroom. It felt dangerous and romantic, but at the same time they were more relaxed together and had soon chosen nicknames for each other. To her now, he was Big Bear.

'But it wouldn't be right, would it? Mixing work and play – and the Old Man'd play hell over it.'

'I know,' Katie said. 'But you don't have to be so cold. It makes me feel dreadful when I'm there all day and you never even look at me. Just give me a smile or a quick wink, and I'll know everything's all right.'

He promised he would, and from then on things had been better. It was rather fun, outwitting Mr Graham – not, as Simon said, that he gave a monkey's really – and more especially Mrs Crosby, whom they had nicknamed 'Misery-Guts'.

'She really could curdle milk with that face,' Simon said one afternoon as they lay together.

He laughed wholeheartedly when Katie began on one of her imitations of Mrs Crosby's resentful tones. 'Yes, Mr Collinge – only my ribbon's wearing terribly thin. Yes, Mr Collinge.' Frown, sniff, toss of head . . .

Katie loved being able to make him laugh. 'I suppose she misses her husband and resents anyone else being happy.'

'Well, good ruddy luck to him,' Simon said. 'I mean, we've all got our problems, but at least he's still alive – not like some. I mean, Gloria in accounts lost her sister in the bombing, but she still manages to put a smile on her face.'

'I think she must just be like that.' Katie laughed at his impatience.

'Don't let's worry about her.' He laid an arm lazily round her shoulders and pulled her close. 'She's not important. She's only a bloody little typist. Now, where d'you want to . . . ?'

She was pulling away, furiously. 'So that's what you think!' she flared at him. 'So that's what I am, isn't it: a bloody little typist!'

'No, no! That's not what I mean. I put it all wrong. I just mean – oh, you know, she's one of those women – compared with you she's . . . I mean, you've got class. You're different altogether. It's not because she's a *typist*, as such, it's just ... She's not in your league at all. Don't be cross, Squeak – I wasn't getting at you.' He gazed at her with round, little-boy eyes until she forgave him.

Spring days came at last, warm and full of green promise.

'One day,' Simon said, as they lay naked together in his bedroom, 'in fact, not one day – lots of days! – we'll go out when it's warm, and we'll make love out in the open air.' He trailed his hands across her ribs and she giggled at the way it tickled. 'We'll make love in haystacks and fields, on the cliffs, on the beach, up trees ...'

She was laughing now. 'Up trees! Can you imagine!'

He turned to her exuberantly. 'I can't ever have enough of you, my Dark Lady. I want to make love to you everywhere and every way ... Hey, I've just thought!' He pushed himself up. 'We can go in the garden!'

'What, now? Don't be daft. It's freezing!'

'It's nearly May – that's almost summer!'

'Well, it may be May, but "the May isn't out". And it's cold. You go in the garden stark naked if you want, but I'm staying in this nice warm bed!'

'Oh, I see – well, would her Ladyship like her Bear to bring her a cup of tea in her nice warm bed?'

'Yes – she would, please.' As he got up, Katie reached up and smacked his bare bottom. 'Double-quick time!'

Sometimes it felt as if the war would just go on and on, and nothing would change. Apart from a couple of lone bombing raids over Birmingham over the past months, the fighting was all far away, and what was close up meant endless inconveniences: the blackout, the shortages of food and cigarettes, razor blades, booze and petrol – small or large considerations, depending on who you were.

And then suddenly the reality of war would burst in and come up close, as it did that morning when they were all working away in the office, Mrs Crosby miserably mopping her nose because of a spring cold and Katie typing until her fingers ached.

They heard running feet and Mr Graham cannonballed through the door, more animated than Katie had ever seen him, going so fast that he had a job not to crash into Lena Crosby's desk.

'Have you heard the news?' Obviously they hadn't. He was hopping from foot to foot. 'They've surrendered, those Kraut bastards! In the desert – in North Africa. The whole bloody sodding lot of them. Monty's done it!'

The victory at El Alamein led by General Montgomery in the autumn had been a huge boost for morale, and this was more cause for celebration. Hope had appeared.

Katie knew this was the happiest time of her life so far. But something was niggling at her. Simon had a very relaxed view of the future, saying that there was no point in thinking about anything permanent until the war was over. After all, everything was uncertain, here today and gone tomorrow: what was the point in making plans? But Katie was beginning to feel she needed more. After all, she had given herself to him and they were, in her eyes – well, just as good as married, weren't they? She wouldn't just lose her virginity to anyone. She wasn't fast like that. It *meant* something.

And for all Simon's reasoning, she thought they should have more to do with each other's families. To satisfy Vera, Simon had been round a couple of times for tea and met her. He was very charming and reassuring, and Vera seemed almost dazzled by him and the happier for it. But Katie had not even so much as met Simon's sister, never mind his parents, in any other capacity than as a typist at the works. Mr Collinge senior was still none the wiser.

'Don't worry,' Simon kept saying. 'We'll tell them in good time. But just for now, I want you too much to spend too many afternoons drinking tea and making small talk.' Then he would pull her close to him and look deeply into her eyes. 'For the moment I want you all to myself!'

And it was very gratifying that he couldn't seem to get enough of her. He had an endless thirst for love-making and this made her feel desirable and, in turn, made her desire him all the more. As spring turned to summer and the flowers blossomed, she resigned herself to waiting – the way they were all waiting, all the time, for the war to end, for things to change.

Seventeen

'What's the matter?' Ann said, seeing Katie grimace as she took a sip of her coffee. 'Dain't you put any sugar in?'

'Yes . . .' Katie stirred it again, but it still didn't taste any better.

'I thought you liked that Camp stuff. Anyway, as I was saying . . .'

Their occasional Saturday-morning meetings for a cuppa were a chance to catch up on Ann's love life, which to Katie's surprise still seemed to involve Gordon. She hadn't thought he'd last long, but Ann seemed quite stuck on him now.

'I had the most terrible fright . . .' Ann leaned close across the table, her eyes wide, voice sinking low. She looked to each side to see if anyone could hear. 'I thought last week that I must be . . .' She was whispering now. *'Expecting!'* For a moment she put one hand over her mouth and laid the other on her chest, rolling her eyes. 'God, I was terrified! What the hell would I've said to Mom? She'd've killed me! My life would've been over.'

Katie's heart thudded so hard that she felt dizzy. She looked down to try and hide her burning cheeks.

'Katie, you all right?'

'Oh yes – course.' She raised her head again to hear Ann's whispers.

'I thought I'd missed – you know, my monthly visitor was late. I mean I've been careful lately, making sure I keep a note, and for three days – oh, blimey.' She sat back, her immense breasts heaving dramatically under her pale-green sweater. 'I can't tell you the relief. I started thinking I had all the signs . . .'

'Well, what would they be?' Katie asked quickly. She arranged her face in what she hoped was a relaxed expression. Ann smiled at this innocence.

'Oh, you know, the usual things: missing your monthly, feeling tired out and everything tasting funny – then morning sickness.' She stopped and thought. 'When my sister Florrie was having little Amy, she kept fainting if she stood up for long, and she said she had this nasty taste in her mouth. In fact she was quite poorly all the way through.'

While trying to keep an interested, calm expression, Katie found her thoughts hurtling round in panic. She had missed. Her period was late. Very late. But she wasn't being sick, was she? Not actually *sick*, although she did feel a bit queasy at times. Quite a lot of the time, if she was truthful. But surely she might just have a chill on her stomach or something? Taking another sip of coffee, she couldn't help reacting to the horrible taste. Was it her? Surely the coffee was just the same? She decided she wouldn't bother to drink the rest.

'Anyroad, I was in a right state for three days, and I think our mom was beginning to suspect something. And then it came – oh!' Ann fanned her hand past her face in relief. 'I don't know what I'd've done, honest to God I don't. I s'pect Gordon would stick by me. He's mad about me. But I don't want marriage and kiddies and all that yet – I mean, our Amy and Raymond are the best of kids, but they are a handful. Florrie never

147

stops. I don't think I could stand all that yet – I want to have some fun first!' Ann narrowed her eyes and looked at Katie again. 'You sure you're all right?'

'Yes – course. It's just been a tiring week: working late and . . .'

'And playing late, I bet, you dark horse. How's it going with your fella – the perfect gent? And are you still getting digs from her Majesty?'

Katie had told Ann a certain amount about Simon – she loved talking about him for one thing, and there was really no on else she could say much to. Ann knew he was the boss's son. And she knew about Lena Crosby.

'Oh, she doesn't change,' Katie laughed. She sat back and took a deep breath, trying to calm herself, though all the time her hands were clenched tightly in her lap. 'She makes all sorts of catty remarks. She keeps making out I'm the favourite in the office, even though they really do treat us the same. If anyone asks her to run an errand, she gets all pointy-faced about it because she thinks I should be doing everything like that, because I'm younger. But Simon and I' – how she loved saying that, *Simon and I* – 'never do or say anything in the office that's not to do with the job.'

'Oh, she's just jealous.'

'Mind you, Simon did mention that he'd been to a concert at the Town Hall the other night, and she gave me such a look because she must have guessed I went as well. And we're going to the Hippodrome on Saturday.'

'You lucky thing,' Ann said good-naturedly. 'He's quite a classy number, isn't he?' Still, so are you, so there you go. Gordon's more of a one for going down the pub and a game of darts. And we have to go to his mom's a lot 'cause she's not very well. She's all right, though, Mrs T. I get on with her. I need to, don't I? She might be my mother-in-law one day. What about your mother: doesn't she mind you gadding about?'

'Well, she makes remarks sometimes,' Katie said. 'But I think she's decided there's nothing she can do about it.'

'Well, that's good,' Ann said. ''Bout time.'

It was good to sit and chat with Ann, and Katie felt herself relax gradually, her mind distracted from the subject she was obsessed with. But as soon as they parted and Katie was walking along New Street towards the bus stop, she felt terror clasp her innards again like a freezing cold hand.

The thought was never far from her mind and her certainty grew. What Ann had said, other bits of information she picked up – she had even been to the library and looked up in a medical book – and the strange, different way she was feeling, all added up. She covered it up from everyone else, but by the time it was high summer she had missed two periods and looked like missing a third, so there was no getting away from it. She had a baby on the way.

The first time she actually allowed herself to say it, she was in the bath at Simon's house. It was a warm July day and they had been out for a walk. Katie felt hot and sticky, but more than that, she needed to be alone. Amid all Simon's cheerful chatter about life in general, the war and golf and his plans for the future – which she couldn't help noticing, more and more, did not seem to involve marriage, or her, or was she being over-sensitive? – she was finding it very hard to keep talking and smiling as if there was nothing wrong.

'BB, would it be all right if I had a quick bath?' she said when they got back to Kings Heath. 'I just feel a bit hot and uncomfortable.'

In the hall he put his arm around her and waggled his eyebrows suggestively. 'Of course it would. The idea of you being all warm and soft from the bath is absolutely delicious to a Bear like me. I'll be waiting for you. Want a cup of tea?'

She was about to say no, because now tea tasted odd to her too, but she gave a faint smile and said, 'Yes, that'd be nice. Thanks.'

Lying in the bath, sunlight from the window flashing in the water and lighting up her pale body in brilliant patches, she moved her hands over her belly. And she felt it – something. Just a little bit, but there was a lump, a fullness.

'Oh my God,' she whispered. 'Jesus, Mary and Joseph!' She was filled with panic. Tears rose in her eyes. She had felt alone in her life many times, but never so much as now. What in the name of heaven was she going to do?

'Katie?' He was knocking at the door. The two Welsh lodgers must have been out for the afternoon and they had the house to themselves. 'Tea – can I bring it in?'

'Yes,' she called, immediately pulling herself together. She couldn't let him see yet, or anyone else.

Simon came in, looking oddly overdressed in the bathroom, since she was naked. He perched the cup and saucer on the corner of the bath.

'You look lovely,' he said. 'I almost feel like getting in with you.'

'I'll be out soon,' she said, not encouraging him. She certainly wasn't in the mood for any playing about of that sort.

150

'OK, I'll just go and run my eye over the paper while you finish off.' He leaned down and kissed her on the lips. 'Don't be long though, will you?'

In his bedroom, wrapped in a towel, her hair hanging loose down her back, she sat on the bed looking at the sunlit poplar tree gently shifting in the breeze at the bottom of the garden. He would soon come up and would want to make love, because he always did. Ever since they had begun on it together, his appetite had never diminished. She was flattered by his wanting her: didn't it show how much he cared for her? But this was something different altogether. Could she tell him? He kept saying over and over that he loved her, but could she rely on him? Why was she so full now of all the doubts she had pushed aside, the ones that didn't fit the romantic picture she had clung to?

She didn't feel in the least like lovemaking, but she knew it was inevitable so that he didn't become suspicious. What she longed for was to be looked after, for him to come up, and for her to spill out the truth to him and have him say that everything would be all right, that he loved her more than anything and would always be with her. It was such an immense thing to say and it would change everything. Why did it feel so impossible to come out with it? Didn't she trust him in this test? He might be kind and sweet and true. But what if he wasn't? What then? She could hardly bear to ask herself the question.

His tread was approaching up the stairs; the door opened. She kept her back to him.

'Oh, look at you,' he said, the desire already evident in his voice.

Unbuttoning his shirt, he came and knelt in front of her and gently tugged the towel away from her. With a sound of pleasure he kissed and sucked at her nipples. They felt tender, more sensitive than usual. His tongue filled her with an ache, a strange, almost unbearable feeling.

'Don't!' She pushed him away, though not roughly.

He looked up startled. 'What's up?'

'They hurt – I don't know why.'

'Oh, sweetheart . . .' This seemed to arouse him, and soon he was naked and drawing her down to lie beside him. He lay looking down at her. 'You know, I think they've got bigger.' Gently he caressed her breasts and the feeling went through her like electricity, a mixture of pain and desire.

She knew he was right. 'Must be something to do with the time of the month,' she said quickly.

'I thought you didn't seem quite yourself today.' He kissed her cheek, then beamed down at her. He was already fully aroused. 'My poor Katie. But God, you are so beautiful.'

He kissed her lips then and soon went to move his hand between her legs, in a hurry, wanting her to be ready for him.

'You're not . . . ?'

'Bleeding? No.' If only she was!

When he came in naked, jerking with urgency, with no horrible-smelling rubber thing covering him, she didn't protest. It was too late now, after all. It had happened before, a number of times. The first time she hadn't noticed until it was far too late. She left all that up to him.

'I took a risk,' he'd said afterwards, sort of in apology. He grinned winningly at her. 'It's just – it feels so nice, just delicious. It's like dying and going to heaven.'

Katie blushed. She found talking about all these sorts

of things very awkward, and when at other times he had neglected to protect himself and had plunged into her, she had been too embarrassed to say anything. He seemed to need her so badly as well, and it felt wrong to stop him.

Now she lay back and felt a hot sweep of desire growing in her belly as he moved inside her. It was not quite like anything she had ever felt before, and after he'd climaxed she felt angry and unsatisfied.

'Don't go,' she ordered, pulling him close in a way that took him by surprise, and moving under him she brought herself to a shuddering, gasping climax, not quite like any she had ever had before, as if her insides were in a melting, volcanic state.

'My God!' Simon said, excited by her reaction, and thrust into her again. At last they both lay back, panting.

Katie felt like spilling words all over him. *Do you realize – do you know what you've done, what we've done? Oh, hold me, hold me and tell me you'll stay with me and it's all going to be all right!*

But she didn't dare. The words, once spoken, could not be taken back. She was going to have to keep her secret – for as long as she could.

Eighteen

She felt it, lying in bed one morning: a tiny pulse of movement inside her, like a bubble bursting. The little lump of her stomach had grown just a fraction. It terrified her, the way it could just grow and grow, with no way of her stopping it. At the same time it was hard to take in that it was real.

For minutes at a time she would forget. When things were very busy in the office and she sat pounding her typewriter, concentrating on the latest schedule, there were blessed moments when it slipped from her mind. And then *he* would speak to Mrs Crosby, or a breeze carried through the open office windows a whiff of smoke from a cigarette or factory chimney. Everything seemed to smell more strongly. Or she would feel queasily hungry. And it all came flooding back, the numbing panic that made her catch her breath and sometimes sit staring, stunned, out of the window at the neighbouring rooftops until something nudged her back to work. For the first time she was glad that Simon did not pay any attention to her in the office, his mind turned to his male world.

The worry wore her out as much as anything, and by the evening she was exhausted. A couple of times she told Simon she couldn't come out with him. She was tired and she found pretending everything was normal a terrible strain. At home she would fall asleep in the chair over the book she was pretending to read, though her mind was usually miles away, worrying, panicking.

'You seem tired,' Vera had remarked several times. She was more careful about what she said to Katie these days. 'Perhaps you're sickening for something? I'm usually the one who's dropping off!'

Katie would try to smile and stifle her yawns. 'Yes, I s'pose I am tired. Maybe it's everything just catching up with me.' Most people were tired. The strain of the war was taking its toll.

It was only when she was in bed alone that the fear took over. Sometimes she lay rigid, her head full of jeering voices: '... O-ho! She's got a bun in the oven! ... Bastard child ... No better than she should be ... You'd never have thought it to look at her, would you?' And above all the voice demanding: *What are you going to do? What in heaven's name are you going to do?*

Over these months while she and Simon had been going about together, she'd lived in a rosy bubble of love and hope, not seeing things she didn't want to see. He loved her and she loved him, and that was all that mattered. This was how it was supposed to be, and she had been able to see nothing but him. But now everything she had put her hopes in seemed to rest on dreadfully frail foundations. She had dreams of marrying Simon and becoming Mrs Collinge, of spending her life with him and, yes, having his children. But now all she could see were the excuses he'd made to keep their affair – she had to admit that was what it was – a secret. He barely acknowledged her at work, and he had never taken her to meet his family. The way he'd put it to her, wanting things to be secret, like an adventure, had all seemed fun and exciting. But now she felt a fool. It was as if she was his dirty secret. She was a complete dupe to think he'd want anything to do with her now that she was expecting a baby – his baby. But still she clung to hope. He loved her, of course he did! He'd make sure everything was all right. Then she would feel ashamed of doubting him.

One Saturday morning she slipped into Sparkhill Library again. Since she didn't dare talk to a real medical man, she found *The Universal Home Doctor* and took it discreetly to a corner of the hushed room, where she sat with her back turned to everyone. She felt as if everyone must be watching her, as if the book was red-hot. Here she was, this respectable-looking young woman, neatly turned out in a sage-green summer frock, jumpy as a mouse in case anyone came and looked over her shoulder and saw her looking up . . . But looking up what?

She flicked through the pages with clammy hands. Surely there wasn't a heading 'Getting rid of a baby'? Soon, under A, she found 'Abortion'. Of course! Her heart was pounding. That was the term for it, and a terrible one. Even seeing it on the page made her tremble. You could go to prison for that, couldn't you?

She read frantically, full of dread, her breathing shallow and jerky. At first she thought that the entry was only about natural miscarriage. Too much activity, it said, or heavy lifting, might bring on the baby. It was the next part that chilled her blood. 'It is well known that abortion may be due to the taking of certain drugs or the criminal use of instruments.' Either of these, it warned, often resulted in the death of the woman.

Her legs turned to water and her hands were shaking so much that she almost dropped the book on the floor. She managed somehow to get it back onto the shelf and stagger out into the pale sunshine of the Stratford Road, the word criminal, *criminal*, pounding in her mind. Life burst in on her, the Saturday-morning scramble to the shops with ration books. As people came towards her they made her jump. They felt like a threat, and she found herself laying a hand protectively over her stomach.

Why on earth am I doing that? she wondered, shivering. She felt very cold and sick. I want it not to be there, I want it to die ... Oh God, she wailed inwardly as tears rose in her eyes, I don't know what I want. She felt as if her life had been taken over and was not hers any more. It was terrifying.

To try and calm herself she went into the park and, taking deep breaths, walked slowly round the green space, speckled with playing children. She found a bench where no one else was sitting and sat staring ahead of her. The *criminal use of instruments* ... She'd heard whispers about wire or knitting needles being used to end a baby, about buckets full of blood. She felt faint just thinking about it. And it all seemed so far from who she thought she was. It was girls in sordid back streets who did such things, girls who had asked for it, who were fast ... Not people like her. How snooty she had been in her thinking! Yet now she was one of them, caught in this trap where to continue with the child or to end it was equally dreadful. For a few moments it all welled up and overcame her and she put her hands over her face, fighting back her tears.

Soon, though, she heard voices coming closer and quickly wiped her eyes. Three boys, all about nine years old, were running round quite close to her, charging at each other like little bulls, then wrestling each other on the grass. Her shock at them disturbing her was overcome by the sight of their cheeky, laughing faces, and a bolt of longing went through her.

Why am I being so ridiculous? she thought, her spirits soaring, after hitting the bottom a moment before. I'm going to see Simon later. All I have to do is tell him. I love him and he loves me, I know he does. Everything in that moment felt very secure and clear. He would make everything all right, she knew he would.

She caught the bus and then walked to his house, churning with nerves, and knocked on the door. She was ready with her words, her thin thread of hope, but the door was opened by Dai, one of Simon's lodgers, a stocky man with wild brown hair.

'Oh – hello!' He seemed as startled as Katie.

'Is Simon in?' She managed to make her voice sound almost normal.

'No, he's not here, I'm afraid. I don't know where he's gone. The works, p'raps.'

Her courage was already seeping away. What on earth was she doing, just turning up on his doorstep when anyone could be about!

'All right,' she said casually. 'Not to worry. Thank you.'

Just round the corner she was grateful for a scrubby hedge edging a garden, because her insides bucked and she was sick until there was nothing left inside her.

Nineteen

October 1943

It was Vera who noticed.

Katie spent the rest of the summer in a paralysis of fear, denying to herself for as long as she could that this was really happening to her. But as the days waned and the leaves turned yellow, then brown, the child moved unmistakably inside her.

That evening it was wet and they had both come in tired and hungry from work, leaving their umbrellas open to dry in the hall. They took off their wet boots, then went round pulling the blackout curtains and turning on the lights.

'There's some of that stew left over from yesterday,' Vera said. 'Where are my slippers? Ah, here they are. It's more potato than meat, but there's a fair bit left, I think.'

'I'll put it on to heat up,' Katie said. She almost said, 'I could eat a horse, I'm so hungry,' but stopped herself. Her mother had been giving her odd looks lately, as if she was trying to work something out.

'There's some carrot and swede,' Vera said. She got to her feet, with a tired grunt. 'I'll get the fire going, then I'll come and give you a hand.'

Vera clicked the wireless on. Music streamed out and

then, as she riddled the fire and Katie was scraping carrots, the news. Italy had declared war on Germany.

'They want to make up their minds, those Eyties,' Vera remarked. 'This is nearly all slack—' The fire kindled and spat.

Katie heard her mother's intake of breath. She was kneeling by the fender, head turned to look at Katie as she stood by the table. Their eyes met and, in those seconds, Katie knew it was too late to deny anything. Her stomach had taken on an unmistakable roundness and Vera was staring straight at it. Katie felt her cheeks burn.

There was a moment of silence as Vera got slowly to her feet. Then she advanced like a prowling tiger. Katie took a step back, horrified at her demented expression.

'*What*' – she pointed an accusing finger – 'is *that*?'

Katie looked down helplessly at her expanding belly, unable to meet her mother's burning gaze.

'Look at me!' Vera shrieked. 'Don't you dare look away from me! What is that ... That swollen ... *thing* doing in this house? It's true, isn't it? I knew something was going on – it's that Collinge chap, isn't it? You *stupid, stupid*—'

The stinging slap her mother delivered across her face forced Katie to look up in shock, tears of pain filling her eyes.

'Ow – don't! Don't hit me!' Holding her cheek, she burst into tears. 'What're you hitting me for?'

Vera was beside herself. 'What d'you damn well think I'm hitting you for, you *stupid*, dirty girl!' She began by screaming, but managed to lower her voice in case any of the neighbours might hear. She came up close, taking hold of the neck of Katie's cardigan, her whole face bitterly contorted. The rest of her words came out as a venomous hiss. 'It's true, isn't it? You've gone and let him have his way with you, and now look at you!'

Katie couldn't deny it. She nodded, but she could feel defiance growing in her.

'Well, what d'you want me to say? I've been biting my lip long enough, but my God, I should've said something before. You'd better get him to marry you right away, there's nothing else for it. I just hope he does the decent thing or you're ruined, my girl – no two ways about it!'

'Of course he will,' Katie defended him. 'We love one another – only he doesn't know yet. I haven't told him.'

Vera gave a nasty laugh, folding her arms across her chest. She was working herself up into more of a mocking rage by the minute.

'No, I bet you damn well haven't! All these years I've brought you up, scrimping and saving, and trying to give us a respectable life amid all the dregs ... And how d'you thank me for it, you little slut? Spreading your legs for the first man who comes along. My God ...' She was so worked up that for a moment Katie thought she was going to have a fit. Her voice turned to a growl. 'Look at you – just like your father. You're like him down to the bone – oh!' She backed away and slapped her hand down hard on the table. Katie saw that the pan of water for the carrots was boiling away, steam pouring into the cold air. My father? Katie thought. What on earth is she talking about?

'Mother ...'

'Don't you "Mother" me!' Vera was wringing her hands. 'Don't think you can get around me. I'm not your mother any more. D'you think I've hauled myself out of the gutter for you to drag us straight back down there again? Do you? Over my dead body! You can get out – take your things and your bastard brat, and get out of my sight. You're all the same: you're an O'Neill to the core, and I'm finished with you – the whole damn rotten lot of you! That's what you are: rotten to the core.'

It was Vera who was sobbing after this bewildering outburst, bent over with her elbows resting on the table, face buried in her hands. Katie stood numbed, in shock as the words poured out of her mother, not seeming to make any sense.

Vera suddenly flung herself away from the table. 'Go on, I mean it – get out! Take your things and go – to him. And I hope he damn well wants you or you'll be on the streets, my girl, and it'll serve you right, and don't think you can come running to me! You'll find out what life's about, won't you, you stupid little bitch. Go on . . .'

She came across the room and Katie ran out, frightened that her mother was about to set about her. Up in her room, she stood at a loss. What was she doing? Surely her mother didn't really mean her to leave, for good? She couldn't mean that! In her panic, the only person she could think of whom she wanted to see was Simon. He felt like her rock, the only safe haven to which she could escape.

'I'll take my night things,' she murmured, opening drawers with shaking hands and gathering a little pile of belongings on the bed, the tears now running down her face.

'Are you ready yet?' Vera's voice grated up the stairs. She came up and stood in the doorway, arms folded, her expression as hard as iron.

162

'Mother, surely you don't mean . . . You don't really want me to *leave*?'

'Oh yes, I do. I've had enough of you and your kind – Judases all!'

'But what d'you mean?' Katie wailed. 'Uncle Patrick wasn't a . . . a Judas. And Daddy . . .'

'*Daddy*,' Vera mimicked in a nasty voice. She looked so strange, so completely possessed by rage, that Katie was frightened. It was as if Vera had become someone she'd never seen before. 'What do you know about *Daddy*. You were too young to remember anything.'

'But . . .' Katie's voice became a squeak. 'What d'you mean?'

They stood staring at each other. Vera's face was working, and for a few seconds Katie felt she was looking at someone deranged. Then her expression seemed to freeze. In a low, intense voice, almost a hiss, she said, 'I don't mean anything. He *died*. Left forever. That's a betrayal – can't you see that? Can't you?'

Their words ran out and suddenly it was quiet. Repelled, Katie turned and stuffed her things into her little suitcase. Vera stood back to let her past. She didn't follow Katie as she went down the stairs, put on her wet boots again, picked up her umbrella and walked out into the night.

It seemed to take forever to get to Kings Heath, though it was not very late. She felt punch-drunk and unable to think straight. On the bus she found herself wondering whether Vera had taken the carrots off the stove or whether they had boiled dry. This made the tears come again, but she tried to swallow them down, not wanting to cry in front of strangers.

At Simon's door she prayed he would answer, and not one of the Welsh lads. It took her several minutes to get up the courage to knock, and when she heard footsteps in the hall she thought she might faint with fright.

Simon's face appeared round the door, squinting into the gloom.

'Squeak!' he exclaimed. 'How lovely to see you, darling!' Katie was sure the cheerful welcome sounded forced, but then she had taken him by surprise.

'Can I come in?' she asked huskily.

'Well, of course you can.' He stood back and she passed him, not sure if he had noticed the holdall in her hand. 'So I take it you can't keep away from me?'

The hall was dimly lit and the house sounded quiet. She took a breath, even opened her mouth to tell him, but instead said, 'I – I've had a bit of a falling-out with my mother. Can I stay here tonight?'

'Ah!' Simon laughed, sounding relieved. 'I did wonder what the luggage was all in aid of. Of course you can, Squeaky. I know what you mothers and daughters are like. Come on in, I was just having some supper. Bangers – d'you want some?'

'No, it's all right, I've had mine,' she lied. In any case she could not have eaten: her stomach was churning like a maiding tub.

She sat opposite Simon and accepted a cup of tea as he tucked into his sausage and mash, looking as handsome as ever, but completely unaware of her misery.

Just look at me, she thought. Look at me properly. But he was too busy tucking in.

'I've been over to Coventry today – see about a new customer. That's why I wasn't in.' He took a swig of tea. 'What sort of day've you had – old Misery-Guts behaving herself?'

Katie told him a few bits and pieces about the office. She was sure Mrs Crosby knew that she and Simon were involved with each other – the woman seemed to have second sense. But though she gave Katie long, meaningful stares, there was nothing she could say. As they talked about the day-to-day life of the firm, and Katie tried to be as normal as possible, the day's upset and even the reality of the baby faded a little into the background. It became more and more impossible to begin the conversation. She knew she was putting it off again. Mother would calm down, she could go back home . . .

But as they prepared for bed later, she was careful to keep herself facing away from him as she undressed, in case he noticed. She saw though, with despair, as he carelessly threw his clothes onto the chair and flung on a dressing gown to go and clean his teeth, that he wouldn't notice. He was blithely oblivious to everything. His life was going along swimmingly, thank you very much. She watched his departing back with utter desperation. She had to tell him – had to . . . *Please, listen to me – help me . . .*

They cuddled up in Simon's three-quarter-size bed, she with her back to him, Simon curled around her. As soon as they were touching she knew he was aroused, his hands beginning to explore her body in a lazy sort of way.

'I think Mac and Les are going to be able to fix up a round of golf this weekend,' he said through a yawn. 'It's a shame you don't play – you should come and learn.'

Katie felt lonelier in that moment than ever before in her life. She said nothing. Simon's hands were lifting the edge of her nightdress, his hands moving higher.

'Goodness, Squeak' – he stroked her bare belly – 'I do believe you're starting to fill out a bit. Is someone getting you extra rations from somewhere?'

Her breath caught in her throat. She turned in the bed so that she was on her back, half facing him.

'BB – Simon. I . . . I need to tell you something.'

'Umm?' She could feel him pressing against her, hard and wanting.

'No – stop, please!' She was so emphatic that his hands stilled.

'Hey, what's up?'

'I'm . . . I'm . . .' Oh heavens, could she get the words out! 'Oh, Si – I'm having a baby – our baby.' They poured out, the sobs starting too.

He pushed himself up on his elbow and his boyish face was staring intently down into hers.

'You are having me on, aren't you?'

She shook her head vigorously. 'I can feel it moving. It's yours, Si – ours.'

He pushed back the bedclothes, drawing up her nightgown so that she felt cold and exposed, and touched her swollen stomach. His interest seemed detached, scientific, as if he was checking the pressure of a set of tyres.

'And you're sure?' he said again. She could see he was completely stunned. That such a thing might really happen had not crossed his mind.

Fearfully, her tears running into her hair, she looked up into his face. 'I'm certain.'

His left eye twitched. He looked away, across the room. Katie felt a coldness grow in her. He was not with her, she knew. He was far, far away. All he said, in the end, was, '*Christ!*'

Twenty

Katie woke the next morning after a terrible night's sleep, sick with hunger. Of course – she had had no tea last night. It all came rushing back to her. She was here, in Simon's bed, after the row with Mom, after his reaction: the fact that he could think of nothing whatsoever to say.

She was alone in the bed. The curtains were still closed and the room very dark. Somewhere she could hear movement in the house, the others getting off to work. Would Simon just disappear to the works and not even come and speak to her? Was that how it was? And she had to get to work as well – she couldn't just lie here! But she felt sick and utterly drained.

What had he said to her last night? She thought back to what it was that had kept her awake, paralysed by worry, by a sense of abandonment. There had been no warm words, no loving reassurance. Yet he hadn't exactly rejected her, either. He had been overwhelmed, she could see, and had nothing to give her when she needed to feel his arms close round her, reassuring her. Instead of which he had spoken in a strange, flat voice, not at all like his usual jaunty self.

'Look, Katie.' No fond nicknames now. That was all gone. 'I don't know what to say. I can't sort this out tonight. Let's sleep on it.'

He lay down, turned away from her and seemed to

167

sleep easily, though she was not sure if he was pretending, just to avoid her.

Sort this out, he had said, as if she was a carburettor that needed technical adjustment. Had she known, in her heart, that it would be like this? That Simon had never truly loved her, and that in her turn she was not sure of him? She had felt herself shut down. She could not bear to let herself feel the bald truth of this. Still she longed to believe in love, that what they had made together was not all false and a terrible mistake.

Footsteps came up the stairs, slowly, reluctantly. He came in with a cup and saucer.

'Are you awake?'

'Yes.' She sat up slowly.

'I brought you some tea.'

'Thank you.'

He handed it to her in the gloom, then sat on the bed, at the end, far from her. His mood seemed even more distant. There was silence for a few moments and she sipped the sweet tea, feeling detached and helpless.

'Look, it's no good,' Simon said, all in a rushed, clipped voice. 'I've been thinking. You'll have to go – you can't go into the works in that state. It's just not on. You'd better give in your notice today – I'll see to it that you get references for another job somewhere, when you're ready.'

'What d'you mean? Just go?' Her voice rose in panic. Even if she did not expect much of him, she had at least hoped for gentleness. She had not thought he would be this brutal. 'What about . . . I mean, this is our baby – yours and mine!'

'Not mine.'

'What d'you mean, "not mine"?' She scrambled up

onto her knees in outrage. 'Of course it's yours – who else d'you think . . . ?'

'I mean, I'm not a part of this. Look, keep your voice down, for God's sake. You can see my position, can't you? I've got the firm to run – there's a war on, in case you'd forgotten. I'll be taking over the firm one day, and I suppose one day I'll have to get married, bring up a family with the right sort of girl. I mean if the Old Man found out – God almighty!' He gave something that sounded like a chuckle. 'Doesn't bear thinking about. But I'm not ready for all that yet, anyway. I'm only just setting out on the road . . .'

The coldness gripped tighter round her heart.

'The right sort of girl?' She could barely get the words out. 'What sort of girl am I then?'

'Well,' he tried to make light of it, 'you know what I mean! There are certain expectations of the kind of person you marry. Look, I'm sorry about it, Katie-kins.' He reached for something and, unable to see in the dark, cursed and went to twitch back the curtain a little. He was dressed for the works, fumbling in his jacket pocket for his wallet.

Her rage and hurt were so deep that the words came out small and tight. 'Do you realize I have nowhere to go? I have no one? This is your baby.' Then she choked. 'I thought you loved me. You've just been *playing* with me – all this time!'

'Oh, now don't start all that!' He turned, the wallet in his hand. 'Playing? Maybe a bit, yes. But what have you been doing? I've given you a good time – very nice being able to hop in someone's motor and be whisked away for an evening out. I'll bet you don't know anyone else in a position to give you that. So don't pretend I've been all take.' He shrugged. 'Fair dos, Katie – we've had some fun, but I can't be seen to be hanging about with . . . Well, we're just not each other's type deep down, are we? Look – I'll see you're all right.' He held out a wad of notes. 'Here's enough to look after yourself for a bit. You can either, well – see to it that there's no child . . . or if you go ahead with the brat, that amount'll keep you for a while until you're on your feet again.'

Brat? This man who had talked so fondly of children. She stared at him.

'You're paying me off? Like a cheap tart?'

'Well, not exactly . . .'

The cup left her hand before she'd even thought. 'I always knew you were a shallow, spoilt, boring . . .' She heard it crack against his forehead. The dregs splashed down his face. She hurled the saucer after it, but it missed and thudded on the floor.

'Ow! Christ, woman! What the hell're you doing? Look, if that's the way you're going to behave, I'm not even going to try and discuss it with you. But it just makes my point – my family expects me to marry a respectable woman, not some easy tart like you.'

Katie gasped, but before she could reply he had moved close and was looking threateningly into her face.

'And don't you go trying any cheap tricks, like going to the Old Man – he won't have any cotter with you, I can tell you right now. Your word against mine is hardly going to wash, is it?'

She was shaking her head now. She would never have done that. She didn't want revenge and trouble – only love, from somewhere at least; and his love, she could see now, she had never had. Her sobs broke into the room.

'Oh, don't start that. Look, I'm going to work. You make sure you come in and hand in your notice. And be out of here by the time I get back, as well. This is for you – luckily I had a fair wedge in the house.'

He put the money down on the end of the bed, picked up something from the chair and went to the door.

'We've had some nice times, Katie. Good luck, old girl. You'll be all right – you'll see.'

She sat in the quiet after the front door slammed, hugging her knees.

'You bastard,' she whispered. 'You cowardly bastard . . .'

Suddenly she was seized by the need to be sick and ran to the bathroom, bringing up a grainy stream of tea and curdled milk. Afterwards she walked back unsteadily and sat on the bed.

I am alone, she thought, exhaustedly. There's no one – just you and me. And for the first time she had fellow feeling for the little life growing in her. Picking up the sheaf of notes, she counted it. He had left her a hundred pounds.

She walked through the old familiar streets in darkness that evening, carrying her little holdall, until she reached Enid Thomas's house.

Thank heavens it's so dark, she thought, groping her way to the front door.

'Who is it?' Enid's voice came through to her.

'It's me,' she hissed. 'Katie – Vera's daughter.'

'Who? I can't hear yer!'

Katie rolled her eyes. So much for trying to come in quietly. Eventually Enid opened the door, looking out cautiously. She was dressed in her old slippers and her hair was looking a bit dishevelled.

'Oh, it's you, bab.' Her gentle voice reached Katie soothingly. 'I wasn't expecting any visitors. Come on then, quick – mustn't let the light out.'

Seeing Enid's familiar figure was a comfort after the lonely, agonizing day she'd had and Katie felt tears rising in her.

'D'yer want a cup of tea, bab? I've got some on the go.'

'Yes, please – I'd love one.'

'Might be on the weak side – you know how it is.'

'Enid . . .' The tone of Katie's voice stopped Enid in her tracks. She looked up, the teapot in her hand. 'I'm sorry to have to ask this, but can you put me up tonight, please? I'll sleep anywhere – I don't need anything much, I just haven't got anywhere to go . . .' She was babbling, her anxiety spilling out.

'Stay here?' Enid put the teapot down and looked closely at her. 'What d'yer mean? Oh, you are in a state – what's happened, bab?'

It was no good pretending and making up some excuse. Enid would find out sooner or later, and Katie was desperate for her help.

'Mom's told me not to come home. She's, well, she's thrown me out. Truth is, Enid' – she lowered her head, her face burning with shame – 'I'm . . . I'm expecting a baby.'

Enid sank onto the chair by the table.

'You? You're *expecting* . . . ?' Seconds passed as she tried to absorb the shock of it, her mouth open. No – not *you*, Katie, surely not? A babby? You're not that sort of girl!'

172

'Well, it seems I am, doesn't it?' Katie retorted bitterly.

It took some time to convince Enid that she was sure, and Enid eventually said, 'Oh, my word, Katie – I'd never, *ever*'ve thought it of you, the way you look so smart and nice and all your books and reading ... Oh my goodness.' She brought her hands up to her face. 'You poor, poor thing.' At last she remembered to attend to the teapot, her instinct immediately motherly and kind, despite her shock. 'Have you had your tea? Are you hungry?'

'Yes – no, I'm not hungry, thanks.' Katie had been to a cafe and had sat eating a meagre mutton stew in a corner, glad to be somewhere where no one knew her. She hadn't wanted to put Enid out any more than she had to. She knew Enid got into a tizzy easily.

Enid looked carefully at her, and Katie was full of gratitude. Now that she was getting over her shock – one of the many shocks life had thrown at her – Enid was squaring up to what needed to be done. And it was such a relief to tell someone who was kind and might help.

'Whatever are you going to do, love? Who is he? Is he going to marry yer?'

Katie shook her head. 'No. It doesn't matter who he is. But he gave me money. And I'll be able to work for quite a time yet. After that – I don't know.'

She'd gone to Collinge's that day, handed in her notice and walked into a job in a typing pool at another machine-tools firm, a job where she could be part of a crowd and not stand out. She already had good references from the Commercial School and didn't stoop to ask for the glowing recommendations that Simon had promised. So far as she was concerned, she never wanted to set eyes on him again, the slimy bastard. She had to close the door on him. He was no help. He was nothing. As the day passed, she felt herself develop a hard shell of protection around herself. To her surprise, she wanted to wrap protection around the child. After all, it was all she had in the world now.

'I'll find another place to live,' she promised Enid. 'Only I just need somewhere for tonight. I don't want to make trouble for you. You've been very kind.'

'Well, Katie – I can't say I'm not surprised at what you've told me. Shocked is the word – I'm shocked. But I've known you for such a time, I'm fond of you, bab, and your mother and I've been friends for years . . .'

'Yes, that's what I mean – I don't want to cause trouble.'

'And she threw you out?' Enid's good-natured face creased with distress. 'I mean, it must've been a terrible blow for her. You've always been such a good girl, Katie. And your mother's a lady. But surely she'll change her mind, she'll get over it. I mean, you're her flesh and blood when it comes down to it. I should leave it a few days and then go and see her. Make it up with her. It's hard for a mother to see this happen – but to wash her hands of you! I should have thought better of her. Give her another chance, and maybe she'll give you one.'

Katie was silent. She remembered the look of vicious loathing on her mother's face and her words: *D'you think I've hauled myself out of the gutter for you to drag us straight back down there again?*

'I don't know about that,' she said.

'Look.' Enid got up. 'You can stay here tonight – of course you can. I mean, I can't put you up for the long term, but . . .'

'Oh no, I know! Thank you so much.' She felt tearful again.

'But do as I say, love – go and see your mother. See if you both can't come to some agreement.'

As she settled Katie into her spare room that night – the room that had once been her dead son's – Enid said goodnight, then added, 'I wish I could say it's going to be easy, love. But the fact is, you're going to have a struggle ahead of yer.'

Twenty-One

There was a thick fog the next evening when she came out of work. People were calling out to one another in exasperation at being bumped into or struggling to find the right turning.

'Oi – watch it!' a male voice snapped as Katie's shoulder collided painfully with someone. She paused in the street to get her bearings.

The firm where she now worked, under the eagle eye of a Miss Poulter, who was in charge of the typing pool, was in Ombersley Road in Balsall Heath. It was not too long a walk to Sparkhill, but at this rate it would take ages.

Gradually Katie felt her way along to where she needed to turn off, coughing in the damp, acrid air, though at least the dark and fog made her feel safely hidden. All the time now she felt as if everyone could see that she was growing out at the front. She had not mentioned that she was expecting when she went for the job, though she did call herself Mrs O'Neill.

She passed a pub on one corner. The door opened to let someone out and for a second she made out a handwritten sign on the door: 'NO BEER' in large letters. But it made her think of cosy evenings she had spent with Simon in the corner of various pubs while he talked to her – yes, she could see, he had done most of the talking; had not, truth to tell, shown much real interest in her. At the time she had overlooked this and not expected anything else. Those evenings out they had had – to the pictures, or the occasional dance – and those stolen afternoons in Kings Heath, how precious they had seemed and how bitterly she remembered them now. It was remembering the good times, as they had seemed then, that hurt the most and made her long for things to be different. She had thought she was in love, that this was how it was. You met someone, fell in love and they loved you back, the way her mother had. But it had all been a lie. The hurt of his rejection bit deeply into her. She kept seeing Simon's cold, contemptuous face as he handed her the money, as he would to a tart. That soon put a stop to any tender feelings she still had, of missing him. She was the one left raw and aching, and frightened and carrying his child. She boiled with the injustice of it. Any time she was alone for a few minutes she found herself ranting at him, pouring out all her hurt in bitter insults and accusations.

'All I was to you was a bit of fun,' she whispered furiously in that dark street. 'A chance for you to get what you wanted and then throw me aside like rubbish! I was just a plaything – I might as well have been a common whore. You never felt anything for me, not like you said. You lied and lied . . . And now my life is ruined, and you'll just go on, having everything on a plate the way you always have . . .' Her hurt and rage rose up and choked her, so that she was weeping, struggling to be quiet about it. She had to stop and recover as the tears blinded her even further. She longed to hurt him back. But she knew it was no good – he didn't care, and nothing she could say would make him care.

*

All day, during the back-aching hours of typing, she had been a bag of nerves thinking about her mother. Surely Enid was right – Vera would come round. If she went to her and talked calmly, told her mother how sorry she was . . . Vera had had all day to calm down – surely she couldn't have meant what she said, so cruel and so final?

Reaching the house, Katie saw that the blackout curtains were drawn closed. She was about to walk in as she would normally have done, but she paused on the step, realizing she had better knock. Somewhere nearby a neighbour's cat was yowling to be let in. Taking several deep, frightened breaths, she raised her hand and knocked.

Vera opened the door slowly. She had left the hall light off, so the only illumination came through faintly from the back room, showing her forbidding silhouette. Katie waited for her to say, 'Well, come in then', but Vera said nothing and stood blocking the doorway. It was impossible to see the exact expression on her face in the shadows, but after a few seconds she folded her arms.

'Mother . . .' Katie was about to embark on her apology, but Vera raised a hand to cut her off.

'Here you are – there's as much as you'll need in here.'

Only then, as her mother turned, did Katie see the suitcase at the bottom of the stairs. Vera dragged it out onto the step.

'There's nothing else here that belongs to you.'

'Mother!' Katie's voice rose to a wail. 'You can't just throw me out on the street like this! For God's sake, have some pity. You can't mean for me just to go and never come back! I've come to apologize . . .'

'Apologize?' Vera derided. 'What use is that? It's a bit late for apology. You've made your bed – now you can damn well lie in it.'

Katie gasped. 'My God, what sort of mother are you? I'm your only daughter – don't you care anything about your own flesh and blood? And this is your grandchild I'm carrying!'

'*Grandchild!*' Vera spat out the word as if it disgusted her. She lowered her voice to a bitter hiss. 'You have the brazen nerve to call it that! A bastard born out of wedlock is no grandchild of mine. Nor ever will be. And what sort of daughter have you turned out to be? Bringing shame and disgrace upon me, after all I've suffered for you. Turning all my hopes to dust and ashes. You *slut.* You're no daughter of mine – not after this!'

She stepped back and the door slammed shut. Katie stood stunned in the darkness. The little cat was still wailing and its cry sounded desolate, but it did not bring her to tears in sympathy. That woman who had been her mother did not bring out gentle emotions. Instead there was another hardening, something in her that had to grow strong if it was not to collapse. Her mother was unhinged in some way – what was all this rage and cruelty? All Vera cared about was herself, her own feelings: wasn't that all she'd ever really cared about? Katie thought savagely. Always telling her what she could say and not say, what she should do.

Katie pulled herself straighter, feeling as if she was already looking back on her younger self from a new position. *Damn her* – if that was all Vera could say, the best she could do as a mother, then she could go to hell. She was filled with rage and a burning resolve. *Damn her, and damn him too!*

'Well, so it's just you now. Us.' To her surprise she found herself talking to the baby inside her. 'You and me. And we'll damn well cope somehow – whatever it takes.'

She picked up the heavy case with an angry strength and lugged it slowly to the tram stop on the Stratford Road.

'I knew it – I knew there was summat the matter.'

It was over a month since Katie had seen Ann, and they were sitting in their usual place with cups of tea and coffee on the table between them. Ann's currant bun lay half eaten and forgotten on her plate since she had heard the momentous news. She leaned forward and Katie saw in her eyes, along with obvious curiosity, nothing but kindness and concern. It was such a relief, to know that she could confide in someone. Away with her airs and graces, she had thought. Away with all the secrecy. She needed help.

'How far gone are you?' Ann whispered. They were leaning close across the table.

'About five months.'

'Well . . .' Ann sat back. 'You won't be able to keep that a secret much longer, will you? And – I mean . . .' She looked confused for a moment, wondering if she'd got it all wrong. 'I mean, when's the wedding? I never knew there was anyone – you're a flaming dark horse, you are! You're not already married and not told me, are yer?'

'No wedding.' Katie looked into her lap. All the time now she was aware of the swell of her stomach. As she was slender, it showed quite a lot already. 'He doesn't want to know. Just turned his back on me.'

'Oh my Lord.' Ann's eyes widened. 'Oh, Katie – I can't take this in. Whatever are you going to do?'

Katie looked up at her, her eyes hard, determined. 'What else can I do? I'm Mrs O'Neill so far as everyone else knows. Thank God for the war – after all, I could have a husband anywhere or nowhere, and no one's any the wiser. I've got a new job and a room – not far from you in fact.'

After a few nights staying with Enid, she had found a room to rent in Balsall Heath, within walking distance of where she worked. It was very small – no more than a boxroom, with space for a bed and a chair – but it would do.

'My husband's overseas in the army. I might even be a widow soon.' She held out her left hand to show Ann the brass ring she was wearing on her third finger.

'Oh, Katie,' Ann said again.

'I wasn't going to tell anyone. Not at first. But . . .' Her tough exterior cracked for a second. 'I need – I can't do all of this on my own.'

'What about when it comes?' Ann asked.

Katie shrugged. 'I don't know what to do. My landlady hasn't spotted that I'm expecting yet, or I don't think she'd have let me have the room. I'll have to get out of there as soon as – well, certainly after it's born.'

Ann reached across and touched her hand for a moment. Katie was moved. Though she was obviously astonished and frightened for her, not once had Ann shown any sign of passing judgement.

Katie blushed then, almost afraid to ask what she needed to.

'Aren't you ashamed to have anything to do with me? My mom is – why shouldn't you be?'

'Your mom?'

'She's disowned me.' It was a terrible thing to have to admit. Tears welled in her eyes. She cried so easily these days. Beneath the smouldering anger that gave her strength, there was such deep hurt.

'I'll help you – any way I can,' Ann said. 'Look, where're you living?' When Katie told her she looked pleased. 'Oh, that's not far from us! Look, Katie, I can't say I'm not surprised – you of all people. I can hardly take it in, to tell you the truth. But I don't s'pose you wanted things to turn out like this, and if I was you I'd be frightened to death. I don't envy you one bit. But we're pals, aren't we? Anything I can do to help, I will. And I'm sure our mom could ask around and see if she can gather up a few clothes for you. I mean . . .' She hesitated. 'You could come to us for a bit, if you needed to.'

Katie wiped her eyes, though more tears threatened to follow at this touching kindness. Ann was one of nine: how on earth did she think they could fit another one in!

'Oh, Ann, it's ever so good of you, but I wouldn't dream of it.'

'Well, who else've you got – what about the rest of your family?'

'There isn't any more of it. There's Mom's friend Enid – she's kind, but I don't like to put too much on her. It's not fair.'

Ann leaned forward fiercely. 'What about *him*? The father? What does he think he's playing at?'

'Playing,' Katie said bleakly. 'That was exactly what he was doing, and nothing else. And I, poor stupid little idiot, thought he actually cared about me. He did give me a bit of money.'

'Mighty big of him,' Ann said. 'God Almighty, men

– some of 'em want stringing up, that they do. But don't you worry, love. I'll find out who the midwife is down your way. No one need know you're not married – we'll all pull together.'

'Miss O'Neill?'

Katie looked up from her typewriter to see Miss Poulter's thin form looking down on her, framed by the long window behind her. Her hair was so tightly curled that it looked as if she set it with glue.

'Mrs O'Neill,' Katie corrected her.

'Ah, yes.' Miss Poulter's mouth twitched as if she intended to smile, but it didn't happen. 'A word, please. Would you come outside?'

They walked across the office together, the other girls typing frantically as Miss Poulter cast her eye over them. Katie walked holding her back very straight, hoping the loose dress she had bought hid the swell of her at the front, but she knew really that it didn't. There were only two months to go.

Out in the passage, the sound of the works below was louder. Miss Poulter led her to the end, by the window, then turned to face Katie with a distasteful expression on her face. In her clipped, well-spoken voice she said, 'Miss, er, Mrs O' Neill, I shall be blunt. Am I to understand that you are with child?'

Katie felt her heart race. She looked down, saw a cigarette stub crushed on the floor. 'Yes, Miss Poulter.'

'The other girls are talking, of course. You did not mention this when first we employed you?'

'I didn't know myself then,' Katie lied. These days she knew she would do or say anything she had to. She had discovered something primitive in herself – for the baby, she would fight, even kill if necessary, she thought. A pink flush had gathered in Miss Poulter's cheeks, and her eyes were blinking nervously behind her spectacles.

'I'm afraid we shall have to let you go, as from today.'

Katie stared at her. She felt her legs go weak. 'Pardon? I'm sorry – what d'you mean?'

'Well, clearly I shall have to find someone else to fill your position, and really I feel you should go as soon as possible. We can't have you round here in that condition. The men don't like it, you know.'

Katie's heart was thudding so hard with shock that she had to put her hand out to lean against the wall. She couldn't lose her job, not yet! She was worried to death about how things would be once the baby was born. Even though she still had most of Simon's money stored away in the bank, she was terrified of not being able to work. She had to keep earning for as long as possible.

'The men?' she repeated faintly. 'What men?' Where she worked there were only Miss Poulter and the other girls in the typing pool.

'The men in the works, of course – it's not right to have the girls in the works flaunting their . . .' She circled her hand in the direction of Katie's stomach.

'*Flaunting?*' Katie held on tight to her temper. *The men don't like it!* 'Miss Poulter, I don't think it's fair to say I'm flaunting anything. Where we work there are no men, and I never have cause to go down into the works. Please, don't lose me my job now. My husband is abroad, I think he's in Italy, but I haven't heard from him for such a long time . . .' She managed to produce some tears, without difficulty as she was so worried. At nights she lay awake, feeling the child moving, and was swamped by fear. 'I don't have any family and I need this job. Things are different now with the war on, aren't they? We all need to pull together in any way we can. Just let me carry on a little longer – at least another month, please. I'll keep out of everyone's way, like I usually do. Only don't make me go now! You'll be putting me in a terribly difficult position!'

Katie could see that Miss Poulter was coming round a little.

'You should have told me,' she said stiffly. 'You haven't been straight with me and I don't appreciate that.'

'I'm sorry,' Katie said, demurely. 'Only' – she lowered her voice even further – 'it's a bit embarrassing to talk about.'

'Quite so.' Miss Poulter looked out of the window, down at the yard where a truck was turning, belching out exhaust fumes. 'If you can be as discreet as possible, you can stay. But any trouble . . .'

'Yes, Miss Poulter. Thank you.'

She followed the woman's stiff walk back to their room, flushed with relief.

Twenty-Two

Winter 1944

Somewhere in the distance, she could hear a baby crying. Muzzily Katie opened her eyes to see pale-blue walls, and a big dark wardrobe. She tried to move, but flopped back, a wrenching pain shooting through her belly. She heard a crackling noise and realized she was lying on sheets of newspaper. Her breasts ached sharply. Between her legs was some sort of cloth pad, and everything down there felt damp and sticky.

'Oh, dear God. Oh, Mom, Mom, why aren't you here?' she murmured in a heartbroken voice, before slipping back into sleep.

'Katie?' It seemed only seconds later that she was woken again. The stickiness had grown worse. A face floated into focus. 'How're you feeling? I've brought little'un up for you.'

No, Katie thought. Don't make me do anything! I can't manage – I can't even get up.

But Ann's mom, Mrs Miller, plump and capable like her daughter, came and sat on the side of the bed – Ann's bed, which normally she shared with two of her younger sisters. Mrs Miller's thin, faded hair was scraped up in a bun and she was missing several front teeth, which gave her a rakish smile. The bundle she was holding in her thick arms gave off snuffling noises, sneezed, then let out a vexed-sounding wail. Mrs Miller wobbled with laughter.

'Hark at him! 'E wants his dinner, 'e does!'

Exhausted as she was, Katie pushed herself up again, full of longing curiosity about the little being who had shared the night's ordeal. The nightmare of the hours of pain in the darkness was still close to her, but now he had arrived, she wanted nothing more than to hold her son. Sitting up, she frowned.

'I'm sorry, Mrs Miller. I seem to be bleeding rather a lot.' She was worried about staining the bed.

'It's all right, bab, I know how it is. Don't you worry – we'll soon get yer sorted out. 'Ere 'e is, look! 'E's a fine lad – look at that hair! Go on, that's it: you give him a feed.'

The little boy took the breast enthusiastically and Katie winced as he started to feed. She stroked the mop of black hair that was slathered to his head. She could see nothing of Simon in him, only her own dark looks, and about this she felt stingingly triumphant.

'That's it!' Mrs Miller encouraged her. 'You've got the idea. You've got a lovely little lad there – a good size an' all. He was well over seven pound.'

Katie smiled faintly. 'I feel as if I've been hit by a tram.'

'Ooh, I know, bab, believe me, I do! Listen, what you'll want is a nice cup of tea. Now, give him a few minutes on each side and you'll stay evened up that way. I'll go and get you some tea and a bit of bread and scrape – that'll set you up.'

'You've been ever so kind,' Katie said tearfully.

'Don't mention it, love. You're our Ann's friend,

and we couldn't have you doing it all on yer own, could we?'

The baby had come early. Katie had calculated that it was due towards the end of February, but yesterday, a fortnight sooner, she had felt strange sensations as she was sitting at her desk at work – a hot, melting feeling of something giving way inside her. It was only later, after she'd walked home, that the pains began.

She had always kept out of the way of her crabby landlady as much as possible, going straight to her room, cooking solitary little meals on the single ring, only having anything to do with the woman if she had her topcoat on, which she hoped hid her swelling figure. As soon as the pains began, she knew there was only one person she could turn to: Ann. The Millers were already keeping an eye out for her. When Mrs Miller heard just how alone in the world she was, she had insisted that Katie go round there for Christmas dinner, taking everything she could in the way of rations, and she had squeezed in with all the family and received a kindly welcome. She was more grateful to the Millers than she could have put into words.

Thanking providence that it had begun in the evening, when she was not at work and it was dark, she put a few things in a bag and walked along to Ann's house on Stoney Lane. Mrs Miller took one look at Katie, bent over, gasping, on the doorstep and said, 'Oh dear – like that, is it? Come on, we'd better get you upstairs. Ann!' she bawled into the house. 'Get yer bed ready!'

She sent one of the younger children out for the midwife, a Mrs Mulvey.

'That'll give Mrs M a shock, us lot calling for 'er,' she joked as she helped Katie to climb the narrow stairs. The younger children were watching curiously from the hall. 'I've 'ad everything taken away down there now – she'll think I've 'ad a little miracle happen!'

Katie gave herself up gratefully into the hands of kindly Mrs Miller and the midwife, and the crushing waves of pain. The only things she was aware of were the squeezing of her drum of a body, and someone wiping her forehead with a cool rag from time to time. How the rest of the family were managing, she had no idea. She was only aware, distantly, that after she had managed at last to push the baby out, feeling as though all her bones would crack apart in the effort, and he was taken downstairs to be shown off in the small hours of the morning, there came the sound of a cheer from the waiting children and it brought tears to her eyes that someone else in the world was pleased to welcome him.

All the next day Katie slept, on and off, feeding and holding the baby in between. The house had gone quiet, except for Mrs Miller moving about and panting up the stairs to see how she was, and whether she wanted another cup of tea or something to eat. Katie started to feel bad that she was causing such a fuss. She'd handed Mrs Miller her ration book of course, but apart from that she was too exhausted to do anything but lie there. She felt tearful and vulnerable to painful thoughts. Her mother's rejection of her played endlessly in her mind. Then sometimes she let herself imagine Simon coming into the room, seeing his son and being delighted and tender towards them both, and for a few moments it made her weep with longing. It was no good. She'd wipe her eyes fiercely. She had to harden herself, finding her bitter anger so as not to dissolve into despair. Never, ever again, she vowed, would she put her trust in a man.

One morning, instead of Simon, she found herself thinking about Em, and dwelling on all that had happened all those years ago. She wondered how Em was, whether the Browns still lived in the same street. There had been a sweet perfection about their childhood friendship – and she had wrecked it. But she knew that it was as much her mother's fault, forcing on Katie her mean, superior ways, and again she burned with hurt and anger towards Vera. *She's no mother of mine . . .* She longed to see Em – for that freckly, smiling face that she remembered to come into the room now and see her, and for things to be all right. She told herself not to be so silly. Em would have grown up and changed completely now, and she certainly wouldn't be pleased to see her, of all people! But *it's funny*, she found herself thinking tearfully, *we were only babies really, but I still think of her as the best friend I've ever had*.

'You'll soon pick up,' Mrs Miller told her on one of her visits to the bedroom, finding Katie wet-cheeked once again. 'There's you, all on yer own – t'ain't right, that. But don't you worry. We'll see yer all right.'

'You're so kind,' Katie kept saying, though the tears kept on coming. She couldn't seem to stop them.

As soon as Ann came in from work that evening she was up the stairs.

'Where is he? Ooh, let me have a hold. I've been looking forward to this all day!'

Katie was sitting up in bed with the baby in her arms. Since the end of school there'd been a trail of smudgy-faced, amiable Miller children up and down to ''ave a look at the babby'. As she held him, he gazed up at Katie with a blurred, confused expression. She found it hard to let go of him when she handed him to Ann. In that one day she had been amazed to find that she had a fierce, tender attachment to him.

'You're looking a bit better,' Ann said. 'You looked ever so pale and poorly this morning.'

'I felt it,' Katie said. 'But your mom's been looking after me so nicely. I feel better.'

'He's *beautiful*. Aren't you?' Ann smiled and cooed down at the little boy until Katie was laughing. 'I feel quite jealous.'

'Oh, I could tell you a few things to talk you out of that for a start!' Katie said. 'Ow, I mustn't laugh! I've never been so sore in my life. It's like going through the mincer!'

They both sat adoring the little boy for a while longer. Katie felt as if she had a glow around her. But there was a whole host of things she was worrying about.

'Look, Ann – you've all been so good to me. But I can't keep taking your bed . . .'

Ann held up a hand. 'Don't even mention it. Tonight, you're sleeping there. You've got to recover properly. Some of the girls are bunking up with Mom and Dad, and the rest of us are downstairs, but we'll manage. We're a hardy lot, us Millers – we can sleep anywhere.'

Katie's face grew very solemn as her fears spilled out. 'I don't know what I'm going to do, Ann. I can't just stay here, imposing on all of you. I mean, I'd like to give your mom some money for a start.' Ann was holding up her hand in protest. 'But I can't go back to

St Paul's Road – I know she won't have me, not now. I've got nowhere on earth to go.'

As soon as she felt a bit better Katie insisted that she move downstairs and let the Miller girls, Ann, Hetty and Dora, have their bed back.

'And the moment I can find somewhere to go, I'll be out of your way,' she promised Mrs Miller. She insisted on paying her rent, feeling guilty that she had Simon's money, yet was living off the Millers.

'One thing I should do is go and see Mrs Thomas,' she told Ann. 'She's a friend of my mother's, but in her way she's been very good to me as well. She told me she wanted to see the babby when it was born. I'll go and see her this afternoon.'

It felt very strange venturing out in the cold winter air after she had been inside for so long. She felt as if giving birth had taken her on a long, strange journey and she had come back to find everything looking slightly altered from how it was before she left. She knew she was the one who had changed. Even her coat was stretched out of shape now that her belly had gone down again. She walked to the tram stop, holding her little boy swaddled up and wrapped in a white woollen shawl and feeling painfully self-conscious – surely everyone she met could tell she wasn't married, that she was a fallen woman! Their eyes seemed to bore through her. But every time she looked into that sleeping little face, she knew that nothing anyone said mattered more than the fact that she was with him and he with her, no matter how hard she had to struggle.

She cradled him in her arms on the tram, caressing his cheek with a finger. Ann kept saying, 'So what are you going to call him then?' So far Katie had not said anything. She knew she would name him, but she could hardly go to a priest and ask to have him baptized, could she? Not in her situation, or not without telling more lies. But then, if she didn't baptize him, would he go to hell? That was what she had been brought up to believe. Would it be better to lie, to say that the father was overseas? She had already lied about that, but lying to one of the Fathers felt worse still.

In her heart she knew what she was going to call him. There was something in the set of his face, the thick, dark hair, that gave her a feeling she would not have named to anyone – that she had given birth to her father, or to someone who was so like him that it was as if, in a strange way, he had been given back to her.

Leaning down she kissed him. 'Michael,' she whispered. 'My little son, Michael.'

She also knew that when she went to see Enid Thomas, her visit would be reported to her mother. And she wanted Vera to know – to realize what she was missing, and to know that she had named the baby after her father, who had not rejected her. Life had rejected him.

'Oh!' Enid gasped in amazement when she opened the door. 'Katie, love – oh, come in!'

She was delighted at the sight of both of them and spent ages admiring the baby and holding him.

'What're you calling him?' she asked as she took a break from cuddling him to brew some tea.

'Michael Patrick O'Neill,' Katie said confidently. 'After my father and uncle.'

'Oh, that's nice,' Enid said. She looked solemnly at Katie. 'You haven't seen your mother?'

Katie shook her head sharply, though she felt tears

193

close to the surface. She swallowed them down. 'But I suppose you have?'

'Yes, love, I have.'

Katie wanted to hear how much Vera was regretting her decision and her cruel treatment of her daughter, how she longed to see her grandchild, but Enid went on, 'I can't believe it really, Katie, the way she is. I'd never've thought it of her. We've had words about it, I can tell you. But she'll never say more than that it's not my business – that she's asked you to go, and she doesn't want to hear any more about it.' She shook her head, carefully spooning tea. 'I can't understand her: that she'd treat her own flesh and blood the way she has. I'll stand by her – we've been friends to each other for too long to do anything else. But to tell you the truth, I can't help seeing her differently after this. You know I lost my son, don't you?' She looked up, her eyes filling with tears. 'I'd give anything, *anything*, to have my William back on this earth alive again. And I look at how she's going on ... I think it's terrible. Really terrible.'

'Thanks, Enid,' Katie said, touched. 'I don't understand it either.'

They sat talking and admiring the baby until Katie realized time was getting on. She gathered Michael up and thanked Enid, before setting out again.

The evening was grey and smoky and she was glad of the gloom as she walked through her old neighbourhood, ghosts of times past all around her. She thought of the old school on Cromwell Street. It had been her favourite school by far, the fun she had had there with Em. Again she felt a deep pang. She pulled the brim of her hat down further and hurried along, lost in thought, wanting to get away from there in case anyone recognized her.

Rounding a corner, she almost collided with some-one. They both stepped back, their eyes meeting for a fleeting moment, then hurried on.

'Sorry!' the other person called.

It only sank in as she continued along the road: the voice, the pale face she had seen in the dusk. It had been Em – taller and older, but otherwise just the same and immediately recognizable. It had been her, hadn't it? Emma Brown. All she could remember of the last time she saw Em was a haunted figure in the street when her mother was poorly, hurrying here and there with no time to stop and join in the other children's games. She ached to think of Em in those days, how skinny and sad she had looked, and how cruel she had been to her.

Sitting on the tram from town to Balsall Heath, looking out at the dark streets, Katie felt very low. She'd lost her father, Uncle Patrick and then Em – and now both Simon and her mother. Was she cursed or some-thing? Was there never going to be anyone she could love who would stay with her? She held Michael close and tight.

'You won't leave me, will you?' she whispered.

He slept on, with complete trust.

1946

II

MOLLY

Twenty-Three

Calais, June 1946

'Molly – are you awake?'

Molly's eyes flickered open in the dark Nissen hut. For a second she was confused. She had slept in so many wooden army huts that she could have been anywhere. Her head felt heavy and her mind dull, as if she had had no sleep at all. Close by she made out her friend Cath's outline, half sitting up in the next bed.

'I am now,' she muttered drowsily. 'What time is it?'

'Almost five. Sorry if I woke you, but we'll have to be getting up in a tick anyway.'

'Sounds as if the wind's dropped?'

'Yes, I think so.'

All night a gale had blown, buffeting the hut so that it felt as if it might lift off the ground and be tossed away. They all had high hopes of crossing the Channel first thing that morning, and as Molly listened it did sound as if the wind had calmed.

By eight o'clock they had been at the quayside for half an hour waiting to embark. Around them rose a buzz of excited chatter from this contingent of ATS and a sprinkling of WAAF girls, some of the number who had volunteered for postings to Belgium in 1944 and were now being demobbed. Molly knew that Cath shared their excitement, though she faced a good deal of uncertainty. Her family were in Ireland and she had long left them behind. Instead of returning there, she had decided to wait in London for Derck, her Dutch fiancé, to be released from the army as well. She and Orla, another ATS girl, were planning to try and find digs together. It was going to be very sad to say good-bye.

In fact Molly was anything but excited. A heavy dread filled her, making her feel queasy, on top of the poor night's sleep. She stood on the quay in that steel-grey morning with her kitbag and the old case with leather straps she had bought in Birmingham before she joined up. Holding tight to the well-worn, familiar handle of the case that had travelled so far with her, it felt at that moment like her only friend in the world. She lit a cigarette, smoked one, then another.

The crossing was calm and quite pleasant, and Molly managed to keep her spirits up while she was still with Cath. The two of them, and Orla, went and walked up and down the deck, looking out over the sea.

'I still can't take it in,' Cath said, her eyes reflecting the grey water. Even her wayward auburn hair looked subdued under the heavy clouds. 'We're actually leaving the army – it's over. I don't know if I'm sad or glad.' She took Molly's arm and squeezed it. 'I'll be glad when I see Derck's lovely face smiling at me, I know that. But my God I'll miss you, Molly. You've got to promise me we'll keep in touch, now? Are you sure you won't change your mind and come and stop in London with us?'

'Oh no – ta,' Molly said. 'And of course I'll keep in touch, you daft thing.'

She was tempted to go and try for a life in London

with Cath, but she just knew it didn't feel right. Had it just been Cath it might have been different, but with both the Irish girls, she felt three was a crowd. And then Cath had her future with Derck and would be gone. Molly found the thought of London overwhelming. Her only memories of it were such painfully sad ones. Tony, the man she had loved when they met at a training camp on the Welsh coast, had been killed in London by an unexploded bomb that had been concealed in a nearby house. London, for Molly, was a place of grief and death.

She had, at that moment, absolutely no idea what she was going to do next with her life.

Even the train ride to the demobilization centre was fraught with painful memories. As chance would have it, they were to be processed at a Release Centre in Birmingham and had to travel up out of Euston, a journey that Molly also associated with Tony and what, for her, had been the darkest days of the war. And Birmingham, although the place she came from, was somewhere she would have been happy never to see again.

As they had so much kit and most of the girls were eventually heading for all sorts of different destinations, they were allowed to leave some of their luggage at Euston.

'You'll be taking all yours, though, won't you, Molly?' Orla asked, knowing that Birmingham had been her home.

Molly looked down at the case and khaki kitbag. In that split second she knew she was making a crucial decision. If she took all her luggage north to the Midlands, she knew somehow that she was opting for that – to go home to Brum. And her whole being rebelled against this. What was there in Birmingham for her. Her mother? God alone knew what state she'd be in by now. And the ghost of her brother, hanged by the neck, as well as the ghosts of her own childhood. Oh no, thanks very much, she thought.

'I'll only take overnight stuff up there,' she said. 'The rest can stay here.'

She saw Cath and Orla look at each other.

'But, Molly . . .' Cath began. She was going to ask once again: *What are you going to do?*

'I don't *know*,' Molly snapped, before Cath even got the words out.

Their company distracted her from her thoughts for the next few hours. On arrival in Birmingham they were met by an army truck, which took them south again to Wythall, where they saw the huts of what looked like an army camp, but was in fact the exit door from the army. Molly found it all comforting, as she found all the orderly ways of the army comforting. They were given a meal and a bed and told to sort out what kit was to be handed in and what they were keeping. The next morning was a rush of activity, as the staff seemed to want to shift them through as fast as possible. They had to hand in their kit and be issued with their demob book, railway warrants and clothing coupons.

And then it really was over. Molly travelled back with the others to New Street Station to say goodbye to Cath and Orla, who were going straight back to London. Already everything felt strange, each of them squeezed into old civilian clothes that they had outgrown in every way. Molly's skirt felt uncomfortably tight round the waistband. None of them had yet had time to take their coupons and choose new ones. In the busy, echoing station, Cath hugged Molly warmly and looked at her in a worried way.

'Where *are* you going to go, Molly?'

Molly smiled bravely. 'Tonight I'm going to go and see a pal of mine. After that – I don't know. I'll keep you posted. Now' – her voice was turning gruff with coming tears – 'go on, the pair of yer, sod off or you'll miss it. You take care of each other.'

'We will!' they laughed, and they all hugged again and said TTFN, not somehow able to bear the word 'good-bye', and tried – not very successfully in Cath and Orla's case – not to cry. Then the two of them boarded their train, waving until it gathered speed along the platform and Molly couldn't see their tearful faces any more.

Only then did the great well of sadness waiting inside her reach up into her eyes.

Molly had joined up early in 1941 to get away from her family. Her childhood in Birmingham had been poor and full of suffering at the hands of her drunken mother, Iris, and sexually predatory grandfather, William Rathbone. Just before Molly joined the army, Iris had told her, with a sadistic kind of pleasure, that William Rathbone – the man whom she had loathed as a grandfather – was also her father, since he had also preyed upon Iris, his daughter. This news along with the fact that Bert, her thieving, cheating brother, lived with them had led Molly almost to a state of despair, which she hid from herself by drinking heavily. She was a big, attractive blonde who always had men buzzing round her, but her relationships with them usually turned sour. On those sickening, hungover mornings when she looked in the murky mirror in her bedroom with a splitting head, she had known that she was beginning to go the same way as her mother.

The army had saved her, given her a place to belong, where she felt safe and where, at least for some of the time, she was recognized as being capable of things – of far more than she had ever dreamed. She had wanted it to go on forever.

But now it was over. There would be a few ATS continuing work for a time, but after that the army would only be for men again. A terrible kind of silence seemed to fill Molly even as she walked through the busy railway station. She made her way slowly out to New Street, oblivious to everything around her, the bomb-damaged streets, the people who weaved around her. All she could see was the greyness of it all. It felt as if life – the life she now knew and wanted – had just dropped away from her, and she was left stranded and alone in a barren place where the colour had seeped out of everything. Only now it truly came home to her. This was it: the war was over, her time in the army was finished and it no longer wanted her. For a moment she stopped, dizzy at the thought. She was back here. Birmingham: where she had begun. In those seconds she felt as bad as at any time she could remember. It felt as if her life was finished.

The ride on the trolleybus did nothing to cheer her. It was still an overcast day, neither raining nor sunny. Everything looked smaller, meaner and more run-down than she remembered. The streets appeared narrower and the bomb scars still looked raw and a mess. She looked out of the murky window, catching glimpses of children playing on the bombsites, of underfed people who looked washed out and harassed after all the months of shortages and worry. Everything looked drab. She was so caught up in looking out at it all that she almost missed her stop and had to push through to get out, causing people to mutter in annoyance.

As if in a dream, she walked along to Kenilworth Street, memories flooding back of the neighbours: Jenny and Stanley Button, who had been so kind to her and who had been killed in the bombing; the elderly twins who ran the sweet shop; Dot Wiggins, another kind neighbour who was now happily remarried to her Italian husband, Lou, in Duddesdon nearby; and of course the Browns, Em and the rest, the family she would have liked to have grown up in, instead of her blighted one. She hesitated at the entrance to one of the back yards where her family had lived for a time. The entry still looked the same, dark and dingy. And there was the ghost of her younger self sidling out onto the street, arms itching with eczema and impetigo, clothes smelly, trying to join in the street games with the other children, hoping and praying they'd let her have a go . . . All of it filled her now with a sense of rage, a furious sadness for her younger self.

I can't come back and live here, she thought. I'll go anywhere – but not here.

Pulling herself together, she stood up straight and went across to knock on the Browns' door. It was Em who opened it, an older-looking but still sweet-faced Em, with her straight brown hair and freckled nose. She held the door back, bewildered at first, then gasped, beaming with pleasure.

'*Molly!* Oh my word!' She rushed to hug her. 'Come on in – I knew you'd turn up one day. Took your flaming time, didn't you?'

Twenty-Four

The Browns' house looked exactly as Molly had always remembered it, and she found this both a comfort and a bit depressing at the same time. She had been here on and off throughout the war, whenever she could, but as she followed Em through to the back kitchen, saw the table and chairs, the stove, the same plates and pots on the shelves, and Em's mom Cynthia sitting at the table with the family's ration books in front of her, she found herself wondering how so little could have changed, when she had been so far and seen so much.

'Guess who's here, Mom!' Em announced, though Cynthia was already looking up to greet her.

'Hello, love!' Cynthia cried, delighted. Molly went over and gave her a kiss. Cynthia had been like a mom to her. 'You back for good now, are you?'

'Well, the army've had enough of me,' Molly joked.

'Here, sit down – Em'll bring you a cup of tea. Don't you look well – it's suited you, hasn't it?'

'Yes,' Molly said, thinking this was an understatement indeed. She knew she looked more healthy and better fed than most of the civilians. She saw that Cynthia had aged a good deal since she'd last seen her, her skin looking tired and her once-dark brown hair a long way towards grey. But her dark eyes were still full of life.

'Good job you came today,' Em said. 'I'm off work

'cause Robbie's not well. He's asleep at the moment. Mr Perry's nice like that, if I need time off.'

They all sat round the table. The rest of the family were out at work. Molly tried to adjust to being here, to the thought that she would not be going back tonight or tomorrow to an ack-ack battery somewhere. It was a dismal thought, even though she was pleased to see them and to have a chance to catch up.

'See your mother?' Cynthia asked, a careful tone in her voice. Molly saw her exchange glances with Em.

'No, and I'm not going to,' Molly said firmly. 'It never does either of us any good. Is she still in the same place?'

'I think so,' Cynthia said. 'Down Lupin Street, though I've not seen her in a few weeks.'

'She'll have taken it hard over Bert,' Molly said. 'He was always her favourite. I s'pose he sort of looked after her, in his twisted way.' She looked at Em. 'Thanks for letting me know about it all – you know, for going along.'

Em had written after Bert was hanged, telling Molly that she had been to Winson Green, that the deed was done. There was nothing much to relate, except that she had run into Katie O'Neill again. Molly had greeted that news with a shrug. She had never liked Katie, whom she thought stuck up and spiteful.

'That's all right,' Em said. 'I just thought someone ought to pay their respects. Whatever he was, he was your brother.'

'Yes, I know.' Molly sighed. She knew Bert had never stood a chance really. His life had been sad and unpleasant, and his response had been to become vile to everyone.

'I think your mother's all right, in her way,' Cynthia said. She hesitated as if not sure whether to go on, but then added, 'There's someone living with her.'

Molly looked up. 'A bloke?'

Cynthia nodded. 'I don't know who he is – a great big fella, and dark . . .'

Molly thought of the last time she had seen Iris, sleeping it off in bed at four in the afternoon, beside a huge, stubbly, pot-bellied man. Was it the same one? It might be, might not. It hardly mattered.

'She'll survive, I expect,' she said drily.

They sat catching up on news of everyone. Em's brother Sid had recently married his girl, Connie, and they were living in one cramped room in Saltley.

'It's the devil trying to find anywhere to live,' Cynthia said. 'They wanted to move out on their own, but since Hitler's done for so many of the houses, there's not much going. They were lucky to find anything.'

'That's two weddings since the end of the war,' Em said. 'Sid's was nice, we had a lovely day, didn't we? And then there was the wedding of Carolina, Dot's stepdaughter and Lou's daughter. Well, I say girl, but she was over thirty: she'd left it ever so late! Anyway that was a real Italian do – hundreds of 'em – it was lovely, though, wasn't it, Mom?'

Cynthia laughed. 'Yes, it was a good day. Dot looked happy – she and Lou suit each other, they really do.'

'Our Joyce'll be next,' Em said. 'She' s a proper one for the boys, but she's been knocking around with Larry for a long time now . . . Hang on' – she cocked her head – 'that's Robbie calling me, isn't it? Back in a sec.'

She reappeared with a very feverish-looking little lad

in her arms. Hot and half asleep, he cuddled up against her, hardly seeming to notice that Molly was there. Em stroked his head.

'Hello, Robbie,' Molly said. 'Oh, he does look poorly. His hair's lighter than I remember, Em – more like yours?'

'Yes, I think it is a bit,' Em said, attentive to every tiny detail about her son. 'Course Norm and I are about the same, colour-wise. Come on, Robbie – have a sip of water before you go off to sleep again.' She looked up at Molly. 'He starts school in a few months – you wouldn't believe it, would you?'

'Where's Norm now?' Molly asked. 'Any sign of him coming home?'

Em shrugged. 'I hope so. But I don't know – they don't tell you, do they?'

'D'you need a bed tonight, Molly?' Cynthia asked.

'Yes, please – if that's all right,' Molly said. 'I'm sorry I didn't warn you I was coming.'

'Well, you couldn't have done, could you? Don't be daft – it's nice to see you.' Cynthia looked concerned. 'Are you going to look for a job then, Molly? Settle down?'

'I don't know,' Molly said bleakly. 'To tell you the honest truth, I've got no idea.'

It was nice to be there, she thought, lying in Sid's old bed that night. Good to see them all. Joyce was really grown-up now, at nineteen, quite sassy and full of it, and Violet, the babby who was fifteen, had grown into a very pretty girl, sweet like Em and quite studious, with more confidence than her older sister.

She had had some time to talk alone with Em, and

Em had poured out her heart over Norm, how she knew he had been in Italy, how much she had longed to have him back, but that now the time was growing nearer – and she blushed confessing this, with a frankness that surprised Molly – she was also frightened of it, dreading it almost.

'Sometimes I just long for him to be here and take me in his arms, and for us to be a proper married couple again. But then I worry that we shan't have anything to say to each other and everything'll have to change. I suppose we've got quite settled here now, into a routine, just Mom and me and Robbie. We're all used to it. And Norm's been away for so long – he might be quite different.' She looked across at Molly helplessly. 'All I can do is wait and see, isn't it?'

Molly lay in the dark, unable to sleep, even though it had been such a long day and the night before so bad. She felt keyed up, worried about everything. Now she was alone, lying there, she allowed herself to think. She cast her mind back over the war, both the good times and the bad. There'd been her first Corporal, Phoebe Morrison, who had in her brusque way, encouraged Molly to carry on, to succeed in the army. Phoebe Morrison had also been Molly's Subaltern in Belgium for the first months, and it had been with great regret that she had parted from her when the war finished.

In the spring of 1945 the ack-ack batteries stationed in Belgium were definitely no longer required and were to be stood down. Some of the staff were sent home. Molly, even while celebrating Victory in Europe with everyone else, was desolate that she would have to go home. However, Phoebe Morrison gave her to understand that this need not be the end: Molly, along with Cath, took the aptitude tests to remain in the force, which was to become the 21 Army Group HQ in Brussels. They were both sent on to the Headquarters of the British Army on the Rhine at Bad Oeynhausen.

It was clear that most of the roles were to be taken by men. The appointing officer seized on the fact that Molly had experience in cooking and told her that she could cook for one of the messes. Cath came to work on the telephone exchange. While Molly had hoped for a more challenging job, by this stage she was just happy to be allowed to stay, and she and Cath and the others had some happy times in the gracious surroundings of Bad Oeynhausen barracks. She had never seen Phoebe Morrison since, but she knew she would never forget her for her encouragement, for the fact that in the end she seemed to have a special place for Molly in her toughly guarded heart.

Amid all the rest of it, of course there had been Tony, the lovely times they'd had together on the cliffs in Wales, and in London. But then came the agony of his death. Any place she had been with Tony was associated with sadness.

After that though, after some other postings, during her greatest time of sadness, she had been sent to Clacton. Lying there that night, Molly's heart began to beat faster. Now that was one place where she felt she could go and see it in a positive light. She thought of her friends there – Cath and Nora and Ann and, strangely, Ruth, a studious girl who had fallen out mightily with Molly in their early days of training together, before they became unlikely friends. None of them would be there, of course: it was no good looking back. But maybe she could find work, away from here, by the sea. A fresh start in a place where at least the memories were good? In her mind she walked the long parade at Clacton, remembering how the guns had fired continually from the practice camp along the coast. She remembered the Viennese Ballroom at Butlin's where they had danced. She fell asleep thinking of it, a smile turning up her lips.

Twenty-Five

Molly flung her case down on the attic-room bed and went straight to the window. The casement was fastened with a rusting catch, but the window opened readily enough, and she leaned against the rotten sill, which was level with her chest, the window being set in the gable. She was pleased to realize that the room faced south, so that although it was dingy and the ceiling low, it would not always be dark. She lit a cigarette and let the smoke stream out through the window.

The Laurels guesthouse was in a side street off the main coast road. Turning to look as far as she could to the left, Molly could just see the sea with the last rays of the afternoon sun on it. She took a long, deep breath. Ahhh – that smell, all that billowing air, the smell of sea water and the wide-open view! Clacton was much quieter and more knocked about than she remembered, but just being here made her feel happier and full of expectation, like a child on holiday.

It had all been easier than she expected, even finding a job almost as soon as she arrived. She had not been walking all that long after coming out of the railway station, with her faithful old case collected from Euston, when she headed straight for Marine Parade, along the sea front. She could see that most of the guesthouses that had been requisitioned during the war were back in business, even though some were in poor repair. Many had signs in the window saying 'Vacancies', but turning up Vista Road, she had not gone very far when she saw a house part-shrouded with dark bushes and a sign saying, 'Housekeeper-cook wanted'.

Cooking, Molly thought. Why did she always seem to end up flaming cooking, however hard she tried to get away from it? Still, there was nothing for it.

A small, neat lady answered the door of The Laurels, saying rather faintly, 'Yes?'

Molly put on her best-spoken voice. 'I've come about the notice – for a housekeeper and cook.'

The lady looked immediately anxious, her brow furrowing. Molly saw that despite the fact that she was dressed like someone rather older, in a floral frock that reached halfway down her shins, and wore her mousy hair in a bun, she was only in her early forties.

'Well,' she said, in a flustered way, flapping the door a little as if she wasn't sure whether to open or close it. 'You'd better ... I mean, good, that's very good. Yes ...' She gathered herself. 'You'd better come in, dear.'

She showed Molly into the room immediately inside, which seemed to be a sitting room, though not a very comfortable one, with a large number of hard wooden chairs arranged in a circle as if they were waiting for a meeting. The walls were the colour of milky coffee and the floor was covered by a thin brown carpet. As a concession to cautious gaiety, there was a vase of faded paper flowers on a stand by the window.

'My name is Mrs Lester.' The lady indicated one of the chairs. 'You'd better sit down.' She sank thankfully onto another one herself. 'I run this establishment with my husband, Mr Lester,' she explained. Molly thought she had seldom seen anyone look so pale. The blue of

Mrs Lester's veins showed through at her temples and her skin looked clammy. 'Unfortunately I am not always in the best of health, since those dreadful days of the war, and I am finding it all too much for me. The mornings are especially bad.' She seemed to suppress a sob.

Molly began to feel as if the walls were closing in, though she did not feel dislike for the woman.

'So my husband suggested that I should enlist some help. You see, some days I'm perfectly all right, and then on others . . . And today is not a good day – I find that I can scarcely get around. You look a good, strong girl,' she commented, looking Molly up and down. She had a nervous way of blinking her eyes.

'I s'pose I am, yes,' Molly said. She had her hair up today, thick and blonde and piled up in a way that suited her, and she felt energetic and ready for anything.

'Can you cook?' This seemed to be the greatest source of anxiety. 'I need help with generally running the house, of course – changing the beds is really too much for me, and now the summer is coming, there'll be more visitors. People are so longing to get back on the sands, aren't they?' She smiled faintly. 'Such a blessing, all that clean fresh air. But you see, it's the cooking. We provide breakfast and an evening meal, and I do find it so hard to keep up. Breakfast is a struggle.'

'I trained as an army cook,' Molly said. 'I know it's not quite the same, but I'm sure I could manage.'

Mrs Lester's eyes widened. 'You were in the army? The ATS? How *brave* of you.'

'I was on an ack-ack battery.' Molly was anxious for her to know that she had not just done cooking. 'In fact we were stationed here for a bit of the time. But I did start off as a cook.'

'Well, that sounds suitable. I'm so pleased.' To Molly's astonishment, Mrs Lester suddenly reached out and grasped Molly's hand. Hers felt very cold and froggy, as if her circulation was poor. Molly felt very large and robust in contrast to her. 'Could you start straight away? You'd live in and have your board – I can't pay you a great deal, but there's a nice little room at the top of the house.'

'Yes,' Molly said, her spirits soaring. Fancy her getting a job so quickly!

'Until my husband gets back later, I can't give you the final say-so. He is the head of the household at The Laurels, after all. But I have a strong feeling it will be all right. May I ask you one thing?'

'I can show you my discharge letter, if you like,' Molly said quickly. 'I don't have any references as such – not for cooking, I mean . . .'

'No, that won't be necessary. That wasn't it – it was just to ask something much more pressing. Are you a Christian, dear?'

'Um . . .' Molly stuttered. She'd got no idea of religion except for army church parades. 'Well, I s'pose I'm sort of Church of England.'

Mrs Lester blinked rather sorrowfully at her for a moment, then said, 'I think that will be all right. My husband is rather a devout man, you see. He likes certain standards met. We have our little meetings here, of course . . .' She indicated the chairs. So they were indeed set up for a meeting. 'On Tuesday evenings.'

Within minutes, Molly was in the attic room, settling in, before Mrs Lester showed her her duties. It had all been so easy! She was feeling quite high as she looked out of the window. She associated the coast with happy times, an open landscape where you could see out. All things seemed possible.

Molly soon realized that the cooking that was expected of her was going to be rather different from that in the army. She was used to cooking mountainous quantities of stodgy, if not necessarily palatable food for hordes of young active people. Despite food shortages, the army had been a priority and they had taken their rations more or less for granted. Now she was out in the civilian world of making do, eking out and watering down.

Once she had settled into her room, feeling quite hopeful, Molly went down, as Mrs Lester had requested, to see her in the kitchen. She found her stirring a pot of some sort of watery stew.

'We've one couple staying,' Mrs Lester said, her eyes blinking nervously. 'So we've got an extra bit of beef on their points. I believe they're on their honeymoon.' She gave a shrill little laugh, then stopped herself with her hand over her mouth as if this was naughty.

'I'm afraid I do add a little water to the jam,' Mrs Lester said later, when telling Molly about breakfast. 'And of course now there's such a shortage of bread – of everything ... Mr Lester does most of the shopping...' Her voice faded again as if all was hopeless. 'Now I do undertake what I can. We shall just have to take it day by day and work together. All we can do is keep going and trust in the Lord: that's true of all of life, isn't it?' Molly thought it best to nod. 'I hope that suits – it sounds a little vague? Mr Lester doesn't like me being vague. He's always so precise.'

Molly felt she could rise to the challenge of watery gravy and stews padded out with vegetables. She realized that she was better fed, and her nerves in a less frayed state, than many people who had been civilians. When Mrs Lester showed Molly her other housekeeping duties, most of which consisted of cleaning and laundry, she felt well able to take them on. She wondered quite what it was that exhausted Mrs Lester so much.

When she met Mr Lester, she began to find out. He was back in the house before the evening meal and came into the kitchen.

'Ah, you're back, dear!' Mrs Lester exclaimed.

Mr Lester gave a curt nod and Molly felt immediately unsure of him. He was quite a small man and, Molly realized, a good few years older than his wife. He had taken off his hat to reveal his balding pate, with strands of grey hair combed neatly over it, which the hat had apparently not even slightly disturbed, and he was still wearing a sandy brown mackintosh. Molly saw his gaze move to her and he nodded commandingly at his wife, as if to say, 'Well, who's that?'

'We've had such a stroke of good luck this afternoon!' Mrs Lester exclaimed, clapping her hands together and holding them clasped under her chin as if in prayer. 'This is Molly – she's an experienced cook and, as you can see, good and strong. Isn't she just what The Laurels needs, dear? I think she'll be a godsend!'

Molly shook hands with her new employer, saying, 'How d'you do.' There was not much response. All he did was nod at her again, not looking especially pleased. He seemed to be examining her carefully. His hand felt small and dry.

'Of course I wouldn't just take her on without your

say-so,' Mrs Lester went on. 'I thought perhaps we should have her for a trial period . . .'

Mr Lester made a sound rather like a cough, nodded abruptly and then smartly left the room.

Molly tried not to let her face show what she was thinking: Well, he's a queer so-and-so, and flaming rude with it.

But Mrs Lester waited until her husband was out of earshot and came closer to Molly. 'I should have explained,' she whispered apologetically. 'I forget that people don't know . . . You see, Mr Lester is not quite as other men. He has a difficulty with his speech, so he is a person of rather few words. He has a deformity to the roof of his mouth. It's the cross he has to bear.'

'Oh, I see,' Molly said. This seemed very sad and made him less forbidding. But, she couldn't help wondering, how did Mr and Mrs Lester talk to each other? How did they even get to know each other?

'He does compensate so well in other ways,' Mrs Lester added.

It didn't become fully apparent what this meant until the next morning. Molly helped Mrs Lester serve the young couple who had come down from London straight from their wedding. The woman was buxom with thick, honey-blonde hair and a big toothy smile, the lad thin and sweet-looking, and apparently scarcely able to believe his luck.

Breakfast involved scrambling powdered egg. It also, as it turned out, involved hymn-singing and prayers led by Mr Lester. Molly had just come into the dining room from the kitchen holding a small milk jug when he appeared from the hall, and before she could even reach the table to deliver the milk, he was handing his customers a sheaf of typed papers, fastened together, which were evidently a home-made hymnal. The young couple, who were not necessarily prepared for this eventuality, looked politely bewildered. To Molly's surprise, a white-faced Mrs Lester then appeared. Molly put the milk on the couple's table and started to retreat.

'Good morning,' she heard Mrs Lester say. Molly stood by the door in her apron, not sure if she was supposed to be involved. 'We like to begin our day by giving thanks to the Lord for all he has given us. If you'd turn to number ten?'

The hymn was 'Lead us, heavenly father, lead us . . .' Mr Lester then erupted into song, with Mrs Lester warbling behind him. It became very obvious, within seconds, that he was capable only of pronouncing vowels, but very little in the way of consonants, so that what came out was a loud, quite tuneful, but completely incomprehensible series of noises, while Mrs Lester sang along determinedly beside him in accompaniment. Molly, herself astonished, and embarrassed by his handicap, saw the face of the young bride in front of her turn from shock to incredulity and quickly to an overpowering urge to laugh. She turned her face to the wall, curtaining it with her long hair while her husband gamely joined in with the singing, obviously ill at ease, but too kindly to refuse. Within a few seconds Molly could see the young woman's shoulders shaking with silent laughter. By midway through the second verse, Molly's own rising hysteria was almost as bad as the other young woman's. Mr Lester's expression was so pompous, his efforts to deliver the singing so earnest, while the sounds he was making were so tortured, that all she could think was: Oh, my goodness, this is *awful*. Why doesn't he just *shut up* and spare all of us?

As the third verse ground towards its merciful close,

the young blonde woman glanced round desperately as if looking for a way out, and she and Molly caught each other's eye. The girl had tears of mirth running down her face, and Molly could see she was on the point of exploding. And then the prayers began. Molly did the only thing she could think of and crept from the room, leaving the blonde woman to her fate while she tore along the hall to the stairs and burst into gusts of laughter. It seemed so bad laughing at someone else's misfortune like that, but why – of all things, she asked herself, shaking with laughter – did he have to sing hymns?

She imagined telling Cath about it, and Em, and the thought of how it would have been if they'd been there made her giggle even more. Was this going to happen every day? How on earth would she manage?

By the time the religious part of the proceedings was over she managed to compose herself, wiping her eyes and going to serve the eggs and toast. She avoided looking at the young woman too directly. She didn't want to get the sack on her first day.

As they were clearing up the breakfast, though, Mrs Lester took Molly aside.

'Now, you've seen our morning routine, dear. It's very important to Mr Lester that we preserve a Christian atmosphere in our establishment. You never know when a lost and searching soul might hear the message of the Lord Jesus. As I told you, I don't do well in the mornings, so from now on I'd like you to take over. I shall rest until a little later – at least while things are quiet. But you will have to assist Mr Lester with our morning devotions.'

Molly stared at her, speechless. Mrs Lester put a hand on her arm. 'A number of our guests have been helped, dear.'

'I...' Molly gulped. 'I don't think I know the hymns.'

Mrs Lester smiled gently. 'Oh, you'll soon learn, dear. I can help you. And Mr Lester is a very patient teacher. He's a good-hearted man when you get to know him.'

Twenty-Six

For someone who could not speak, Mr Lester managed to communicate a powerful sense of his personality. There was something about his bearing – very upright, always dressed in a poorly fitting grey flannel suit, a little too short in the leg so that his brown socks were exposed – and his intense stare through his watery blue eyes, a stare that suggested a furnace of feeling within him, which made Molly nervous.

She stood beside him at breakfast the next morning, with the dog-eared collection of hymn sheets that someone – probably Mr Lester – had taken the trouble to type out. He was not the best of typists and there were a lot of overtypes and XXXXX-ings out. Mrs Lester had called Molly to her the previous night and sat her down in the brown front room.

'I wanted us to choose a hymn for the morning,' she said, with the faintest air of apology. 'Now you look through, dear, and see which ones you know.'

'I'm not really a church-goer,' Molly said, shrinking with dread inside. To her, church was just something you did with the army, like PT or drill. It meant nothing to her beyond its form. But there was something about Mrs Lester that was so put-upon and actually sweet-natured that Molly found herself not wanting to offend her. She also wanted to keep her job. Leafing through the worn sheets of paper, she dimly recognized a few of the hymns, but there were none that she could have sung through – except for one.

'I think I know that,' she said, pointing at 'Fight the Good Fight'. They had sung it on Church Parade a number of times.

'Oh, thank goodness!' Mrs Lester said, laying a hand over her heart. 'And that's one of Bernard's favourites. I can certainly teach you some of the others. I can't tell you what it means to me to be able to lie a little longer in bed in the mornings. I know it looks like idleness . . .' Her eyes blinked in that nervous way she had. 'But I do wake feeling so very unwell . . .'

So here was Molly – who had been having nightmares for half the night about singing hymns to Bert, her dead brother, in a prison cell – standing trembling beside Mr Lester, amid the smells of porridge and burnt toast. With a sinking heart she saw that there was still only the same couple staying in the guesthouse. Why must Mr Lester force this on them? Molly wondered. They obviously didn't want to know. Even before she'd started singing, she thought mutinously: I'm never, *ever* doing this again. I'm going to look for a new job!

The buxom young bride was wearing a tight, pink frock. Molly carefully avoided her eye. If they looked at each other, she was done for. All she could do was to get through this somehow. She'd hardly ever felt such a fool in her life before, standing with this overbearing, fanatical man. Mr Lester swivelled his head and looked meaningfully at her and Molly, using the words that Mrs Lester had taught her, said, 'We will now sing hymn number twenty-two.'

Mr Lester was off almost before she'd got the words out of her mouth and she had to tune in with him: 'Christ is thy strength and Christ thy right!' She found a surprisingly strong voice coming out of her mouth and, to her surprise, quite enjoyed it, apart from the sheer embarrassment of it all. Mr Lester insisted on reading the prayer, which was a scrambled agony, though Molly realized that if you tuned in hard enough, you could just about make out what he was saying.

At last Molly was freed to serve the breakfast.

'You've got a very nice voice,' the young husband said to her. Though his wife was smirking a bit, she was not in anything like the state she had been the day before. Molly wondered if her kindly looking husband had told her that she should behave better.

'Oh – thanks!' Molly said, surprised. 'I've never done this sort of thing before.' She was anxious for them to know that.

'I don't s'pose you have,' the woman said, exposing her teeth in a big grin. She looked a handful, Molly thought, and not just in the curves department.

'Where've you come from?' Molly asked, trying to change the subject.

'Wandsworth. We're on our honeymoon,' the young man said eagerly.

'Can we have a cuppa tea now?' the girl asked abruptly.

'I'll get it straight away,' Molly said, tempted to wish the young man luck.

'Mr Lester told me that it all went very well!' Mrs Lester told Molly later. She appeared by eleven o'clock, seeming more rested and with the faintest hint of colour in her cheeks. Molly had been clearing break-fast and then cleaning in the house, vacuuming the stairs and cleaning the two bathrooms. Mrs Lester found her cleaning the bath on the middle floor. 'I'm very grateful to you – and he said your voice is a treat!'

'Oh!' Molly stood up. All these compliments in one morning! 'Well – thanks.'

'Now, I'd like to send you out with a list,' Mrs Lester said.

It was a nice day and Molly was more than happy to go out shopping, away from the dark house. She set off with a basket over each arm, the list, money and ration books. As soon as she was out of the house she felt more cheerful. The combination of Mr Lester's oppressive presence and the poorly Mrs Lester tiptoeing round him was already beginning to get her down.

Clacton felt very bare compared to how she remembered it. All the wartime obstructions to holidaymaking had taken up a lot of room. The beach had been wired off then, and all the roads leading off Marine Parade had been blocked by more wire and concrete pyramids across the roads, known as 'pimples', to discourage invaders. The town had been bustling full of forces personnel, especially army. Now they were all gone and, though there were people going about their business, they were each in their own little world, not like all the group endeavours of the war – no army lorries roaring up to collect a gaggle of them for the practice camp at Jaywick. Life felt quiet and shapeless. What was the point in anything now that the war was over?

Taking a short detour, she walked along to the house where she had been lodged with Cath and a group of other ATS on ack-ack training. She stood across the road, staring. There it was, just the same, with its wrought-iron railings at the front. A piece of deep-blue carpet was draped over them. Otherwise it looked much the same, though it now seemed to be back in business as a hotel. Any minute, Molly expected Ann or Nora or Cath to come bouncing out of the door and wave across at her. But no, those days were over. All gone.

Walking along in the sunshine, Molly's spirits began to sink and she was filled with an aching loneliness. Although it was only a matter of days, it seemed a lifetime ago that she had said goodbye to Cath and the others. Was this her life now? For the first time she questioned her decision to come back to Clacton. She saw herself staying here, in this place where she knew no one, cooking and cleaning in the dark guesthouse for the rest of her days. The future looked very bleak and full of boredom. For the first time in a long time, she found herself longing for a drink when it was only half past eleven in the morning.

'You know,' Mrs Lester told her as they unpacked the shopping, which Molly had carried home with aching arms, forcing back the tears that were threatening to come. 'Apart from those years of the war, I've lived in this house all my life.'

Molly realized how happy Mrs Lester was to have someone to talk to, and she wasn't sorry herself. It was a way of taking her mind off her dismal thoughts today. Apart from her employer, she realized with another stab of gloom, there was no one else at all here that she could talk to.

'Have you, Mrs Lester?' she asked, surprised.

'Oh yes.' Mrs Lester turned, with a packet of flour in her hand, blushing a little. 'I should rather like it if you called me by my Christian name – after all, that is why we are given them! It's Jane.'

'All right then,' Molly said awkwardly. They exchanged faint smiles.

'But, yes, my late parents ran this establishment for years, and then my father departed this life, and Mother and I continued as Father would have wanted. He was a very devoted Christian man.' She stopped unpacking the groceries and looked ahead of her. 'You see, you never know what the Lord has in store. When the war came and the army requisitioned a lot of our guesthouses and hotels, it seemed to us the greatest disaster. You can imagine, I expect. We had to get out and go somewhere. Clacton was overrun with barbed wire and khaki uniforms, or so it seemed to us. So we went to Mother's sister in Hendon – hardly safer really, but there was no choice. It was all too much for Mother in the end ... she suffered with her nerves; I'm afraid I'm rather like her. But a chill turned to pneumonia. My poor, dear mother is buried in Hendon, but at least I have the comfort of knowing she's near her sister. But while we were there, I was attending the chapel of course, as I do, and there I met Mr Lester.' She smiled a realistic smile at Molly. 'I never thought I should be able to marry ... And Mr Lester is so on fire with the Lord – he could see that this work would be an opportunity to evangelize, as well as to earn our living. He's so brave a man. He has a cleft palate, you see – from birth. But it never stops him trying to share the Good News.'

It certainly doesn't, Molly thought. But she was touched, and couldn't help liking Jane Lester with her pink nose and worn face. Her thoughts of rushing to find another job began to waver. After all, it could be out of the frying pan into the fire.

'And you were here, you said, during the war?'

'Yes!' Molly felt herself lighting up. 'Our battery was doing ack-ack training. I was lodging just off Marine Parade. I went to have a look at it this morning, you know, for old times' sake.'

'Fancy,' Mrs Lester said. 'All I did was join the WVS – but with Mother being so ill and Auntie Vi being rather demanding ... I don't know. I'm not a very courageous person, I'm afraid. Rather a mouse. Oh my goodness – is that all the bacon? That barely even looks like the ration to me.' She turned suddenly to Molly. 'I hope you don't *mind* helping Bernard with the morning devotions?'

'Oh,' Molly hesitated. Did she mind? Yes! She found it all embarrassing. But she'd quite liked the singing, and she didn't know any of these people who passed through the guesthouse. What did it matter? And she did like the feeling of pleasing people. Mr Lester even smiled at her occasionally now. 'It's all right. I expect I'll get used to it.'

While out shopping, Molly had bought three postcards and some stamps. That evening, after a session with Jane Lester who had been teaching her 'Love Divine, All Loves Excelling' for the next morning, she sat on her bed in the attic room and wrote cards to Em and to Cath and Ruth, both of whom had been with her in the ATS. To the last two she wrote, 'Here I am in Clacton again. Wish you were here!'

III

EM

Twenty-Seven

June 1946

'Em, quick. Get down here – it's for you!'

Em heard her mom's voice shrieking up the stairs while she was getting Robbie ready. Heart pounding, she ran, picked up Robbie and, holding him on her hip, ran down the stairs.

'What's up?'

Cynthia, with trembling fingers, was holding out a telegram, and for a second Em stared, appalled, thinking the worst.

'Well, take it!' Cynthia cried.

Sinking onto a chair by the table, Robbie on her lap, she opened it up:

Reached London. Home soon. Norm.

'Oh my God – he's back in England!' Em found she was breathless. She'd gone quite wobbly. 'Ooh, I thought they must send him home soon. Oh, Robbie – you're going to see your dad!'

Cynthia's eyes were full of tears. 'Oh, love – I'm so pleased for you!' She too sat down suddenly. 'Funny how you always think it's going to be bad news, isn't it?'

*

235

'When's my dad coming home?' Robbie asked so many times that Em almost began to wish she hadn't told him so soon. At three years old, now means now; not sometime soon, but I'm not sure when. 'When's he coming? When's my dad coming?' On and on. Em wondered if he even knew what a dad was.

'He'll be here soon,' she kept telling him, until her patience snapped. 'Look, don't keep on, Robbie – your dad'll be here as soon as he can, all right?' She was glad that the news had come on one of the days she didn't work, but as the day passed she almost wished she was busy in Mr Perry's shop, to take her mind off the butterflies in her stomach.

She was full of excitement and also of nerves. This was the moment she had been waiting for, for so long, since she last waved Norm off before Robbie was even born. She knew she loved Norm, but sometimes now she struggled even to remember clearly what he looked like or the sound of his voice. She so longed for him to be here, reassuring old Norm, to take her in his arms, but she was afraid he'd have changed. That's what they all said: war changed people. The Great War's survivors had been men who were never the same again – what about this war?

'Oh, Mom,' Em said to Cynthia later, 'I feel all churned up, I really do.'

'I don't blame you,' Cynthia said. 'But it'll be all right, bab. You'll see.'

'D'you think he'll be here today?'

'I'd've thought it'd more likely be tomorrow. They have to go through a whole lot of rigmarole, don't they? D'you want to put a flag out for him – you know, I s'pect we could get hold of some bunting, make a banner?'

'I don't know that I do,' Em said. 'I know it's silly, but I feel superstitious – as if it might bring bad luck. Let's just get him home, not count our chickens.'

A bit later she changed her mind and, calling Robbie, she took him down the road to buy some chalk, and on the wall by the front door she wrote, 'WELCOME HOME, NORM' in big letters. Robbie drew a thick, wonky line underneath and something that was meant to be an aeroplane. Neighbours saw her doing it and came and asked.

Em stood back to look at it. 'Just hope it doesn't rain now,' she said to Cynthia. 'He most likely won't be here today anyhow.'

But that evening, as the last of the light was going, there was a brisk tap on the front door. They all looked at each other: Em, her mom and dad, and Violet. Joyce was out gadding as usual.

'I'll go,' Em said, her pulse picking up. Don't be stupid, she told herself. It'll just be one of the neighbours.

There, on the step, stood a man in a suit. Em stared, not taking it in.

'Em – love, it's me!'

'Norm!' It came out as a gasp. He looked like a different person – except for the ears, sticking out as ever, unmistakably his.

'Are you going to let me come in?'

'Oh my God, Norm!' A great pool of emotion broke open in her and their arms were round each other, she clinging to him, sobbing into his chest. All this time he'd been away, and now having him here seemed overwhelming, as if she had never believed he would come back, that they might have a future and a normal married life.

'Oh, love,' he said, stroking her back. 'Oh, I've been dying to do this: to hold on to you for – well, forever! That's it, love – I'm back now. Don't cry, there's a girl.'

Em collected herself and took his hand, dragging him into the house.

'Watch it – there's my bag!' He picked up the kitbag and then all the family were coming to greet him, Bob slapping him on the back and saying, 'Welcome home, son', Violet shyly saying hello, Cynthia kissing him and exclaiming at how he'd filled out, how she'd never've recognized him.

'I thought they'd sent us the wrong fella,' Em laughed through her tears. 'Let's have a proper look at you.'

Norm stood straight and tall in the back room as they all looked him over. In the more than three years he had been away, the gangly youth Em had married had filled out and turned into a man – and, Em saw, a more handsome one than when he left. His shoulders were broad and muscular, and while he was still slender, he looked strong and stood upright. Even the 'car-doors' ears, as Sid used to call them, looked slightly less comical now, because his face was fuller, the jaw seeming more pronounced. And he looked tanned and healthy.

'My, my,' Cynthia said admiringly. 'Well, I can't say it looks as if it's done you any harm – look at you! Anyroad, let's all stop gawping at him and give the poor lad a bite to eat. Not that there's much to go on – that'll be a shock to you,' she added.

'What about Robbie?' Norm said. He took Em's hand again, couldn't seem to stop touching her.

'He's asleep.' She looked up at him, clinging to him too, still drinking in the sight. She was still almost unable to believe he was here. 'D'you want to come up and see him?'

'Nothing'd stop me,' Norm said. 'Hang on a sec . . .' He crouched down. 'I'll take these bleeding shoes off first. I got them in the demob and they squeak like hell.'

Still holding hands, Em going first, the two of them crept up the stairs in their stockinged feet. She pulled him into the room where Robbie slept in her bed, and they left the door open so that some light could spill through.

'I should've brought a candle,' she whispered.

But they could make out a shadowy Robbie, curled on his right side facing them, one hand under his plump cheek and fast asleep.

Norm bent down. 'Hello, son . . . Oh, look at him, Em – oh God, he's lovely . . . I'd best not wake him, but . . .' He stopped. Em could see that he was moved and she burned with pride that she had carried Robbie and brought him to life and looked after him this far, so that her husband could come home and find him safe and beautiful and asleep.

'He *is* a lovely boy,' she murmured. 'You'll see soon enough.'

'Oh, Em.' Norm turned to her and took her in his arms, clutching her close. 'I can hardly believe I'm here. I've wanted you that bad.'

His lips brushed her cheek, searched for her lips, and now she remembered him properly, the feel of him. She gave a little sigh of desire. Home. Norm was home.

Brimful of desire, but knowing they mustn't let things go further – not yet – they hugged each other close.

'Home with my family,' he said. And suddenly he was the one sobbing in her arms.

Twenty-Eight

Everyone was keen to listen to Norm as they ate, and Cynthia made cups of tea and they chatted late into the evening. Joyce came home and said in her jovial way, 'Oh, so you're back, are you?' and then grinned, showing her big teeth, and gave Norm a kiss. Em saw the admiring looks that Joyce gave Norm – Joyce who had always been the first to tease about boring Norm and his ears. Yes, Em thought proudly – Norm had changed. He was different from Sid, who had married and been in a factory all through the war.

They listened to some of Norm's tales about Italy and all the while, even when they were eating, Norm kept one hand on Em's knee under the table. He kept looking at her, as if he couldn't believe she was there. After they'd all had cups of weak tea, and washed up and sat for a bit, Cynthia got up, saying, 'Well – we'd better leave you to it', and after the goodnights were said, Em and Norm were able to be alone at last, with the sounds of the others getting ready for bed upstairs, the noises gradually quietening.

'Come 'ere,' Norm said, sitting in the one armchair by the unlit fire. He patted his lap. 'Come and sit with me, love.'

Gladly Em went and sank onto his lap, leaning against him while he held her tight. Norm nuzzled against her. She could tell how badly he wanted her, but they needed a few minutes first to talk and be close.

'Getting your letters – that was what kept me going,' he told her. 'Meant the world to me, that did.'

Em laughed happily. 'Me, too. Least I knew you were still alive.'

He looked up anxiously into her face. 'You've been all right, love, haven't you? You tell me – I've been doing all the talking for the two of us.'

'I've been all right,' Em said. She felt tired suddenly, thinking of it. There had been so many days, so many tiny details that Norm had missed. She couldn't possibly tell him all of them. In that moment she felt very far away from him, as if they could never catch up. 'Robbie's been a good boy. And we've seen your mom and dad every week, of course. And I've had my little job . . .' She rested her head against him, breathing him in, but his demob suit smelled alien to her. 'Sometimes I just thought it would go on for ever. That we'd never see you again, and Robbie wouldn't have a father.'

'Oh, love . . .' He cuddled her. 'Well, it hasn't turned out like that, has it? I'm here now, and we've got it all in front of us. 'You done a marvellous job, girl – he looks a fine little lad.'

'He is.' She smiled. 'I can't wait for you to see him properly.'

After a time Norm said, 'Where're we going to sleep? In with littl'un?'

'We'll have to,' Em said. 'Joyce and Violet are in Sid's old room now.'

'Or we could just stay down here' – Norm was stroking her arm, seductively – 'make us a bed up on the hearth here . . .'

There was a rug by the fire. 'Tell you what,' Em said.

'I could put a match to it. There's a few bits of kindling left and a bit of slack. It won't last long, but it'd be cosy. And I'll get the spare blanket from up in our room.' She crept up and fetched the old rug and a pillow. The boards creaked, but the rest of the family were sleeping soundly. When she went down, Norm was kneeling, skilfully coaxing the fire into light. She watched him for a second, the light flickering on his face. My husband, she thought. That's my husband. The fire was taking, licking round the knots of newspaper.

'Shall I make us another cup of tea?' she asked, knowing that although she longed for what was to come, she felt shy again, not sure what to say or do. It was a way of putting it off.

Norm turned. 'There's no need.' He held his arms out. 'Oh God, love – just come here, will you?'

Moved by the longing in his eyes, she went to him and, ravenously, he began to make love to her, urgently tugging at the buttons of her frock as they sank to the floor by the fire.

'You'll tear it – let me do it!' she laughed, taking his hands to restrain him.

He needed her so badly that he could hardly contain himself until he was inside her, and she held him, finding her own pleasure reawakening and bursting in on her too, so that they were both gasping, trying not to make too much noise. As they calmed, she held him, kissing him tenderly, feeling how much broader and more substantial he was than the gawky boy to whom she had waved goodbye.

'My man,' she whispered into his neck. 'Oh, Norm, you're here – you're really here.'

He raised his head and looked down at her, eyes full of love. 'And you're my girl. My wife.' Emotionally he added, 'You're so lovely, Em. I told them all out there, showed them your picture – my girl, I said, she's the best. I can't believe I'm back here with you.'

They lay with him inside her for a long while, close in each other's warmth, as if they couldn't bear to come apart. There had been too much being apart. But once they separated, they snuggled up side by side by the last flickers of the fire, pulling the old rug over them and sharing the pillow. Em rested her head on Norm's chest, her hand stroking his taut belly.

And now it was easier to talk, as if they had more fully come home to each other. In low voices they told each other something of the past years. Norm talked about his squadron, about the terror of flying at night, how one of his mates, Rodney Mapple, had come down over the Med, never to be seen again. But he also told her about the good times, the jokes and pranks, and that somehow, poor and war-torn though it was, he had liked Italy.

'There were some nice people,' he said. 'We'd give 'em food or fags or whatever we could, when we could. And they'd ply us with the old *vino*, teach us how to say things like *buongiorno* and *grazie*. Some of the lads got quite good at it – much better than me. I wouldn't mind going back some time – seeing it when there's no war on.'

Em told him about the family, about how Molly had gone off and joined the army and seemed to be thriving.

'Molly Fox?' Norm said, surprised. 'Blimey – I wouldn't't've thought she'd've lasted five minutes in the army, the state of her. Mind you, they've probably seen worse. Maybe it was good for her. I've seen quite a few lads licked into shape.'

'She's in Clacton now,' Em said. 'I had a postcard.'

Mostly, though, she told him about Robbie, about his birth and little stories about him. She knew she'd written some of them to Norm before, but he still liked to hear them. It was a way of getting to know his son, as a baby and as a growing boy.

'Sometime back – in the spring, I think it was – Mr Perry had the first lot of bananas in that we'd seen in years. Course Robbie had never seen one before, so I brought one home to give him. And I said, "D'you know what this is?" It was a bit green, mind. And he looked at me and said, "Is it a gun?"' They both laughed.

'One of them dirty Jerry tricks,' Norm chuckled. 'Guns disguised as bananas!' He turned and kissed Em yet again. 'Oh, I can't wait to see him in the morning!'

It was well into the small hours when they finally slept, but what felt like only seconds later, Em was wakened by the sound of Robbie crying upstairs. It took her a few seconds to work out where she was. The sound didn't seem to have wakened Norm and she sat up, gently moving his arm away from her, and went up to her little boy. He had woken to find the bed empty when she had always been there before.

'It's all right, pet . . .' She sat and cuddled him until he calmed. 'Mom's here, ssshhh – you go back to sleep now, darlin'.'

But he wouldn't settle again without her getting in and holding him, and Em, though longing to go back downstairs to Norm, climbed into bed and lay down with Robbie, holding him close. She had pinched the pillow to take downstairs, so it was not very comfortable, but despite that she found herself falling asleep beside her son's warm body, leaving her husband on the floor downstairs.

She only woke a few hours later, to find Norm perched on the edge of the bed looking down at them both. Once again she was struck by the tanned, healthy look of his face.

'So that's where you got to!' he said.

'Sorry.' Em sat up immediately to give him a hug. 'It's just he's got used to me being in the bed with him. I'm glad he didn't wake you.'

'Oh, I was that tired I could've slept anywhere,' Norm said.

He was looking hungrily at his son, whose dark-lashed eyes were just beginning to flicker open. Robbie looked around, dazed, then sat up.

'Robbie,' Em said gently. 'D'you know who this is? This is your daddy.'

Robbie, only half awake, stared at Norm in a dazed way. Norm reached out as if to pick him up, saying, 'Hello, son.'

But Robbie pulled away, his face creasing, and flung himself against Em, bursting into tears. He hid his face against his mother's body.

'Oh dear!' Em said. 'I'm sorry, love – maybe this wasn't the best moment. He's not even awake yet, and he is sometimes a bit grumpy in the mornings.' She saw how hurt Norm looked. 'He'll be all right when he's had a bite to eat, love – just give him a bit of time.'

She coaxed Robbie through his breakfast.

'He's not sure about Norm,' Em whispered to Cynthia. She couldn't help feeling upset, even though she could see that it was all a big shock for the little boy.

'That's your dad,' Cynthia told Robbie, going to him and stroking his hair. Norm was sitting at the table with him, watching him eat. 'Don't you want to say hello to your dad?'

Robbie pursed his lips and gave a firm shake of the head.

'Leave him for now, Mom,' Em pleaded. 'Just let him eat.'

When he had had his bread and milk and seemed a bit more awake, she took his hand and said, 'Would you like to say hello to your dad now?'

Round-eyed, he allowed her to lead him from his place at the table around to where Norm was sitting.

Norm played it gently. 'Hello,' he said again. He held out his hand. 'I'm Norm. I'm your dad.'

Robbie stared, then slowly held out his hand and took Norm's.

By that evening news of Norm's arrival had got around and seemed reason for a party. He had been to see his mom and dad, who were all for Norm, Em and Robbie moving in with them, and Em could see that in the end they would have to, though she knew it was going to be a wrench. In the meantime, they spent the evening celebrating with the family – Norm's parents and Dot and Lou Alberello, old friends of the family. Dot and Cynthia had been neighbours when their children were young and Dot had been a staunch friend, someone whom Em, as well as her mom, had always been able to turn to.

They brought in beer from the Outdoor down the road and sat drinking and celebrating until Robbie's head was nodding and Em said, 'I'll just take him up to bed.' She scooped him up and laid him on the bed upstairs, but as he lay down his eyes opened again.

'No, Mom – don't go . . .'

'Oh, Robbie.' This time Em felt exasperated. She knew she'd always given in to Robbie before, and that it had not been an easy day for him, but she still wanted to get back to the company downstairs. 'All right – shove up a bit then. Just for a few minutes.'

It took some time before he had fully gone off again, and by the time she got back downstairs she was half asleep herself, and Dot and Lou had got up and were preparing to go.

'Lovely to see yer, bab,' Dot said, picking up her bag. She was looking quite smart these days, Em noticed, and had filled out. Dot, tall and dark, had always been a thin, rangy woman, but now she looked quite curvaceous. Em was glad to see her so happy.

'How's little'un taking to Norm coming home?' Dot asked.

Em pulled the corners of her mouth down. 'Not too well yet. He won't really go near him.'

Dot put her hand on Em's arm. 'Give him time, love – it's bound to be a bit strange for him.'

Up in the bedroom, Norm and Em debated in whispers what they were going to do. The bed was narrow enough, without three of them trying to sleep on it.

'Can't we move him onto the floor?' Norm asked.

Em felt a pang go through her, the pain of having to be separated from her son, whom she had shared a bed with ever since he was born. But she knew Norm was right.

'I'll put the spare blanket down,' she said. 'We can make a little bed for him.'

She folded the blanket to make a mattress for Robbie

on the bare boards. They gave him a pillow and Norm went to fetch his coat. Then very carefully they moved Robbie onto his new bed. It seemed like a miracle that he didn't wake.

It seemed cosy, all of them in the same room. Em and Norm got into bed and lay crushed close together. Very quietly they managed to make love, wincing every time the springs squeaked.

'When we get to Mom's we'll have a proper bed,' Norm said happily.

Em felt another plunge of dread. 'That'll be nice,' she managed to say.

They slept, slotted together spoon-like, Em facing the wall, with Norm curled protectively around her.

She woke to a yelp of pain from Norm. It was already light. Turning her head, she could see a shoe banging up and down against Norm's head.

'Ow! For Christ's sake – what're you doing! Stop it!'

Robbie was whacking Norm with a hard, determined face.

'Don't like you!' he shouted. 'Don't like you. Go away – you go away again and don't come back!'

Twenty-Nine

'Don't say I didn't warn you' Cynthia shouted, over Robbie's hysterical screaming. 'You've made a rod to beat yourself with, that you have.'

Em was standing over her son, trying to persuade him to eat his breakfast.

'Come on now, pet. You know Mommy's got to go to work – and you'll be here with Nanna, just like you always are. Now just calm down . . .'

Her quiet pleading suddenly cracked open and she snatched him up frantically from his chair, holding him in her arms and shouting into his tear-stained face, 'Just stop it, Robbie! Stop this shrieking. You've got to eat your breakfast and behave yourself – I can't stand any more of it!'

And then it was her turn to cry, all the strain and tension of the past week since Norm had come home pouring out.

'Oh, Mom – what'm I going to do? He's like a different child since his dad came back. I can't stand to see him like this!'

Robbie, seeing his mother's tears, cried even more.

'Oh now, stop that, the pair of you. Come 'ere Robbie.' Cynthia, still in her pale-blue nightdress with a cardie over the top, came and took her distressed grandson from his mother. 'Look, I said this would happen, didn't I?' she grumbled, her own nerves on edge with all the screaming. 'You've given in to him all the way along the line, sleeping with him, letting him have it all his way, as if the world revolved round him . . .' Realizing that this lecture was not helping especially, she buttoned her lip.

'Look, bab,' she added more gently, stroking Robbie's quivering back as he clung to her. 'You get off to work. We'll be all right. He'll calm down once you're gone.'

'Mom, MOM!' Robbie started to scream again at the top of his voice, kicking and struggling.

'Robbie,' Cynthia cried firmly. 'Just stop that – now! D'you hear? Go *on*, Em, for heaven's sake.'

Em, still crying, left the house, with obvious reluctance. Cynthia stood watching, jiggling her grandson on her hip. Now that Em had gone, he quietened gradually and she sat him down at the table again.

'There you are, you silly thing. What was all that for, eh? Your mom's just gone to work, that's all. She'll be back. Now you eat up – there's a good boy. What a kerfuffle!'

Cynthia's words rode on the back of a sigh. She began to clear the breakfast things away. Some days it felt as if the end of the war had made things more difficult instead of less. All that hope and expectation they'd had: that the war would make everything better, everyone trying so hard and doing without, in the grand cause of beating Hitler. And now look at us! she thought, going into the scullery to fill the kettle for washing-up water. We're all crammed into this house, there's even less to eat than before and no end of it in sight. What was the carrot now, to keep them all going?

Within days, Em and Norm were due to move in with Norm's mom and dad, Edna and Bill Stapleton, though Cynthia would still be looking after Robbie on the days when Em worked. Though Cynthia dreaded them going, and the wrench of not having her grandson living there any more, at moments like this she felt the day could not come too soon.

Em wiped her eyes, hurrying along the road to Mr Perry's grocer's shop, where she had worked through the war. Mr Perry was a widower and his one son was still serving out east, so her nice little job had just carried on.

She felt like sobbing her heart out, but didn't want to be seen crying out in the street, so she swallowed her emotions. But oh, how sad and upset she felt. For the past three years and more, since she had had Robbie, he had been her closest relationship, the love of her life. She had invested everything in him, all her affection and energy, telling herself that she had to be both a mom and dad to him until Norm came back – if he did. There was always that terrible thought. She had let Robbie share her bed, needing the feel of his warm little body beside her as much as he needed her for reassurance. The thought of moving him out into a cold, lonely little bed of his own was unbearable to her. Nor could she bear his tears if he was upset. The sound of his distress cut right through her and she would do almost anything to mollify him. She knew Cynthia was right: she had warned Em and told her that she was spoiling him. But without Norm home, there didn't seem to be any point in doing anything else. She'd do all that in due course.

Norm had been patient at first. 'It's bound to be hard for the lad,' he said, when Robbie screamed when he came near and tried to hold the door shut, so that Norm couldn't come into the bedroom. 'I mean, to him I'm a stranger. He's got to get to know me.'

Em could see that he was hurt, but was trying to make the best of it. At first, torn in half by the needs of her son and husband, she suggested that Robbie sleep in the bed with both of them. But the bed was only a single one, so she and Norm were cramped enough as it was. And Robbie wouldn't let Norm get into bed anyway. He would start up as soon as Norm appeared and would kick and scream. Norm tried hard, speaking nicely to him to try and calm him down, but it didn't make any difference. On the third night, Norm stormed out.

'For Christ's sake, get that child in order. What a welcome – in my own home! How's anyone supposed to get any sleep with all that going on?'

And Em was left to get into bed with Robbie and soothe him, until at least they could move him into the little makeshift bed on the floor. It took a long time some nights, as Robbie would not settle and go to sleep. Em was up and down the stairs while the others sat together down there.

'Just give him a bit longer,' she kept saying, her own nerves in shreds, seeing Norm's disapproving expression and with the memory of Robbie's tearful, betrayed-looking face.

At last, they'd be able to creep into bed, terrified of waking him.

Norm, who was looking forward to good times with his wife and had not grown used to life with a child in any form, kept suggesting they go out.

'We could go out for a dance,' he'd say. Or another night, 'Come on – let's go to the pictures tonight.'

Neither time had they made it, because Em didn't

feel she could leave until Robbie was settled, and it all took so long that it was too late by then.

'I'm sorry, Norm,' she'd whispered the night before, when they were finally curled up in bed together. 'I know it's not how things should be. Just give us a bit of time.'

'Don't worry, love.' Norm cuddled her, but she heard his stifled sigh. 'There's no rush. We've got our lives in front of us, haven't we? Anyroad, when we get to my mom and dad's he can have a proper bed of his own. It'll all be different, you'll see.'

Em's heart shrivelled at this. She was dreading moving out to the Stapletons', even though she quite liked Norm's mom and dad. But Em, who struggled with any kind of change, had got very settled in her routines in her own family's house over the past years, with her mom always there. She knew it would upset Robbie too, and she was chilled by the way Norm spoke about moving over there, as if that would put him in charge of everything. There was an 'and then we'll see an end to all this nonsense' tone to his voice.

Reaching Mr Perry's, she tried to put these gloomy thoughts of out her mind. It was early days. Things weren't easy for anyone. There were rumours about some of the other men who'd come home, the state some of them were in, and she counted herself lucky in that. Their first week together had contained extremes of great anger and frustration, but also great tenderness between them.

I must look on the bright side, she thought.

'Morning, Mr Perry!' she called out cheerfully, finding him outside, still setting up. The summer veg were coming in now, so the place was not so bare.

'Morning, bab!' Mr Perry touched an imaginary hat.

''Nother fine one!' She expected him to add, 'And you're a sight for sore eyes.' But just for once, he didn't.

There was so much to have to get used to that week. Em could see that Norm was restless, having to adapt to civilian life, to rationing and shortages and restrictions. Norm kept a lot of his feelings to himself, but she noticed changes both in him and in herself that they were having to get used to.

For a start, Norm was bossier than he'd used to be: more commanding. Even though he'd only been promoted to Corporal in the RAF, he had had people to order about. There was more confidence in the way he expressed his opinions, both about Robbie and things outside.

'They're going to sweep all this away, you know,' he'd said one evening over tea. 'All this area'll go. It's a new era, now we've got a Labour government – they've got to do better for the working man, better houses. The lads've been talking about it all through the war. They won't let them get away without doing it now.'

'Swept away?' Cynthia said.

'All these old houses – they'll have to go.'

Em and Cynthia looked at each other in dismay. They knew that the powers that be had plans, but they weren't at all sure that they wanted their house swept away.

'Equal shares – none of this government by the rich. We've all had more than enough of that.'

He tried to draw Bob, Em's dad, into discussions, but Bob, though obviously not in any disagreement with him, was not a great talker. Last year, in the elections after the war, they had voted Labour, even though they were grateful to Winnie Churchill. But it was just odd, hearing Norm suddenly giving off opinions like that. The war had changed him.

'I've seen blokes killed,' he said tersely to her, when she accused him of being on a soapbox one evening. 'And I'll be damned if they're going to have died for nothing – for it all just to go back to how it was before, with *certain people* lining their pockets.'

He had also come home with other high hopes – of independence, of starting something up.

'I'd like my own little business,' he said to Em, when they were alone in bed, soon after he came back. 'Not have a boss – to be the one in charge.'

'But what could you do?' Em asked. The thought seemed extraordinary to her, and well out of reach.

'That's the trouble – I don't know.' He sounded frustrated. 'A shop, maybe?'

But very quickly he was coming down to earth. There was no money for anything new. Norm was having to come to terms, within those first days home, with the fact that the only obvious thing for him to do was go back into the police force, where he'd started out.

Last night, lying with her in the darkness, he'd said sadly. 'I dunno – I thought things were opening out. That was the feeling I had: I wanted to keep it up, carry on like that. In the war things felt important. *We* felt important. Now it just feels as if things are closing in, getting smaller, as if there's nowhere to turn.'

And Em stroked one of his arms, which were wrapped around her, and felt desperate, because it felt as if she and Robbie were part of that closing down and hemming in. As if they were making life for him feel like a prison, shutting him away from his new, high hopes.

IV

KATIE

Thirty

June 1946

She didn't think she could face knocking on yet another door.

Katie stopped for a moment in the street, trying to hold back the tears that were stinging her eyes. Her throat felt sore with the effort of not crying. The light was at last beginning to die on this long June evening, but there were a few people about and children still playing out, and she didn't want anyone to see the tear that oozed over and ran down her cheek.

So far, all she had met was suspicion and hard-faced rejection. It was all very well when they opened their doors and saw her, smart in a sage-green shirt-waister with its matching belt, and her white cardigan and neat navy shoes. She wore her hair swept back stylishly so that she looked every inch a reliable working girl, the sort who would have money to meet the rent and no trouble.

'I'm enquiring about the room,' she'd say. 'It says you have one to let?'

The landladies could afford to be fussy: there were far more people in need of a room than the accommodation to meet it. A quiet, single woman – that's what they all wanted. Or, second best, a quiet, single man. So far so good. Seeing Katie's respectable look, some of their faces broke into cautious smiles. But sooner or later in the conversation she had to tell them the full truth. That wiped the smiles off them. The last one had been the worst, the one who'd really got under her skin.

'I have regular work,' she'd begun. 'With solicitors Rowan and Johnson on Bennett's Hill...' This always impressed them. This last lady had been in her apron, middle-aged with tight brown curls, genteel but hard-faced in a thin, tight-lipped way. The sort who could damn you with a look or a whisper. She stood twisting her wedding ring round and round her bony finger, as if to emphasize how respectably married she was.

'A solicitor – oh well, you sound *just* the sort of person I'm looking for,' she said in an affected way, even managing something almost like a smile. 'Tell me – where are you living now?'

'Not far away,' Katie explained. 'In Holly Road.' It was another street nearby in Handsworth. 'I'm lodging with a lady there, but her husband will be coming home soon and I need to give them their privacy and find somewhere else.'

The lady looked her up and down again, sniffed, then said, 'I'm very strict about use of hot water. But you look a sensible sort of girl. If you're serious, you'd better come and see the room.'

'The thing is,' Katie felt her legs turn weak again, having to say this, 'I'm not completely on my own.' There, the words had to come out. 'I've my little boy: he's nearly two and a half, and he's no trouble...' She babbled fast, trying to make a good impression, but all the while aware of the expression of disdain taking over the landlady's face. 'He's a quiet little lad, ever so good, and he'll be looked after during the day while I'm at work . . .'

But the woman was retreating furiously back into her doorway.

'Oh no, I don't think so. I don't want any children, all noise and mess. No, you'll have to find somewhere else. Coming here, disturbing people at this time of the evening! I mean, how do I even know you've got a husband? You never can tell these days. Off you go now – away from my door!'

'But . . .' Katie called out, as the door slammed shut. 'You don't understand. My husband – he was killed at Arnhem.' Her voice sunk to a whisper. 'You stuck-up, cold-hearted bitch.'

No, she thought, standing in the dusk, she couldn't face any more. She felt cold and shrunken inside. The woman's words had sliced into her. It was her mother all over again, that stone-hearted sanctimony. Because it was all true: she wasn't respectable. There was no husband, killed at Arnhem or anywhere else. She was going to be burdened by her shame every day of her life, no matter how much she lied and pretended and put on a brave front. How was she ever going to find a place for herself and her little boy? Somewhere they could just live in peace and make some sort of life? She had hoped to find a place in Handsworth, to be close to her present lodgings, because Maudie, her current land-lady, was going to carry on looking after Michael. But maybe that was a vain hope – she'd have to find a place that wasn't quite so respectable, where people were more desperate for her rent. This dreadful thought sunk into her: the idea of returning to the sort of place where she had grown up, surrounded by poverty.

Trying to pull herself together, she turned for home. She'd go back to the cosy little house near the park, to Maudie and the children. That would cheer her up.

Crossing over the main road in the falling dusk, she headed home along a side street of tall Victorian houses. Even after all this time it still felt like a novelty being able to walk the evening streets and be able to see, after all the war years of blackout when some nights you could scarcely see your hand in front of your face. The neglect that most houses had suffered through the war was shrouded now by the encroaching darkness, and Katie thought how cosy some of them looked, the lights on behind the curtains in the wide windows, many of them with a pretty border at the top, of coloured glass flowers and fruits. These were the sorts of houses where they would have had maids before the war, and maybe a few still did. But all that sort of thing seemed to be dying out. She peered curiously at each house as she passed, hoping to catch a glimpse of the lives going on behind the glass, aching at the thought that she would never have a proper family now, or a normal life.

A movement caught her eye in the downstairs window of a house halfway along. A plump arm and shoulder appeared through the curtains, and something white. There was some operation going on with a pot of glue, a card being stuck into the window. For a moment she shrunk down behind the hedge, waiting until the card had been attached and the person had withdrawn. With curiosity, but not much hope, she crept up the path.

'ROOM FOR RENT,' the sign read, and then in smaller letters: 'SIZEABLE BUT MUST TACKLE STAIRS. SUIT WORKING MAN. Half Board, £1 a week. Apply Within.'

'Must tackle stairs,' Katie murmured, frowning at this rather odd condition. 'That must mean it's the attic.'

Still not sure that she could face another ordeal with a hatchet-faced landlady, she was turning to back away when she realized someone was standing on the path behind her.

'Oh my goodness!' She laid a hand over her thudding heart. 'Did you have to creep up on me like that? You nearly made me jump out of my skin!'

A youngish man in a suit, with a sorrowful-looking moustache, was standing patiently, apparently waiting for her to move.

'I was just coming home,' he said. 'This is where I live.'

'Sorry,' Katie said, calming down, 'only I didn't hear you.'

'That'll be my room,' he added, nodding at the card, adding tragically, 'They're moving me to Manchester.'

'Oh – I see. Well, yes. I'm looking for somewhere. Should I ask, d'you think?' She wanted to say: *What's she like?* But didn't dare.

'You could apply within, as stated.' He produced a key and, before she could protest, swung the door open. A nice smell floated out, of meat cooking. 'Allow me.'

A shrill barking also broke out as soon as the door opened, and Katie heard the tac-tac of a dog's nails coming along the hall. A wiry-haired Jack Russell came to the step and stood barking for all he was worth.

'Hello,' Katie said to the dog, hoping it wouldn't bite her, and it did more important barking.

'Archie?' A deep, well-spoken voice called. Light spilled into the hall as a door opened inside. 'Oh, Archie, what are you doing?'

Katie saw a woman coming towards her, limping on

263

obviously sore feet and wearing a shapeless, billowing frock.

'Archie, for goodness' sake, *stop it*! Now, out of the way.' Opening the door of the room beside her, the woman put her foot against the dog's backside, directed him in there with a firm shove and closed the door. The barking continued, then stopped, defeated. Katie found herself being observed. As the woman had her back to the light, Katie could only get an impression of her: hair in some sort of bun, but straggling, a surprisingly masculine-looking face with black brows, then the rest of her shapeless form lost in the green frock, which was belted loosely at the waist. On her feet were thick stockings and broken-down sheepskin slippers.

'Oh dear,' the woman said at once. 'I see you really aren't a young man.'

'Well, no,' Katie agreed, almost feeling she ought to apologize.

'I see – and you have come about the room? Good heavens, I've only just put the card up. Were you standing out in the street waiting, or something?'

'In a way I was,' Katie said. 'I've been looking for a room, and I was just passing.'

'But really I want a young man . . .'

'I can climb stairs,' Katie said. 'If that's the problem. I'm very strong and I don't mind at all . . . In fact,' she added desperately, 'I'd be willing to help you – I mean, in the house, if you need it.'

She decided to lay everything bare, instead of waiting. After all she might as well be turned away sooner rather than delaying the agony. All her pride had been shaken out of her by now.

'I'm really desperate for a place to go, you see. It's me and my little boy. I'm a widow – we're on our own:

he's only two – and my present landlady, her husband's being demobbed and they don't want a lodger, and no one will have us. I'm afraid if it goes on like this, I'm going to be on the streets . . .' The emotion she had been keeping down all evening began to pour out and she burst into tears. 'Oh, I'm sorry – I never meant to carry on like this, only I've been looking for days and everyone's been so nasty . . .'

The woman leaned against the doorframe. 'Oh, dearie me,' she said, almost huffily. 'I do wish you hadn't told me all this.' There was a silence as Katie composed herself.

'You've really nowhere else to go? What about your family – can't they help?'

Katie shook her head, wiping her eyes. 'Not a hope.'

'What's your name? And the boy?'

'Katie – O'Neill.' And my little boy's Michael. He's no trouble, honestly. He's a quiet little chap, and I wouldn't cause you any noise or bother.'

There was a silence. The woman folded her arms and let out a long, considering sigh.

'It's against my better judgement,' she said. 'I prefer male lodgers really – they're handier, and not so hard on the plumbing. But you do seem to be in a jam, and one must try and be Christian about these things. Come round tomorrow and bring your boy. If you like the room, and I like you, we might be able to come to some arrangement.'

'Oh – d'you mean it!' Katie felt like throwing her arms around the woman. 'Really? Oh, thank you, thank you!'

'I haven't said yes yet,' she said crustily. 'Come round tomorrow – it's number twenty-six. Don't come so late. Six o'clock would suit. Then we'll see.' She had almost shut the door when it opened again. 'My name is Miss Routh, by the way. Sybil Routh.'

'How d'you do,' Katie said.

Sybil Routh stared a moment longer, shook her head as if baffled by her own foolishness, then shut the door.

Thirty-One

Within days of Katie giving birth in the Millers' crowded household, something lucky had happened. Ann came in from work one afternoon while Katie was feeding Michael, wincing at the child's strong pull on her.

'Ooh,' Ann looked sympathetic. 'Does it hurt yer?'

'A bit – he doesn't half suck.' Katie smiled. 'Never mind.'

'Look!' Ann was waving a copy of the *Mail*. 'I'm not trying to get rid of you – not as such, of course. But there's summat here might be just the thing.'

A service wife in Handsworth was advertising for a lodger-cum-companion while her husband was away. Well-behaved infants were welcome, not more than two, sharing care of the children.

Katie read it and looked up at Ann, her eyes full of hope.

'The only thing is,' Ann said, concerned. 'How will you pay the rent – it does say it's neg . . . negotiable.'

'Don't worry,' Katie said. 'I can manage – until I can get back to work again.' She had Simon's money. Anger and hurt swelled in her, as it did every time she thought of him, as well as a defiant determination to survive without him, whatever happened. To *show him* she didn't need him – even if he didn't know or care! Anyway, it was the least he could do: put a roof over their heads.

That was how she came to be living with Maudie Grant in Holly Road. Maudie and her husband John were schoolteachers, though John, a history teacher, had decided to 'do his bit' and had joined the navy in 1940. Maudie's parents, who lived nearby in Handsworth Wood, had helped and supported her with the little ones and she had had a lodger for a time, but she had moved on.

'As my two have got older, I find it even more of a handful in some ways,' Maudie told Katie on her first visit. 'I thought it might be fun to have someone else in the house with children – but then, you see, I love babies. Oh, I'd so like another one, but of course with John not being here...'

Maudie was a curvaceous, lively, scatty young woman who hardly ever stopped talking. She had straight brown hair, yanked back into a wayward ponytail, and an artless way of dressing – frumpy almost, Katie thought, taking in Maudie's calf-length brown skirt and cream blouse with three-quarter length sleeves, and a button missing so that the blouse gaped, giving a glimpse of her white brassiere. Yet the overall effect of Maudie was not of a frump, because there was something so individual about her shapely, restless figure that gave her her own style. And she was very pretty, with a scattering of freckles across her nose and wide grey eyes. Her children – Jenny, six, and Peter, four – were blond and angelic-looking.

Katie, wanting to hide nothing and spare herself any disappointment, carried Michael along with her. In any case, she didn't like being separated from him and didn't want to put Mrs Miller to the trouble of looking after him. He lay sleepily in her arms, his cheeks pink and firm.

'Oh, now he's adorable!' Maudie said softly, looking down at him. 'What lovely colouring: those dark lashes. He's ever so like you, isn't he? But so little – when on earth did you have him?'

'A week ago,' Katie confessed.

'Gracious heavens!' Maudie looked at her, aghast. 'You must be all in – here, have a chair. And I'll make tea: you must have biscuits! I'll run and turn up the gas! Course, I used to have a daily, but she's gone off to work in a factory – more money. And quite right of course, naturally. We must all do our bit...'

Katie was more than grateful to sit down. She felt shaky, and the journey had taken it out of her.

'And you're having to look for a new berth so soon after?' Maudie bustled back in. 'You poor, poor thing! And where's your husband, may I ask?'

Katie had told so many of these kinds of lies that they came easily now. 'Oh, he's out east somewhere. I haven't heard from him in a little while now. I don't know if he even knows about Michael yet – probably not. I can't help worrying.'

'Well, of *course*.' Maudie said. 'I know with my John – I mean he's very good, and he writes whenever he gets the chance, but it's so erratic, and of course when they're at sea...!' She gazed down at Michael again. 'What a heavenly baby – oh, the kettle!' She dashed back into the kitchen.

By the end of this 'interview' Katie had hardly had to say anything, but she knew a great deal about Maudie and John Grant, and about little Jenny's schooling, which was a homespun business these days, taking place in the house of a Mrs Grey where sometimes Maudie went to help, and about Peter's tendency to sleepwalk. And Maudie had said, of course, that Katie could move in if she could stand the chaos, and that they would muddle along together.

And they had done, for more than two years. Katie was more grateful to Maudie than she could put into words. Until Michael was two months old she had stayed home with him, paying Maudie for her board out of Simon's money. The girls pooled their rations. Katie found a new job as a typist then, not too far away, in Hockley, and paid Maudie to look after Michael. She had to start giving him formula from a bottle in the daytime, and Katie was always longing to get home after a long day slogging at the typewriter, her breasts still tingling and seeping with milk, to feed him herself.

It was hard at first, uncomfortable, and she hated being away from Michael. She was envious of the time Maudie spent with him, pushing him up to the shops on the Soho Road in Jenny's and Peter's old perambulator, and sitting with him in the afternoon. But Maudie was so kind-hearted and never at all possessive about Michael, because her hands were already quite full enough with her own children. And soon, since Katie always came home to find him safe and well cared for, she trusted Maudie with him completely.

In return, she sometimes took Jenny and Peter out for a walk at the weekend to give Maudie a break, although Maudie often said she wanted to come too and they ended up chatting together in Handsworth Park; or Maudie's mother came round, so Katie didn't have to do much. But as she was of an orderly nature and Maudie was anything but, Katie did try to keep things tidy in the house. She made lists for shopping and jobs that needed doing, until Maudie would say, 'How on earth did I manage before you were here?' And Maudie sometimes took things rather over-seriously and Katie could make her laugh. They found that they were good for each other.

On Sundays, Katie often went over to St Francis's parish for Mass while Maudie joined her mother at Handsworth Old Church, by the park. Maudie was not especially religious, but going to church was something they had always done, and she liked to read bits of the Bible to the children. Katie found it a comfort to go to Mass. As things settled, as her body recovered and she continued this new life, she began to dwell more on the past. She missed Uncle Patrick, and going to Mass was a reminder of him. It was painful thinking of him, but not as painful as thinking about the other people who had bowed so cruelly out of her life. Many of her memories of him were happy ones, and Mass brought some of those back. Sometimes, in the evenings, when Maudie was settling the children down, reading to them, Katie would sit on the stairs of the little terraced house and listen. Maudie always read a story and then, as they were lying down to sleep, a psalm.

'The rhythm of them is so beautiful,' she told Katie. 'It doesn't really matter if they don't understand the words.'

So Katie sat, if Michael was settled, in the almost darkness at the top of the stairs and listened: 'The Lord is my shepherd: therefore can I lack nothing . . . But thy loving-kindness and mercy shall follow me all the days of my life: and I will dwell in the house of the Lord forever.' Psalm 23 was her favourite, but there were many others that took her back to Patrick's gentle, musical voice. She found it soothing.

And there was something else for which she was

especially grateful to Maudie. At first it took some getting used to. All Katie's life she had been schooled – first by her mother, then by circumstances ¬ to be secretive, even to lie if necessary, so that shameful truths should not be disclosed. Anyone who asked questions was seen as suspect. But Maudie asked questions – lots of them. And not only that, she talked, straightforwardly and with an artless trust that Katie found astonishing.

'The thing is,' Maudie told her one afternoon, while the children were napping, not long after Katie had arrived. She was perched on a low stool, looking rather like a little girl, in ankle socks and with her hair hanging loose. She was working on a long skein of green knitting, though it would have been hard to say what kind of garment was meant to be developing from it.

'My brother Wilfred is the black sheep of the family. What with Daddy being a headmaster, of course, there was always a lot of school and a lot of bossing about. Being a headmaster did make Daddy rather pompous, I'm afraid. And Wilfred reacted badly. That wife of his, Glenda – well, you won't meet her because they've moved away – but she was *well* on with their first baby before they tied the knot. Mummy and Daddy were furious with him. You can imagine! Anyway – oh, bother, I've lost a stitch again – there was this awful shotgun wedding, and she's clearly not at all right for him. Simply ghastly woman! They've two children now, but oh my goodness, Mummy and Daddy *loathe* her, even though they try to be polite!'

Katie was astonished to be told such family secrets, but somehow hearing about them like this made them seem not quite so bad. Maudie seemed to regard most human foibles with a detached amusement, rather than sitting as judge and jury. *Ah well*, her attitude seemed to be, *it'll all be the same in a hundred years! People, compared with geology, are very short-lived – and aren't people* funny?

Katie started to see just how obsessed her own mother had been with keeping things secret: Uncle Patrick's condition, and even the details of her husband's death, which was hardly something to be ashamed of. As the weeks passed, under Maudie's interested questioning Katie found herself, for the first time in her life, beginning to talk.

At first it was about her father dying, and about sharing the house with Uncle Patrick. For the first time ever she voiced the words, 'I suppose you'd have to say he wasn't really very well . . .'

Maudie put down the mending she was doing that afternoon and listened raptly. 'It sounds as if he was a manic depressive,' she said.

'A what?' Katie had never heard the words before. If only she could have turned to that medical dictionary in Sparkhill Library and known what to look for. Would it have made any difference?

'I couldn't give you chapter and verse,' Maudie said. 'But I know Daddy worked with someone once who was like that. Sometimes he just sat in the darkest corner of the staffroom as if he had no life in him at all, then next time he'd be brim full of energy, fomenting revolution! He drove all the rest of them round the bend. It really became very difficult – you know, beyond managing. They had to ask him to move on in the end.'

Katie could feel things falling into place in her mind. Tearfully she described what she knew of Patrick's life to Maudie, his suddenly leaving the White Fathers, the dark days when he would barely move, the over-excitement and pacing at night, the long walks, his coming home soaked to the skin and famished, with his shoes worn through.

'And he was so kind,' she found herself sobbing. 'He was like a father to me, even though he wasn't. You know, I still make sure they say a Mass for him every year, round the anniversary of his death.'

Maudie was interested and sympathetic. Gradually Katie found herself talking about Vera. She had been tempted to tell Maudie that her mother was dead too, but she owed it to her to be more truthful than that. And eventually – because it soon became obvious that there were no letters arriving from her husband, and Maudie kept worrying for her – Katie could not keep up the pretence of pining for an absent spouse. She told Maudie about Simon Collinge. Maudie was shocked, but then furious on Katie's behalf.

'You mean he paid you off – just like that?'

Katie nodded, her face burning. 'I felt . . .' It was so strange, so wonderful to pour all this out for the first time! 'Well, I felt cheap – awful. Maybe I shouldn't have taken the money, but . . .'

'Of course you should!' Maudie insisted indignantly. 'If he was just going to abandon you, instead of doing the decent thing. What a complete cad!'

'Yes,' Katie agreed. Even though it hurt, she could see Simon Collinge for what he was: a spoilt, shallow young man who had used her for what he could get and then cast her aside. 'I wouldn't have been able to pay my rent without it.'

'And he's not interested in seeing his own son?'

Katie shook her head miserably, looking down to hide the sudden tears.

'Well, you poor girl. We women have to stand up for

ourselves, you know – we didn't get the vote by giving in to them. All I can say is, we'll stick together here, at least till the war ends. We'll have to see after that, won't we?'

Katie nodded gratefully, wiping her eyes. 'Yes – thank you very much.'

Thirty-Two

The two years had flown by. Their household had been a very female one, with some of Maudie's friends visiting. Katie's old friend Ann Miller came very occasionally to see how she was getting along, and she went to see the family in Balsall Heath sometimes too. They were always delighted to see her and Michael. In its way it had been a happy time, and she had put a lot of her bitterness over Simon Collinge behind her. He had become irrelevant.

But in the summer of 1945, after peace had been declared and celebrated in Europe, Katie realized that although the men would not be home for some time yet, she had better get out of the typing pool and look for a better-paid job. She had soon found her new post at Rowan and Johnson, Solicitors, and was pleased at the thought of working in town for a change. In celebration she went to a draper's in Handsworth – never Lewis's, in case she ran into her mother – and bought a length of vivid jade-green cloth, off the ration, to make herself a suit. It had been that first morning, reporting for work, as she had walked across Cathedral Square in high spirits, that a young woman in a pink frock – so busy gazing up at the cathedral that she was not looking where she was going – had collided with her. The past echoed at her immediately. It was Emma Brown, from Kenilworth Street.

Katie's heart beat fast with delight at seeing her. She wanted to put the clock back and return to that friendship they had had in the Cromwell Street School classroom, their jokes and games, before all the hurts and difficulties. But despite her new relaxed openness with Maudie, in those seconds the old habits fell back into place. Don't say anything. Don't give anything away. So she put on a bright and breezy manner, friendly, but closed, and told Em nothing. And then Em started on about Molly Fox and that disgusting brother of hers and how he'd been hanged, and there'd been no chance to say more, or change anything. She'd tried – she'd smiled and hoped Em would ask more. She needed to be asked – to be invited back in. But then Em was gone, and so had her chance.

'Never mind,' she told herself. 'You've got Maudie. She's the best friend you've ever had!'

But the sadness of what happened with Em still stayed with her.

The attic room that Sybil Routh showed to Katie did indeed involve climbing a lot of stairs, with runners of old carpet up the middle. She carried Michael, feeling her leg muscles pulling. This would keep her in trim all right! Archie, the little dog, followed this time, seeming quite happy with Katie's presence now that she had been let into the house. When they reached the top and looked into its large, airy space, she felt immediately that she could live in it, even though it was still occupied in a sparse, masculine way by the man who was going to Manchester – Mr Bell. The bed was rumpled and there were clothes thrown carelessly on the chair.

'Mr Bell will be gone by the end of the month,' Sybil told her, still panting from the climb.

The room extended across most of the top of the house, which was built of generous Victorian proportions, with a high ceiling and two dormer windows overlooking the street, so that the front of the room was bathed in light, with the back end, where the bed was, more shadowy. As well as the bed, which seemed to be three-quarter-sized, there was an old leather armchair, its brown surface rubbed pale where countless heads and hands had rested on it, a small writing table and chair, and a wardrobe that, Sybil showed her, also contained shelves. The floor was of worn brown linoleum. Even without any female touch, it felt cheerful and inviting.

'It's very nice,' Katie said. Michael chattered, smiling and waving his arm excitedly, wanting to be put down to play with Archie, who was sniffing round the room.

'He won't hurt him,' Sybil said, as Michael made straight for Archie. The dog's little docked tail wagged at him. 'He's all sound and fury – look, friends already.'

'Just be gentle with him, Mikey,' Katie said. But the dog seemed happy and Michael too.

'Think you can do all these stairs – with him?' Sybil Routh nodded at Michael, then gave an unexpected smile. 'Yes, little fellow: this is your new home!'

Katie was warmed by this. Sybil seemed in no doubt about them.

'I'll be perfectly all right. I just don't want to disturb the people underneath – if he were to run up and down.'

'Well, you're above the Gudgeons, both of whom are fortunately rather deaf. You won't see much of her – she's an invalid. Tell you what, I've got a mouldy old rug somewhere in the back there, if you don't mind it. That'd muffle things up a bit, wouldn't it?'

On the way down again Sybil Routh showed her the bathroom at the back of the second floor, with a huge claw-footed bath. It was the best bathroom Katie had ever seen.

'There's a meter for the water – I know what you girls are like for baths; go easy on the lavatory flush – and no more than two squares of Izal at a time: the plumbing objects to it . . . Now, I'll show you what's what. That room – well, rooms – at the front, that's the Gudgeons'.' Her voice dropped to a whisper. Katie had to strain to hear over Michael's happy crooning. She had put him down and was having to hold on tight to his hand. 'They're a nice old couple, but very frail. She looks as if the wind would blow her down, and he's quite devoted. Then there's Mr Treace in the back room. He'll be in any minute – works in Lloyds Bank – rather a dull fellow, I'm afraid, but of frugal habits, which is what we landladies like, of course! A modest bather. Now, I know you'll need to bath the child . . . We'll have to see what we can do.' She led the way downstairs. Michael was wrapped up in the dog, playing with him along the hall.

'The bottom floor is all mine. There's a little parlour at the front, which I never really use and it's cold as the grave in there. This room is where all life happens.'

She led the way along the lovely tiled hall and into a very large back room. Katie was aware immediately of moss-green walls beneath a picture rail, above which everything was creamy-white, and of a room crammed with intriguing things. At one end was a dining table and chairs and, beside it, a dark old sideboard on which rested a huge china soup-tureen and various silver jugs and salvers. There was a dresser, the top half of which had glass doors, crammed with leather-bound books, and beside it another set of deep shelves, which held a mixture of books and glass cases. In them Katie saw a variety of stuffed birds: pheasants and grouse and other game birds. Her eyes were drawn to the very top shelf, where she could see something with very big teeth.

'Ah...' Sybil saw where she was looking. 'That is the Bengal tiger, or was once, poor fellow – skull of one.' Its jaws were stretched wide open, the teeth curved like sabres. 'It was my brother Anselm's – he died in India, alas. And these others...' A sweep of her hand took in the birds and various glass cases of coloured butterflies, which were attached to the wall by the door. 'Those are Cuthbert's: another brother, but he's *gorn orf*, as they say, to Australia.'

Nearer the back end of the house, from which glass doors led out to the garden, there was a fireplace with a couple of comfy old chairs covered in green-and-white flowered chintz beside it and, against the wall behind, an upright piano.

'Oh,' Katie said, surprised. 'It's lovely! And a piano – can you play it?'

'I was just about to ask you the same question. I live in hope!'

'No, I'm afraid I never learned,' Katie said.

'It's beyond me now,' Sybil said. 'My sister Cordelia is the real pianist and I used to play around a bit on it, before my wretched hands seized up.' She held her hands out, swollen and gnarled-looking, and Katie felt for her. 'Mr Treace can tinkle a bit, but nothing that you'd really want to listen to exactly, I'm afraid.' She chuckled. 'Yes, young man,' she said and Michael came and peered curiously at it. 'Have you seen a piano before?' She opened the lid. 'Look, I'll show you something. That's middle C – that's right, you press it.'

Michael looked up at her, fascinated as the note sounded out.

'You'll have to learn to play, won't you?' Sybil smiled, closing the lid again. 'Now, this room is where we all eat – breakfast and evening meal. Lunch is your affair, of course. I'll have your ration books off you. I've a girl does some shopping for me and a few odd jobs. Better that we all share – I like my house to be a home, not a doss-house. I don't hold with all this crouching in little rooms over a solitary electric ring. It's wasteful and uncivilized. Now, we can arrange for you to feed the boy separately, if you wish him to have tea early, but otherwise food will be on the table at seven. You'll hear the gong. In fact, I need to go and finish it off now. So – d'you want the room or not?'

Maudie laughed wholeheartedly when Katie told her where she had found new lodgings for the following month.

'Old Sybil Routh? Oh yes, Mummy and I know her from the church. In fact I think her father was a clergyman, though not round here. There are quite a few Rouths scattered around somewhere – I think she was one of six or seven. She's quite potty, but actually rather nice. Such odd clothes! But how funny that you should go there. I think she runs a bit of a home for waifs and strays, even though she tries to pretend she's terribly businesslike about it. She's an interesting lady – used to be some kind of social worker, I believe. Or was it a nurse? Well, that's lovely, Katie – you're not far away and you, little M, can come round and see me while your mummy's at work, can't you?'

In her sweet, spontaneous way, Maudie swept Michael up into her arms and kissed him and Katie laughed, suddenly amazed by how good life felt.

V

MOLLY

Thirty-Three

10th July '46
Hello, Molly,
   Norm is home. We're living at his mom's now.
All going all right, though Robbie not very settled.
We're going along. Are you ever coming up this
way to see us? Please write.
   Love Em x
PS Robbie drew this for you.

Em had sent a plain white postcard on which she had
got Robbie to do a drawing. It was only in two colours.
Molly looked at the square, red house with swirls of
angry black smoke pouring from the chimney. And
there was a dullness to Em's message and, reading
between the lines, a lot of things not said. At times
Molly envied Em's staid, family life, never far from her
mom and dad and her sisters, husband home from the
war, a child. All the things Molly didn't have, could
never even imagine having now. Once she had, for a
time, with Tony, during those sunlit, dreamlike days in
1942 before he was killed. She still tried to imagine
that it might have worked for them, had he lived. But
not now. None of that was for her. But for all that,
she didn't think Em sounded especially full of the joys,
either.
   She did not hear from Em often. To her surprise the

person who kept in touch with her very faithfully was Ruth Chambers. Every couple of weeks a blue envelope would slip through the door, addressed in Ruth's neat, sloping hand. Molly found she had started to look forward to the letters very much, even though she had a little smile at some of Ruth's expressions.

Molly and Ruth had begun their basic training in the ATS together and immediately loathed each other. Molly thought back with shame and embarrassment on her first weeks in the army. Feeling very unsure of herself, and inferior to a lot of the other girls in every way, she had played up and been loud and rude, and got a lot of people's backs up. Ruth, a staid, studious girl from a sheltered middle-class background, had been about to start studying natural sciences at Cambridge. Ruth was rather buck-toothed and awkward, and had absolutely no idea how to cope with someone like Molly, whose behaviour had been mostly noisy and as crude as possible. They had hoped never to set eyes on each other again after basic training, but had met up several times – including at Clacton. Ruth had been trained in technical work as a kiné-theodolite operator and Molly ended up in ack-ack. The very last time she had come across Ruth, the girl had been badly frightened by unwanted advances from a man and had confided in Molly. The two had managed to get past some of the barriers of prejudice that separated them and form an unlikely friendship.

Molly realized to her astonishment that Ruth was genuinely fond of her and was missing her. She wrote letters about adjusting to Cambridge. She was enjoying the work, but finding it hard to settle to such a quiet life.

'As soon as term ends I'll be down to see you,' she

wrote. 'I do hope that's all right? I can come and stay in your guesthouse and we can go on the beach. How funny it will be to be in Clacton again. I suppose you've got used to it in peacetime now, but I can only think of it with all those guns going off all the time and the beach closed off. Actually I remember Clacton awfully fondly.'

'*Aw*fully fondly,' Molly murmured, grinning affectionately as she slipped the letter back in the envelope and laid it with her other letters from Ruth. They felt like something to hold onto, because the truth was, soon after her excitement at escaping Birmingham and arriving back in Clacton, her spirits had plummeted.

She had in fact got used quite quickly to the routine at The Laurels. They had their evening 'praise meeting', as they called it, in the house, which the guests could join in or not as they pleased. Ten or eleven people would start to appear at eight o'clock, all of them drably dressed and wearing expressions of anxious enthusiasm. Molly longed to wrap colourful feather boas round each of their necks and paint the women with lipstick. The sounds of hymn-singing interspersed with silences sometimes filtered up to the attic. And every Sunday evening the Lesters attended church.

And, of course, there were the mornings. Molly had gained some respect for Mr Lester, even though he was clearly a fanatic. She appreciated his courage and felt almost protective of him. She had also realized that she had a good strong singing voice, so she belted out the hymns and, she thought, if people laughed, they laughed – that was up to them. Most people just joined in the hymns and were polite; there was just the odd one now and again who would collapse into incredulous laughter. Molly had thought about leaving and moving on, but to what? She'd only have to find some other boarding house. And she knew Mrs Lester would find it hard to cope without her.

It also would not make any difference. She felt herself sinking, day after day. The army had given her life a structure: the day organized for her, the orders, the tasks, the ready-made company and chances of approval and promotion. It had contained her and made her feel safe and purposeful. Ever since she had taken off her uniform, with her Corporal's chevrons worn proudly on the sleeves, it was as if she had lost a part of herself – her better self, who had a place to be in the world. It was a world that had a shape. Now, though, she felt as if she had been let out into a wide, bleak plain and did not know where she belonged, or which way to turn. She could keep on forever with the drudgery of The Laurels. That at least was a routine. But, all the time, all that kept coming to her was the hurt and grief of the past, dragging her further and further down.

On one of her afternoons off she walked along the front at Clacton. It was quite a nice day, hazy but warm, the sea calm and flat, but Molly's spirits would not even lift with the weather. Her head ached slightly, and she felt heavy in herself, ambling along in the shapeless afternoon. She made her way along to where there were fewer people about, found a bench looking out to sea and sat down to have a smoke. All the stark facts of her life began to crowd in, reported in her head like newspaper headlines: Molly Fox, child of a Birmingham back yard, mother a drunkard, father . . . ? Well, that was a hard one. Father a broken casualty of war. Real father? Her grandfather – a filthy old man who had molested her and spawned her with his own daughter. Brothers? One vanished, one a vile crook, hanged for murder. The one chance of real love, Tony, dead from a delayed-action bomb in London . . .

Stinky little Molly Fox . . . All her childhood she had been the outsider. The poorest, the smelly one, with problems – she realized now – stemming from her grandfather's attentions, so that she could not always hold her water. Thinking back on her past self, she was filled with an anguished fury. What a family! Round and round in her head it all went, until she could stand no more. She pushed herself up and, walking as if propelled by a will stronger than her own, went up a side street and found the nearest pub.

'I'll have a whisky,' she said abruptly.

The landlord gave her a look, but served her anyway.

She sat in a dark corner while a row of men nursed pints along the bar. She saw them eyeing her and turned away, looking as unfriendly as she could. Men always paid her attention: her figure, her blonde hair. It was as if they couldn't help themselves, had some picture in their minds, ready-made, that was really nothing to do with her.

Molly drank quickly, going to the bar for another, turning away from their comments. The drink reached down into her, warm and numbing. It was a long time since she had drunk. In the army she had made a fresh start. She was going to make something of herself, break away. The very last thing she was going to do was turn out like Iris. But now . . .

Not wanting to go back to the bar for a third drink, she went to another pub, then another. By the time she weaved her way back to The Laurels she couldn't walk straight. She climbed up to her room and flung herself on the bed. Thoughts battered her, despite the drink. Tony, and Len, with whom she had had a desperate love affair after Tony's death – Len who had been promised to someone else, and she had ruined it, all of it ... And she had lain with them and coupled with them: Len and others. And she had taken no care, yet there had been no child – not ever.

I can't even do that, she thought, sinking into a despairing sleep. Can't do men, can't do children: barren. When she woke it was dark and her head was pounding. She just made it down to the bathroom and was sick, her body heaving painfully. She drank some water and sat groggily on the toilet trying to pull herself together.

Whatever was the time? The house seemed to be completely quiet. Molly crept down to the hall and switched on the light to look at the clock. It was a quarter to one in the morning. She had slept through all the serving of dinner! She would dearly have loved a cup of tea, but there was no chance of that now, so she crept back up and crawled into bed again, feeling doubly ashamed.

'I told Mr Lester that you were ill,' Mrs Lester said the next morning. She was up in time for breakfast, looking pale and strained, and Molly realized that she had dragged herself out of bed in case Molly hadn't made an appearance. She wasn't sure what was wrong with Mrs Lester: she realized it was probably mostly in her mind.

'Well, I wasn't feeling too well,' Molly admitted. 'I never meant to just sleep the evening away, though. I'm ever so sorry.' Molly had managed to get down and carry out her breakfast duties, including singing, with a throbbing head, the smell of powdered egg making her feel even more sick.

Jane Lester went and closed the kitchen door, careful to check that her husband was nowhere within earshot.

'Molly,' she said sternly, 'I came up to look for you. The smell of drink was overpowering. You might have been sleeping in a distillery. If Bernard had smelt it . . .' She rolled her eyes. 'He's very strong on temperance – oh, you've no idea.'

Molly did have some idea, because Mr Lester seemed to be strong on everything. But she was ashamed. Blushing, she hung her head, trying to think what to say.

'We cannot have strong drink in this house!' Mrs Lester declared with a passion. 'Do you understand? I had no idea that you . . . You never seemed that kind of person!'

Molly bit back a bitter reply. *Well, that's what you think – but I am, so there!*

'I'm not really – I just . . . I can't really explain.'

'You must pray for strength against temptation.' Mrs Lester's face took on a zealous shine, but Molly could see that she was also frightened of her husband. 'We can't have this here, Molly – and if Bernard finds out, you'll be sacked immediately. Pray to the Lord, and don't ever let it happen again!'

It was easier said than done. Just those few drinks had started Molly off again and it felt as if her body craved a drink – even that next morning. It developed a taste for it all over again, and so quickly.

I can't start off doing all that again, she thought, frightened of herself and what she might do. She remembered some of the more humiliating times she'd had as a result of drink – in the army and before it. The thought made her feel even more lonely. Everything was slipping away from her.

She tried desperately hard in those following days to pull herself together. Though at times she was almost screaming for a drink, Jane Lester kept her very busy and she didn't have much free time. She managed not to do anything she would regret. But it did not stop the craving. And as the days passed, her mood sunk lower. At night, when she finished work, feeling utterly worn down by the task of keeping going, she fell into bed only to find her mind full of terrible thoughts: memories of the past and her own jeering voice telling her she was no good, that anything that might have worked out well for her was all over now, and there was nothing left to look forward to. The past pulled at her, sucking her down like a foul, bony hand, and the present didn't seem to offer her anything of hope to pull her up against it. She was a prisoner of all the bad things of the past, and that was that. And it was unbearable.

She sneaked out one afternoon when she knew Jane Lester was resting and bought a bottle of Johnnie Walker. Just a drop every night – I won't have much. It'll just help me sleep. The nights had become restless, full of uneasy dreams.

Carrying the bottle home in a shopping basket, she crept back into the house and almost jumped out of her skin when she saw Bernard Lester standing at the other end of the long hall, watching her.

'Oh my goodness, you made me jump!' she said, laughing to cover up how much her heart was thumping. Suppose he looked in the basket. She had covered the bottle with her cardigan, but wasn't it obvious what she had been doing? He watched her climb the stairs.

Hands shaking as she reached the room, her resolve

to have only a nip from the bottle last thing at night went straight out of the window. She closed her door and, without even sitting down, opened the bottle and took a long swig. God, seeing that creeping Jesus down there had given her a start!

'Aah.' Molly sank down on the bed, cradling the bottle. 'That's better!' She took one last swig and put the top back on. Then she hid the bottle under her mattress at the head of the bed and sat down with her eyes closed for a moment, to let the drink really take hold. She was warmer, suddenly, and comforted. Now she could face the rest of the day.

And that was how it was the next day, and the next.

Thirty-Four

'Molly – over here!'

Molly had caught a glimpse of Ruth's long, pale face and dark hair behind the glass as the train pulled in, and it made her even more jittery. She'd already had a nip of her secret supply of the hard stuff to ease her butterflies. Ruth Chambers, whom she had known in the ATS, was coming to stay for three days – they were like chalk and cheese. Writing letters was one thing, but what on earth was she going to say to her?

But seeing Ruth here, Molly felt a sudden great rush of fondness for her. She was in civvies of course, some rather sludgy-coloured slacks and a short-sleeved white blouse, her long hair tied back in a schoolgirlish pony-tail, just as she always had, and giving her buck-toothed smile. For a second the two of them stood in front of each other, uncertainly, then Ruth held out her arms and they embraced.

'Well, well,' Molly joked to cover her nerves. 'Fancy seeing you!'

Ruth pulled back with a grin, picking up her case. 'It's so nice to see you, Molly.'

She looked closely into Molly's face and seemed about to say something, but held back. As they moved towards the exit Molly said, 'So – back here in Clacton.'

'I know,' Ruth said, excited. 'It feels so strange. I

suppose you've got used to it, but I've never seen it except with the army all over it.'

Molly smiled at hearing Ruth's distinctive voice, well spoken and somehow always sounding rather strangulated, as if her throat was tight. But it was truly lovely to see her – one of the people she had shared that intense time of her life in the army with, which she could not talk about with anyone else.

'It's still quite busy,' Molly said. 'There's a lot down here on holiday. Our place isn't the most popular, not being on the main parade . . .'

'And they do sound a bit sent,' Ruth said.

'Sent – how d'yer mean?'

'You know, overly religious. It's not what everyone wants, especially if they're on holiday.' Ruth was only religious in a reserved, Church of England way.

'You're telling me!' Molly laughed. 'And they have to put up with my singing. It's really embarrassing at times. But I suppose you have to hand it to him – it takes some guts. And some people seem to come back specially to hear 'im!'

'Well,' Ruth said drily. 'I can hardly wait.'

They had reserved a single room for Ruth on the second floor, as she had come as a normal paying guest.

'Oh my goodness,' she said, seeing the small, simple room. 'It's our billets all over again, isn't it?'

Having her there helped Molly feel that same sense of adventure again, of the army, of moving from place to place, with a purpose, a real job to do. It was as if, in those seconds, they could recapture that.

'You'll want the window open,' Molly said, wrestling with the stiff catch. 'The cooking smells come up, and it gets stuffy. When you're ready we'll go and get you a cup of tea.'

She explained to Ruth that she would have to work some of the time, but on Ruth's last day there she would have the whole day off.

'Oh, that's perfectly all right. I'm quite happy to go off and wander round. It's lovely to see the sea – a change from Cambridge, I can assure you.'

The girls spent the next two days catching up and reminiscing. Because Molly was working for most of the day, she only saw Ruth in snatches. The first morning she felt even more nervous and awkward than usual when facing the breakfast hymn-singing. That morning Harold Lester had chosen 'Soldiers of Christ, Arise!' Ruth, who was a little late, hurried in as they reached 'From strength to strength go on, wrestle and fight and pray!' and took her seat. Molly felt herself blushing, but gratefully saw Ruth pick up her hymn sheet and, with a calm, polite expression, join in the singing.

'I see what you mean,' she laughed afterwards. 'It takes courage to do that all right! For him, I mean. But you, too – it's the very last thing I'd ever 've imagined seeing you doing! But you've got the most lovely voice by the way, Molly.'

The days stayed fine, and Ruth – sometimes with Molly, sometimes without – visited some of the old haunts: their billets and the Butlin's camp. They met up when Molly had finished, in the evenings, went out for a drink and then sat curled up on the bed in Ruth's room, sipping cocoa and talking over old times. Molly told Ruth that she heard on and off from Cath, who was in Holland and seemed very happy.

'Oh – I forgot, how silly of me! You'll never guess who I ran into on the way here,' Ruth told her the first night. 'Win!'

Win had been with them in basic training, a bright girl with a natural gift of leadership.

'She's at King's, London, doing her degree in history. She seems quite happy,' Ruth told her. 'I met her at King's Cross – she said she was on her way home. But the point was, guess who *she's* seen, working not far away?'

'Who?'

'The Gorgon!'

'*No* – has she?' Molly felt her heart beat faster. The Gorgon was the name they had given to their first Lance Corporal, Phoebe Morrison. Though she was a gruff, prickly character, she had developed a soft spot for Molly, even though Molly had given her all sorts of trouble. Molly – who, given the right encouragement, was always eager to please – and Ruth had in the end found Phoebe Morrison an inspiration. By the time she volunteered to be posted to Belgium in 1944, she had been promoted to their Subaltern and went with them.

'Yes! The Gorgon's back in Civvy Street, working in some admin role in the Civil Service apparently. Sounds pretty dull. Win said she met her in the Strand, and the Gorgon was smoking her head off as usual. Win didn't seem to think she was overly thrilled with her peacetime occupation.'

'Well,' Molly said lightly, 'is anyone?'

Ruth's stay at The Laurels felt like a lifeline to Molly, literally. It was as if she was suddenly connected back to herself, to the real self that had flourished nowhere else as it had in the army.

During those days she felt no need to resort to drink. Before, she had been relying more and more on alcohol to see her through, even though she hated herself for it. She had tried not to let it get out of hand and, above all, not to get caught. She hid her habit by deviousness, and peppermints to veil the taste on her breath, especially if she had secretly run to her room in the daytime for a sip to keep her going.

Since Ruth had been here, she hadn't felt the same desperate need to drink to fill her emptiness. But the time flew by. On the third day, Molly's day off, they could at last spend all of it together. The day dawned fair, and the girls decided to spend the time on the beach.

'We can take some sarnies and buy a few other bits on the way,' Molly said.

'I've got my sweet ration coupons still,' Ruth said with a giggle.

'Me too!'

'We can get sherbet lemons . . .'

'And toffees!'

They were like children.

They set off with their towels and rations, in the Jaywick direction, and found their place to settle on the pale sand amid the other holidaymakers. It was quite crowded as so many people were celebrating the freedom of the end of the war by coming to the sea at last. There was a constant playing of games and children screaming and splashing, and that was all part of the pleasure. The sun came out hot and strong and the two of them alternated between paddling and lounging back lazily in the heat.

'Aah, this is blissful,' Ruth said, as they strolled back

over the warm sand from another toe-tingling visit to the sea and settled on their towels, drinking in the heat.

Molly looked across at Ruth's slender limbs, her quaint, rather severe face with its closed eyes, the lids a pale mauve. She smiled faintly, remembering how much she and Ruth had antagonized each other when they first met. How odd it was that they should be here now, as friends! The day passed all too quickly. They ate their picnic and sunbathed. Ruth went and bought ice creams from a passing barrow and they licked them, staring out at the blue. Ruth made a face.

'Ugh – evap! And what on earth else is it made of? It feels at if it's got porridge in it!'

'Probably has,' Molly said. It really was a very odd ice cream.

As the afternoon waned and some of the families started to pack up, Ruth said, 'Shall we go for a wander along? It's been heaven lazing about, but I could do with a walk and it'd be nice to see a bit more. It still feels so astounding, even being allowed on the beach!'

They strolled along the water's edge in the mellow afternoon light, talking once more about the old times. But after the jokes about army food and some of the characters they'd known, Ruth – as if she had been needing to say it for some time – came out with one of her sudden bursts of forthrightness.

'You know, Molly, my family think it's marvellous, my being at Cambridge and doing science. My mother would have loved to have had the same chance. And it *is* such a privilege – there's no more beautiful place, and it's so old and scholarly. There's that powerful feeling of all the people who've been there racking their brains over things before you. I mean, at Girton, where I am, there've been all those brave, pioneering women – so inspiring. Except that thinking about them makes me feel all the more ordinary and inadequate. I'm so grateful for it all, I am . . . But there's hardly a day when I don't wish in some ways that I was back with all you ATS girls. Ridiculous, isn't it? But d'you know what I mean?'

'Yes,' Molly said faintly. She couldn't begin to explain just how much she understood, and how lost she felt now. How she had had a life where every fibre of her felt challenged and involved and useful, whereas now everything felt empty, bewildering and without purpose.

Now Ruth had started, it was like the floodgates opening.

'Gosh, I hope you don't mind me banging on like this, Molly. The thing is, I can talk to you. If you're at Cambridge, especially if you're a woman, you're expected to be so *grateful* all the time. And I am, of course . . . But I can't seem to communicate properly with anyone. There are other ex-service girls, of course – quite a few Wrens and WAAFs. But somehow we all seem to be on our own as to how we feel about things. Perhaps I'm just – I don't know . . .' She made a frustrated movement with her hands. 'I expect it's just me. I've always felt like a misfit: at school, then in the army and now in Cambridge, as if I'm outside looking in through a window, and everyone inside knows what's going on and how to behave. Just for a while, a blissful while towards the end of the war, I began to feel I fitted in a little bit, but now . . .' she ended desolately. 'My goodness, we've got victory and peacetime and so much of what we were supposed to be fighting for. So why does everything feel so flat? I say, Molly – gosh, are you all right? I didn't mean to upset you.'

Molly's shoulders had begun to heave and she was full of a bursting tightness, as if a great howl of anguish were trying to escape from her. She began to sob.

'Oh my goodness, Molly dear – what is it?' Ruth took her hand and gently pulled her closer to the waterline, away from other people. 'I thought you were looking a bit strained and peaky, not like your blooming self at all. But I didn't like to ask.'

For a few moments Molly could only cry, and Ruth slipped an arm round her back, squeezing comfortingly.

'You know Molly,' she said with a gentleness that made Molly weep all the more. 'You've never told me much about yourself. Why don't we just keep walking and you can tell me about things – um?'

Molly shook her head, 'You don't want to know, Ruth,' she sniffed. 'Honest – you wouldn't want to know me if I told you.'

Ruth stopped and turned to Molly to face her, her expression very solemn. 'You think I'm just a sheltered, namby-pamby girl with all the privileges, don't you? Well, you're right, I am. I've had a sheltered, comfortable life and we're not short of money. I've had a good schooling and a nice house, and one brother who I get on reasonably well with, but the truth is, even if we were pulling each other's heads off, it wouldn't make much difference...' Her voice was rising. 'Because neither of our parents would pay the slightest attention anyway; they don't even take any notice of each other because they're so busy being hard-working and worthy and charitable ... And yes, on the surface it's all very polite and civilized...' Ruth shrugged.

'You might think you're going to shock me – and perhaps you will. But what if I am shocked? Some things *are* shocking. But I can hear you out, that's all. I'm your friend.'

'That's nice of yer.' Molly wiped her eyes. She felt ashamed, as if she didn't deserve this.

'*Nice?*' Ruth was almost shouting. 'I'm not being nice. Just *speak* to me, Molly – don't be another of those people I always seem to be surrounded by, who never say anything, until I think I'm going insane!' Molly was touched to see that Ruth was actually trembling with emotion.

'All right.' Molly felt shaky herself. 'I'll try.'

As they walked, paddling in the shallows, she talked about Iris and Joe, and tried to explain what life with them had been like. She told Ruth about Em, and what had happened to her mom after she'd had Violet, and how she and Em had become friends; and about Jenny and Stanley Button and their deaths. One thing she couldn't just come out with was about Old Man Rathbone and his filthy habits, but she hinted at it and Ruth didn't pry. Molly explained it by saying that was why she had had infections and problems with her waterworks.

'I've never been so well as I was in the army,' she said. 'They really looked after us.'

She could feel Ruth's quiet attentiveness.

She told her about Tony and how he had died, and finally about Bert, his crooked dealings and what had happened with Aggie, the girl he murdered. I might as well, she thought. Just go the whole hog.

'When we were posted to Dover, remember? I saw it in the paper. My brother's name, Albert Fox, there in black-and-white. They hanged him, last July while we were still in Belgium.' She shuddered. 'He was never nice – not that I remember. Always cruel and mean. I suppose he didn't stand a chance.'

'But you're not cruel and mean,' Ruth said.

'I s'pose I had other people who were kind to me. I had Jenny and Stanley, and Em's family. Bert never had any of that. Anyroad, everyone's dead now, except Mom. Well, and Tom, my other brother, but he might just as well be. I'm not going back there again, for all the tea in China.'

Ruth was silent for several paces, then quietly she just said, 'My God.'

'Not pretty, is it?'

'No, it's not – but, Molly, you're truly remarkable.'

'Not really,' Molly said dully. 'I thought for a while I might've made summat of myself. When the Gorgon promoted me and we went to Belgium – it was the most exciting thing that's ever happened to me.'

'You were a Lance Corporal!'

'Yes.' She was pleased that Ruth remembered. 'It felt like the beginning of something. As if it was meant. Then the war ended and now . . .' She shrugged again. 'It's all gone. I don't feel as if there's anything for me now, as if I'll just be stuck down here forever.' More tears of bereavement ran down her cheeks.

'But, Molly,' Ruth said urgently, 'you can't just let yourself get stuck. You're so intelligent – honestly, I'm not flattering you. You could be doing something more than being a cook or a chambermaid, I'm sure you could.'

Molly sighed. 'But what? I've got nothing, and no money.'

'What about night school? You could get qualifications – shorthand, typing or bookkeeping, that sort of thing. I don't know if you could do it in Clacton, but . . .'

Molly was shaking her head. She felt almost angry at hearing these possibilities put before her.

'No, that sort of thing's not for me.'

'Why not?'

'It just isn't. Anyway, I work evenings. I couldn't get out.'

Ruth looked at her uncomprehendingly. 'Don't you want to get out of here and do something else, Molly?'

'Well, yes . . .' But she couldn't explain. Ruth came from another world, no matter how much she was trying to help. The army had been one thing; it had given her a false confidence. Doing something better sounded nice in theory, but thinking of who she was, where she'd come from – it didn't seem like a real possibility. She felt her time had passed. Better things were not for her.

Ruth didn't insist. She seemed to sense that she wasn't getting anywhere.

They turned back, facing into the sun, which was about to disappear behind the land, and wandered along.

'You know,' Ruth said, 'something'll turn up, Molly. It has a way of doing that – don't be downcast.' She touched Molly's arm. 'In the meantime, let me treat you to fish and chips, can I?'

Molly smiled, glad to change the subject. 'Go on then – let's be devils, shall we?'

Thirty-Five

'Did you have a nice time with your friend?' Jane Lester asked the next day, after Ruth had left on a morning train. 'She seemed ever such a nice girl.'

'She is,' Molly said. 'It was very nice, thank you.'

Ruth's visit lifted Molly's spirits for days, especially Ruth's parting words: 'Do keep in touch, won't you, Molly? It means a lot to me.'

And though Molly found it hard to believe it of herself, Ruth thought she was intelligent and capable. She had said so, hadn't she?

But as the days passed her mood began to slide down again. Throughout the day's routine of cooking and cleaning, the bottle of Johnnie Walker – still with a couple of inches left at the bottom – which she had pushed away at the back of the cupboard, loomed in her mind until she could think of nothing else. Whenever she could sneak up to her room for a nip of it, she did, more and more. And the next bottle, and the next.

The worst thing was thinking about what Ruth had said. That she, Molly, could do better than this. Her thoughts raced round and round, but she couldn't find a way out. She didn't know how.

'Molly – I need a word with you.'

Jane Lester's voice was very solemn. It was a month

after Ruth's visit and summer had ended. The days were already beginning to close in. Mr Lester had just gone out and the two women were in the kitchen. Mrs Lester firmly shut the door. Though only eleven in the morning, Molly had already had several goes at the bottle. Only a sip here and there, she reasoned. It wasn't much – just a little pick-me-up, like a tonic.

Jane folded her arms and gave Molly a pitying look.

'I've been putting off saying this, hoping things would right themselves, but I've got to say something. You may think I haven't noticed. I'm not that much of an innocent, you know.'

'What d'you mean?' Molly asked. She lost her balance for a second – on an uneven bit of lino, she told herself – and swayed back against the table.

'The drink: I can smell it on you now. It's no good thinking that sucking a mint will cover it up. Look, Molly, I've been giving you the benefit of the doubt. I'm not so hard and fast about these things as Mr Lester. After all, my own father enjoyed a little drink now and then, with no harm done. But not at this time of the morning! And Bernard has strong feelings – very strong. If he finds out, you'll be sacked and no second chances.'

Oh, very Christian, Molly thought savagely, but said only, 'I'm sorry' and hung her head.

She didn't want to drink, not really. She just couldn't seem to help it. It drew her as if it was more powerful than her and as if a strong hand was pulling her towards it. And the more she had, the more she needed it.

'Look, dear, you've been a great asset to us here, especially to me. You're a good, hard-working girl when you put your mind to it. Why must you persist in giving in to the devil's leadings? You need to renounce it – put it behind you and ask for forgiveness. Tip the

306

rest of it away and begin anew. Otherwise you'll be out on the street! Bernard won't have it – and he's a man of his word!'

Molly knew she was right, but still childishly resented being told so.

'I'll try,' she said, resentfully.

She really did try. All the rest of that day she was frightened enough of losing her job to stay away from her room, even though she was almost desperate at times to run upstairs for the comforting liquor, which helped to dull her unhappy, restless feelings.

'I'll do it gradually,' she thought as she mopped a bathroom floor. 'I'm not throwing away the rest of the bottle – it cost a lot of my wages! I'll have a little drink tonight, then one tomorrow, then it'll almost be gone...'

By the time she got up to her room that evening, closing the door and tearing to the cupboard, her hands were trembling so much that she could hardly get the bottle open. Even in her agitation, the lonely emptiness of the room seemed to echo round her. Was this her life – is this how it would be now for ever and ever? She sank down on the bed, taking a deep slug from the bottle and closed her eyes with the old, familiar relief of feeling it burn down inside her.

'Oh, thank God,' she murmured, then gave a little giggle at the thought of what Mr Lester would think of her giving thanks for the devil's brew. But she wasn't having him telling her what she could and could not do: if she wanted a drink, she'd damn well have one! And there she'd be in the morning, standing beside him singing hymns! She lay back with a cackle of laughter and cradled the bottle against her. One more mouthful, then she'd put it away.

By the end of the night the bottle was empty. The next day she managed to sneak out and buy another one.

Winter closed in fast. Molly's army training in Clacton had been during the summer months, and though she had heard about the east-coast winter, she was still not prepared for the grey bleakness of it, as the days grew colder and Siberia-born winds whipped across the water. She also knew that Jane Lester was watching her like a hawk. Molly tried to contain her drinking to the evening, and to times when she knew there was no one about. But she found herself caught in the old tussle between wanting to be obliging and gain approval, so that much of the time she did her job very well, and wanting childishly to rebel and behave badly, to lash out and destroy any good thing that she had created.

She still hardly knew anyone in Clacton, other than shopkeepers, just by sight. The only other person who could just about be called a friend was a girl called Liza, a Londoner who worked as a chambermaid in one of the bigger hotels. Occasionally the two of them had time off together or met for a drink.

One such October day, Molly was due to meet Liza in the evening. All that gloomy day the sky seemed to be sitting on the tops of the houses. Molly went out to do some shopping and pulled her coat around her, looking at the cheerless streets. The holiday season was mostly over, very few guests arriving now, though Jane Lester had decided to keep Molly on more or less as a home help for herself. She supposed she was lucky to have a job really. Though Molly was glad to be relieved of her singing duties, she missed having other people passing through the house, where now the puritanical habits of the Lesters and their fellow evangelicals were unrelieved by anyone more joyful.

She dawdled over the shopping, even though it was cold, glad to be out and about. Thank goodness she could escape for a bit tonight! The afternoon passed, slow and dull.

When at last it was time to go, she sneaked down the stairs. It wasn't that she wasn't allowed out, but she didn't want to have to explain to either of the Lesters where she was going. But as she reached the hall, Jane Lester appeared out of the back sitting room.

'Oh, are you off out?' she asked, suspiciously.

'Yes,' Molly said breezily. 'I'm just meeting my friend Liza – we'll have a cup of cocoa and a chat. I shan't be late.'

Jane smiled, looking relieved. 'Good. Well, you have a nice time, dear.'

Liza, a solid, black-haired girl, who had surprised Molly when they first met by telling her that she had been a Land Girl, was already waiting outside the pub when Molly arrived.

'I didn't think I wanted to go in without yer,' she said, standing with her coat pulled tightly around her. 'You know what it's like – you only get a lot of old-fashioned looks!'

Molly laughed. 'Oh, you don't want to take any notice! Come on, love – let's go and get settled in.'

As soon as the two of them walked in, a host of male eyes fixed on them. Molly, who had already drunk quite a bit before she came out, could feel herself acting up, giving pert looks and swinging her hips as she and Liza crossed the room with their drinks: whisky for Molly, half of mild for Liza. It was as if all her old habits, which she'd fought to drive out of herself in the later years in the army, were all coming back. They found a corner and sat chatting, but didn't remain unpestered for long.

'How're your Holy Joes?' Liza asked, offering Molly a cigarette. Both of them lit up. 'Still singing all your hymns, are yer?'

'Not when there's no one staying,' Molly said. 'It's all a bit quiet.'

'Ours too. I'm lucky to have a job. Hey, you know what I'm gonna do? If it all dries up, I'll go back up London, but come the spring I'll be back. I like it down 'ere, out of the smoke, and I thought I'd go and get a job at the camp – at Butlin's. They need tons of people there!'

Molly was about to reply when two lads approached them and squeezed in next to them, whether they were wanted or not. One was tall and thin with a cheeky expression, the other stockier with strong, dark brows.

''Ello, girls!' the stocky one said. 'All alone, are we?'

'How d'yer mean, alone?' Liza quipped. She was prickly towards men, or at least the pushy ones. 'Can't yer count, then? There's two of us, so how can we be on our own?'

'Ha bloody ha,' the skinny one said. 'What's your name?' he asked Molly.

'I'm Molly,' she said archly. 'And that's Liza.'

'Well, I'm Brian,' the skinny one said, mimicking her. 'And that's Roy.'

Molly could tell Roy was interested in her at once. Most blokes were.

"'Nother drink, ladies?' Brian asked, though there was a sarky tone in his voice.

'Johnnie Walker for me, love,' Molly said immediately.

'Anything in it?'

'Oh no, ta. As it comes.' Molly could feel herself moving back into it, the pub talk, the men, the way she had always been with them – she knew she provoked men, led them on, so easily, unless she was determined not to.

'Another half for me, ta,' Liza said, a bit more friendly now.

The lads settled down with them and they had one drink after another, the men paying. They each told Molly and Liza what they did for a job, but Molly had soon forgotten. She was very well oiled, and everything was distant and mellow and she didn't care about anything. She heard herself laughing at their jokes, telling them where she worked, doing an unkind imitation of Bernard Lester's singing, which made them all laugh. She told them she'd been in the army. Roy, the dark one, said he had been too. Molly decided she liked him best of the two. Someone started up singing and they joined in. The evening passed in a haze.

'I'm off now, Moll,' Liza said at some point.

'I'll see yer back,' Brian said, getting up, and soon Molly realized they had gone and that Roy was sitting closer and had his hand on her thigh. She thought about telling him to get it off, but somehow the words wouldn't come to her. What the hell did it matter anyway? She was warm and contented and it was nice to have someone near.

'God, it's been a long time,' she murmured.

'Whatcha saying?' Roy asked, leaning down to her.

'Oh – nothing!' She looked up and laughed, suddenly. 'Let's have another drink. I'll get this one in.'

When she got up, she was taken aback by how odd her legs felt. They weren't hers – someone had stolen them. She only just managed to get back to the table without spilling the drinks.

'Dunno how much I've had,' she giggled, falling back into her seat again.

'Quite a bit, by the look of yer,' Roy said.

'What's your name again?' Molly said. And she started laughing and couldn't stop.

There was rain falling on her face. Molly lay letting the drops fall and slide, trickling down her cheeks. Gradually, as she came to, she noticed that she was cold to the bone, that she was lying somewhere very hard and uncomfortable, that her head was reeling even though she was lying still and that she was half undressed.

She groaned softly, managing to push herself upright. It was neither light nor dark and she had no idea of the time or where she was. She was wet through, shivering. Somewhere in front of her she heard waves breaking gently; she felt the wet sand with her hand and cursed repeatedly. How had she got there? Those lads – had she come with them? What had happened? But it was obvious. She was no longer wearing knickers, and her stockings had been torn away from her suspenders. She only had one shoe on: the left one. As she sat there her teeth began to chatter unstoppably.

Groping around with her hands she found her knickers, one of the stockings and her other shoe. Her underclothes were so soaked that she didn't bother putting them on, but she put her shoe on and stood up, shakily. As soon as she tried to walk, her heels clagged in the sand, so she stooped with a whimper at the pain in her head and took them off again, turning to walk away from the sound of the sea. It was just growing light, the early east-coast dawn, so that she could make out the outlines of things, the top of the beach, the pier stretching away behind her. She stood and got her bearings for a moment. A lone gull cried overhead. She would walk back along the beach.

Shivering and feeling ill, she scuffed her way along the sand, carrying her shoes, her knickers stuffed into one, the stocking in the other. Things gradually became clearer as the sun came up, casting a pale morning light that knifed into her eyes, making her screw them up. Only one person was about, a man with a dog, coming back up from the sea, who avoided looking directly at Molly, then disappeared up to the promenade.

How must I look? she thought, washed with shame. She felt sticky between her legs, her clothes were soaked and dishevelled and her hair was full of sand. After a while she realized she was near the place where there were public toilets. She needed to go, and also maybe she could have a bit of clean-up before going back to the Laurels? She'd have to sneak in without them hearing.

Climbing up off the beach, she stepped inside the even colder atmosphere of the toilets. It was quite dark inside and, as she stepped towards the basins, someone loomed towards her, a tall, dark figure that she recognized with a horrible shock. The big-boned face, hair pulled messily to the side, the slouching walk, the drunken, sullen expression . . .

'Mom!' she gasped. What the hell was Iris doing here,

lurking in a public convenience, waiting to jump on her, give her one of her beatings?

Heart thumping with shock, she moved closer to the mirror, reached out and, with a small intake of breath, touched its cold surface.

'Oh! Oh God!'

Her reflection stared back at her in horror. The darkness had stolen the blonde colouring from her hair so that it looked darker, like Iris's. And the puffy drunkard's face: her mother's face looking back at her, full of disgust at what she saw.

'I can't,' she whispered. 'Can't go on like this.'

Molly leaned queasily against the basin in front of the mirror, put her hands over her face and began to sob from the depths of herself.

VI

EM

Thirty-Six

'Come on, Nanna, open the door!'

Robbie rapped his knuckles impatiently on the door of number eighteen.

'Get back under here,' Em said, leaning over him with the umbrella. 'You'll get soaked else.'

Even now, after a month of living with her mother-in-law, there was a lump in her throat as she stood on her mother's doorstep. Cynthia looked after Robbie in the daytime most days, and for the first few days of her own and Norm's move to Saltley, Em had cried when she had had to come back as a visitor.

'Back again!' Cynthia said, opening the door, for Robbie to push inside. She was already dressed and ready for them.

'I'm wet, Nanna!'

'Well, you should've stayed under the umbrella,' Em grumbled, putting it down and shaking the drops off outside the door.

Breakfast was still on the table, and Joyce and Violet were both on their way out to work. 'Bye!' they yelled, hurrying out into the wet.

'D'you want any more to eat, Robbie?' Cynthia asked. 'Not that I've got much.'

Robbie, who was on the floor, getting his marbles out of his pocket, shook his head emphatically.

'Don't get those out in here!' Em said. 'Nanna'll fall

over them and hurt herself. I've told you – only outside.'

'Has Granddad finished the moke yet?' Robbie
asked, scrambling up off the floor. A moke was a little
car made of pram wheels and leftover bits of wood, to
sit in and push along with your feet – unless your mates
would push you. Bob was in the middle of making one
for him.

'You know, Norm calls them goeys,' Em said.

'Does 'e?' Cynthia said absently, clearing things from
the table. 'You can go and look at it, Robbie – he did a
bit more last night. It's in the privy, but don't go getting
wet!'

'I wanna take it out!' Robbie squeaked excitedly.

'Well, what you want and what you'll get're two
different things,' Cynthia told him tartly. 'Now be
quick, and don't get wet. You got time for a cuppa?'
she asked Em as Robbie scurried out to the back.

'Not really, but he won't mind if I'm a bit late.' Em
sat down wearily. Her mother seemed in better nick
than she did herself these days. All the inconveniences
that during the war were a heroic sacrifice were now
just a tiresome nuisance.

'All right?' Cynthia looked at her and handed her a
cup of stewed tea.

'I'll survive,' Em said, stirring sugar. '*He*'s getting to
be a handful, though.'

Over the time she had been living with the Stapletons, Robbie had been a constant worry. At first he had
refused to settle there, suffering from the separation
from his grandparents and aunties and from the only
home he had ever known. He took against Norm and
his mom and dad, and screamed for ages when Em
tried to put him to bed. It was only Edna Stapleton's

kind firmness – which Em had found almost unbearable, even when she knew her mother-in-law was right – that had got him to begin settling in.

'Don't just give in to him every time,' Edna told her. 'I know it sounds bad and that, but if you just give in and go up to him every time, he'll have you wrapped round his little finger. You have to be firm. He'll get used to it soon enough.'

It had taken weeks, and a heavy toll on Em's nerves. Sometimes she felt that Norm and the other Stapletons were ganging up on her, coming between her and Robbie. But at the same time she could see that if Robbie didn't settle and carried on demanding so much of her, it would drive a wedge between her and her newly returned husband. Even now, at times she felt torn in half.

'He's got in with a lot of boys in the road,' Em said.

'That's good, isn't it? Have him make some friends.'

'They're older, though. But they're not old enough to know to look out for him. He loves it – thinks it's all a big adventure.'

Robbie was not yet five, and a lot of the other boys were eight and nine. Sometimes it felt as if Robbie wanted to be a baby at night, but far too grown-up in the daytime.

'Aren't there any others he can play with?' Cynthia said. 'Girls?'

'*Girls!*' Em made a wry face. If there was one thing in the world for which Robbie had complete contempt, it was girls.

She and Cynthia laughed.

Robbie came bursting back into the room, hair spattered with droplets of rain, knees all muddy. 'It's bostin! Is it finished – can I go on it?'

'I've told you: no!' Cynthia said. Wait till Granddad

319

gets back later, and then we'll see. Anyroad, you're going to have to come to the shops with me today.'

'Again?' Robbie groaned. 'That's boring!'

'You can say that again,' Cynthia said. 'Queue after flaming queue. But it's got to be done. We'll see if we can find you a big aniseed ball, eh, Robbie?'

'I'd best get off,' Em said, downing her tea and picking up the umbrella. 'Bye-bye, darlin',' she said to Robbie, but he was sulking about the unfinished moke and wouldn't look at her. Em felt rather crushed by this.

'We'll be all right,' Cynthia said. 'Won't we, Robbie? Off you go.'

Em set off into the wet, cursing the hole in her left shoe. Her spirits were low. Though she was trying to put a brave face on it, she loathed living with her mother-in-law. Edna and Bill Stapleton had both been kind to her, though she knew Edna thought she was soppy over Robbie. Bill was a quiet, capable man and there was no reason to be ungrateful. But now – especially now that the war was over and Norm was home – all Em wanted was for them to have a home of their own, not always be living with other people.

The other reason she felt drained and disappointed was that her period had come on that morning. Somehow she had thought that, with Norm back, it would happen straight away – another baby on the way. She knew she was being silly, but it had happened so easily the first time that she just expected things to repeat themselves. Robbie was growing up fast and she didn't want him to be on his own. He would already be a lot older than any brother or sister who came along.

'Ah well,' she told herself as she walked to work. 'I mustn't get silly about it. It's early days yet.'

Thirty-Seven

When Norm came home off shift that Friday afternoon, Em was waiting to surprise him. As so often now, he came in with a tired, morose expression, longing to get out of his uniform and in need of something to eat.

'I'll get the kettle on,' she said. 'Then I've got something to tell you.'

'Oh yeah?' Barely listening, he glanced over the paper that was lying on the table. What's that then?' He glanced round the room. 'Where's the lad?'

His words cut through Em. 'The lad' – almost as if Robbie was someone else's, not his.

'That's what I was going to tell you. You know you've got the day off tomorrow? Well, Mom said Robbie could stay over tonight, partly to give us a break. But Dad's nearly finished making his moke: he's going to let him take it out tomorrow, so Robbie's gone off happy as a sand boy, and we can have a lie-in – or maybe go out somewhere.'

She saw Norm's face relax, which both encouraged and saddened her. She wanted to make him happy, but it tore her up to see how hard he was finding it coming home and adjusting, not just to life in Civvy Street, but also to the fact that he had a son and that life was not free as it once was.

'That's nice.' He came towards her and took her in his arms, was about to kiss her when his mom came in

321

from out the back with a bucket of coal. Em suppressed a sigh. There wasn't much privacy to be had. But she could at least see that Norm was pleased. She knew he felt squeezed out, that she spent so much time with Robbie that even the few opportunities for lovemaking they had were often prevented or interrupted by him. Em was used to her life revolving around Robbie – Norm wasn't, not yet.

She asked him if he wanted to go to the pictures, but Norm said he'd prefer just to go out for a bit of a walk with her, that they never seemed to get time alone.

'Tell you what,' he said. 'Let's go up to Aston Park – get a bit of fresh air.'

Em was flattered by this, that he'd rather spend time with her than lost in a story on a screen. They caught the train at Duddesdon and went for a lovely stroll, arm in arm round the park, with the old mansion in the middle, relaxing together and talking over old times. She tried not to think about Robbie, how her mom would be putting him to bed about now and was he all right? And about the questions and doubts regarding Norm that nagged at her: *Do you love Robbie? Do you, really?* she wanted to ask, because she really wasn't sure if he did. But she knew this was not the moment.

She found it hard going back into the little terraced house, with Norm's mom and dad sitting in their chairs – Edna knitting, Bill with the paper – asking them how they'd got on and where they'd gone. They were only being kind, they were good people, but she longed for an empty house, a house of their own where they didn't have to answer to anyone.

*

Norm was very loving that night and Em woke later than usual, with no Robbie pulling at her. Though she found it a wrench leaving him, it was also a relief and she felt rested and content. She went down and made them both a cup of tea and, once they'd drunk it, luxuriously still in bed, Norm put his cup down and said, 'Now then – come 'ere, Mrs Stapleton. You needn't think I've finished with you!'

Their bed was two single beds pushed together, so they had to watch the crack down the middle. Giggling, hoping her in-laws next door couldn't hear anything, Em snuggled up on Norm's side of the bed, cuddling into his arms. They were soon making love again, and things felt close and warm just as they used to, before the war when they had had such a short time together as husband and wife. Maybe, Em thought, as she held her husband in her arms and they loved each other, maybe this time, we'll make another baby . . .

She kissed Norm's neck, the combination of soft skin and hard muscle beneath, which she loved.

'Em,' he nuzzled her. 'You're my girl, my woman, that's what you are.'

She told him she loved him, over and over, stroking his back, his strong buttocks, and suddenly tears sprang into her eyes because things felt right again, when they had been tense for so long.

'You glad to be home?' she asked.

She saw the slightest hesitation before he said, 'Course I am. Where else would I want to be, eh?' He turned and looked at her. '*You're* home to me. It wouldn't matter where.'

They curled up together, warm and happy, and asked each other things about their long separation – things there had scarcely been time for, with all the adjustment to living that they had had to do. Norm told her more about some of his times in Italy, about how beautiful the country was.

Em smiled, listening, 'I'm glad you liked it there. I always wondered – it seems so far away and so foreign. And then you didn't write . . .' She leaned on her elbow for a few seconds and looked down accusingly at him. 'I was flaming worried.' She pretended to thump him, then lay back down again in the warm.

'Sorry,' Norm said.

'So you broke your leg? Falling off a truck?' she snorted.

'All right – you can laugh.'

'Sorry, love . . .' She stroked his bare tummy appeasingly. 'Only what I don't understand is what happened next. I thought you were in hospital – how come you got so ill?'

'Well, you know what they say: don't go to hospital if you want to keep in good health.'

'But what happened?'

Her question was met by such a long silence that Em lifted her head again and saw that Norm was blushing red to the roots.

'I don't want to tell you,' he said.

'What d'you mean, you don't want to tell me?' she demanded indignantly.

'I want to, sort of, 'cause I feel I ought to.' He was stumbling over his words. 'But there's some things you're maybe better off not knowing.'

She was fully alert now, still thinking he was joking. She sat up and pummelled his chest. 'You can't say that and not tell me – come on, out with it!'

'OK, well, here goes. You won't get cross, will you?'

'I don't know yet, do I?' She started to feel worried. What on earth was he going to say?

'Oh dear,' Norm said. 'Look – lie down again. I'll tell you, but don't keep looking at me!'

Obediently she settled in the crook of his arm again and waited.

'Thing is,' he said. 'After I broke my leg – I mean, it's not as if I was sick really, I just had my leg in plaster – they moved a couple of us into this other place. It had been a big house, just in a street, and they'd requisitioned it to use as a sort of convalescent rest home. I had a nice room looking out the back, over a little garden, more like a courtyard really, with a couple of trees, oranges and lemons – lovely, it was. Anyroad . . .' Here she heard him sound more reluctant again. 'My bed was by the window, so I could look out, and over the other side of the yard – well, I thought I was imagining it to start with, but then I knew I wasn't – there was this girl – well, woman. She kept whistling and calling out to me, over and over, beckoning me, you know, all coy-like.'

Em stiffened, but didn't interrupt.

'Anyroad, this kept on, and course I was a bit bored by now and she never left me in peace, so . . . Well, I went over. I mean, I couldn't just go, I had to sneak out: through the window . . .'

Her head shot up. '*With a broken leg?*'

'Well, yeah. It weren't easy, I can tell you. There was this big vine thing, growing up the wall . . . Don't look at me!' Firmly he pushed her head down again. 'She came down and let me in and, well . . . The thing is, Em, it wasn't anything – not that *meant* anything, not like you and me. I was just passing the time! And anyroad, I got what I deserved because she was a naughty girl, that one, I had to pay her a bit and give her my ciggies and' – he finished in a rush – 'whatever it was I caught, I got it off her.'

'You mean . . . ?' Her first reaction was to snort with laughter.

'The clap – and it's not funny, that I can tell you. The cure's not funny, either . . .'

'Did I say I thought it was funny? You carrying on with someone – some Italian bird with great big—' Em made a gesture at her breasts.

'I never said she had . . . !'

'But I bet she did, dain't she?' Em shot out of bed, hurt and furious. 'There's me stuck here worrying about you, bringing up *your son*, when all the time . . . Well, you got what you bloody deserved, didn't you?'

'Oh, Em, don't – look, I told you, it wasn't like that . . . It was all stupid, a mistake. She was just a tart on the make, and I fell for it . . .'

But she was out of the bedroom door, running downstairs in her nightdress, full to the brim with fury. The bastard! The filthy, unfaithful, cheating . . .

She paced up and down the back room, arms crossed over her chest, shaking with hurt and anger. She kept thinking about that woman's big breasts, which he hadn't told her about. After a few moments she burst into tears. She'd never even thought of being unfaithful to Norm, and yet look what he'd done – and so easily! And all the time here she'd been, waiting, worrying. She sank down on a chair, feeling very sorry for herself.

After a time she was cold. She wiped her face and tried to think. What was she going to do? Hold this against him and leave him? Move back in with Mom and Dad and have to explain to everyone? Her heart sank at the thought. She couldn't exactly go anywhere at this moment, because she had nothing on but her nightie. There was nothing for it: she was going to have to forgive him – but not too soon! A moment later she started to see the funny side of it. It was so like Norm to get in a scrape like that.

Soon she heard movements upstairs. Her in-laws would be down any moment and she didn't want to see them. She crept back upstairs and went into the bedroom, trying to keep a straight face, but her lips were twitching. Norm was still in bed, but he eyed her warily. He looked rotten.

'Look, I'm sorry, love,' he said wretchedly. 'I know it was wrong and stupid. It's not as if I felt anything for her. I don't even know what her name was, to tell you the truth. It's just – you know what us blokes get like. And she was on at me, morning, noon and night . . .'

'Were you very poorly?' Em asked, sitting on the edge of the bed, keeping her face straight.

Norm winced. 'Ooh – yes.'

'I'm surprised you didn't break your flaming neck getting out of the window in the first place!' The laughter erupted out of her then, at the thought of Norm shinning out of the window with a plaster cast on and trying to creep quietly across some courtyard. In a moment more tears, of mirth this time, were running down her face. 'Oh my God, you really are the end!'

Norm, relieved and surprised, started laughing too.

'You are properly better now, aren't you?' she asked. 'I don't bloody well want to catch anything!'

'I'm all right,' he said. 'They gave me some of the new stuff – penicillin. It's marvellous. God knows what it would have been like without it. The stupid thing is, they was always on about it, VD this and VD that.

Films and talks, and that. There was this girl in the films who they were always telling you to, you know, beware of, called . . .' He started to chuckle himself, so at first he couldn't get the words out. 'She was called Susie Rotten Crotch!'

'*What?*' Em fell back on the bed so that her head was resting on Norm's stomach, both of them howling with laughter.

It was a while before either of them could speak again, but eventually she managed to roll over and look directly at him. They searched each other's eyes and, knowing that what they saw was true, put their arms around one another.

'You,' Em said, wet-faced, 'are the daftest bugger alive, but for some reason I love you. I can't seem to help it.'

1948–1949

VII

KATIE

Thirty-Eight

June 1948

'Bye-bye – see you tomorrow. Say goodbye, Michael!'

Maudie, heavily pregnant, stood at her door waving them off, a smile on her face, which was for the moment plumper than usual.

'Thanks, see you in the morning!' Katie called.

Michael waved and then, without looking what he was doing, reached out for his mother and almost fell down the step.

'Careful! I'm here, silly,' she laughed, taking his hand and walking along with him. 'Have you had a nice day?'

Michael turned his serious, deep-brown eyes up to hers, nodding. 'We did plasticine. Can I have a bun?'

Katie showed him a little white paper bag. 'I got a currant bun. But you have it for your pudding. You'll spoil your tea else.'

'Oh, Mom – I'm hungry!' Michael protested. 'Please. Can I?'

As they turned into their road she relented and broke off a bit of the bun. 'Here, that'll keep you going. But you're not having it all, so don't ask me. 'Ey-up – what's going on?'

Usually when she got home from work the house was quiet. On a nice day like today, Sybil would be out

333

at the back, tending her beloved garden. But in the distance Katie could see Sybil out at the front, and the neighbours, Edna Arbuckle and her daughter Susan, were at the wall that divided their houses, all deep in conversation. Both Arbuckles were large, fleshy women, especially Susan, who was thirty-five and still lived with her mother. She was big-boned and beetle-browed, her thick hair cut savagely into a bob around her heavy jaw. Her mother's one reigning obsession was to find her a husband.

They all turned as she and Michael reached the gate, and Edna Arbuckle, a paler-haired, softer woman than her daughter, said portentously, 'You're going to have to tell her, Miss Routh.'

Katie's pulse quickened. What on earth was the matter? Michael was perfectly fine, as obviously were Maudie and Sybil Routh, and there was no one else she could think of to worry about.

'Ah – Katie,' Sybil said, limping towards her. She suffered with her feet and was, as usual, wearing slippers with her smudgy green frock. In the bright sun, her grey hair seemed to have a yellow tinge. 'Bit of a do, I'm afraid. We've lost Mr Gudgeon.'

'Lost him?' Katie wondered for a split second whether he had ambled off somewhere.

'Dead in his bed,' Sybil said with her usual directness. Katie heard Edna Arbuckle make a slight sound of protest. Edna would always have whispered *passed away*. Or even *fallen asleep*, which would only have confused things further. 'I had to have him carted away in an ambulance.' This phrasing provoked another squeak from the other side of the wall.

'The poor, poor man,' Edna said, mopping her eyes. Susan looked weepy and pink-cheeked too. If Sybil was upset, it would have been hard to tell, but Katie knew that was the way with Sybil. She didn't wear her heart on her sleeve. Michael, still chewing on his bit of bun, was staring up at them all in fascination.

A thought made Edna perk up. 'I suppose you'll be looking for another lodger now, won't you, Miss Routh?'

'Oh, I dare say.' Sybil held the gate open for Katie and Michael and, as if grateful to have a reason to escape, ushered them into the house and shut the door.

'Oh!' she declared. 'That woman – how she does keep on! I'm all behind myself, but I have got a stew pot on. I expect you need a cup of tea . . .'

Katie followed her shuffling figure – so familiar now, with her baggy clothes, hair pinned up in a bun – to the back kitchen, from where there was a delicious smell of stew. Sybil was good at making food tasty, even on short rations. In fact, despite her bad hands and feet, Sybil ran the house very competently.

She made tea, then fished about in the kitchen cupboard. 'I could do with a nip of something stronger . . . Want some?' She held out a bottle of malt whisky, which she only ever drank on very special occasions.

'Oh, no thanks,' Katie said. She didn't like even the smell of whisky, and certainly didn't want to deprive Sybil.

'Ah!' She took a nip and sank down on a chair with an outrush of breath. 'That's the ticket.'

Katie sat Michael down and poured a helping of tea into her saucer for him.

'So – whatever happened? To Mr Gudgeon, I mean?'

'Oh, well, the old boy never got up this morning is the long and short of it. Must have gone in his sleep. The awful thing is, I didn't notice, because as you know

335

he didn't always rise early, and I was going up to the shops myself today. I went off smartish, so as not to be right at the back of that beastly meat queue – hence . . .' and she gestured at the stew pot. 'It was only later, when I'd got back and was looking to see if I had any pearl barley . . . I realized the house was quiet. You know, a different sort of quiet from usual. Eventually I went up and tapped on his door, and there was no reply. The poor old fellow was stiff as a board by then, no teeth in – oh dear, oh dear. I mean, he was going on for eighty, but it's always a shock when it happens.'

'Poor you,' Katie said sadly. 'What a thing to happen.' She had liked Mr Gudgeon, who had been a timid, kindly man. They had seen more of him after the death of his wife, last year.

'And now,' Sybil said, knocking back the last of her Scotch and rallying herself, 'as Edna so rightly predicted, I shall have to look for a new tenant.'

'You won't have any trouble there,' Katie said. 'There'll be a queue.'

'I know.' Sybil grimaced, before her lined face broke into a wicked grin. 'But will any of them be *a husband for Susan*?'

When Katie first moved into the household of Sybil Routh, it had taken her some time to get used to it, and to what was expected.

'I think it's going to be all right,' she reported to Maudie the first week, as they had a cuppa together. 'The room's lovely, now I've got a few of my things in it, and Miss Routh is *so* much nicer than some of those other miserable old bitches I could have had as land-ladies. She even lets Michael tinkle on the piano sometimes, and it's quite a racket. And she's very pleased if I lend a hand, which I'm quite happy to do. Her feet look so sore for moving around much. But she is rather odd, isn't she?'

'I think her background was quite bohemian,' Maudie said, frowning as she tried to remember what she'd heard about Sybil Routh. 'At least on her mother's side. Father was a clergyman of course, but with his own ideas to some extent, and I think her mother had come from a family of arty types. So what with the missionary input and the artistes, she's a bit of a rum mixture.'

At first, Katie was nervous of Miss Routh. Her posh, outspoken manner was not what Katie was used to, but she quickly discovered several things that made life in the house a very good experience. The first was that while Sybil Routh was interested in what was going on in the world, and in humanity in general, she was not nosy about people in particular. She did not pry, nor did Katie find herself cross-questioned about her past or feel that her privacy was going to be invaded. But she realized, over time, that if she did tell Sybil things, she would not been shocked or judgemental – she seemed to treat people with a broad, breezy objectivity.

Secondly, the fact that she demanded that the household share their evening meal together meant that life was not lonely, that Michael got to know other adults, and that the atmosphere in the house was gently, if eccentrically, friendly. They all assembled in the evening after Sybil banged the mellow-sounding gong on the hall table. At first there had been the quiet banker Mr Treace, who over time had been replaced by various harmless young men, clerks and salesmen requiring lodgings in what was the smallest room on offer in the house. None of them really stuck in the memory. The latest was a slightly older man, Mr Jenkins, who was doing the accounts in a firm on the Soho Road. Then there were the Gudgeons. Mrs Gudgeon scarcely ever left her room, but Mr Gudgeon had taken his evening meals with them, before carrying a portion up to feed to his sickly wife. He was a faded, shy person with clicking, badly fitting dentures, but had a genuine and kindly nature. Sometimes he told them stories about his past out in Barnt Green as a boy.

Katie began to relax and realize that she and Michael could have a safe, settled life here. Sybil had a gift for uniting this rather unpromising group of people into a household with character. Katie also began to have time to take more interest in the outside world. Sybil was forever listening in to the news. When the Mahatma, Mr Gandhi, had been assassinated earlier that year, Sybil was so upset that none of them could have avoided hearing and learning about the man, and all that he had meant.

The other thing was that Sybil soon cottoned on to the fact that Katie could sew. Anxious to please, Katie offered to do various bits of mending.

'I was always a cack-handed seamstress at the best of times,' Sybil admitted. 'But now of course my hands are no use for anything delicate at all.' Both her hands and feet were gnarled and painful with arthritis.

'Oh, I'm quite happy to sew,' Katie told her.

'In fact, if you're that keen ... Can you tailor garments as well?'

'Yes, my mother taught me! She was – is ... a seam-stress ...'

Sybil bypassed an opportunity to be nosy here, for which Katie was very grateful. 'There's an old Singer out in the privy at the back. We could bring it in and get it cleaned up and oiled. You're welcome to use it. I expect you could do with making things for the boy.'

Katie soon turned her hand to getting the machine working. It was perfectly all right, apart from dust and cobwebs and in need of a dash of oil.

'Thank you so much, Miss Routh!' she said. 'I'd thought about trying to get hold of one somewhere, but I shan't have to now. And if you'd like me to sew anything for you, you only have to say.'

'Well now,' Sybil said, 'I do have some cloth that would make a frock – so if you wouldn't mind . . . And do call me by my Christian name, for heaven's sake. I feel like a schoolteacher being "Miss Routhed" all the time.'

'Of course, er, Sybil,' Katie said. 'I can make you something based on one of your other ones, can't I?'

Sybil produced a bolt of cloth from somewhere upstairs, of dark-blue swirls on a yellow-and-white background.

'I'm sure it's meant for curtains really,' she said. 'But beggars can't be choosers, can we?'

'She thinks you're marvellous,' Maudie told Katie a few weeks after she'd moved in. 'She was singing your praises to several of the others after Communion on Sunday.'

Katie wondered nervously whether Sybil would expect her to go to church as well, and what she'd think if she knew Katie was a Catholic. One Sunday, when she saw Sybil getting ready to go out, in her large straw hat, she took courage and said, 'I haven't been very good about keeping it up, as I've been so busy. But I might start taking Michael to Mass soon.'

She waited for the ceiling to fall in. Sybil glanced round, then back into the glass where she was adjusting her hat.

'Ah, you're a Holy Roman, are you? I did wonder, with a name like O'Neill.' She tidied her collar, putting her head on one side. 'Queer business, church. Still, I was brought up to it, you see.' She pressed her hat harder down onto her head. 'And I do find that if you can stick it out, it can be frightfully entertaining.'

Thirty-Nine

Katie's regard and fondness for Sybil Routh had increased over the months that she was a tenant in her house, but it was last winter's freeze that had really created a bond between the two women.

The snow began in late January, so much of it that the country was gripped by a terrible freeze and a state of emergency. The novelty of the first day or two – Michael out in the street with the other children, snowballing and pulling each other along on trays – quickly wore off.

'Well,' Sybil announced one morning at the beginning of February. 'It's happened – everything's frozen up. I can't get any water out of the tap. Don't go trying to flush any lavatories until I see if the downpipe is frozen as well. We'll have to think what to do.'

'Thank goodness!' she announced shortly afterwards. The downpipe was still working. Soon they were all helping to melt snow in an old tin baby's bath over the range, for flushing the toilets and having a wash. Basic living became a huge operation: melting snow, trying to get anywhere, buying food. Evenings were spent swathed in coats close to the fire in the dining room, though Sybil had insisted that the Gudgeons must have the little electric-bar fire in their room.

'She can't be moved, and the pair of them will freeze to death else,' Sybil said. 'They're like a pair of little birds – no flesh on them.'

Soon, because enough coal could not be brought from the newly nationalized mines, the Government was rationing electricity. By early February there was to be no electricity allocated to industry and thousands of workers were laid off. Those at home would have no power between nine and midday and between two and four in the afternoon. Coal itself was in acutely short supply as well. Even sitting huddled up inside, listening on the wireless to news of twenty-foot drifts in country areas, it was hard to keep warm. The offices where Katie worked kept going on most days, and she struggled in when she could get a bus and worked wrapped in her coat and scarf, blowing on her hands to keep warm.

When she wasn't at work, Katie did everything she could to help Sybil. She felt responsible, somehow, as the only other woman in the house, and she was always keen to earn Sybil's approval. Sybil was also a person with resources that she could tap. In the storeroom behind Katie's attic bedroom there seemed to be a stash of all sorts of things.

'Old family stuff,' Sybil told her. 'Heaven knows what's in there! The siblings won't bother with it. It's hardly been touched for years.'

Sybil's five surviving brothers and sisters were scattered widely from Perth in Australia to Cape Wrath in Scotland. Only one lived anywhere near – a brother in Bournemouth. She seemed to have a regular correspondence with them all, but they scarcely ever saw each other.

It was in this cluttered storeroom, after ferreting about a bit, that Sybil had found the material that Katie made into a frock for her. She had been very pleased and admiring of Katie's sewing. And one day during the great freeze, when Katie came home, Sybil announced,

'I've been having a clear-out – found some things to burn. There are chairs up there that are full of worm, and I never want to see them again, ugly old things. So there'll be some extra firewood for a start. There are still a few logs out in the garden. If we could get Mr Jenkins busy with an axe . . .'

Geoff Jenkins, the accounts clerk, did not, on the face of it, look the axe-wielding type, but he dutifully set to the next Saturday morning with surprising energy and produced a heap of chunks of wood to keep them going.

When Sybil and Katie stepped outside to see how he was getting on, Sybil suddenly stepped close to Katie and said, 'Take a glance up at next door's window.'

Katie looked up, as instructed, to see Mrs Arbuckle at the back window, staring fixedly at Mr Jenkins's striving figure.

'Susan-fodder, d'you think?' Sybil murmured.

'Isn't he a bit young?' Katie objected. Geoffrey Jenkins must have had ten years on Susan.

'Oh, that's never stopped her yet,' Sybil said.

'That's a fine specimen of a man you've got there,' Katie said, imitating Mrs Arbuckle's breathless voice.

Sybil guffawed, then called out, 'Fine work, Mr Jenkins! Keep it up – I'm most grateful to you!'

Geoff Jenkins straightened up, pink in the face, and smiled. He looked as if he was rather enjoying himself.

'Makes a change,' he said. 'You know – from sitting at a desk.'

'You're being watched, by the way,' Sybil said. 'From next door. I expect she wants you to marry her daughter.'

The look of alarm that spread over his face sent both of them inside in a fit of giggles.

'Poor Susan,' Sybil spluttered. 'It must be rather like

having a shark for a mother!' Her face sobered. 'Actually, though, Katie – I rather think it's you he might be interested in.'

'Well,' Katie said tartly, though she had realized this, as Geoff Jenkins had started paying attention to her, 'he can forget about that *right* away.'

At the height of the freeze Mrs Gudgeon was taken seriously ill and had to be moved to Dudley Road Hospital, where she died two days later. They tried to be kind and helpful to the bereaved Mr Gudgeon.

'Oh, the poor man!' Edna Arbuckle had cried, appearing on the step to find out what was amiss. She was bundled up in a huge tweed coat, a mustard-coloured hat like a large pie sitting on top of her head and a pair of little boots with zips up the front. 'I suppose he's all on his own now!'

'Well, we'll do our best to see that he doesn't just hibernate,' Sybil said drily.

For several months afterwards Mrs Arbuckle had pursued Mr Gudgeon with what he appeared to find a horrific amount of interest – not this time on Susan's behalf, but for herself.

'He could move in with us, you know,' she told Sybil, who relayed the offer to Katie with twinkling glee. 'I know how to look after a man, even though my Harold has been on the other side for a good many years now.'

The only flaw in her plan was that poor Mr Gudgeon fled every time she appeared, and eventually she gave up on him, declaring him too old and set in his ways.

'He'd only take advantage,' she confided to Sybil. 'You know the type – ask them in for a cup of tea and the next minute they've installed themselves, slippers and all.'

Mr Gudgeon continued to live in the big room at the front on his own, but because of its size it was also a cold room. The warmest place in the house was Sybil's dining room, where she kept a fire going. In these days of extremity she made it clear that they were welcome to sit there whenever they liked, to keep warm. Coal supplies had to be eked out, the wood was soon going down and it was a case of making do, rugs over their knees, wrapped in layers and layers of clothes while the house was muffled in snow and spiky with icicles, the ground hard and slippery as glass. Mr Gudgeon usually disappeared upstairs first, and Geoff Jenkins – who seemed to have taken the hint quite quickly that Katie was not interested in him – stayed to chat for a while, before leaving Katie to talk to Sybil.

One night in late February they had settled as usual, chairs pulled in close to the fire. Sybil treated herself to a nip of malt, Katie refusing as ever.

'One day,' Katie sighed, cradling a cup of tea between her hands, 'we'll be able to have a proper bath!'

Sybil laughed. 'Surprising what comes to seem a luxury, isn't it? We're all right though, really. Think of all those poor people still laid off at Longbridge, not getting paid. And some of the houses – so inadequate. Goodness knows how some people are managing. The wind's bitter out there tonight.' She grimaced. 'I used to be a midwife. I've seen some sights in my time.'

She paused to take a sip of her whisky.

'My father used to say, after we came home from Africa, "We take too much for granted!" He was really quite vicarish at times. "We live a life of comfort, and we don't even know it." There was always a bit of finger-wagging that went with that.'

'How long did you live in Africa?' Katie asked.

'Oh, I was born there, stayed until I was seven, when we came back here, the whole gaggle of us: seven children. If you're not careful, I'll bore you with the family albums – of which I seem to be custodian.'

'I'd like that,' Katie said. Sybil's life seemed so exotic.

'Oh, I'll dig them out one of these days . . . Anyway, my parents thought I needed rescuing. I had no concept of race – you don't, until someone tells you you're supposed to, I don't think, though of course they start on you very young. But I used to play with anyone and everyone. I was quite native, really! Much more so than my other siblings. My best friend, Nancy – well, that was her English name; I expect she had another one – was the cook's daughter. We were of an age. But that wasn't the reason we left. I was about to be sent home to some ghastly boarding school anyway. No, my mother was having my youngest sister, and her health grew worse and worse. The missions were all a great trial to her really. Not that she wasn't an open-minded woman – she liked to see the world, and she was some sort of Christian. But she did get so poorly at times. One of the mission doctors said to my father, "You have two options, Cyril. You stay with the mission here in Uganda – or you go home and save your wife." So home we came, I'm glad to say. Which saved me from boarding school and proved to me that my father was sensible at heart and not a religious fanatic. He was stern at times, but he didn't put his ideals or his so-called vocation before real people – that's always such a bad idea.'

Katie had been listening, fascinated. 'I had an uncle who was a missionary in Uganda,' she said.

Sybil's head swivelled round, eyes gleaming with curiosity under her dark brows. 'Oh? Who? Do tell!' Then she remembered. 'Ah, of course. He wasn't one of ours.'

'He was a White Father. Well, Brother. But they sent him home – it didn't suit his health, either.' Katie found tears spring unexpectedly into her eyes.

'You were attached to him?'

'Yes. You see he lived with us while I was growing up. My father died when I was very young, and Uncle Patrick came and helped look after us. He suffered ... Well, mentally, really.' Again, this tough admission. Blood flooded her cheeks. 'And then he ... He died as well ...'

'Leaving how many?'

'Oh, not many – just my mother and me.'

There was a silence. Sybil, circling her glass round between her hands, stared into the fire. Her familiar smell, of lavender water mixed with whisky, was comforting.

'That's why she – my mother – took up sewing, you see. Even when Uncle Patrick was alive she needed a living. She made lovely things.'

'She taught you excellently. And she passed away as well?'

Katie quickly wiped her eyes, her cheeks still burning. 'No. Not so far as I know. We had a disagreement. I haven't seen her for some time.'

'I see,' Sybil said, considering this. 'And is there no mending the situation?'

Katie didn't want to say more, to go into what had happened with Michael's father. She had tried to bury

Simon Collinge in her mind, even though she suspected Sybil must have guessed some of it. 'She told me to leave,' she said abruptly. 'So I suppose I feel that the situation is hers to mend. She could find me, if she tried. She doesn't seem to want to.'

Whether because of tact or lack of further interest, Sybil did not push on with the conversation and soon, as the fire died down, she struggled to her feet.

'Ah!' She gave a grunt of pain as her feet took her weight. 'Blast this wretched rheumatism. Time to turn in, I think. Up the wooden hill. This weather takes it out of you.'

'Yes, it does. It's making Michael sleep like a log, that's one thing!' Katie tidied the room a little to save Sybil's sore feet.

'I heard a good bit of advice today for keeping warm in bed,' Sybil said, limping to the door. 'Take you knickers off and put your feet in them. You won't wear your socks out so fast then.'

'Oh,' Katie said, startled. 'Yes – well, thank you. Perhaps I'll try that.'

'Goodnight, dear.'

'Goodnight, Sybil.'

Lying as instructed, with her feet tucked into her knickers, which turned out to be not a bad idea at all, she stared, shivering, up into the darkness, full of uncomfortable feelings.

The conversation about her mother brought it all back, the hurt and shame. Should she go and find Vera, make amends if she could? It was more than four years now. A cold, sad feeling filled her. Most of the time she tried to put it all out of her mind. Michael was her precious kin now – the only one – and she loved him fiercely and proudly. But her mother? When had things ever been close or loving between her and that fearful, angry widow, even when she was very young? Even in her dimmest memories of when her father was still alive, it was him she remembered running to, where there was a memory of warmth. If only he hadn't died – things would have been so different!

Now, in this house, she realized that she felt more fondness for funny old Sybil than she ever could now for her mother. It seemed wrong, unnatural, but, she knew, as her eyes slowly closed, that was the truth of how she felt. Sybil had been kind and made her feel welcome in this house – and that kindness was worth its weight in gold.

Forty

After Mr Gudgeon's funeral, a very quiet affair, Sybil advertised for a new lodger in her usual way. She didn't have to wait long.

On the Sunday afternoon, on a still, balmy day, Katie was getting ready to take Michael out to his favourite place: Handsworth Park. He loved to be able to run freely in the wide-open space. But as she was squatting down to help him put his shoes on, Katie heard voices downstairs. There was something different about them that caught her attention.

'Sssh, Mikey – listen!' She held up her finger to stop her son's chatter. Eyes wide, he listened with her. There were male voices down in the hall, interspersed with Sybil's gruff tones.

'Stay there,' Katie instructed Michael. She crept over and opened the door. The voices floated up more loudly, though still muffled. There were two men, both foreign, and she could barely make out anything they said. They sounded polite and rather earnest. Then she heard Sybil say, 'There's a gentleman in the room next door, a Mr Jenkins – he's quiet and hard-working. And up in the attic is Mrs O'Neill, a young widow with a little boy. She's a very nice, reserved person and the child is quiet. You won't be disturbed.'

One of them asked a question, in a deep, bassoon-like voice that fascinated Katie. She had never heard a voice quite like it before. They were clearly struggling to understand everything.

'Yes,' Sybil went on. 'It's one room only – but it is large, so if the two of you are wanting to share for the time being . . . Why don't you come up and see?'

As the sound of footsteps advanced up the stairs Katie quickly shut the door. When it was clear that the three of them were inside the room below, she took Michael's hand and led him speedily downstairs and out into the sunshine, wondering who the prospective new lodgers might be.

Sometimes she found the weekends hung heavy and she felt lonely. She loved Michael with a passion, he was her everything, but even so, the hours spent in just the company of a four-year-old could seem very long. Last weekend she had been to see the Millers. She didn't like to call on Maudie at the weekend when her husband was at home as it felt like an intrusion, so she made the best of it, spending a bit of time with Sybil and sometimes chatting to other young mothers in the park.

She had bought Michael a little blow-up ball with bright-coloured stripes around it and they played catch, Katie waiting patiently for his clumsy catches and throws. Then they kicked it to each other for a bit. Another little boy came and joined in and Katie exchanged a few words with his mother, a blonde woman with a rounded figure and friendly manner.

'Nice to see some sun, isn't it?' the woman said, eyeing Katie's summer dress enviously. 'That's nice – did you make it yourself?'

The dress was fitting at the top, with a fuller skirt, in a narrow navy-and-white stripe.

'I did, as a matter of fact,' Katie laughed, as to her

the dress seemed drab now. 'But a long time ago – before the war. It's quite faded.'

'Well, it looks very nice on you,' the woman said wistfully. 'You've kept your figure, haven't you? Oh, I wish I could sew. I'm like a bull in a china shop with a needle.'

The two lads were getting along quite nicely and their mothers passed the time for a while, sitting on a bench nearby and drinking in the sun. An ice-cream barrow came into the park and Katie and her new acquaintance bought wafer sandwiches for themselves and their boys. The ice cream, still always made from substitutes like evaporated milk, tasted a bit odd. But it was better than nothing.

'I have to come out with Peter to get him out of my husband's hair,' the woman confided. 'He says he has enough going on in the week without having his Sunday disrupted. He likes to sit and read the paper after his dinner – and of course Saturday's his cricket, in the summer anyway.' Without actually complaining, she sounded wistful. 'What about your husband? Is he having a sit-down as well?'

'Actually I'm a widow,' Katie said. It was her story, for most people.

The woman's good-natured face creased in sympathy. 'Oh, I *am* sorry. And there's me having a little moan . . . Was it the war?'

Katie nodded, feeling guilty. 'Yes – at Arnhem.'

'Oh, and your poor little lad as well. Well, I do hope you meet someone else – I'm sure you will.'

'Oh no, I doubt it,' Katie said. Her voice came out bitter. 'I don't want to – we're all right as we are.'

'Well, I think you're very brave,' the woman told her.

When they had said their goodbyes and ambled back home, Sybil was just coming in from the vegetable patch in her wide-brimmed hat, secateurs in hand and Archie at her heels. She met Katie in the hall.

'Ah, hello, dear – I'm just battling the brambles. Did you hear our callers earlier? I've got replacements for the room. Two Poles – not long demobbed. About time too, one might add. Still in uniform, after all this time . . .'

'Poles?' Katie said, alarmed. So that explained the strange accents!

'Yes – two chaps. They seem pleasant fellows. They're coming tomorrow.' She was drifting through to the kitchen. 'Actually one of them is waiting to meet his sister, so his friend is bunking up with him until she arrives.' She vanished out to the back.

Katie led Michael upstairs, suddenly feeling cross and out of sorts. She wasn't pleased to hear about the new lodgers. Somehow her safe little haven here felt threatened and she found herself wishing that Sybil was a bit more choosy about who she allowed to live in her house! Nervously she remembered the sound of the deep, ringing voice she had heard rising from the hall. All she had heard about Polish servicemen was quite contradictory – that they were rude and rough on the one hand and terrible womanizers and that, on the other, they were charmers who were forever kissing women's hands.

Well, I've had enough of male charm to last a lifetime, she thought sniffily, going into her room. But she did have to remind herself that if Sybil hadn't been so open-minded about her lodgers, she wouldn't be here, either.

*

353

By the time she came in from work the next day they had moved in. Creeping upstairs, she could hear muffled voices and the sound of something being scraped across the floorboards. Katie rolled her eyes. It seemed too soon, their arrival. She hadn't had time to get used to it yet. Archie kept letting out little woofs downstairs as well, not sure about all these strange new noises.

'Sybil's gone and rented out the middle room to a couple of Poles – soldiers,' she complained to Maudie, interested to test her reaction.

'Really?' Maudie was jiggling her third child, a little blonde girl called Elizabeth, now a year old, on her hip. 'Well, that'll be interesting. John says the Poles were marvellous in the forces, the ones he came across.'

Sybil had evidently explained to them about the communal eating arrangements and, as soon as the mellow sound of the gong rang out at six-fifteen, there was an almost instant thudding of feet down the stairs.

They must still be wearing army boots, by the sound of them, Katie thought. What a racket!

She had decided that Michael should eat with them tonight, instead of having his tea earlier. Somehow having him beside her made her feel less of the shyness that suddenly came over her, in the face of these foreign newcomers.

Mr Jenkins followed her down.

'Have you met them?' he mumbled to her in the hall. He seemed ill at ease.

Katie had a sudden feeling that the men they were about to meet were likely to be altogether more full-blooded and vigorous than Mr Jenkins. However, he did seem to be walking out with someone at last – a girl called Dolly, whom they hadn't yet met.

'No, not yet.' His shifty nervousness made her feel impatience of her own. 'But now's our chance.'

In the dining room Katie found two men standing rather formally to one side of the table. Her first impression was of the difference in their sizes, one very tall and lean, with prominent cheekbones, the other short and stocky, looking as if he was made of pure muscle. Both had hair of varying shades of brown – the taller one's a slightly lighter shade than his more ursine companion, whose hair was a thick brush covering his head, and his eyebrows equally bushy. She could not have begun to guess their ages.

'Ah,' Sybil said, limping to the table with a pot of something that smelt discouragingly fishy.

The tall Pole immediately held out his arms saying, 'Please – I help.' As his face caught the light, Katie saw that he had vivid, ice-blue eyes.

'No, it's all right – I'm there now.' She put the pot on the table with a grunt and laid the towel she had used to carry it over the back of a chair. 'Here we are. Now you can all be introduced.' She turned to Katie and Geoff Jenkins. 'These are our new lodgers. This is' – she indicated the taller one – 'Marek. I don't think we'll go into surnames for the present.' Marek gave a faint smile and a rather military nod of the head. Katie thought he looked rather forbidding, and that beneath his formal manners there was a sadness about him. 'And this' – indicating his shorter friend – 'is Piotr. Is that right?'

The man gave a broad smile and nodded very agreeably. 'Piotr – yes, that is me.'

'I imagine that means Peter, to us,' Sybil said. 'Now – this is Mrs O'Neill. Katie O'Neill, and little Michael.'

Marek, who was standing further away, again gave his nod of acknowledgement and Katie could only think to nod back. Piotr seemed on the point of stepping forward and taking her hand, but she saw him restrain himself.

'Hello,' he said, smiling again. 'Hello, little Michael. He is lovely boy.'

'Hello,' Michael said. Katie had her usual feeling of pride, seeing her son's lovely blue-eyed face turned up to them so trustingly. She was glad she had brought him down for tea.

Sybil introduced Geoff Jenkins, who said a rather shy hello, and then they all sat down. Katie was at one end, seated between Michael and Geoff Jenkins and facing Sybil, who had the two newcomers on either side.

'Now,' Sybil took the lid off the pot and the fishy smell increased. Michael wrinkled his nose and Katie gave his hand a warning squeeze. Sybil did not take kindly to fussiness over food. 'This is a recipe of my own invention . . .' Katie saw the two Poles making a visible effort to keep pace with Sybil's English. 'The meat ration has been cut almost to nothing because of the dock strike, so I thought, there's nothing for it: I had two tins of snoek – fish,' she explained unnecessarily as, by the smell, it couldn't be anything else.

She served each of them a helping of a mushy fish-and-tomato mixture, which had a few other bits of stray vegetable in it – carrot and a good deal of onion and cabbage. They ate it with potatoes, and when Katie tasted it she realized it did at least taste a bit better than it smelled.

Sybil did most of the talking, asking the Poles questions, which they struggled slowly to answer while the others listened, and Katie quietly goaded Michael to eat some of the food.

'So,' Sybil spoke slowly and with care, 'where have you come from?'

'We?' Piotr was the one who seemed most eager to answer. He had a naturally smiling face and dark-brown eyes. 'We are come from . . . Black . . . Shaw – yes Blackshaw Moor . . .'

'Where is that?' Sybil asked, before a forkful of boiled potato.

'Where is . . . ?' Piotr glanced uncertainly at his companion, whose sculpted face was working, chewing on the fish stew.

'Blackshaw Moor – in Staffordshire,' he said, a little more fluently. Katie was already warming much more to Piotr, of the two of them, as he seemed more relaxed and amiable. 'It was army camp,' Piotr said.

'Yes, of course – but where were you before that?'

Piotr looked to his friend for help.

'We come . . . We came from Austria, and Italy,' Marek said.

'Ah – Cassino . . .'

'Yes,' they both agreed. 'Monte Cassino, yes.'

'And before that – before you were in Italy?'

For a moment they looked helplessly at each other as if overcome by the enormity of the question. Eventually Piotr shrugged, holding his fork, and said, 'Everywhere, we have been. Before that – *Polska*, Poland, our homeland.'

'I see, yes, of course,' Sybil said. She had the sense not to push her questioning too far.

Piotr suddenly looked down the table at Michael and grinned. 'Hey – little Michael! You like it? It's good?' He pointed at the food, grinning and nodding.

'Yes,' Michael fibbed, nodding back, unable to resist all this good humour. He had barely touched the snoek and was eating only the potato.

'And you say your sister is coming?' Sybil asked Marek.

For the first time Katie saw his rather mournful face lift and become more animated. He put his fork down and turned to Sybil.

'Yes, I think this month. She is coming from Africa – I hear through the Red Cross that she is there. She will come, but first, before she will be coming to this house, she goes to camp . . .'

'Ah, I see,' Sybil nodded. 'To acclimatize – I mean, get used to this country . . .'

The two of them were nodding solemnly.

'She learn English,' Piotr added.

'And how old is your sister?'

Marek considered, head on one side. 'Now – she will be twenty yearses old.'

'I see.' Gently Sybil asked, 'When did you last see her?'

'Er – I see her four years ago.'

Katie saw the solemn look on Sybil's face. She felt the years of the war open out a fraction in her under-standing. All of them had been so taken up with their own concerns, their families, the bombing and shortages and, in her case, Simon Collinge and all that had hap-pened to her, that the newspaper headlines and Pathé newsreels had so often felt distant and hardly real. She realized she had only the barest idea of whatever turmoil had taken place across the great span of Europe and beyond.

Very gently Sybil asked him, 'You are from a large family?'

Marek looked down for a second as if counting, then raised his head. In a flat voice he said, 'We were seven. Now, I think, we are but two.'

Katie felt the words sink into her.

'And you?' Sybil asked Piotr.

He shrugged. 'My family is six people then. Now – I do not know.'

This led to a silence, filled with questions that it did not seem possible to ask. Then Marek broke it, gazing longingly across the room.

'You have a piano,' he said.

'Oh yes!' Sybil looked pleased. 'Why – do you play?'

'Yes,' he said in his serious way. 'In my home, I play piano. I have not played since . . . For a long time.'

Well,' Sybil invited. 'You must feel free to play. I don't think one ever forgets completely. I should love to have a pianist in the house.'

'Thank you – I will try,' Marek said. His smile lit up his face.

VIII

EM

Forty-One

Summer 1948

'Tara, Mr Perry – see you on Tuesday!'

The forced smile faded from Em's face as she hurried away from work after her Saturday half-day. Her head was throbbing and she felt weary and a bit queasy. When the sick feeling started, it had given her a momentary jolt of excitement. Did that mean ... ? Could she be ... ? So often that had happened over these past two years, some small thing giving her hope. But no, of course there was no baby. Her monthly visitor had only just finished. She was just a bit tired, and churned up, that was all. If she took a couple of aspirin she'd feel better.

There might even be a few things left to buy in the shops before she went back to Norm's mom's. Even now she struggled to call the place 'home'.

The long years of rationing had not improved anyone's temper. The only thing derationed so far was bread, and everyone was worn out and fed up with it all. The war had been over for three years and nothing much seemed to have improved! She knew Edna Stapleton would have done the main food shop, but she wanted to get Robbie his sweets, and Edna had asked her to go to a particular shop for eggs.

There was no luck with the eggs, but she managed to get Robbie's sweet ration, then headed back, feeling weary and irritable. Turning into Reginald Road in Saltley, she met with a sight that did nothing to improve her temper. Ahead of her along the road was Norm, dragging a sobbing Robbie by the hand.

Em tutted. Norm was supposed to have taken Robbie to the barber's – early on before it got too crowded. He had obviously left it until the last moment and they were only just on their way back. And why was Robbie blarting? she asked herself crossly. God knew, Norm didn't have to do much for him – couldn't he even manage to keep the child happy for the short time that he did spend with him?

She reached the house just after them and was all ready to be snappy.

'What's the matter with him?' she demanded, as they all crowded into the tiny hall. She could hear her mother-in-law somewhere at the back, calling, 'Now, now – what's all that noise and fuss about?'

She could see that Robbie had been to the barber's and received a severe short back and sides. Then she caught sight of his ear.

'He cut me!' Robbie howled even harder for his mother's benefit. 'He cut me with the scissors and then put 'is stingy pencil on it and it hurt!'

'Oh dear, let's have a look.' Ignoring Norm, on whom she still, rather unreasonably, blamed all the trouble, Em squatted down and looked at Robbie's smarting ear. The barber had nicked it and then tried to ease the damage with a styptic pencil, which tended to sting even more than the cut. 'Ooh, that looks sore – never mind, we'll see if we can find a plaster. And, look,

I got your sweeties for you. You can have one before dinner, just as a treat.'

Robbie brightened up no end at the sight of a pineapple chunk. Em stood up as Norm disappeared out to the back.

'I s'pose you're off fishing this afternoon?'

Norm turned, half shamefaced. 'For a bit. Me and Wal. Looks a good day for it.'

Most Saturdays now he was either out fishing with a mate or two or, in the winter season, playing football with the lads. There was a police team. It was something new that the army had given to him – that he had more need of male company. And, Em thought bitterly, to be away from her, from having to bring up a child. It felt a long time since they'd done anything together, just the two of them.

'What're you going to do?' he asked.

Fat lot you care, she thought. 'Well, I suppose I'll be looking after Robbie – just for a change,' she said sarcastically. Turning away, to go and fetch aspirin and a plaster, she said. 'I'll go to our mom's.'

'All right then,' Norm said. As if trying to make things better, he followed her and pecked her on the side of the head, adding, 'It's nice for them to see him. See you later, love.' And off he went with his rod and sandwiches.

Em's mother-in-law, Edna Stapleton, was a kindly woman who had always made them welcome in her house. She had had a long and stable marriage, her husband Bill employed at Metro-Cammell ever since his working life had begun, and, having had only two sons, they had been reasonably comfortably off. Their terraced house was neat and always immaculate.

The housing shortage was so extreme, the queues for council properties to rent so long, that it was a good job she was so even-tempered, as they were all stuck with each other for the moment. Em was ashamed of the fact that, however kind her mother-in-law was, Edna Stapleton was also rather interfering and got royally on her nerves.

Edna meant well. She was cheerful, energetic and fiercely house-proud, forever scrubbing at something and always convinced she knew best.

'Oh, I don't think you ought to be feeding him again yet, ought you?' she'd say when Robbie was a baby. 'You don't want to spoil him.'

'You don't want' was one of Edna's phrases. 'You don't want to put that on there,' when Em put a little vase of flowers in her own and Norm's bedroom. 'It'll make a stain.' 'You don't want to put him in that – it's still damp . . .' Or 'You want to make sure you turn that mattress . . .' Em was sick to the back teeth of being told what she did and didn't want. She knew really that her in-laws were far better than many, but she longed to live in her own house, where she could decide what she wanted for herself. Where her married life could start properly, instead of being stuck with Norm's parents.

After a quick dinner of bread with pickled beetroot and a wafer of cheese, Em was still in a bad mood.

'Come on, Robbie,' she sighed. 'We'll go and see Nanna and Granddad.'

'Oh!' he protested, grimacing. 'I wanna go and play out with Don and Eric!'

'Well, you're not going with them today,' Em said firmly. She didn't like the way Robbie was hanging

366

about with a lot of the older boys these days. He was mad to be with them, scouring the bomb pecks for shrapnel and other treasures, playing games of shooting Germans.

As they walked along in the muggy afternoon, Em glanced a few times at her son's shorn head. She wasn't sure she liked the haircut. It was very short and made him look too grown-up, and somehow harder in the face.

'Your hair'll grow back soon,' she said, rubbing a hand over it. Robbie shrugged her off impatiently.

He was in a world of his own, pulling on her hand, trying to get her to walk faster and muttering to himself. He was in some war game now as well, she could tell. Suddenly he caught sight of a skinny, red-haired boy across the street.

'Eh – Tommy!' he yelled.

'All right, Robbie!' the lad, about ten, bawled back.

'Shoosh, Robbie,' Em scolded. 'Don't shout across the road like that. It's rude.'

Robbie shrugged. He was starting to walk with a swagger, she saw with a pang. He wasn't like her little boy any more, soft and biddable. These days he was off out, the first chance he got, and came home filthy with cuts and grazes on his legs, full of the big boys and all their adventures. It had hit her hard when he first went to school, even though it was to Cromwell Street where she had been herself. She sometimes felt he'd outgrown her, even though he was only six – that she was a bore who spoiled his fun. It was only at night when he was half asleep, or if he was poorly, that he felt like her sweet little boy again, the boy who needed her comfort.

Here I am, she thought resentfully, with the two of them, husband and son – and neither of them take the blindest bit of notice of me. Norm had taken a while to settle back to life at home after the army. Over these past years his restlessness had died down a bit, but he was not the man who had gone away, devoted to her and wanting nothing but to be with her. He was off and out with the lads far more. Sometimes she looked back with nostalgia to the days of the war, when she had missed him and longed wholeheartedly for him to come home. Now he was here, everything felt so flat. She found herself longing for a daughter who might give her more company.

As they crossed the cut, Em pulled Robbie to a stop and looked down into the water.

'I can't see, Mom,' Robbie said, jumping at the wall and scuffing his shoes. He held up his arms, little again suddenly. 'Lift us up.'

With an effort she hoisted him up in time to see a filthy joey boat containing coal slide out of sight under the bridge.

'There – gone,' she said, and kissed the soft skin at the back of Robbie's neck.

'Mom, don't!' he cried, wriggling. 'That's sissy, that is! Put me down!'

As she bent to let him down to the ground Em felt tears start in her eyes. Here she was, twenty-five years old and she felt like an old matron, stuck in her ways. There was nothing to look forward to. And she knew deep down that her resentment and anger towards Norm stemmed from the fact that she had still not caught for another baby. And so far as she was concerned, it was all his fault.

*

'D'you fancy going up the park?' Cynthia said when she arrived. 'It's quite a nice day – I'd like a bit of a breather.'

'All right,' Em said listlessly. She knew it was a good idea, but she could really have done with a sit down.

'Just give me a minute.' Cynthia said. 'Come on, Robbie, you can come up with me while I change my shoes.

Bob was in the back room, and Violet was sitting at the table, peering at the newspaper. She looked up, squinting at Em.

'Oh, hello,' she said smiling.

Bob, who had been snoozing, opened his eyes long enough to say, 'All right, wench?' and slid back into sleep again, snoring gently. Even though she saw him nearly every day, Em was aware that her father was ageing fast.

'You coming up the park with us, Vi?' Em asked, hoping she would. Violet was good with Robbie and took some of the pressure off her.

'Can't – I'm going out with Sue and Peggy.'

'Oh.' Em was disappointed. But she knew there must be more exciting ways for her seventeen-year-old sister to spend the afternoon. 'Anywhere nice?'

Violet shrugged. 'Dunno really – we might go into town.'

'Vi, you've nearly got your nose on that news-paper . . .'

Violet straightened her back for a moment, then sunk down again. 'I can't see unless I sit close.'

'Well, that's no good, is it? You need glasses. You can get them free now, you know that, don't you?'

Violet looked round. 'Can I?'

369

'So they say. Norm's mom's talking about getting glasses.' Edna was full of the new National Health Service. Some of her friends were going to see a doctor for the first time in years, after suffering in silence. 'You ought to go and see.'

Cynthia came back down again. 'Come on then,' she said. 'There's a chance Dot might come an' all. We can meet her up there.'

'All right,' Em said. She was fond of Dot, her mom's old friend, but the thought of going all the way to Aston Park to listen to the two of them canting didn't fill her with enthusiasm. Still, she had to get through the day somehow.

Thank goodness for my little job, she thought. She was still working Tuesday, Thursday and half of Friday and Saturday with Mr Perry. It got her out of the house. Otherwise, she thought, I'd be going off my head by now.

Norm scraped into the house just in time for tea, having been down the pub after the football. Em thought sourly that he could always manage to be in time for his mother, if nothing else.

Edna had made a fish pie and the room stank of fish, but it tasted quite good, padded out with a lot of potato and carrot.

'Nanna,' Robbie said in the middle of tea. 'Can we get a dog?'

'Don't talk with your mouth full,' Edna corrected him.

'A dog?' Bill chuckled. He picked up his teacup, which looked like a toy in his big hairy hand. He worked an overhead crane at the factory – had done all through the war, while they were making tanks instead of railway carriages. 'You'll never get that one past yer nan.'

'Please, Nanna?'

'Ooh, no, I'm not having animals in my house – they're dirty,' Edna said.

Em immediately felt that she wanted Robbie to be able to have a dog, even though she wasn't too fussed about animals either.

'One day, son,' Norm said. 'When we've got our own house – then you can have a dog.'

Robbie's face lit up with excitement. He looked tanned and healthy from their afternoon in Aston Park. 'Can I, Dad? When? When're we going to get our own house?'

Norm ruffled his son's cropped hair. 'I don't know, son. When our boat comes in, I think – that'll be the time.'

Robbie's brow creased. 'We ain't got a boat – have we?'

When Em and Norm went to bed that night, Norm was chattering, as if to break through the silence that seemed to have grown up between them. He talked about the fishing and his mates, and what they'd seen going along the cut and the people they'd met.

The big bed took up most of their room and there was just space for a couple of chairs and a chest of drawers, which they shared.

Em stood barefoot on the lino, brushing out her hair in front of the tilted mirror on the chest of drawers. She took her hairgrips out and laid them out carefully. Without her hair pinned back, and in her nightdress, she looked younger. She turned and got into bed.

'All right, love?' Norm asked, when she pulled the bedclothes up rather huffily.

Underlying her anger was the answer she never gave him. *We can't have a baby, because you went with that woman and caught some horrible disease, and now you can't make babies.* She had laughed at the time – well, in the end – and tried to forgive him. Norm thought that was all long forgotten. But they had made Robbie before – *so why not now?*

But she knew she wasn't going to say it – not that. She lay back, looking at the ceiling for a moment. Things could be better between them, even despite that. They had to be. She turned to him suddenly.

'Norm, you know what you said tonight, about us getting our own house?'

'Huh, yeah. Pigs might fly.'

'But d'you want us to get our own place – really?' Sometimes she thought he'd be just as happy living here forever with his mom.

'Well, yes, course. But you know what it's like.'

'But if we really tried – there must be places to rent if we looked around. If we tried a bit harder.'

'Oh, I dunno,' Norm said fatalistically. He gave a huge yawn. 'We're on the council list. I don't know there's much else we can do about it.'

Em lay back, suddenly burning with determination. 'But if we tried,' she insisted. She could tell Norm was almost asleep. Norm nearly always seemed to go to sleep whenever she wanted to talk about anything.

'Night, love.' He patted her haunch and turned on his side, soon dead to the world.

Well, you may not be prepared to try and make it happen, but I've had enough, she thought. I don't want to go on like this, so something's got to change!

372

Forty-Two

Em's determination to try and find a new place to live unfortunately could not overrule the reality – that there was nowhere to be had. The odd room would come up for rent, but precious little else. The bombing had destroyed many houses, and others were rotting away of their own accord. Families anxious to settle after the years of war were having babies at a rate of knots, and many were in her position, crammed in with parents and in-laws, or even living in old prisoner-of-war camps or disused railway carriages. There was simply not enough to go round. The council had tens of thousands on the waiting list. The newspapers talked about slum clearance.

Bob, her dad, kept saying, 'They'll have this place down, then – you wait and see.'

'We're not living in a slum, Bob!' Cynthia would protest crossly. 'I've always kept our house nice.'

There was much talk by the city planners, but the action was very slow. Set against all this, Em felt guilty.

'It's not so bad where you are,' another young mother reproached her, when she talked about her longing to find somewhere else. 'You don't even have the babby sleeping in with you – that's flaming luxury, that is! Some people don't know when they're well off.'

It was true, Em thought. There were so many worse off – and Edna's house was clean into the bargain. And it wasn't as if Edna was a tyrant, like some. Em felt almost ashamed of her sense of frustration. After those war years, married but stuck at home with Mom and Dad, was it asking too much to hope for a married life where she could run her own house and be in charge of her own kitchen?

'What about one of them prefab places?' she said to Norm one night, once they were alone. 'They look quite nice.'

'Aren't they on the council list like the rest?' he said.

Em sighed, knowing he was right. Suddenly she started crying, curling up on her side in bed.

'Eh, Em! What's brought all this on?' He sounded bewildered.

'I just want things to be different,' she sobbed. As usual what she wanted to say came out wrong. She couldn't seem to say what she really meant: that she wanted to feel that the two of them were close again and that, despite living with all these people, she was lonely. 'I wish we had our own house.'

'Oh now, love,' Norm said. He snuggled up behind her. 'I know you do – but we haven't got a magician with a wand to find one just like that. We'll have our own little place eventually. But it's not so bad here, is it? Mom and Dad've been good to us and they could've kicked up a fuss, having us foisted on them. I think our mom's enjoying having her grandson living with her. Come on – let's look on the bright side, eh?'

He leaned over and kissed her cheek and she twisted round and cuddled into his arms, sniffing.

'D'you still love me, Norm?' she asked sadly.

'Course I do – you're my wife!' He pushed his body against her. 'D'you want me to prove it?'

Em edged away. 'No, it's all right. Let's go to sleep.' Why did Norm think that doing *that* would always

374

make everything all right? In some ways it made things worse.

She lay awake once he was fast asleep, the darkness broken by a dim streak of light from between the curtains. More tears ran silently down her cheeks. If only they could have another baby. If Norm was there to see it grow up this time, things would be different and he'd be more enthusiastic than he had been about Robbie. Em had loved looking after a baby, feeling its need of her. With a heavy sigh she turned on her side to try and sleep. It was no good moaning. She'd just have to keep going and make the best of things.

A few days later, when the front doors were all open to let in the warm evening air while they were eating tea, there was an urgent hammering from the front.

'Sounds like trouble,' Edna said, getting up.

They all listened. Em heard sobbing from the front door.

'That's our Vi!'

She hurried to the door and had time to take in Edna's sorrowful expression before Violet burst out, 'Oh, Em – it's our dad. They've taken him to the hospital! He went all funny and he can't speak or walk properly or anything.'

'Sounds like a stroke,' Edna said, half to herself.

Norm had joined them in the hall by now. 'You go back with her, love,' he said. 'Go and look after your mom.'

'Joyce is with her,' Violet said. She was shaking from the shock.

'You'd best take a few things in a bag – you'll need to stop over,' Edna said.

Em did as she was advised, glad suddenly of Edna's practical nature when she couldn't think straight.

'Go on, love,' Norm said, when she came down.' He kissed her cheek. 'You do what you've got to do. Robbie'll be all right.'

Em looked gratefully at him. 'Thanks, love – but I'll be back soon. Thanks, Edna. Come on, Vi – let's get over there.'

Bob had been taken to Dudley Road Hospital.

'I could see in his eyes how frightened he was,' Cynthia wept when Em and Violet got back to the house. She and Joyce were sitting at the table, both red-eyed. Cynthia dabbed her face with the hem of her apron. 'He's never been in a hospital in his life, except when I was – you know – when I was in there. But that was different. And that place ... To him it's still the workhouse. I hated having to see him go in there.'

The three girls exchanged looks. They all hated the thought of it too.

'We must tell Sid what's happened,' Cynthia was fretting. She got up and then sank back down again, wanting to busy herself with something, but unable to think what.

'Just sit down and have a rest for a bit, Mom,' Em said. She felt older and, as usual, as if she was the one who had to take charge. 'Tell us what happened?'

'It just came on, when he came in from work – gradual like. He couldn't seem to find his words to start with, and then suddenly the side of his face went all sort of twisted and funny...' More tears came as she recalled it all. 'He was all mithered – I could see there

376

was something really bad wrong with him. I said, "Bob, what is it? Can you tell me?" And I could see he couldn't ... That was when I sent Violet down to the phone box ... Oh!' She looked round at them all, frightened. 'I don't think he's going to come home!'

The next days were spent waiting, taking it in turns to visit the hospital with Cynthia.

The first time Em visited the hospital she felt sick with nerves. They went through town, and it would have been nice, a trip out with her mom on their own, had it not been for something so sad. The day was warm, but drizzly, the sky grey and oppressive. They walked along the Dudley Road together in summer frocks and cardies, sharing an umbrella.

'Mom, your bag keeps banging against me.'

'Sorry – here, I'll put it on the other arm.' Cynthia had a string bag containing some offerings for Bob, including bananas that Em had got from Mr Perry and a few sweets.

'I don't like it round here much,' Em said, peering out. 'Gives me the creeps.'

In that small area just north of the centre of Birmingham, the hospital, which had once had the workhouse attached to it, the prison and the asylum had all been built huddled together, almost like one vast and forbidding red-brick institution. The asylum in particular brought back too many dark memories, though Cynthia had never been in this particular one.

'I know what you mean,' Cynthia said. But her face was tight and preoccupied. She had aged overnight, little lines round her mouth.

'Will it be different now?'

Cynthia glanced round. 'Different? How d'you mean?'

'Well – with all this National Health Service thing coming in.'

'I wouldn't say all that different, except ... The doctor who was there when he first came in – I went with your dad, because he couldn't say anything. He was full of it: said he was proud to be a doctor now, and how everyone'd be looked after. I was in that much of a state I'd forgotten it'd all changed, and I told him Bob was on the panel – you know he'd paid up over the years. So he said that didn't matter any more, and how if I was taken ill, it'd be free for me too now. I'd just forgotten. I was too mithered. He looked ever so pleased with himself. Here we are, look.'

They turned into the grand, forbidding entrance and walked the corridors to the ward. Em didn't recognize her father at first. Cynthia led her to a bed just inside the ward, where a stubbly cheeked, grey-faced man lay with his eyes closed.

No! Em wanted to cry out. *That's not our dad!*

The sight of him really frightened her. Mom had kept saying he wasn't going to come home, and she thought it was just her panic speaking. But as Em took a seat by the bed she could see, with a chill to her bones, how ill he was. He was dressed in a pair of green pyjamas that she'd never seen before, and which made him seem more alien.

'Bob?' The way Mom spoke, gentle and caressing, nearly broke Em's heart. For a moment she imagined Norm lying there like that. She leaned forward and touched his hand. It felt cool and lifeless.

'Dad – it's Em.'

'Can you hear us?' Cynthia asked.

He stirred, and his eyes slowly opened. For a moment he looked at the ceiling, obviously not sure where he was.

Cynthia clasped the hand nearest hers and stroked it. Em heard her father make a noise in the back of his throat, but no words came out. A desperate look passed over his face, and Em swallowed down the tears that threatened to take over.

A nurse appeared beside them, pretty black hair just showing from under her white veil. Em found her awe-inspiring. With a pang she wished for a moment that she could have been a nurse.

'He's really not very well today.' She spoke quietly, to Cynthia. 'We're just hoping to see an improvement. But you're doing the right thing. Do talk to him.' With a smile she moved away.

Cynthia began to talk to him, telling him they were all getting on all right and that various of his pals had asked after him. Then Em took over for a bit. She was in full flow, telling him about Robbie and his pranks with the other lads, some of which had upset her at the time, but she made them into a joke for his granddad.

Then her eyes met her mother's, both of them stricken, when they saw Bob's welling eyes, and a tear roll down the side of his face to the pillow.

Forty-Three

'You come in if you can, bab,' Mr Perry said. 'But if you can't, I'll manage for a day or two, or find someone to stand in for yer.'

'I'll try and get here, Mr P,' Em promised. 'I think I'd rather be busy. But Mom needs some help, and it's not easy for our Joyce or Vi to get time off.'

'Don't you worry.' Mr Perry patted her shoulder in a fatherly way. 'Family comes first. I remember when my missus was taken bad – you've got to do your bit.'

Em was touched by everyone's kindness. Bob, in his quiet way, had been a popular man. He'd worked in the same place, at the power station, for most of his working life and had made loyal friends, who came and asked after him. Most of all, though, Em was humbled by the way her in-laws treated her.

'He's no age,' Edna said sorrowfully when she went back after her first visit to the hospital. In fact Edna and Bob were almost exactly the same age: fifty-three. 'But there we are, bab – there's no telling. He might be right as rain in a few months. Now, don't you worry about things here. Robbie'll be all right with us. You go and look after your mother.'

Em, with a pang, realized that Robbie would indeed be perfectly all right without her. She hated handing him over to anyone else to look after, but was grateful for Edna being so kind and capable. Her father-in-law,

Bill, was also quietly concerned and asked after her dad.

When Norm got in late that afternoon, he held her close in their room while she had a little cry. 'It's awful seeing him like that,' she wept. 'Just lying there – I didn't even know him at first. He can't speak and he can't move: all down one side of his body . . . He knew us all right, but oh, Norm – he was so upset. I've never seen him like that before.'

Norm seemed to come into his own. He stroked her back and said, 'Now look, love – our mom's right. You need to pay attention to your mom and dad, the way things are at the moment. Don't you worry about anything here.'

'Everyone's being so kind,' Em sobbed, ashamed of the moaning she'd done. 'I don't deserve it.'

'What're you on about?' Norm stepped back and looked into her blotchy face, laughing. He leaned in to give her a peck on her freckly nose. 'You're a daft thing sometimes. Now, come on – I'm going to walk you over to your mom's, and you can stay there for a day or two till we see how things go.'

She looked up at him, full of emotion. 'Oh, Norm, I do love you.'

He kissed her lips this time. 'Love you too, silly.'

Days passed. They visited the hospital and tried to get on with things. Em did go into work, at least for the mornings. There was nothing much else she could do, and the hanging about was worse than being busy. And she popped home to see Robbie and Norm when she could.

But she knew she was in the right place for the

moment – with her own family. Violet was relieved to have her there. Though Joyce still lived at home, she and Violet had never been close and Joyce spent nearly all her time out with her boyfriend, Larry. Violet would have found it hard to be on her own at home just with Cynthia.

As the days passed, Bob showed very little sign of improvement and all they could do was wait and hope. They got through the evenings together, trying to distract themselves, but in the end there was only one topic of conversation and all of them were full of their memories.

'I remember the first time I saw your dad,' Cynthia said, as the three girls sat in the back room one evening, spinning out weak cups of tea. Now summer was here, they didn't need to light the fire. They all knew this story, but they loved her telling it. 'I'd moved out to get away from my stepmother...' Her faced creased with bitterness. 'Mom was dead – and Geoff, my brother, who was killed in the first war. Anything was better than living with her. I had a factory job, was earning my keep just about – no great hopes. Then I met your dad on the tram.' Her lips curved up at the memory. 'The way he was looking at me – oh, it makes me blush even now, thinking about it!'

'Love at first sight,' Violet said dreamily.

Cynthia got up, seeming to move more slowly, as if stunned and disorientated by what had happened. She fetched the old wedding photograph that had been sitting on the mantel for years. Two handsome faces smiled out of it, young and full of hopes.

'Let's see,' Violet said. She drew the picture right up to her face.

'For heaven's sake, Vi,' Em said. 'I told you: you need to get some specs – look at you, squinting like that! I'm going to take you and make sure you get some.'

'All right,' Violet said, gazing at the picture. 'You look so pretty, Mom.'

'And happy,' Joyce said, leaning in to look.

'It was a happy day.'

The tears came without warning. She put her hands over her face. 'Oh! I can't stand seeing him like that!'

'Oh, Mom,' Violet said, starting to cry as well. These last years their mom had been like a rock, always there. They hated it when anything upset her: it shook them, bringing back the days when she had not been able to be there always, when she had been taken into hospital.

Joyce, biting on one of her fingernails, looked helplessly at Em.

'It'll take time, Mom,' Em said. 'But they said he could get better.' She could only just speak, through the lump in her throat.

'I know,' Cynthia said, wiping her eyes. 'But he looks so poorly. I don't see how he can get better.'

During those days, because of her father's illness and being back in her mom's house, Em found more of these painful memories kept coming back to her: things that had happened when they were all very young, things that usually she tried to forget. The years of her mother's worst illness, when Em had been left to look after the others, were the most awful. Bob had taken comfort in the arms of another woman and Em had been like a worn-out, harassed mother at the age of eight. In those days they hadn't known if their mom would ever get better and come home. Bob had been so sad, so lost without her.

One dinnertime, when it was just Em and Cynthia at home, they had been cleaning the house, trying to keep themselves occupied. They'd done upstairs most of the morning, Em cleaning her old childhood bedroom. She stood for a moment, thinking back. She remembered once, when things were really bad with Mom away, she had lost her temper with her father. That time he had come and sat on her bed while she wept bitter, desperate tears, and he had been sorry, and kind in his rough way. The memory brought her to tears again now. He'd been a quiet man all their lives, just always there, sleeves rolled up eating his tea, or in his chair, tired and mucky from work. But she knew his life revolved round them – all of them, but especially Cynthia, his wife. He was lost without her.

Em leaned on her broom, tears rolling down her cheeks, and a sudden extra dread seized her. How might she be without him? If Dad didn't get better, would it make Mom poorly again as well? They had all hoped those days were over, and Em prayed from the bottom of her heart that they were.

Downstairs, at dinnertime, they listened to *Worker's Playtime* and cleared up a bit. Cynthia cut some bread, holding the loaf under her arm. She fetched a couple of plates, then clicked off the wireless. Not looking at Em, she said, 'I've always loved him. Your dad. Even with what happened.'

Em was completely taken aback. From the day Dad had come back home, after his time away with *that woman*, until now, none of them had ever mentioned it or her – Flossie Dawson – again. Everything about that heartbreaking time had been locked away in the past as they tried to heal and keep going as a family. But Mom must have been thinking back, just the way she had. Em felt the blood banging in her ears.

'I know, Mom . . .'

'See, it wasn't his fault, what happened . . .' She looked towards the window, her face full of pain. She seemed smaller suddenly, Em realized. In that moment she could see how her mother was going to look as an old lady.

'It wasn't yours, either, Mom.' Em felt as if her chest was going to tear open as the grief of it all rushed back to her. 'You were just poorly, that's all.'

Cynthia turned to her, eyes welling. 'I know. But I always felt I should have been able to help it, to stop it. And leaving you and the others . . .' She put her hand over her mouth and shook her head for a moment, then reached for a knife to spread margarine on the bread. 'Bob's a man – he didn't know what to do . . .'

'Mom.' Em couldn't stand any more. She went and took the knife off Cynthia. 'You sit down – I'll do this. Look, we'll go and see Dad this afternoon.' Her words came out in a rush. 'Don't go over it all. We've been all right, haven't we? Don't make a rod to beat yourself.'

Cynthia looked up at her and bravely pulled herself together, even managing a smile. 'All right, love. Yes – you're right. Let's talk about something else. You heard from Molly?'

Em pulled the corners of her mouth down. 'Not for months. I had a card, from Skeggy – she was at another of them camps, working, I s'pose.'

Cynthia took a mouthful of bread, resting her elbows on the table, frowning a little.

'She does seem to drift, that one.'

'Yes,' Em said sadly. 'I don't know what she's think-ing of, really. I thought she was going to get on all right – in the war and that. But now . . .'

Cynthia shook her head. 'Poor Molly.'

That afternoon they found Bob looking a bit brighter.

'He's trying to say more,' the nurse told them when they arrived. 'And I think there's a bit more feeling in his hand.'

Encouraged, they went to his bedside, finding that he had been moved a bit further along the ward. As they approached, Em saw him catch sight of them and recognize them. He raised his right arm, the good one, in greeting.

'Hello, love,' Cynthia said softly, leaning to kiss his cheek. He was propped up on pillows, looked clean and had been shaved, but his face seemed sunken and had not yet regained its normal colour. He tried to say something in reply, but could not manage the words and looked stricken when all that came out was a kind of groan.

'Never mind,' Cynthia said. 'It'll get better – you just wait and see. Look, we've brought you a couple of bananas, love – those'll do you good.'

Em smiled at him, but Bob laid his head back against the pillow suddenly, as if he was already worn out. They told him little bits of news, though there was not much to tell. It soon became clear that he was very tired and started to doze as they sat with him, his mouth dropping open.

'I think we might as well go now,' Cynthia whis-pered, anxiously. 'But I don't like to leave him without saying goodbye . . .' She didn't add *just in case* . . . She leaned over him and very gently kissed his forehead. 'Bye-bye, love.'

They slipped away along the ward. At the door they turned, and Em saw her father still sleeping in the same position.

'Bless him,' Cynthia said, distressed.

Em took her arm and together they walked back along the echoing corridors.

It was the last time they saw Bob alive. The next day, they were told, he had had another enormous stroke in the night and had not woken up again.

They left Robbie with Edna when they went to the funeral.

'I don't want him to have to come,' Em said. 'I know he's old enough to understand, sort of anyway, but it's a lot for a little one.'

She knew she also needed room for her own grief, without having to explain things to him all the way through.

It was a heavy August day and Em and her sisters, all in summer dresses, walked red-eyed along the peaceful path, lined with tilting gravestones, from Witton cemetery. Sid, Em's brother, was arm in arm with his wife Connie, while Violet and Joyce walked together, and Em and Norm walked either side of Cynthia. There were no tears from her now: she was numb and heavy with sorrow.

They saw Cynthia into one of the waiting cars and, before getting in themselves, Norm put his arm round Em's shoulders.

'All right, love?' His eyes searched her face and she looked back at him, deeply. It felt as if, over those days since her father had died, she and Norm had come back together and were really seeing each other properly. She was so grateful to him.

'As I'll ever be,' she said, managing a tiny smile.

'Oh, love.' He held her close for a minute and she closed her eyes, face pressed against him. Her Norm. He was a good'un – she knew that really.

'Come on,' he said, releasing her. 'In you get.'

She slid in beside her mother, who was looking out of the far window, up at the trees. Norm got in last, beside her. The car moved off and she felt him take her hand, and in those moments all that mattered was the warmth of his hand and the knowledge that he was there and that he loved her.

IX

MOLLY

Forty-Four

August 1948

'Molly – how lovely to see you!'

As Ruth leaned to kiss her cheek, Molly observed that Ruth had become socially a little more confident and less awkward. She had taken to wearing her long, dark hair swept up and fastened with a big slide at the back and looked a little more sophisticated.

'Nice to see you too,' Molly said, feeling awkward herself, as she always did when she first met Ruth, beside whom she felt herself to be an odd mix of glamorous and rough, with her big curvy figure, eye-catching hair and down-to-earth ways. 'Come on – I'll show you where your billet is!' She eyed Ruth's little shoulder bag. 'You haven't brought much with you, have you?'

'Well, enough for a long weekend, I'd say,' Ruth laughed, looking around her. 'This is lovely! It must feel like old times, moving from camp to camp!'

Molly was becoming a regular in summer-camp jobs – this time at Bracklesham Bay, a Pontin's camp near Chichester.

'In some ways . . .' Molly grimaced. 'Not in others, though. But it's all right. Keeps me going.'

'You look very well on it – all bronzed and healthy. How's the swimming coming on?'

'All right – I get a bit of practice in my time off.' One of the lads at a Butlin's camp where Molly had worked last year had started teaching her to swim, and she loved being in the water and how good she felt afterwards. 'We can go in a bit, if you like. You can swim outdoors or in – take your pick! Here we are, look.'

They reached the cabin that Ruth had rented for a long weekend. Ruth lifted the strap of her shoulder bag over her head and put it down, looked around inside the little cabin with its simple furniture, excited as a child.

'Oh, this is so nice!' She turned from looking out of the little window. 'It's wonderful to be here. I love Cambridge dearly, but it can be a bit of a hothouse.'

Molly smiled. It was a constant source of wonder to her that Ruth kept in touch, still apparently wanted to be her friend.

'But you've just been to France – that must've been a lot more exciting?'

Ruth had been on a jaunt with two Cambridge friends.

'Oh yes, it was nice, of course – and that reminds me . . .' She went and unfastened the buckle on her bag and pulled out a little package. 'For you: from gay Paree!'

'Oh, Ruth!' Molly was overcome. 'For me? That's ever so kind of you . . .' Unwrapping it, she found a cream silk scarf with a red border and Parisian scenes drawn on it in dark-blue ink and coloured with patches of turquoise. 'That's beautiful – is that the Eiffel Tower?'

'Yes, and the Arc de Triomphe and Notre-Dame – I thought the colours would suit you. There . . .' She snaked it round Molly's neck. 'It looks lovely!'

Molly was delighted. 'It'll dress up anything, that will – oh, thank you!'

'Don't mention it. Now, why don't you show me around?'

Molly had made sure she had a day off while Ruth was staying, though it was the busiest holiday season and she was working hard a lot of the time.

'Bloody cooking again!' she groaned as she and Ruth at last got some time to relax together on Saturday afternoon. They sat at the edge of the little boating pool, dangling their feet in the water and drinking in the sunshine. 'I never get away from it, do I? Course, once you've done it before – like I did at Butlin's last year – they just want you to do it again. Breakfast's the worst: two shifts, so you're always trying to hurry the first lot to get out, so that the next lot can get in. It's bedlam!'

'Sounds it! Rather you than me. A boiled egg is still about the most complicated thing I can cook!' Ruth, her neat figure dressed in navy slacks rolled to the knee, with a white short-sleeved blouse, was also looking tanned and well. She put her head back and closed her eyes. 'Ah, this is bliss – at least it will be, if those children keep their distance. I don't want to get splashed!'

Molly screwed up her eyes against the sunlight dazzling her from the water. The lake was busy with little blue-and-yellow pedaloes. The water felt silky as she moved her feet in it.

'Have you seen Win?'

'No – not for ages. I had a card from her, though, from Rome. It all sounded very cultural – you know Win. She's going into her final year now, like me.'

'What'll she do then?'

'Oh,' Ruth smiled mischievously. 'Something frightfully sensible, I expect.'

'And what will you do?' Molly could scarcely imagine their lives. A university degree was hard enough to picture, but then what? 'Will you be a teacher or summat like that?'

Ruth straightened up, eyes open. 'I don't know. More and more I think I'd like to stay on and do research – if I get a good enough degree. Otherwise, I suppose I'll go and work for some firm – or hospital laboratory . . . I have no desire to be a teacher. They'd run rings around me—'

'Hello, Molly!' a male voice cut in, making them both jump. A lively, sandy-haired young man planted himself beside Molly.

'All right, Trevor?' Molly said. 'This is my mate Ruth – she's come for a long weekend.'

''Ello, Ruth!' Trevor held his hand out, grinning. 'Are you the brainy one?'

'Oh, I don't know about—' Ruth began.

'Yes,' Molly said, proudly. 'She's doing a degree at Cambridge University.'

'Blimey,' Trevor said. 'Most of us are stuck with the university of life, eh?' He seemed put off and got to his feet. 'See you later, Molly?'

'Maybe,' Molly said.

'Bye, then – bye, Ruth.'

He went off cheerfully.

'That was Trevor,' Molly said.

'Is he your boyfriend?' Ruth could be very direct.

Molly blushed. 'Sort of. For now, I s'pose.'

'Not a great romance then,' Ruth said drily. In all the time Molly had known Ruth, so far as she knew Ruth had never had a boyfriend. She just didn't seem to be the type.

'Nah. Not me.' Molly made a splash with her toes.

Ruth looked curiously at her. 'But you're such a honeypot! Don't you want marriage and babies, things like that, Molly?'

Molly looked down at the bright water. Abruptly she said, 'I can't have babies, Ruth.'

'*What?* Whatever makes you think that?'

Molly was really blushing now. It was the first time she had ever said it, admitted it properly, even to herself. It was one of the things that tied her to Ruth – the fact that they could both say things to each other: there was that kind of bond.

'Put it this way,' she said, still not looking round at her friend. 'If I was going to have a babby, it would've happened by now.'

Ruth was silent for a while. Then, quietly, she just said, 'I see.'

'I haven't been a good girl. You know I haven't.'

'Well, I didn't know for sure . . .'

'So now you do. I could've had Tony's baby.' Tony, the one man she had truly loved. 'But it never happened. Then the others. There's summat wrong, Ruth, it doesn't happen for me. Not that I've wanted it to – it's the last thing I've needed. But I've taken that many risks, usually when I'd had too much to drink, and I never thought about it. But I started thinking about it a while ago. I put two and two together and – I knew.'

'Surely there are tests . . . ?'

Molly shook her head. 'There's no point. I just know that's how it is.'

'I'm so sorry,' Ruth began.

'No. I'm not. Best not pass on my family's seed,

that's my way of looking at it.' Her voice was bitter now. Had her grandfather ruined her, somehow? All those infections she'd had? She would never know. It was just the way things were.

She turned her head now. 'What about you?'

'Oh – me! I don't know. I can't really imagine it at all. I think I'm too much of a bluestocking for most men.'

Molly smiled. 'We can be old maids together then.'

'That's about it, I think!'

'Talking of old maids – have you seen the Gorgon?'

'No, but Win has. I think they meet for a coffee every month or two. She's a rather lonely soul, I think. Win says she seems ever so pleased to see her when they meet up – still smokes like a chimney. There's another one for our club, I reckon!'

Molly laughed, though she felt sad for Phoebe Morrison. She had never seemed a very happy person.

'Not Win, though,' Ruth said. 'I'm sure she'll marry someone very decent and sensible, and they'll live in a nice little house and have two children called Janet and John!'

'Yes!' Molly laughed. 'She will – like Honor!' Honor, another of the ATS they had done basic training with, had married someone very rich and was now leading a graceful country life near Oxford.

'Oh, I think for Honor it's more of a mansion!' Ruth laughed.

'She was all right though, she was,' Molly said. 'Hey – fancy a cuppa?'

'Now you mention it,' Ruth said, 'there's nothing I'd like more.'

Forty-Five

That October day when Molly had stumbled into the public toilets at Clacton and saw in the mirror her shambling, dishevelled reflection, another horrifying premonition of ending up like her mother, she promised herself that she was never going to drink again. The way she had sunk so low, waking half naked on the beach, unable to remember much about the night before, had frightened her badly.

She managed to pull herself together enough to work out that winter in Clacton, staying on at the Lesters' boarding house, keeping rigidly away from the bottle. But she had to go out sometimes, or she would have gone mad. Once or twice a week she met Liza, who was at first very confused by Molly's sudden turnaround.

'I'm no good to myself on it,' Molly told her. She made herself tell Liza about waking on the beach. She knew she mustn't pretend. 'If I go on like that, there's no knowing how I might end up. If I start, I can't stop.'

'Oh, go on, one quick half won't hurt yer,' Liza would say at first. It seemed to make her uncomfortable going out with someone who didn't drink alcohol. 'You're not turning into one of them Holy Joes yourself, are yer?'

'Look,' Molly said one night when Liza had been on at her. 'My mom's a drunk. I've seen the way it goes, and I don't want to end up in her shoes – got it? So don't keep on, or I shan't bother coming out with you.'

'Ooh, so-*rry*!' Liza said huffily. But she got the message. She also craved company in these deadly winter months and didn't want Molly to forsake her. They often found themselves the centre of attention from some lads. Molly's looks always drew admiring glances, and Liza was curvaceous with a brunette bob, full lipsticked lips and a come-hither expression. And it was nice to have some young company. But Molly stuck to lemonade, acted as prim as she could manage and made sure the lads walked her home, quite early on in the night.

On their own, the girls laughed about the fellas they'd met, moaned about their jobs and gradually began hatching plans.

'I'm sick to death of working in a hotel,' Liza said. 'I like to be outside more. Come the summer, I'm going to go and work at the camp – Butlin's. You coming with me?'

Molly thought uneasily for a moment of all the memories she had of the Clacton camp. Did she really want to stay around here? But it seemed the best thing on offer, and as the winter passed she and Liza had begun to see themselves as beginning an adventure.

'There's more camps, aren't there?' Molly said. 'We could get work at one, then another.'

'There's Skeggy and Filey. And there's other ones, not just Butlin's,' Liza said.

Possibility seemed to open up in front of Molly. She liked the idea of keeping on moving, on and on, not stopping long in one place.

In the spring she had said goodbye to the Lesters, despite Jane imploring her to stay.

'I feel if you were to stay on, I should get better,' she said desperately.

'I'm sorry,' Molly lied. In the circumstances it seemed better than the truth, which was how stifling she found it living there. 'But I've got to go home for a while. My mom's ill and I've got to look after her.'

'Oh, I see,' Jane said stoically. 'Well, of course, family must come first.'

Soon she had a job in the kitchen at Butlin's and Liza was a chalet maid. About halfway through the summer they moved to the Skegness camp and worked there. Molly liked the freedom of this, the way it indulged her sense of restlessness. And in the main she liked camp life. Some of the staff were local women who came to work in the kitchens or as cleaners, but many – the Jaffas in the dining halls in their orange coats, the Redcoats and all the others – were like themselves: single and young and looking for a job and a bit of fun. There was a sense of camaraderie – in that respect Ruth was right, it was a bit like the army, and Molly liked it for that. There were also a good many fights and fallings-out among the staff, and filching and cheating, but it was nothing that life hadn't prepared Molly for and she was quite able to cope. Camp life gave her some security. It was much less lonely than life at The Laurels.

What was harder was the constant attention of men – both other staff and, quite often, the campers themselves. But Molly was learning gradually that she could put up a barrier: be friendly, but distant. It was a discovery to her that she wasn't obliged to please any man who came along.

Life in the camp was very busy, and it would have been quite easy to forget about anyone outside. She sent Em a card from the Skegness camp, remembering guiltily that it was a long time since she'd written. But she was better at keeping in touch with Ruth. For all that their lives were so different, they somehow needed each other, and so long as Molly let Ruth know where she was, sooner or later a letter or card would arrive, addressed in blue ink in Ruth's neat, sloping hand.

Sometime last summer a card had arrived saying:

Any chance of your getting into London for a day?
I'll be there for a few days – thought I'd meet Win.
It would be fun if you could come too.

They'd gathered on a warm day, in a cafe in one of the streets leading off Trafalgar Square. Ruth had met Molly's train, and they rattled round the Circle Line on the Tube. Molly enjoyed walking the streets of London again, trying not to dwell on the last time she had made her way round here in a light cotton frock – the days she had stayed with Tony and his family. London, to her, meant both acute pleasure and agonizing grief.

'They're coming at half past eleven,' Ruth said, as they ambled past the fountains in the square.

'They?'

'Ah – I didn't tell you. I think she's bringing the Gorgon along with her!'

Molly's pulse quickened. Why? She asked herself. Why should I be nervous now? She regarded Phoebe with a mixture of awe and affection – and still saw her as a superior officer. It was hard to imagine her as anything else.

'It'll be funny seeing her.' Molly was trying to get used to the idea.

'In Civvy Street? Yes, it will. It's been a long time for me, of course.'

Ruth had not been in the battery that went to Belgium – she had returned to England and been demobbed sooner than Molly.

They sat at a sunny window table in the cafe, where they could see the street, and ordered cups of coffee.

'Ah,' Ruth said, after a few minutes. 'There they are – bang on time, of course!'

Through the window Molly saw a slender, elegant young woman in a pastel green shirt-waister, wearing a white cardigan on top and white low-heeled sandals. Her dark-brown hair was still much as she had always worn it, cut into a neat collar-length bob and caught behind one ear. It was unmistakably Win Leighton. And in those seconds Molly took in that Win had, in a kind, subtle way, established a protective relationship with the dumpy, awkward-looking woman walking beside her, dressed in a belted suit of brown-and-tan tweed, which looked too heavy for the weather. Once more it wouldn't have been possible to mistake Phoebe Morrison for anyone else – there was the black hair scraped up in a bun now, the solid, busty figure and the strong, determined face. Yet she looked smaller, as if, Molly sensed, she too had been diminished by civilian life.

They were all saying hello then. Molly was taken aback to be kissed on the cheek first by Win and then, as if following her example, by Phoebe Morrison. She caught the old smell of stale cigarettes as they were close together for a second.

'Ruth, Molly – how absolutely wonderful to see you!' Win gazed, beaming from one to the other of them, and Molly realized she was genuinely moved to be back with them again.

'Hello,' Molly said, nodding and smiling at them both shyly, realizing that she had no idea what to call Phoebe Morrison now. She couldn't keep calling her 'Ma'am', could she?

Win did a very good job of making everyone feel comfortable and at ease, while they sat and drinks were brought. And Molly, who had Phoebe Morrison to her left at the little round table, saw her draw her cigarettes gratefully from her bag and light up.

'For you?' She held out the packet to Molly.

'Thanks very much.' She accepted a light as well, glad to have something to do with her hands.

'So . . .' Win beamed round the table, taking charge as she always had done. 'We must catch up. Do let's share what we've all be up to!'

Win seemed exactly the same, Molly thought, as during that first week in the ATS, when she had been self-appointed head of dorm and had taken charge of switching off the lights. She felt a warm gratitude towards her. Back then, when she had no idea how to fit in, Molly had resented this automatic public-school authority. Now, she just felt fond. She knew from experience about Win's considerable good side.

As they sipped their drinks, Win and Ruth talked about university life and, having most in common, soon fell into conversation. Molly found herself being looked at closely from the left by Phoebe Morrison.

'So,' she puffed out smoke. 'Did you say you're working in *camps*?'

'Yes, Miss, er . . . Morrison . . .'

'Oh, for heaven's sake, do call me Phoebe. We're not in the army now.'

'I'm at Butlin's,' Molly said, thinking it sounded silly. 'Skegness at the moment – but I've been at Clacton. Before that I was in a boarding house.'

'Ah yes, I think I'd heard that. Clacton – fancy that. Has it changed much?'

She asked her questions in a clipped way, seeming ill at ease.

'Well, yes a bit. The beach is open – the hotels have all opened up as well ... And the camps are very busy. There are lots of holidaymakers now.'

'Ah yes. Well, no doubt you have a lot of fun and are kept busy.'

'Busy enough,' Molly agreed. She sipped some more of her cooling coffee. 'You should come – have a holiday yourself.'

Phoebe Morrison gave a snort of laughter. 'Ah well, perhaps!'

There was a pause, so Molly asked, 'And where are you working, er ... Phoebe?'

'Oh, Civil Service: roads and transport. Very dull. Well, I say that – it has its moments of course. There is at least some purpose in it.' Abruptly she asked, 'What shall you do in the winter? Presumably the camps don't stay open all the year?' She pulled out another cigarette and lit up. Molly heard Win laugh at something Ruth had said.

'I don't know,' Molly said. 'I'll just have to think of something.'

Win, who was looking at her now, leaned across the table. 'Perhaps we should all come down in the summer and work at Butlin's too? They take students, don't they?'

'Er – yes,' Molly said. She thought about some of the behaviour of the other staff, the fights and rivalries, the state of some of the kitchens. 'I'm not sure you'd like it really, Win.'

Win laughed. 'Perhaps you're right.'

They sat talking for an hour or so, before Win said they would really have to be going. Molly was relieved. She had found it hard going with Phoebe Morrison, despite being very pleased to see her. All in all, the meeting had made her feel sad. Phoebe's crustiness seemed to stand out more now than it had in the army, where it merged with her commanding role. And apart from her work, she had very little to talk about.

Molly sensed in her an aching loneliness, akin to that she felt herself. Of course, it was not the done thing to miss the war. Everyone had to be glad it was over, overjoyed to be getting on with their lives – getting married, having families, building a life. But what if you were not destined for any of those things? She could see that Phoebe missed the army with the same endless ache as she did herself, knowing, as she felt it all slipping away, that it had been the best time of her life, and that it was over now. And that somehow you had to go on.

As they were all getting up to leave, though, Phoebe surprised her by slipping her a piece of paper.

'My address. I don't suppose you have a fixed address – but do drop me a line if you think of it, will you?' There was a hesitant smile on her face.

'D'you really want me to?' Molly spoke lightly, jokingly, to cover the fact that she was so touched by the request. She could see that Phoebe Morrison had not found it easy to ask. 'Course I will – I'll send you a card now and then, let you know where I've got to next!'

'Do,' Phoebe said briskly, turning away. 'I'd like that.'

Forty-Six

All that winter she had kept running. That was how it felt now. Keep moving: don't settle to anything for too long. That was the way to keep life feeling like an adventure, like being on the road – a place where no one could expect or demand too much of her or get to know her too well.

At first she had been with Liza.

'You can come back to Mum's with me,' she said, as Molly wondered what to do at the end of their first camp summer. The season ended in September. 'See what we can find.'

After a few nights sleeping downstairs on a lumpy couch at Liza's house in Plaistow, where her thin, harassed mother was bringing up eight other children, Molly moved out to be a paying guest in another house. Liza's mother also put in a word for her at Tate & Lyle, where she worked, and Molly got a job packing sugar. It was all right for a bit and helped her get on her feet. But she didn't like factory work and some of the women got on her nerves, forever taking the rise out of her accent ('Ow! Yow from Birmigum, boy any chance?'). Liza, back in London now, where she had other friends, began to treat her in a very offhand way. Molly knew when she wasn't wanted and moved on.

In her bag she had a scrap of paper with the address on it of one of the guests at Clacton, a married man who had taken a blatant fancy to her. But he had also offered her a job in a cinema in South London. Molly had been surprised. He was a big, beefy, red-faced man who looked more like a butcher.

'You're just the sort of girl I could do with,' he'd said, ogling her shamelessly, even in front of his wife, while tucking into his roast chicken. 'You'd bring in the crowds all right – wouldn't she, Rene?'

Rene looked mildly across the table. 'I s'pect she would, Bert, yes.'

'You'll want somewhere to go – yer can't stick here all the year round.' He had insisted on writing the address down and Molly took it, with no thought of doing anything about it – until now.

'Albert Carter,' the paper said, 'Gaumont Cinema', followed by a scrawled address. She had to ask someone to decipher it for her.

'Oh, I get it – that's down Walworth way,' the man told her. 'Bit of a way from 'ere, love.'

She had thought Bert Carter might have forgotten about her by now, that he used his chat-up line wherever he went, handing out his address, but he had seemed very pleased to see her. She arrived at the Gaumont, a dark old fleapit of a place, and, heart sinking, asked the girl in the ticket kiosk for him by name.

The girl looked her up and down with a snide, knowing glance and said pertly. 'Who shall I say it is?'

'Molly Fox,' Molly said, trying to sound dignified.

Anyway, if he doesn't remember or he's rude, he can stuff it, she thought.

But Bert Carter soon appeared, in his shirtsleeves, red-faced as if he had been hurrying, and seemed delighted to see her. A job? Of course! Hadn't he promised? Within a day Molly was installed as an usherette at the Gaumont and had a room in the house of a Mrs Willetts a few streets away.

The work was all right, and she liked to see parts of the pictures as she stood waiting. But she waited to see what the catch was. Sure enough, it was the obvious one. Bert Carter's line of suggestive remarks – 'You're looking very lush-civious today, my dear . . .' – and attempts to grope her in dark corners whenever he got the chance were no more than she expected. But, as Mavis, the rather superior girl who worked at the front, told her world wearily, 'Oh, you don't want to take too much notice – 'e's all mouth, that one. Some of 'em like the girly papers for a bit of an eyeful; 'e just likes to 'ave it walking around, that's all. It don't amount to anything.'

Molly fended him off and made friends with the other usherettes, all of whom were pretty, buxom girls, and comparing notes, they realized they had all been employed for the same reason. As Lily, one of them, said with a cackle one day, 'We're just 'ere to 'elp 'im keep 'is right hand busy!'

It was all right until Christmas. Christmas Eve was hectic, but Molly could feel it building up: the sense of dread of the next lonely day. Why had she come back to London of all places? She'd burned her boats with Liza, so there was no invitation there. That evening, on the way home, she broke all her rules and bought a bottle of Scotch.

'I can't get through tomorrow without you,' she whispered to the bottle, tucking it under her arm in the foggy, dimly lit street. As she stood there, she had a moment of complete giddy panic: a vision of herself, all alone on the vast, spinning world. She had to right herself against the front of a shop.

Her landlady, a reclusive woman, didn't seem to be celebrating Christmas either. Molly spent the day alone in her room, sinking lower and lower. For lunch she heated a tin of soup and ate a ham sandwich. Too late she realized she should have done something about it, gone to Birmingham and asked Em if she could be with them. But the thought of Birmingham – and of being anywhere near her mother – oppressed her.

She thought of past Christmases, army Christmases with all the laughter and entertainments. Faces flashed before her mind, especially from that final Christmas, in Belgium. They knew it was all coming to an end, and that had that lightened the pressure on everything. She remembered a group of them singing round an old piano in a school hall; Cath's face, pink and joyful, knowing that soon she might be with her beloved Derck; the pianist, a plump girl called Susan, so close to being helpless with laughter that she struggled to play; and in the background – as usual – Phoebe Morrison, singing, her face alight as she watched everyone with an almost maternal air. She had looked happy. Molly thought of the dulled, almost bitter woman she had seen in London, the gruff cards she had received with sardonic references to 'keeping on keeping on'.

It was that scene among many memories that floated through her mind as sat on her bed and stared at the bottle. Johnnie Walker. It was the same spirit that her brother Bert had plied her with that night during the war when she went to the house, until she was almost too drunk to know what was happening. She saw his bony face in her mind, then her mother's bloated one.

She thought of the men whom she might have ended up with, had things been different, had *she* been different – Tony, and Len. All the sadness and regrets of her life, which she usually tried to run away from, welled up in her today and she couldn't seem to stop them. Look at me! I might as well go and walk the roads like a proper tramp – I'm living like one anyway. Tears came, sharply, making her sob. The rest of the day was a haze. She slept for most of it. On Boxing Day she woke feeling terrible and her first thought was: *I've got to get out of here.*

She left the Gaumont and her lodgings and got a job as a school cook. Her landlady, in a little terraced house, was a Marion Letts, a petite, dark-haired woman in her thirties whose husband had deserted her, leaving her with two young sons, Jimmy and Alan. Though harassed, she was keen to have a bit of company, and the boys, who were six and eight, liked having Molly in the house, especially as it was also at their school that she worked. Together they struggled through that bitterly cold winter, knitting balaclavas for the boys while pipes burst in the school where Molly worked, and spent every evening sitting on top of the fire, in all the clothes they could find, smoking all the cigarettes they could get hold of, to keep warm.

'You'd make a nice mum,' Marion said one evening, head on one side. 'Haven't you got anyone in your life, Molly? You're so pretty, I'd've thought they'd be swarming around you.'

'Oh, there've been one or two,' Molly said lightly. She didn't go into any real detail about her life to Marion. 'But I've been moving about a fair bit lately. I'll be off again, come the spring.'

'That's a shame,' Marion said, and Molly could tell

she meant it. 'You've been such a help, and the boys like having you here an' all.

'Maybe I'll be back next winter,' Molly said. 'We'll just have to see.'

But she had enjoyed the boys' company too. They were friendly little lads, and during that hard winter she knew she had been a real part of the household. 'Almost like a husband!' she had joked to Marion, who replied drily, 'Yeah – but more use!'

By the spring she had been restless again and, as soon as the camp season was about to begin, she decided to head for somewhere new: this time, Butlin's at Filey. She knew the drill now, so doing it without Liza didn't feel difficult. Getting on a train at King's Cross, travelling up the east coast, reminded her of the war, when the length of the coast had bristled with camps and ack-ack batteries and every kind of operation for prediction and security. Now the beaches were innocent again, dotted with holidaymakers. All the urgency and heightened intensity of that time was gone, and Molly knew she mourned it.

I'll give Filey a few weeks, she promised herself, sitting beside her little holdall on the train. And then see where I might go.

When Ruth came to Bracklesham Bay, Molly had been there for three weeks. She always let Ruth know where she was, dropping her light-hearted postcards in a 'Guess what I'm up to now!' sort of tone. She had also sent Em and Cath cards too, ashamed of how long it was since she had been in touch. They always wrote a note back, but they were busy with husbands and children. They lived another sort of life. She could hardly admit to herself how much it meant that Ruth had become such a good friend. In all the dashing here and there and the changes in her life, Ruth had become a fixed point – almost like a sister. Ruth was the one person now who cared enough to take Molly to task.

'So,' Ruth demanded, the last evening of her visit as they strolled along the beach, 'how long are you going to keep this up, Molly?'

'Keep what up?' Molly pretended innocence.

'This life you're living – shifting here and there with no aim in sight. You're like some kind of gypsy!'

Molly turned away, looking out across the mauve evening water.

'You can do better, Molly,' Ruth insisted.

Tears in her eyes, Molly said, 'I don't know. I don't know how else to do it.'

X

KATIE

Forty-Seven

1948

Over those next days, the household with its new members had to settle in and get used to one another. Everyone was busy, and most conversations took place over the evening meal. They all sat round in Sybil's dining room – the two Poles, quickly becoming familiar to them, at first peering curiously at the food and sometimes conferring quickly in Polish, as if trying to make out what they were about to eat. (*Corned beef – this is same as Bully Beef? Baked beans?*) At the sight of green haricot beans their eyes lit up. 'You grew these on your land? Ah – marvellous!' They were very polite, making sure everyone had what they needed, passing dishes across the table, Piotr with his strong, beefy hands, Marek long-limbed and long-fingered, the shadows cast by the lamp showing up his sharp cheekbones.

Katie learned things gradually, listening to the teatime conversations. She discovered that the Poles were not free to come and go as they pleased; that if they went anywhere new, they had to register with the local police. They were also not allowed to work in any job of their own choosing. Their employment was restricted, for the time being, to menial jobs and 'dirty' industries. In the Displaced Persons camps scattered across Britain, Polish ex-soldiers and airmen and civilian arrivals to the country were being taught English and had often been learning trades. Piotr had trained as a barber.

Soon after the men arrived, Katie met Piotr on the middle landing one morning, as she was on her way out to take Michael to Maudie's house.

'Ah, hello!' he said. 'How are you today?'

They exchanged polite greetings. Katie still felt shy of both of them.

'And how are you, little Michael?'

'All right,' Michael said. Both the men made a fuss of him. They seemed very happy to be living in a home, and with a child about.

Katie was about to move on past when Piotr took a lock of Michael's hair between his finger and thumb.

'I can cut for you, if you please . . .'

'Oh!' Katie was startled. It was true, Michael's hair was getting rather long. 'Can you?' she said doubtfully. She felt Piotr's eyes on her for a moment, unmistakably sizing her up, and found herself blushing.

'I am barber – I train. Now I get work in barber shop. So I can do . . .' He made a scissor motion with his hands.

'Well, that would be very nice, wouldn't it, Michael? Would you like Mr . . . Mr Piotr to cut your hair?'

'Yes!' Michael said excitedly. He had taken to Piotr. Marek always smiled at him in a kindly way, but was more reserved.

'OK,' Piotr said happily, 'OK – I cut! Tonight, yes?'

That evening they took a plank from the shed outside and, to Sybil's great amusement, set it across the arms of one of the chairs in the dining room to make a high seat. They tucked a towel round Michael's neck, and Piotr lifted him onto his makeshift chair.

'You can take the mirror down,' Sybil suggested, as she sat, smiling at this spectacle. 'That's it...' Katie lifted the oval mirror from its hook on the wall near the door and held it, so that Michael could watch while his new barber gave him a short back and sides. Piotr kept up a run of little jokes.

'Now, this needs to be cut,' and he tweaked the boy's nose. 'And this' – one ear, until Michael was squirming and giggling. 'Oh, you must be still!'

But Piotr tickled the little boy's neck so that he wriggled all over again.

'How're we going to finish – huh?'

Katie found herself laughing at his antics. Then, as Piotr was snipping away, over his shoulder she noticed a movement. Marek had come to stand in the doorway and was watching with a gentle smile on his lips. Their eyes met for a moment, then she turned away, blushing, wondering what this quiet, lean man was thinking.

A moment later, looking very grown-up, Michael slid down off the chair.

'All finished!' he cried, triumphant.

'Bravo!' Marek clapped.

'Don't you look grown-up?' Sybil said. Katie saw that she was thoroughly enjoying all these comings and goings in her house.

Marek had found work at Lucas's in Great King Street. When Sybil asked him, over one evening meal, what he had done before, in Poland, he listened to the question in his polite, intent way, then shrugged.

'I was student. When the Germans came in thirty-nine – then Soviets – I was sixteen years. I have no job.'

'No, of course, how silly of me,' Sybil said, while Katie realized, to her surprise, that she and Marek were the same age. She had thought him to be older. He seemed older – both of the Poles did.

'And what about your sister?'

'She was then twelve years.'

Since the war Lucas had stopped making parts for Beaufighters and Stirling bombers and had returned to the production of parts for cars and peacetime aeroplanes. Marek had a quite menial job in assembly.

'But surely,' Sybil said, 'a bright young man like you could be apprenticed?'

'Perhaps one day.' Marek nodded. 'But not now. Is not allowed.'

'Should you like that, d'you think?' Sybil asked. And in a rare moment of probing for facts, 'What was your father's occupation?'

'He was chemist. Not in a factory – I mean . . .' Marek put down his knife and fork. 'He was teacher.' After a moment he added, 'My mother too.'

'A chemist?'

'No.' A faint smile reached his eyes. 'She teached small children.'

'Taught,' Sybil corrected.

'Ah yes, taught. Thank you.'

'Was it she who taught you to play the piano?' They had heard Marek play, haunting tunes and infectious dances that made Katie want to tap her feet immediately, his long body leaning into the piano, relearning things he had not played for years. Gradually they were

418

coming back to him. It was lovely to listen to, and Sybil was delighted.

'Er, no – it was a lady, a neighbour. My mother, she played, but only little bit – in the school.'

'Ah, songs for the children, that sort of thing?'

'Yes,' Marek nodded, 'that sort of thing.'

Further questions about his family seemed to hang in the air, but it didn't feel right to ask them.

About his sister, though, Marek was more forthcoming and they soon found out more about her. Agnieska's ship had docked at Southampton at the end of June and she had been taken, with many of the others who had travelled from Mombasa, to Daglingworth Camp, outside Gloucester. Soon after they moved in, Marek had visited the camp to be reunited with her, coming back to report that she had been placed for the moment in the care of a Polish family, and that she had some problems with her health. She would stay in the camp for at least a few months to learn more English and become acclimatized.

Katie struggled to imagine Agnieska's journey. 'Mombasa?' she had asked. 'I'm afraid I don't know where it is.'

'See on that shelf . . . ?' Sybil pointed. 'That's it, below our Mr Tiger – there's an old atlas. Your legs are younger than mine, dear.' Katie fetched the atlas, and Sybil pushed some dishes out of the way to make room. They all gathered round. 'There . . .' She pointed with a soil-grimed fingernail to the east coast of Africa. 'Mombasa.'

Katie, bewildered in her ignorance of all this, became aware of Marek standing over her shoulder, his breath on her ear as he bent down to look.

'Well, what was she doing in Africa?' she asked, feeling foolish.

'She was in another camp for displaced persons,' Sybil said. 'Some of the Poles have made journeys that you would hardly believe.'

'Before – she was in India,' Marek said. 'Another camp. And before that...' He pointed north and Sybil turned the pages to another map. 'Arctic Circle. Soviet camp.'

'And we, to start with, here...' Piotr got up too, suddenly eager to join in. 'Soviets come – they take many of our people, from here, in East Poland. Then we go to – where is? – ah yes, here – near to Sverdlovsk, in Russia. They want my father for working in steel works.'

'Blimey,' Geoff Jenkins said, looking at the map from the other side of the table. 'That's a long way.'

Piotr flashed a glance at him, an angry one, Katie thought. She had had no idea of any of this. Was he angry with them for being so ignorant? Even now she hardly knew what questions to ask, or whether they wanted to be asked anything. They would say a little sometimes, then clam up.

Most of the time the two of them were more concerned about the present. They were also full of questions about Birmingham, and English life. Their preparation in the camp had taught them about general aspects of life in Britain.

'They tell us,' Piotr said another night, with a twinkle in his eye, 'not to kiss the hand of the women. That it is not good – that the women will be, er...'

'Suspicious?' Sybil chuckled.

420

'Er, yes – suspicious!' They all laughed.

'Our men are a little more reserved,' Sybil said, picking up the serving spoon. 'Now, there's one more potato – are we going to fight over it? Or cut it into five?'

'I think give it to the men,' Katie said.

'Ah, yes,' Sybil said. 'Into three then?'

'No, no,' Marek argued courteously. 'The women must not be hungry. Into five!'

The two Poles were curious about Geoff's work, and asked Katie about herself, her job. Sometimes their questions were very blunt.

'So, Katie,' Piotr said at one of the first mealtimes. 'Where is your husband? He is dead?'

Katie avoided Sybil's gaze and looked coolly back at him. She was not used to being asked things in such a way.

'Yes. He was killed in the war. At Arnhem.'

'He was a soldier?'

'Yes.' She could feel a guilty blush rising right up through her. She hoped they couldn't see it. How awful it was to pretend, when they had truly lost so many loved ones.

Everyone was watching her sympathetically.

'Michael has never seen his father,' she said. This at least was true.

'Mr O'Neill,' Piotr said.

'Er – yes.'

'That reminds me . . .' Sybil seemed to come to her rescue. 'Mrs O'Neill is a Catholic – I assume you are too?'

'Catholic? Yes, of course,' Marek said. He seemed to see Katie with new eyes. 'You are Catholic?'

She nodded.

'You can show them where to go to Mass on Sunday, can't you?' Sybil suggested.

Katie felt her heart sink, though she knew it was only because of shyness. It felt hard work being with them. But she could hardly refuse.

'Yes, of course,' she agreed, and made herself smile.

Forty-Eight

'Are they coming with us?' Michael asked, excited, as they waited in the hall before setting off on Sunday morning to an early Mass.

'Yes – that's nice, isn't it?' And it was, in a way, not to feel like the only exotic foreigner in the house because she was a Catholic. Katie knew a lot of people regarded the church as the 'Italian mission to the Irish'.

There were sounds of movement upstairs and soon the two of them came hurrying downstairs.

'We are not too late?' Piotr said.

'No – we've got plenty of time.'

Both of them looked appreciatively at her best Sunday dress, a neat navy shirt-waister with a tiny white spot, and her straw hat – also in navy, which she knew was a colour that flattered her.

'You are looking very nice.' Marek half bowed at her to usher her out of the front door.

'Thank you,' she said. Though wary of them, she found herself absurdly pleased by the compliment and couldn't help smiling at their courtly manners.

'It is lovely day!' Piotr said in a stilted way, as if this was something straight from a phrasebook. But they seemed in a good mood, glad that it was Sunday – no work and time to look around and get acquainted with the place. And it was a lovely still, sunny day. It would not take many minutes to walk across to the church in Hunters Road.

'Did you have Mass at the camps?' she asked.

'Here, in England?' Marek said. Walking beside him, she realized just how tall he was, with a loping, wiry strength, and his voice was strong, booming. 'Oh yes, of course.' He explained that in the camps every attempt had been made to keep up precious aspects of Polish culture – the Church, the national dancing – to help people feel at home, yet strengthen their sense of Polishness. 'Our people have lost so much,' he said. 'Their lands and country – and now they belong to the Soviets.' She thought for a moment he was going to spit, his voice was so bitter. 'They keep what they can, in this country.'

'Can you not go back?' she asked.

It was Marek who answered. 'No, we can't.'

'Are you sure?'

'Yes,' he said abruptly. 'Sure.'

A silence followed and then, changing the tone completely, Piotr bent towards Michael. 'Come here, young man – take my hand. Marek . . .' He added something in Polish.

Michael found himself between the two men, being swung high by each hand, and he was soon excited and shrieking with laughter. But soon Marek said, 'Now, it is enough' and handed him back to Katie. She smiled gratefully at them. It was lovely, and sad at the same time, to see Michael with them. He had never had a father to play with him.

'In England there are not many Catholics?' Marek asked her.

'Some. A lot of us are Irish – my father was Irish, you see.'

'He is dead?'

'Yes. When I was very young. His brother took me to Mass.'

'Not your mother?' They seemed curious.

'No – she's English, and not Catholic.'

'She is here: you live close to her?'

Katie hesitated. How could she explain to these men, who seemed to have lost so much of their family?

'No, she lives a long way away,' she said. 'Look – here we are.'

The high brick church loomed over them and they quietened. Walking inside, it took a few seconds for their eyes to adjust to the shadows. She saw Piotr and Marek genuflect deeply and make the sign of the cross, and she did the same as they all found a seat. Michael knew that this was a place where he had to be very quiet and behave. Katie had already started taking him to Mass more often. She felt that the faith that her uncle had passed on to her should be his as well. She had begun to take Michael swimming sometimes too – another good memory of Patrick. When she was standing listening to the altar boys and the priest, taking in the familiar words and the scent of incense, she often thought of her uncle.

Though the Poles struggled with their English, the words of the Latin Mass were common to all of them. Looking along the Victorian church, Katie wondered whether the churches in Poland were the same. Standing beside the two men, she was very aware of all that she didn't know about them and what had happened to them. She found herself praying for them.

As the priest gave out communion and the Mass came to an end, both men stood with their heads bowed. She saw Marek quickly flick each of his eyes with his finger, as if there were tears forming. Piotr's eyes were closed. She felt very moved, sensing the strong emotions flowing through them, brought out by the familiar rituals.

Afterwards they had a word with the priest, who welcomed them.

'Where are you living?' he asked. They explained: in the house of Miss Routh, the same house as Mrs O'Neill. Katie already knew that the priest had some idea who Sybil was. Everyone seemed to know her.

On the way back they walked in silence for a few minutes, and the men seemed lost in thought.

'Why did you leave the camp?' she asked, thinking there they could be among their own people, the comfort of it.

'Too much camp,' Piotr said.

'We will have to leave one day,' Marek said. 'We want to find job, have life in house and street – find woman!'

Again, the bluntness startled her. 'Not a Polish woman?'

'Um, perhaps,' Piotr said with a grin. 'But for Poles, there is shortage. Too many soldiers – not so many women.'

'Ah,' Katie said, then laughed suddenly as they were approaching Sybil's house. 'I think I might have the answer for you.'

Standing by their front gate, very obviously waiting, were Mrs Arbuckle and Susan, all in their Sunday finery. Both of them wore wide-brimmed hats made of white straw. As the four of them came up to the house, the Arbuckles' attention was riveted by them.

'Woo-hoo – good morning!' Edna called out. She was wearing a voluminous purple frock. Susan's was of a swirling pink-and-white pattern. Both were smiling broadly. 'We were just off to church! I don't think we've been introduced?' She stepped into their path.

'Morning, Mrs Arbuckle,' Katie said. 'These are Miss Routh's new lodgers: this is Mr . . .' Once again she realized she had no idea what their surnames were and was sure that, even if she had, she would not have been able to pronounce them. 'Mr Piotr. And Mr Marek. This is Mrs Arbuckle from next door – and Miss Arbuckle.'

'Oh, you can call her Susan – we don't need to stand on ceremony!' Edna seemed almost overcome by the two strong handshakes she received, the polite nods.

'How d'you do?' they both said. In the sunlight Katie realized suddenly just how handsome Marek was, his eyes a vivid blue. And Piotr looked strong and masculine. Susan appeared shy and uncomfortable when faced with the two of them, but her mother was smiling from ear to ear.

'Well, we *are* pleased to meet you,' she gushed. And, after dithering for a few seconds, 'Well, we'd better be off. Come along, Susan.'

As they turned to the house, Sybil was coming out as well. She smiled.

'Ah, so you've been introduced, have you? Mrs Arbuckle is our neighbour – and she is looking for a husband for her daughter . . .' Sybil limped on past them. 'I expect one of you would like to volunteer? Cheerio, I'm off to church. See you later.'

Marek and Piotr were looking rather bewildered.

'What did she say?' Piotr asked.

Suppressing a smile, Katie said, 'She thinks one of you ought to marry Susan.'

The boys looked alarmed.

'Oh, not me!' Piotr said.

'No, not me,' Marek added. 'I don't think this is right lady for me.'

Katie grinned then. 'Don't you think so? Well, maybe not.'

The fine weather drew everyone outside that afternoon, and Sybil was happy for them to be in the garden. Her whole approach to life seemed to be communal, like a puppy that likes to lie in a heap. The top end of the long garden, with the old shed extending from the back of the house and a brick path running alongside it, was baking hot today. Further down grew two large apple trees, both dense and in need of pruning, and so close together that the ends of their branches were entangled, making a kind of bower, which cast a cool shade over the grass. Katie settled there with Michael on an old rug, trying to read him storybooks they had borrowed from the library, but his attention kept wandering to the bottom of the garden, to where the two Poles had been drawn, as if to a magnet, by Sybil's large vegetable patch.

This was now in full bloom, so that every night they were feasting from it on new potatoes, carrots, runner and French beans, beetroots, lettuces, radishes, spring onions and chives. Against the sunniest wall lazed a tangle of tomato plants, hanging with red fruit. Sybil undoubtedly had green fingers. But she was elderly and needed help. As she pottered, pulling up weeds and depositing them in a trug nearby, Sybil noticed Marek and Piotr watching her, pointing, conferring in Polish as to the names of things.

'Ah, now if you two like gardening, I've plenty for

you to do,' she announced, straightening up, pink in the face, despite the shade of her straw hat.

'Yes!' Piotr enthused. 'We like. We can help you! We do dig – everything!'

'Well, the digging will be later in the year, but there's plenty of weeding and hoeing. I'm stopping now – it's too hot. I'm going to have a snooze in the shade . . .'

'Snooze?' Furrowed brows.

'A sleep. We can work later.'

'No – is OK. We do now.'

'Well, as you please. You know which are the weeds?'

'Of course!'

Sybil came and joined Katie, pulling up her deck-chair. 'Ah!' She sank into it and released her swollen feet from her mannish sandals. 'That's what we need – some young male muscles. And they seem frightfully keen.'

'I want to go there,' Michael said.

'No, you'd better stay here,' Katie said, trying to restrain him. 'You'll get in the way. What about this nice story? Look – Goldilocks came to the cottage . . .'

'No!' Michael squirmed out of her grasp.

'Oh, I don't suppose he'll do any harm,' Sybil said through a yawn. 'Let him go and watch.'

'Go on then,' Katie said. 'But don't get in their way, will you?'

She watched as Michael advanced importantly on the vegetable patch and stood shyly at the edge. There was something touching about the way he was so fascinated by the men, and it made her heart ache. His father had been an absent ghost, just as hers had.

'You want to help?' she heard Piotr say.

Michael nodded and, as Piotr beckoned him forwards, Marek carried the large trug over and laid it at Michael's feet. 'You guard this, OK? When it is full, we go and put over there.' He indicated Sybil's bonfire pile further down.

Katie felt herself relax. After a hard week in the office it was nice to have a little time just to sit, for someone else to look after Michael. Sybil soon fell into a doze, her hat down over her eyes. Katie sat hugging her knees, watching as Michael solemnly accepted the fistfuls of weeds that the two men thrust into his trug. She wondered if gardening made them feel more at home, and felt sad for them. For a few moments she watched Marek's strong limbs bending and straightening, tackling the weeding with a speed and strength beyond anything Sybil was capable of. Piotr started working with the hoe. Michael was happy and Katie smiled, realizing that she was too. With a grateful glance at Sybil, who in her odd way had created a home in this house for various stray dogs, she lay back on the rug and enjoyed the warm, languid afternoon until she fell into a snooze herself.

Forty-Nine

As the summer passed things fell into a routine. Everyone would come back from work, and Marek and Piotr
would almost always head straight out into the garden.
The supply of vegetables began to thin out, and Sybil
was busy bottling and stewing apples and plums from
her trees. They gardened sometimes at the weekend too,
and Michael was usually keen to help, to be anywhere
where the two Poles were. One afternoon they promised Sybil that they would creosote the shed and found
a little brush for Michael to help, with careful warnings
about not getting the acrid-smelling stuff in his eyes or
mouth. Katie had never seen him so proud as when
standing beside the two men with his brush and the
little tin into which they had poured some creosote.

Katie, though she could not admit it to herself, was
drawn to them as much as Michael was. It was lovely to
have some people of her own age around her, other than
Geoff Jenkins, whom she found dull. Piotr, she had
discovered, was a year older than herself and Marek.
The two Poles approached everything with a cheerful
vigour, joking and mucking about in between the hard
work, teasing and cursing in Polish, or sometimes laughing so hard they would end up sitting down.

On Sunday they went with her to Mass. On payday
they disappeared to one of the pubs, where sometimes
they met a few other Poles. Katie assumed they also met

women, though there had not been talk of anyone in particular. They would arrive home late and in high spirits, although one night Katie heard a loud, bitter-sounding argument between them in the room below. The rest of the time they worked hard and stayed in, and sometimes when everyone lingered over the evening meal there would be longer conversations, or they went up to their room.

Katie had made her own attic cosy and had arranged a little corner, a lamp placed next to the armchair where she often sat and read while Michael slept. But when they were all in their rooms, it was difficult not to be aware of the two men living so close to her, the sound of their voices rising from the floor below, sometimes laughter – a loud bray from Marek, or Piotr's deep, rumbling chuckle. She heard glasses clinking, and occasionally there were heated discussions, shouts even, but all in Polish. They soon cooled down. They had too much respect for Sybil to want to cause any trouble.

The sound of them was a distraction. She would sit in her chair, looking across the room with the book in her lap, listening, thinking about them, despite herself. She had shut away any thoughts of men or marriage. Her life now consisted of bringing up Michael. But she couldn't help thinking.

At first when they came she had related more easily to Piotr, who was more talkative and friendly. Marek she had been less sure of. He was more distant, with an intensity about him that made her feel shyer of him. And both of them had come from a different country that was mysterious to her and had experienced things that she knew she did not understand.

Yet as time passed, she found her gaze drawn more and more to Marek, and every so often she would turn to find his quiet gaze fixed on her. She liked watching him in the garden, when his back was turned, that long, strong spine bending and straightening as he forked over the now-empty potato patch, sometimes holding up in triumph a stray potato, which they'd missed first time round. She would look hard at him, wondering. Often she was overcome by the sheer strangeness of a life so brutally uprooted, of their having to come and begin again somewhere new and foreign to them. She was moved by their courage and cheerfulness.

At first she had told herself she was imagining it – the way each of them sometimes looked at her. It was the same way Simon Collinge had looked at her. Wasn't it? Or had she got it wrong. These men were foreigners – perhaps they did everything differently.

Then one warm afternoon, just as she was walking in from the garden, she met Piotr coming from the other direction, by the back door. Both of them dithered, in each other's way.

'Sorry!' Katie laughed, leaning back against the wall to let him pass.

'Thanks!' Piotr smiled, but stopped, fixing her with a stare. To Katie, pressed against the wall, the back corridor suddenly felt very narrow and her summer dress felt thin, and rather too low in the neck.

Piotr faced her, looking into her eyes, his dark-brown ones full of longing. Then he said, 'I would like to kiss you.' And with no further ado she found herself in his arms, his warm lips on hers, his strong, manly smelling body pressed against her. Pushing his tongue in her mouth, he gave her a long, hungry kiss. She was too taken aback to react at first and did not feel repelled by his kiss, just embarrassed. She began to push against him. Piotr drew back.

'Don't,' she said crossly.

'But you are beautiful woman.'

'Well, thanks . . .' She couldn't help being flattered, and she liked him too much to want to offend him, but she felt panic-stricken as well. She had to put a stop to any ideas he might have! 'But you can't just announce that you're going to kiss someone and simply grab them! It's not very polite.'

'Polite?' Piotr looked offended. 'So you did not like my kissing?'

'It was . . . Well, yes – I mean, no . . . Look, it's not that I didn't like it. It's just not right – I mean we're not . . .'

'So, we can be . . .' He made gestures pointing back and forth at her, then himself. 'You, me' – he seemed to rack his brains, then said in triumph – 'we can be courting!'

'No!' Now she really was panicking. 'The thing is, Piotr, I'm not free just to be, well, courting. I have a child . . .'

'So what?' He shrugged, genuinely baffled. 'I like childs . . . children . . .'

Katie edged a little further along the wall, feeling its roughness snagging the cotton of her dress. Piotr gazed longingly and sorrowfully at her breasts.

'You are lovely . . .'

'Yes, but . . .' She would have to be blunt. 'I don't want to be courting with you. I'm sorry.'

He frowned. 'I am not man enough?'

'Man enough? Of course you are. I'm just – I'm sorry. I just don't want it, that's all.'

'We are good friends. You marry me?'

'No!'

'I tell Marek same? He like you too.'

Katie's heart thudded hard and blood flooded her cheeks. Marek – did he really like her? More than like? For a moment she was filled with enormous joy, before it was overtaken by panic. She had to put a stop to this! 'Yes. Tell him the same. We are friends – yes? Not courting.'

Piotr looked disappointed. 'You do not want a husband?'

The question, as well as Piotr's strong gaze, drilled into her. Did she? She tried never to think about it, or allow herself to think she might be loved or have a life with someone. Until now, everything had led to rejection. Better to put up with being lonely than the pain of all that. And even if Marek did like her, could he not tell her himself? None of this felt right, and her main feeling was wanting to get away from it. She was happy how she was – she had Michael and Maudie, and this house. What more could she want?

'No.' She shook her head. 'I don't think so.'

She told Maudie about it the next day, when she'd had time to think, making a joke of it. Maudie, who had only met Marek and Piotr in passing, smiled at first, but then eyed Katie seriously over the ironing board.

'It's a pity, though,' she said.

'What d'you mean?' Katie was indignant.

'Well, they seem rather nice. I know people say things about the Poles, but these two seem really decent – all they do to help Miss Routh and everything. Do you not think you could develop *some* feelings for one of them?'

Just then, little Petie, Maudie's son, came roaring up in fury at some falling-out with his sisters. Most of their conversations happened in broken threads, in between the needs of children. In those seconds Katie thought of Marek's eyes, his gaze often quietly resting on her. When Maudie returned, having sorted out the squabble, she looked squarely at Katie.

'Well? You don't want to be on your own forever, do you?'

'I don't know,' Katie protested, though she knew Maudie's remark had hit home. 'I mean, what's the use in thinking about it? *Que sera sera.* And they're – well, I don't really know them very well. So much has happened to them, and I don't really know what, and . . .'

'Well, why don't you ask?' Maudie said, as if it was obvious.

'I don't like to. It's not that easy. And they're so – well, foreign!'

'Of course there'll be differences.' Maudie hung one of John's shirts rather haphazardly over the back of a chair, and Katie straightened it. 'But it's not as if they come from Outer Mongolia. And they're both Catholic – and so are you.'

'But I don't feel anything: not for Piotr, the one who kissed me.'

'What about the other one?'

Again Marek's face, so often in her mind. That was the truth. But she was so shy of him and he was reserved, not forward or easy like Piotr. She felt drawn in and terribly afraid all at once.

'Maudie, stop being a matchmaker, for goodness' sake! I just don't know, so stop keeping on! And anyway, I'm a disaster with men. I'm much better off as I am – without them!' She knew she sounded really huffy now. 'And by now Piotr will have told him that I'm not interested.'

'Well, aren't you?'

'*No!* I keep telling you.'

'Ah,' Maudie teased. 'The lady doth protest too much, I think . . .'

'Oh, stop it. You're just being ridiculous.'

That night, at supper, Katie asked Marek again how his sister was getting on at the Daglingworth Camp. She knew he had letters from Agnieska sometimes. She did not often start conversations at the meal table, and he looked across at her surprised and obviously pleased. Partly she just wanted him to speak. She enjoyed the deep sound of his voice.

'I think she is OK. They are looking after her and she is feeling a little better. She has . . .' He placed a hand to his belly. 'Sometimes she is sick – I mean her . . .' He ran his hand up and down his front, fumbling for the right word.

'Digestion?' Sybil suggested.

'Yes, I think it is. Her digestion is not so good. Because in the camp, and in Tashkent, everyone was very hungry and sick. Many are dying. But for her, something has been wrong . . . inside . . .'

Katie felt her heart go out to him at this description. What on earth had happened to these people? From the very small amount she had heard it sounded appalling and, to her, unimaginable.

'I hope she feels better soon,' she said gently.

Marek turned to her. 'I hope so too. Thank you.' He smiled.

Every so often she was woken in the night. The first time she had been terrified, jolting upright, the blood banging round her body, unable to identify the noises coming out of the darkness. It did not sound like Michael. It was too far-off and unearthly, a howl of anguish and a cry of terror mixed. It brought her flesh up in goose pimples and she sat hugging her knees. She could not tell which of the men had cried out. It was a sound of distress that touched her to the core, that begged for the offer of comfort.

After a moment she heard a voice from below, quiet and soothing, and the sound began to die away. For a time then she heard the two men talking in low voices, before it all went quiet again. She felt very stirred up by it and lay awake for a long time afterwards.

None of them ever mentioned it in the daytime.

Fifty

'There you are – didn't I tell you?' Maudie said distract-
edly as she wiped Elizabeth's nose. 'Goodness me, we're
drowning in snot in this house – all three of them and
me! I'm astonished Michael hasn't caught it yet . . .
Anyway,' she looked up, 'I told you they'd soon get
paired up. They're far too handsome a pair to be single
for long.'

It was a Friday evening, in the cold of November,
and Katie had come to pick Michael up after work and
have her usual end-of-the-week cuppa with Maudie.
Katie made the tea and Maudie came to sit down at
the kitchen table, mournfully blowing her pink, sore-
looking nose.

'Oh!' She sank onto the chair. 'I feel really grotty
today. And so do the children, of course. Michael's been
angelic, I have to report, amid this sea of pestilence –
and at least they weren't ill enough to stay off school.'
She had Michael and Elizabeth to look after during
school hours.

'Poor you,' Katie said. 'You look all in.'

Maudie pulled back her long hair and retied it in a
rough knot at the back. 'Well, it sounds worse than it
is. It's good for getting sympathy. I think I felt worse
about three days ago. Anyway . . .' She stirred her tea.
'Tell me then – you say there are women in the offing?'

Making light of it (why was she actually aching

inside?), Katie said, 'I think Piotr is fixed up. He keeps talking about a girl called Patsy. And another one called Gina.'

'Ah, a fast worker! And what about the blue-eyed giant – I don't know how you can resist him! Now, if I was single . . .' Maudie gave a mock-pining look, then laughed.

'Marek? Yes, I'm sure there's someone – I don't know her name. I mean, I can't exactly ask.'

'Why not? If it's nothing to you, why should it matter?'

Katie blushed. Maudie's eyes lit up with amusement over the rim of her teacup. 'There you are, you see – you *do* like him! So it matters! Honestly Katie, you're hopeless. What're we going to do with you?'

'Marriage isn't everything,' Katie said grumpily.

'No, it isn't.' Maudie agreed, serious now. 'But if it's a good one – I mean, for all my grumbles, I wouldn't be without John – it can be lovely, honestly.'

Katie walked home through the winter evening, warmed by her chat with Maudie.

'We're lucky, aren't we?' She looked down at Michael, who was holding her hand, muffled up in his coat and balaclava. There was a cold, mean wind, but at least it was clear, no fog tonight. 'Having a nice friend like Maudie.'

'She's my auntie,' Michael said.

'Well, yes – she is, sort of. She's very kind, isn't she?'

A bitter thought of her mother crossed her mind for a moment. Kindness – not one of Vera's gifts. In the end, didn't it matter more than blood ties, for all that people said blood was thicker than water? Not very thick blood in my family, she thought bitterly. Sybil was more of a mother to her in her odd way than her own had been.

They reached Sybil's gate.

'Let's get in out of the cold,' she said to Michael.

As they walked up the path, a voice behind said, 'Hello, we reach home together.'

Katie turned, her heart thumping hard on hearing Marek's voice. *For goodness' sake*, she said to herself. She couldn't seem to help her physical response to his presence, no matter how hard she tried. What on earth was the matter with her!

'Oh – hello!' She smiled in the darkness, trying to sound casual and banged the heavy knocker. 'I'll be glad to be inside – it's very cold, isn't it?'

Marek shrugged. 'Oh, a little bit. Not so bad.'

'Ah, the world's workers,' Sybil said, swinging the door open. 'Oh, and Marek too. Jolly good.'

They all went thankfully into the dimly lit hall.

'We'll just get our things off,' Katie said. Thank goodness she had Michael to busy herself with.

'Are you going to give him his tea, or let him stay up with us?' Sybil asked. 'It is Friday.'

Katie considered, one foot on the bottom step. Marek was standing back politely to let them go first. 'Oh – he's very tired. Maudie's lot have all got awful colds. I think I'll get him to bed in case he's coming down with it too.'

'Right-oh,' Sybil was disappearing out to the back. 'Come down when you're ready then.'

There was another banging on the knocker.

'I expect that's Piotr. Open it, will you, Marek?' Sybil called. 'Save my poor old feet.'

Halfway up the stairs, half dragging Michael, Katie

441

heard Marek open the door, then voices. It was not Piotr, but another man. She paused to listen, only just hearing a voice say, 'I'm sorry to trouble you. I hope I've got the right house.'

Dimly, in the recesses of her memory, the voice seemed familiar, while her more conscious mind only detected a stranger.

'Mrs O'Neill,' Marek called to her with unusual formality. 'There is a visitor for you.'

Katie came down again into the dimly lit hall to see a man standing just inside the front door. All she could make out was a pale face, a head of thick hair, perhaps grizzled, dark eyes, a long, dark coat and in his hands a black trilby, which he held, looking very ill at ease.

'I go . . .' Marek started to say, but she quickly responded, 'No – don't!' Who was this person? She didn't want to be alone with him, whoever he was.

'I . . . The thing is . . .' The man began, then stopped, capable only of false starts. He seemed in a terrible state. Something about him was familiar and Katie was filled with the oddest sensation, half dread, half trembling. She had wondered if one day Simon would come – would he ever? – to find her, find his son. But this was not Simon Collinge . . .

'Are you Katie O'Neill?' the man said at last. She saw him staring hard at Michael, who had also come back down and was standing beside her, holding onto her skirt.

She nodded. 'Why – who are you?' She glanced at Marek, who was also looking bewildered.

'My name . . .' He stopped, in difficulty, and cleared his throat. 'My name is Michael O'Neill.'

'No, it isn't!' Katie heard her son pipe up crossly from her side. 'That's *my* name!'

442

The man smiled faintly. 'Is it now?' She heard the Irish in his voice. She was finding it hard to breathe.

'What d'you mean?' she asked faintly. 'Who are you? Why are you here?'

'I think I must be your father,' he said with an air of humble apology. He was turning the hat round and round in his hands.

Katie heard Marek gasp, or had she gasped herself? She wasn't sure. Her legs were suddenly so useless that she stepped back and had to sit on the bottom step.

'Mom?' Michael sounded panicky. 'What's the matter? Who's the man?'

'But...' All Katie could say was, 'No. *No.* You're dead. You died. She told me.' She was shaking her head, her whole body beginning to tremble.

'Is that what she told you? Well, I suppose it was for the best – I might as well have done, I suppose.' There was a long pause as they stared at each other. 'You're mine all right,' he said. 'You're the girl I remember – and look at him.' He nodded at Michael. 'He's the image of you.'

'Why ... what ...? But you were in bed – you had TB. I saw you. You were sick ... And then you went to the hospital and you never came back...' She clutched at the wooden banister, needing something to hang on to. 'I remember it – I swear I do.'

'It's true, I was sick at one time – I remember. I had some chest problem, bronchitis or something. And I was in bed. She must have told you ... Or you got it muddled. But I didn't die. I' – he held his hands out helplessly – 'I left. I had to; she was ... impossible...'

Katie's mind was spinning. She couldn't think what to ask about the past. Everything she had believed was exploding into pieces. She felt as if she too might fall apart. Why should she want to know about him? Why ask? But she couldn't seem to stop staring at him.

'You've been alive all this time?'

'I've been in Coventry, most of the time. But I always knew that I had a little girl in Birmingham somewhere – a lovely little girl . . .'

Pain flared harshly in her. 'Go away!' She jumped up, screaming at him. 'You just go away and leave me alone! Why have you come back now, when you've been dead to me all this time? What use are you now, after . . . after everything? Get out – just go away from me!'

The sobs started to break out of her and Michael, terrified by his mother's emotion, clung to her, crying too. She pulled him close, clinging to him, dimly aware of Marek and that man – *that man* – talking in low voices. She put her face in her hands and sank back down on the step, crying so deeply that she was aware of nothing until a warm presence materialized beside her, and strong arms were round both her and Michael and she was being held tightly and lovingly.

'It's OK,' Marek said, as they perched side by side on the step. 'It's OK, he's gone, he's gone. No need to worry.'

He let her cry, saying little, just holding her and rocking her slightly until she came back to herself, as if up into the light, and reached into the sleeve of her blouse for her handkerchief. As he released her, she felt him gently kiss the top of her head. She raised her eyes to him. For a moment they looked at each other.

'Thank you,' she said, wiping her eyes, but still barely able to stop crying. 'That was a shock.'

Marek kept his arm round her back and it felt so reassuring. Katie became aware that Sybil was standing

444

close by, drawn from the kitchen by the screams. She said nothing, but her face was full of enquiring sympathy. Michael was quieter now too, watching her.

'It is true, what he said?' Marek asked. His sensitive face was close to hers, his eyes full of tenderness.

'You mean is he really my father? Yes – I think he must be. In some way I knew, as soon as I saw him.'

'But when did you see him last?'

'When I was two – or three. Somewhere in between. She told me – my mother . . .' She wrung her hankie in her hands. 'He was my dad. He was good to me.' She began to weep again. 'And she told me he was dead. That he died of TB . . .' She turned her face up, bewildered. 'Why did she do that? Why?'

Sybil considered. 'The truth was that he left her? Maybe she was too proud to admit it.'

'And he never came back,' Katie said, bitterly. 'Not once, to see me, see how I was. Why has he come now?'

'Who knows?' Sybil said. 'Guilty conscience? My goodness, what a thing – you poor girl.' She became practical, holding her hand out to Michael. 'Now, little man, you come along with me and we'll find you some tea. Mummy will come and join you in a minute.'

Michael took Sybil's hand with complete trust, and Katie and Marek were left sitting side by side on the stairs. She went to pull herself up, but he held her.

'One minute, Katie. I spoke to him, this man, when he is leaving. He said to give you some time to think. Then he said, he like to see you. If you like too, he will meet you – next Saturday.'

Katie stared into his face, searching it for help. 'I don't know what to do – or feel. What should I do?'

A nerve in Marek's cheek twitched, as if some pain was being registered.

'Perhaps you should think for some days. But he is your father. That he is alive is good – no? Perhaps you should meet with him.'

'Yes,' she said slowly. She stared ahead of her.

'Katie?'

'Umm?' She looked round, dazed, into that beautiful face.

Marek couldn't seem to speak, except with his eyes. They drew closer together, and lovingly, gratefully, she allowed herself to be drawn into his arms again and their lips met, both warm and searching.

Fifty-One

Of all places, Michael O'Neill had suggested that Katie meet him in Lewis's that Saturday morning.

By the time she was on the bus into town, leaving Michael with Sybil, she had been through a week of stormy and conflicting emotions. It had been difficult to concentrate at work, and there was scarcely a moment in the day when her father's sudden presence in her life didn't batter at her thoughts. At first there was the sheer shock of finding out that he was alive, yet had not seen him from that day to this. Even more bewildering was that nothing in her family was as she had believed. As her thoughts spun round and round, this realization was followed by a rage that took her over to such an extent that it had sometimes forced her from her chair or bed to pace up and down the room.

They lied to me – the pair of them! Just lie after lie! the voice roared in her head. *He just buggered off, abandoned his wife and child without a word, no help, no money – just turned his back on us without a care!*

Yet she felt just as furious with her mother. Vera's hurt pride at being deserted by her husband had made her concoct all these self-pitying stories – *lies*, call them what they were! And, for her own comfort, she had turned her absent husband into a dead saint. God, what a pair they were!

Some nights Katie actually punched her pillow to let

out some of her anger. All those years she had spent trying to keep Vera happy, feeling sorry for her, doing her bidding and bowing to her moods – only to have her reject her own daughter so violently when she had got into trouble herself, had made *one mistake* . . . Once again, the only person who came out of the situation in innocence was Uncle Patrick, who clearly believed his story that his brother was dead and had been sent back to Ireland for burial. Patrick had still been in Africa when Michael 'died'.

Other emotions would follow the anger. She thought of his remark about her mother. 'Impossible,' he had said. Of course Vera *was* impossible, and how strengthening to hear someone else say so. It wasn't just that Katie had somehow failed as a daughter! Three years he had lived with Vera – was that all it had taken to drive him away? And Katie was filled with curiosity both about exactly what had happened and about him as a man. What was he really like, other than in her mother's fantasies? But then the anger would axe through her again. *You went off and left me with her!*

At times, though, there came other tender feelings. She ransacked her memory, that of her two-year-old self, who held an image of him as kind and loving. Her daddy. These thoughts flooded her with simple longing for all that she had lost or never had. She wanted her daddy – for him to love her.

It had been a tumultuous week. With all this had come the miracle of Marek, another kind of shock, beautiful, warming, that they had spoken their feelings for one another. He had been very kind to her, and considerate, seeing the state she was in. Through the intimate tenderness they shared, she trusted him very deeply already. Yet there were so many gaps in his life and in her knowledge. She did not yet know what had happened to Marek's family, but she was almost sure that it was he who suffered from the terrible nightmares.

'One day, I tell you,' he said, as they sat one evening, perched on the edge of her bed, holding hands as Michael slept. The little lamp was on and the room felt cosy. She looked round at Marek's thin, sensitive face and even in the gloom could see that mixed with his longing to talk was the fear of it – of facing it all again, and the emotion that went with it. It made her feel very tender towards him.

'You shouldn't bottle things up,' she told him, squeezing his hand, so big and warm. 'It'll only make it worse.'

He looked at her. 'Usually people do not ask. They do not want to know. Or I think they would not believe.'

'Well, I'm asking. But only when you feel like it.'

'Yes,' he said, looking down, almost as if ashamed. She stroked his back. He gave a rueful smile. 'Thank you.'

She assumed that most of his family had died, some-how. For him, the idea that you might find a parent when you believed them dead would be a miracle indeed, even though he could see that the situation was different. He encouraged her to go and see Michael O'Neill with an open mind.

'Maybe there was good reason,' he advised. 'Give him a chance. He is your father – that doesn't change.'

Sybil counselled the same. Katie realized that week just how much things had changed in her life. She was openly sharing her problems and concerns with others who cared about her. It felt a new, happy experience.

As she walked into Lewis's tall, imposing building it

was with a prickling feeling of dread. What if she met her mother? Did she even work here still? Surely not, after all this time? And what, more disastrously, might happen if *he* met her? Katie slipped up the stairs, giving the drapery department a wide berth.

There was no sign of him in the Ranelagh Rooms, where they had agreed to meet. She sat feeling very nervous at a table facing the door of the smart room, amid the Saturday shoppers who had come for a breather and a cup of coffee, and told the waitress she would order once her friend arrived. That morning she had chosen her clothes carefully, dressing in her navy business suit, her coat and smartest navy hat, her hair taken up into a neat pleat – almost as if for a lover, she realized, her emotions still flitting between defensive anger and tremulous need. Whatever else, she wanted him to see the best of her. Pulling off her navy gloves, she sat back trying to look composed. Was he going to be late?

He was bigger than she remembered, more imposing. As soon as he entered the room he was noticeable, hurrying a little, his brown coat swinging open, hat perched slightly at an angle on his head, and a scarf in brown-and-faun checks hanging over his lapels. He saw her and seemed to hesitate for a second, his confidence faltering. He gave a slight smile and came towards her, pulling off his own gloves, large and black, and holding out his hand. Katie stood up, her hammering heart making her breathless, and felt her hand gripped in his.

'Well, hello again, Katie,' he said. She could hear the misgiving in his voice. Did he wish now that he hadn't said he would come, she wondered painfully? But he looked closely at her – hungrily almost, did she imagine that? – as she returned his greeting and they released hands and both sat down.

The waitress whom Katie had waved away before approached immediately and they both ordered coffee.

'Anything to eat, Katie?' Michel O'Neill asked. He had a soft, well-spoken voice.

'No – thank you.' She felt as if she might never eat again at that minute.

There was a moment of silence, during which they eyed each other and she tried to build up her inner defences against him. He was looking at her, curious, as if trying to work something out, and she was examining him. Moved, she saw hints of her son in the shape of his brows, the way his eyes crinkled at the corners and the curling black hair, even though the hair of the man in front of her was halfway to grey. It was astonishing, his physical reality, here in front of her. And he looked nervous, vulnerable. For a moment a lump came up in her throat, quite unexpectedly. She had wanted somehow to keep the upper hand in any conversation. This wasn't the moment to start blarting all over the table!

'You must be angry with me,' he said finally.

This was even more unexpected. The lump grew and her eyes filled, and in desperation she looked down into her lap. It took her a moment to be able to say in a strangled voice, 'Yes. I s'pose I am.'

There was another interruption while the coffee cups were arranged on the table and Katie managed to gain control of herself. When they were alone again, she said, in a stronger tone, 'You'd better explain. Start from the beginning and tell me what happened.'

He nodded. 'I will. Here, let's have some coffee.' He leaned forward and poured for them both. Katie grasped the handle of the cup, grateful for its warm contents and for having something to cling to.

Michael O'Neill looked up at her as he sat back. 'You're mine all right. I can still see the little one you were once.'

Oh God, Katie thought as the tears rose in her eyes again. She gripped the cup until she thought she might smash it and swallowed hard.

Perhaps he could see her distress, but he didn't invade it. He took a sip of coffee, followed by a deep breath, and let out a long sigh of preparation.

'The long and short of it was, I couldn't go on living with the woman. Three years, and she'd almost squeezed the life out of me. Do you have any idea?' he asked hopefully.

Katie nodded. 'Yes. Yes, I do. But ... why did you marry her?'

He dragged a hand over his eyes for a second. 'She was a looker. You'll know that. A real lady – full of charm and good manners. Genteel family, but my God what a snakepit they turned out to be. And she was besotted with me – I was exotic, I suppose. Irish boy over here, trying to make good. We were in love, to be sure, but I think in some way she wanted to spite her family. That's a powerful combination, Katie. At the time I'd never met anyone quite like her. I was not long over here, and she seemed to represent part of the whole promise of this country. We made a handsome pair – everyone said so. And she seemed eager to do anything for me: even being received into the Church and ready to bring you up as a Catholic. Of course, that did it with her family – they cut her off. Not one of them even came to the wedding, d'you know that?'

Katie shook her head. But she could have guessed it.

'Well, there was trouble from the start, as you see, but what I hadn't reckoned with was her – just her. What she was like! I think the rift with her family turned her head a bit. Then having you. She was . . . How can I say it? She became fixed on things – I suppose you'd say obsessed. She wanted to manage every single aspect of my life. She was jealous – of nothing! Before she had you, she took to following me to work, although she must soon have seen that there was nothing to look at when she got there – well, except life in an engineering works! At the same time, though, she had me on a pedestal. She'd call me her angel, her saviour . . . all sorts. That time I was sick – the time I think you'd be remembering – my chest was bad, I was in a state. And she was sweet as pie to me, nursed me with every care.' He shook his head, fumbling in his breast pocket and offered her cigarettes. 'Smoke?'

'No, thanks,' Katie said, watching him light up. With a deep pang she found that she knew his hands intimately, the shape of them, the shading of dark hairs on the backs of his fingers, hands that she had once, many years ago, seen close up and been held by. The feeling of longing they gave her was so acute that her chest ached. She distracted herself, watching the way his lips moved round the tip of the cigarette. He blew out a mouthful of smoke and went on.

'The thing was, then, when I was sick, she had me just where she wanted me: in her power. She was truly happy. I heard her singing round the house. I think it would have suited her if I'd been an invalid and she could have had full control over everything.' He gave a visible shudder. 'I don't know – I'm not sure how I can explain it all. How it all added up, so that I couldn't stand being anywhere near her. It was as if she had her

453

hands round my throat, day and night. I thought when she'd had you she might be better, have someone else to take her mind off it. And she *was* obsessed with you. Any mother would be, you were beautiful.'

Katie flushed with pleasure, hearing the genuine affection in his voice.

'I could go on trying to explain. There was something *crazed* about her. It wasn't that she flew into rages or tantrums all that often – it was that quiet, terrible, stifling atmosphere she created.' Katie was forced to nod in admission. Oh, she knew that all right. 'I couldn't stand it, the look she had in her eyes sometimes.' He drew on the cigarette. 'Makes me go cold thinking of it, even now. It wasn't that I was afraid of her harming me – or you. It was something more ... More about just *being* with her.'

He shifted in his seat to cross one leg over the other and gave a tut of frustration as he looked across at Katie.

'How d'you talk about the force of another person, the way they can press on you? Do you know, in any way, what I'm talking about?'

'I lived with her for twenty-one years,' Katie said, meeting his gaze.

'And you left to marry?'

Time for truth, no pretence. 'No. I left because I was having Michael. She refused to have anything further to do with me – or him, it seems.'

Michael O'Neill's eyebrows lifted. 'No? Dear God – just like her own mother. Heaven knows what a nest of miserable puritans they were. And the father?'

'He never married me. He deserted me – just like you.'

She saw him flinch, but the truth could not be denied.

'Then why ...' he asked hesitantly. 'Why did you call him Michael: my name?'

That was when she lost control. 'Because . . .' *Because I remembered you, because I wanted you, wanted you to be a good thing in my life . . .*

But instead all she managed was to put her hands over her face as her shoulders began shaking with sobs.

Fifty-Two

'I can't make it up to you, I know that,' he said later, when she was calmer and they were on their third cup of coffee. 'I can't change the past. But we can start with something – can't we?'

Katie stared at him, then nodded. She sat back, feeling tired from all the emotions inside her.

They had talked for a long time, as others around them came and went. He had told her that he had set up home with another woman soon afterwards, in Coventry, and that he had two more children, a son and a daughter.

'But, did you marry her?' Katie asked.

'No – how could I? At first, I didn't feel I could tell her what the situation was. And then I saw a long line of twisted lies following me throughout my life, if I didn't own up early on. By then we were ready to get married, if it had been possible. She took it badly at first – you can understand it. But in the end, when I'd tried to get across what Vera was like – *is* like – we had to find our own way. We set up as Mr and Mrs O'Neill . . . and *are* so, except under the law and in the eyes of the Church. She wore a ring, but we've never had a ceremony.'

'So,' Katie said brutally, for those children had had their father all this time – *her* father, 'your children are bastards – like mine.'

Michael O'Neill looked shocked, but had to concede that this was the truth. 'You're very straight-talking, aren't you?'

'I suppose I've learned that I might as well be.' She leaned towards him. 'Could you not have come – just once? Or got a message to me, let me know somehow that you were alive? All these years ... And then you turn up out of the blue.'

He looked away for a moment, then back at her. 'It wasn't that I didn't think of it – to start with. But...' He made a helpless gesture with his hands. 'At first it was too tricky. You were so young: how could I see you without her being there? And then time passes – there's a distance. It seems better not to disturb things: you, them ... There's shame in it – it's all difficult. Our situation was already so irregular. A clean break seemed the best. I left you alone. I mean, you might have—'

'Made trouble for you?'

Again he shrugged, uncomfortable. 'It was a possibility ... So you leave it, year after year ...' He did not meet her eyes.

'What're their names?'

'My, er, wife's name is Anne. Our son Thomas is twenty-one now and apprenticed. And our girl is nineteen: her name is Josie. She's soon to marry. That was part of it, I suppose – seeing her now, wondering about you ...'

Katie digested this, her emotions a swarm of jealousy, anger and curiosity. So she had a half-brother and sister!

'Will you tell them about me?' she asked, jutting her chin at him.

'I might,' he said cautiously. 'Only if you'd be wanting me to.'

'We'll see,' she said. 'Maybe.' She looked sharply at

him. 'There's nothing very regular in our family, is there? I was brought up by your brother – and you never even knew.'

Michael O'Neill had been utterly shocked to find out that his brother Patrick had played such a major role in Katie's life. But it was because of Patrick that he had found her. Michael admitted that he and Anne had moved back to Birmingham a few months ago, when he was offered a good job at Wilmot Breeden in Tyseley. They were living off Shaftmoor Lane.

'I went to Mass – I don't go regularly, you know. Not communion, of course – I just slip in the back once in a while, and I went that very first Sunday we were here in Birmingham. And who is the Mass being offered up for, but one Patrick O'Neill? Well, granted, we're not the only O'Neills in the world, and I assumed Patrick must be still with the Fathers in Uganda. It set me thinking about him, though. He was never quite right, you know, my brother. We weren't close – he was a good few years older than me, but he was a good man, a gentle soul, you'd say. They thought the missions would sort him out. He was packed off there – it seemed the thing to do. But because of the name, I had a little word with the priest, expecting to be told that Patrick O'Neill had been some old local fellow. But the Father was quite expansive – he'd known Patrick for a short time before he died, said he was a good man and an asset to the parish.

'So then I asked who had requested the Mass for him. "Oh," says he, "that'll have been his niece, little Katie. She's not living in this parish any more, but I gather she was here as a child. She likes to have a Mass said for him in the parish where he passed away. So far as I know, she's over in St Francis's parish now, in

Handsworth." Well, it all came as a shock to me. You – him.' Michael seemed to run out of words, shaking his head. Again Katie found herself watching his hands, the sprinkling of dark hairs on his fingers. The sight made her ache. Patrick's had been thinner, the skin papery and dry.

'He was good to me,' she said, tears filling her eyes again. 'As far as he could manage.'

Michael looked searchingly at her. 'Was he ... all right? In himself?'

She shook her head. 'Mom tried to hide it – to hide *him*. He was, well, up and down in himself. I didn't understand when I was small. Well, I'm not sure I do now, but I can see it differently. It was very bad sometimes, poor man – he used to disappear. He was a bit like a dog, you know? Going off to lick his wounds, then coming back when he could manage. But he was always kind. He was a tormented soul – no one should have to live like he did. There must be an answer to it. I suppose you wouldn't know ...' Somehow this was news she didn't want to give harshly, and she spoke in a soft voice. 'That he took his own life?'

'Dear God. Oh dear God!' She could see he was truly shocked and grieved. 'Now you say it, the way that priest talked about him ... He didn't mention it, but there was a shadow in the way he spoke of him. Patrick was a sweet lad as a youngster – too sweet for this world.'

'Yes,' she agreed. 'He drove Mom to distraction, but she needed him – and he needed someone, and somewhere to be.'

'In that case, I'm glad. He did something for me that I would never have guessed, God rest him.'

*

459

They sat talking for well over two hours. As they passed through the big department store out into the cold street, Katie had a prickly feeling that Vera was there, somewhere, watching. And she said so to Michael O'Neill.

'Heaven forbid!' was all he said.

Outside there was a light drizzle and for a moment they were both at a loss. Then both went to speak at once.

'You first,' she said.

He seemed wary now, his eyed veiled. 'I've told you – I can't offer you anything much . . .'

Her anger flared. Was he implying that she was after something, might be on the make? 'Why would you think I need anything from you after all this time?'

'I just mean . . . Look, I don't know. It's a difficult thing, to disturb a family after all this time.'

'Your wife, Anne – she knows I exist?'

He looked down at the wet pavement. 'No.'

Bitterness filled her. 'I see. So you were only truthful up to a point?'

He looked up. 'You've grown into a tough woman, Katie.'

She felt her mouth twist. 'It's what life has taught me. Mother's milk.'

He seemed to soften. 'I'd like us to see each other. I'd like everyone to meet each other, for it to be good, but we can't be sure of that. They might take it very badly.'

Despite her anger, Katie could see that this was costing him something. After all, he could have stayed away forever. And she realized that she didn't want her own life disturbed too abruptly, either.

'Let's meet again like this, shall we?' he said. 'Take it slowly?'

And she agreed. That would be a start. They arranged to meet in three weeks' time.

He looked down at her, with an open gaze now. 'I'm sorry, Katie – for all of it.'

Something in her relaxed a fraction. She had needed to hear his apology.

'So am I,' she said.

She longed to go back and pour it all out to Marek – all that they had said, and how she felt. It was the first time she had ever felt that way, that she could say everything she needed to say without fear.

When she got back to Sybil's house, Sybil was in the kitchen and Michael with her, standing on a stool, making pastry. He was wrapped in a large apron liberally dusted with flour.

'You look busy,' she said, kissing his warm cheek.

'We're making tarts,' he said.

'All right?' Sybil asked her cautiously, and Katie nodded. They would talk later.

'Is Marek in?'

'No – they've both gone out for a while. I believe they're looking for a room for Piotr. It's a shame we don't have more space here, but short of putting him in the storeroom, we can't really manage. But the sister will be arriving soon – around Christmas, I gather.'

Katie wasn't completely sure how she felt about Agnieska's arrival. She was pleased for Marek, of course, but also a little jealous of his company. She told herself not to be so selfish.

'He left you something, I believe,' Sybil said with a twinkle. 'Go up and see.'

Puzzled but excited, Katie went upstairs. Outside her room she found a jam jar of Sybil's and, in it, a bunch of pink carnations. He must have gone out and bought them!

Picking them up with a cry of pleasure, she took them into her room and put them on the chest of drawers. Then she sank onto the bed and sat looking at them, full of wonder. No one had ever given her flowers before.

They had no chance to be alone until later that evening. After Michael was asleep and they had all had their meal, she let Marek into her room. They both sank onto the squeaky bed, laughing quietly. She had the little side-light on that stood by her armchair.

'See – the flowers look lovely,' she whispered, and kissed his cheek. 'Thank you, thank you!'

'It is a pleasure.'

'Where's Piotr?'

'Ah – he is out with lady. Her name is Polly – I think. Or Brolly . . .'

'That's an umbrella,' Katie giggled. 'Maybe Molly?'

'Ah yes, umbrella. Yes – I think it is Polly.'

They were close, side by side and he reached over and took her hand. She stroked his long-fingered, strong hand in both of hers, then looked up into his eyes. The expression in his, and the intense way he looked at her, made her lurch inside.

'So you tell me – about your meeting with your father. It was OK?'

'Yes, it was all right.'

He put his arm round her and she snuggled closer to him, marvelling that this was possible, at how lovely he was.

'All right? Is that all you English can say? All right – all right?'

'Well,' she protested, 'I don't know where to start. It was so strange.'

'Come here . . .' Marek lay back and urged her to lie beside him, in his arms. It was not the first time they had lain kissing and touching. Both knew they longed for more, but it was just not possible or right, in the circumstances.

She settled beside him and he rested his big, warm hand reassuringly on her head. And she began to talk.

Fifty-Three

'It's a shame it's not a nicer day,' Katie said. 'A bit of sun would have made everything look more cheerful.'

'It does not matter,' Marek said, and for a second he took her hand. He needed to touch her often, to be physically close to her. He wanted to do everything with her – shopping and errands, taking Michael swimming, which they now sometimes did together.

Every so often the sun did break through for a few seconds, but it was a blustery December morning of racing clouds. Katie had hung her umbrella over her arm just in case. She and Marek, with Michael sitting between them, had ridden across town and climbed down from the bus in Nechells into this buffeting wind. She had expected Michael to complain, but he was too excited at having an outing to pay any attention to the weather. It was a very unusual Saturday morning for him, especially as Marek had promised that on the way back they'd stop off for a treat – a bite to eat in town.

Katie had watched with tender amusement as Marek spoke to her small son. Sometimes she found Marek remote, mysterious, locked into quiet moods that she could not read. But today he himself was almost childishly excited, out on a treat, sweet and affectionate to her and indulgent with her son, bending his tall frame down to listen when Michael spoke to him. She could see how much this meant to him: being a family, and having found someone to love. It tugged at her heart, thinking about all he must have lost.

'This is Nechells?' Marek asked, pronouncing it carefully.

'This is it.' She watched his face for a reaction. After Sybil's house, among the large villas of Handsworth, the place looked cramped and mean. Here, bomb-damaged streets of tightly packed houses mingled with factories small and large. There was little space for trees or gardens, and many of the houses were grimy and in very poor repair. She could see that Marek was surprised.

'You were poor?' he asked bluntly.

'Yes – we were. My mother was left on her own. My uncle tried his best but . . . well, I told you.'

'And your mother – she still lives here?'

'No. Remember, we moved to Sparkhill. I don't know if she's moved again by now, though. Come on, I'll show you our old house.'

As they walked around she pointed out to Michael the power station in the distance. He gazed at the huge cooling towers and, as they went along Rupert Street, at the gas works, the rusty gasometers of which they caught glimpses. Marek seemed fascinated.

'Such a big city,' he said. 'Where I come from – is small town. Quiet. Many farmers and activities like making bricks, or tools for the fields. You like here?'

'Yes. It was OK. I'd never known anything else. My mother didn't like it – she thought she was too good for it. But I remember some nice people.'

She led Marek along Kenilworth Street, feeling conscious suddenly that they might be being watched. Would anyone have recognized her? No, of course not. And if they did, why should she feel she had anything to hide now? The street let them pass, oblivious to their presence.

Katie exclaimed over all the details of the street that she remembered: the raw gaps where bombs had fallen, the timber yard and, further along, the cycle finishing works. She stopped, aware with the prickling feeling that she was standing by Em's old house.

'That was where my friend lived . . .'

She pointed, seeing the old green door, which looked much the same, and felt a deep pang for all the times she had run to knock on it for Em to come out and play.

'See that entry there?' She pointed to the alley going along into a yard. 'Another girl from my school lived up there – Molly Fox she was called.' Katie shook her head. Looking back now, she could see how hard she and everyone else had been on Molly – except for Em, who had been kind. Poor Molly, she'd never done anything wrong, she'd just been unlucky in her family. Now she was able to give Molly credit. She had always tried, heartbreakingly hard it seemed now, to join in, to make friends, however much they all teased and rejected her. 'You know, her brother was hanged . . .' She had to explain to Marek. 'Put to death by the law – he murdered a woman.'

'Oh!' Marek said. 'Well, that's not good!'

'No – he was vile, even when he was six years old. Poor old Molly, I heard she joined up in the war.'

They walked on towards the old house. So many things remained unchanged. Except, of course, for the gaping hole in the row of houses where that funny old couple lived. Katie struggled to remember them, their names. That was it: Jenny and Stanley Button. Kindly souls – and how she had been encouraged to look down on them by her mother! Vera, who had been scraping a living just as Jenny Button did with her bakery, yet thought she was so superior. Katie felt full of indignation. Life had certainly taught her a thing or two about who was worthwhile in this world!

'Oh, and look – that used to be the pawnshop.' She explained what that was. 'It's closed, by the look of things. And our little sweet shop! There were two old ladies used to run it: twins. Funny old ducks. I wonder if they're still there? They can't be – they used to look as old as the hills when I was young!'

They walked slowly past, peering in.

'Oh!' Katie stifled a cry. 'I saw her – one of them! Heavens above, I'd've thought they'd've been long gone. They can't have been as old as I thought. Yes – the Misses Price: Lucy and Madeleine. It was ever so hard to tell them apart, they used to dress the same and everything. Well, fancy that. And this' – she turned round – 'is where we used to live.'

They looked up at the narrow house, two storeys and an attic on top. It was in poor repair and the windows were dark and uncurtained. It did not look inviting.

'Uncle Patrick lived there, where that window is, and up there my mother did her sewing in the attic . . .' She could imagine walking into the house, going up the dark stairs, every tread of them still familiar, Vera, back ramrod straight, sitting at her sewing table. She moved closer to Marek and took his arm, squeezing it. He looked down at her.

'So – your childhood home.'

'Thank God it's now, not then,' she said passionately. She wanted to get away from it, the memories of the house were oppressive. 'Come on, we'll go and have a

467

mooch round. I'll show you the baths and a few other things, and then we can go back into town.'

It was tiring walking. Katie kept having to hold her hat on, and Michael was beginning to whine in the cold.

'This is mostly where we went to the shops,' she said, along Great Lister Street. 'OK, Mikey – we'll be getting back on the bus soon. This is where your mom used to do her shopping when she was little.'

A figure caught her eye suddenly, standing by the greengrocer's shop. Katie squinted, blinking her eyes, which were watering in the wind that was bellying up the awnings of the shops. She didn't think she knew the woman, who was talking to someone out of sight under the awning, but she seemed familiar: a quite tall, rather splendid figure with a head of thick, metal-grey hair pinned up in a thick pile on her head. Curious, she walked closer, racking her brains to think who it was. She had dark eyebrows and a strong, handsome face. That was it! That lady who lived next to Em, such a kind, energetic person – Mrs Wiggins!

As they moved up close, she saw the woman eye her, though without recognition. She realized that she and Marek made a striking couple walking along the street: she with her dark, pretty looks, and he tall, with his unusual chiselled face and blue eyes. On impulse, Katie said quietly to the woman, 'Excuse me – sorry to bother you. Are you Mrs Wiggins, by any chance?'

The woman looked curiously at her. 'Well, I'm not, as it happens, she said; but I used to be. I'm Mrs Alberello now – have been for years. Do I know you, bab?'

'I used to live in this road,' Katie said. 'Years ago—'

'Katie?' a voice said.

Ducking her head under the awning, Katie saw the

468

person to whom Dot Alberello had been talking. Standing by a pile of parsnips in her working overall, looking much the same as ever.

'Em?'

'Who's this then?' Dot said. 'Your face does look a bit familiar.'

Katie explained where she had lived, that they had moved away. 'Em and I were pals at school,' she said.

Em smiled. 'Yes,' she agreed softly. 'Best friends.'

'How are you, Em?' Katie asked. She saw forgiveness and welcome in Em's smile and felt flooded with happiness.

'I'm all right, thanks. Living with my in-laws, which is a mixed blessing – I was just telling Dot.'

Dot gave a comical, 'Oh well, can't be helped' sort of grimace. 'I'll be off, Em, she said. 'I'm popping in to see your mother. Take care of yerself, bab – don't do anything I wouldn't do! See you soon.' She nodded at Marek, with a curious air, and departed with her shopping.

'What about you, Katie?' Em asked. 'You're not living round here, are you? And is that your . . . ?' Em nodded towards Marek and Michael.

'Marek,' Katie said, 'come and meet my friend Em – Emma . . . not Brown any more then?'

'No – Stapleton.'

Marek smiled and shook her hand and they both said nice-to-meet-yous. Katie saw that Em was intrigued by Marek.

'My friend,' Katie added. There would be a chance, she hoped, to explain about Marek – about everything – some other time. She told Em that they were lodging over in Handsworth.

'And this is my little boy, Michael.'

469

'Oh, isn't he lovely!' Em made much of Michael, and Mr Perry came out and said hello as well and handed Michael an orange. 'Don't tell anyone.' He winked. Em told Katie about her own boy, Robbie.

Katie knew it was up to her, if she wanted Em's friendship, to do something about it now. She owed Em. And she did want it – she was full of need for the friendship, and felt happiness at the prospect. And now she felt able to reach out.

'It'd be nice to see you properly sometime, Em,' she said, nervously. 'That's if you've got time, and everything. Maybe on a Sunday?'

Em's kindly face lit up. 'That'd be lovely,' she said. 'Of course I've got time. And you can bring Michael round to meet Robbie. Robbie's a bit older of course, but we'll find something they can do.'

She wrote her address down for Katie. Saltley. 'It's a long way for you to come,' Em said. 'You could come here instead – to our mom's.' She too was eager, joyful. 'We'll have to come and see you one day.'

'Come and play in the park,' Katie said. 'It's very nice over there. But I'll come first – you've got enough on your plate.'

They said their goodbyes. Michael walked along proudly holding his orange, the brightest thing in the street.

'An old friend?' Marek said.

'Yes.' Katie felt like skipping, she was so happy. Already something felt healed, as if a load had fallen off her. 'An old friend.'

Fifty-Four

'Penny for them – you look full of the joys!' one of the other shorthand typists said one morning the next week at work. 'Are you here with us?'

Katie, who had sunk into a daydream in front of her typewriter and was gazing out at the clouds, jolted back to reality. Everyone seemed more friendly at work suddenly.

'Yes, I'm here, just about,' she laughed

Her friend was already passing on with her filing, but Katie kept smiling. Her life had suddenly become so full that she could hardly keep up with it. There was Marek, and now the reunions with her father and with Em, both of whom she hoped to see again soon. Bubbles of joy, excitement, apprehension rose in her. Would it be all right? Would she see them? Could she trust that things might be better? It was all so much, suddenly, when she had had so little, had lived her life in a closed, starved way. This new happiness seemed to make her able to be more open with everyone.

As Christmas approached, the day was drawing closer when Marek's sister Agnieska would arrive. Katie was apprehensive. Would she like Agnieska? She felt rather in awe of the young woman, because of the astonishing journey she had made and all that she had endured, even if Katie was not sure exactly what that was.

She told herself not to be selfish, worrying that Agnieska would draw Marek's attention away from her. She knew she was in danger of being jealous. Now she had found someone she could be so close to, she didn't want it taken away. But she knew that she, too, had demands on her time and emotions, and that Marek was having to make allowances for that. While they wanted to spend every moment they could together, there were other people in their lives who had to be given attention.

On the Saturday before Christmas, Katie and Michael O'Neill had arranged to meet. Once again they met at Lewis's, but this time she took little Michael.

'We're going to see someone very special,' she told him. 'Your granddad.'

Michael was less astonished by this information than she had imagined he might be.

'Children are funny, aren't they?' she said to Sybil. 'You suddenly produce a grandfather out of the air, and they just take it in their stride. I was worried about them meeting, but Michael seems quite happy about it.'

Sybil laughed. 'Yes – at that age, if you tell them something's normal, they believe it. Besides, it must be nice to discover you've got a grandpa suddenly.'

'Well, yes, Katie said. 'I only hope he turns up. He might have got cold feet. I don't even have his address. It's somewhere Hall Green way.'

When they got off the bus in town she was still full of misgivings that he would not keep their date. How disappointed Michael would be. And though she told herself it wouldn't matter so much – after all, she'd got through all these years without him, hadn't she? – she knew she would be desperately disappointed if he let her down again now. He had said to meet her in The Minories, the walk-through that ran under Lewis's building. As they turned the corner to walk below the building, her heart was thumping uncomfortably and she felt queasy with nerves. But immediately she saw him, waiting for her to one side of the 'rubber road', as it was known, near the wall, standing very straight and tense. When he caught sight of her, he made a slight bow from the waist and tipped his hat. Katie took a deep, relieved breath.

'Mikey, this is your granddad,' she said, her hand on her son's back, urging him towards the stranger.

For a moment, tall man and small boy, both with remarkably similar Irish blue eyes and dark hair, regarded each other. Michael's head was tilted slightly back. Then Michael O'Neill senior squatted down and held out his hand. Katie smiled, tears pricking her eyes as her son shook that familiar hand and she heard her father say, 'Well, young man, it's a great pleasure to meet you.'

'To meet you too,' Michael repeated, unsure. 'Are you my granddad?'

'I am that,' Michael O'Neill said.

And little Michael gave a wide-eyed, trusting nod.

'Come on then, young fella.' The newly found grandfather stood up. 'We've a few things to do.'

It wasn't a morning for a lot of talking. Instead they took Michael to see Father Christmas, and Michael O'Neill treated them to a cup of tea and a cake afterwards. Katie was still shy with him, a bit unsure how to behave. But the fact that he had come to meet her again, had kept his promise, meant the world to her.

'How are your family?' she asked.

'Oh, they're well, thank you,' he said. *Have you told*

them about me? she wanted to ask. But not with Michael present. And in fairness, even she could see that it was early days. That could wait. He was here. He was her father and Michael's grandfather. She enjoyed him watching Michael tuck into his cake, eyes alight with amusement at the boy's blissful enjoyment, cream oozing around his lips.

'He's a fine little fella,' he told her, and Katie blushed with pride. She could see that he genuinely liked children and was taken with Michael.

As they left that day, they were just approaching the stairs when a figure crossed in front of them, seeming in a hurry, and passed down the stairs. A middle-aged woman, slender, elegant. Katie gasped: the faded hair, the smart look. Was it...? But then she saw the woman's walk, something about the angle of her head – it was wrong. It was not Vera O'Neill.

'What's the matter?' Michael O'Neill asked. Katie had stalled giddily at the top of the stairs.

'That woman – I thought for a moment it was her!'

He looked down after the disappearing figure. 'Ah, no,' he said easily. 'Not her, too small.' He seemed so certain after all this time. 'If it was her, I'd have known.'

Katie felt shaken, though.

'What about your mother?' he asked quietly as they went on down. 'Will you go and see her?'

'Why?' She was furious suddenly. 'Will you?'

'Me – no! What would that do? Only harm.'

Katie was quiet as they went out of the store and into Corporation Street. Then she turned to him.

'She's my mother,' she said. 'I feel I ought to see her. As if I owe her, out of duty. But she ditched me. She hasn't once come and found me. And as for harm – well, I feel as she's the one who'd do harm to me!'

474

'Look, I wasn't saying you should.' He looked down kindly at her, but his voice sounded weary. 'I'm in no position to preach, am I?'

'No,' she agreed. 'You're not.'

'I'll be on my way now, Katie. Happy Christmas – and I'm so glad you've found someone good ... for yourself.'

For a moment it sounded as if he was saying goodbye, forever. She was afraid he had had enough!

'Will I see you?' she asked in panic.

'Of course.' He squatted down again for a second. 'Goodbye, little fella – see you again soon.' To her, he added, 'You have to understand, it's delicate. But I give you my word, Katie – I wouldn't have come back into your life unless I'd intended to stay, in some form or other. We just have to wait and see what form that is. That's all I can say.'

She felt a pang. *But I want all of you. I don't want to share you!* Then she thought of Marek. Take what there is and be glad, she told herself. You have more now than you ever dreamed of.

She turned as they walked away, and she and Michael waved at the tall figure who stood watching them, one arm raised.

On Saturday morning, Sybil opened the door to find the Arbuckles on the front step. Katie, who had been halfway up the stairs, paused on hearing their voices.

'Oh, good morning, Miss Routh,' Edna gushed. 'Sorry to disturb you so early, only we wanted to be sure he hadn't gone out or anything.'

Then came Susan's deep voice. 'What Mom means is, we've come to see Mr Pee-ot.'

475

Though, as Polish names go, Zielinski – Piotr's surname – was not the most difficult to pronounce by a long chalk, Piotr was always known by everyone as 'Mr Piotr' or just 'Mr P'.

'Ah, I think he's still in,' Sybil said. 'Why don't you come in a minute?'

Continuing up the stairs, Katie said, 'I'll call him. Just a minute!'

'Ah,' Sybil said. 'Thank you, dear.'

From below she heard Edna Arbuckle say, 'The thing is, we heard that he's been looking for a room, and we thought: Well, what a stroke of luck – he need look no further!'

Katie ran upstairs and knocked on Marek and Piotr's door, and in a second Marek appeared.

'It's the neighbours,' she hissed, with a mischievous grin. 'For Piotr.'

'What?' Piotr came to the door, bemused.

'Those ladies – from next door,' she whispered. 'I think they want you to go and live with them!'

Piotr's eyes widened.

'They've got a room for you!'

'Go on then.' Marek shoved him towards the stairs. 'You have no luck so far . . . Now is here on a plate for you . . .'

'I expect you'll have to marry Susan,' Katie added. 'As part of the arrangement.'

Piotr rolled his eyes. 'What – they are here?'

Marek and Katie were finding it difficult to control their laughter.

'Go – you are keeping them waiting.'

While Piotr went off downstairs Marek pulled Katie swiftly into their room and into his arms.

'Good morning, my darling!' He beamed into her face, then kissed her enthusiastically on the lips.

'Ooh, you're terrible!' she laughed. 'Come on – let me go. I only came up here to get Michael's shoes!'

But for a moment she snuggled into his arms and kissed him back.

'Listen – Piotr's coming back.'

Footsteps thundered up the stairs and he came rushing into the room, grinning. 'Aha, caught you. I knew you two would be all "lovey-dovey"' – he said the words as if reading them mockingly from a dictionary – 'behind my back!'

Marek said something in Polish that sounded fairly ripe, then went on. 'Come on – you are going to marry Miss Susan?'

Piotr became solemn and gave a little bow.

'As matter of fact there is big news . . .' He paused for effect. 'Miss Susan has boyfriend!'

'WHAT?!' Katie and Marek reeled in exaggerated surprise. Marek fell back on his bed, legs waving in the air as if poleaxed by this information.

'Yes, she has man called Percy who is fish man – he is coming to collect her today for taking to pictures.'

'Oh, well, that's lovely!' Katie said. 'You mean he's a fishmonger? Oh, *I* know who you mean – he's a great big, strapping bloke!' She laughed. 'Oh yes, just right!'

'Her mother is very happy,' Piotr said.

'I bet she is! Oh well, that's nice news, it really is. So what did they want you for?'

Marek sat up, still grinning.

'They offer me a room. We have many rooms, they say. Why you not come and live in one of them? But, I am thinking, why do I go and live in room of these nice ladies? Why not Agnieska live next door with nice ladies, and I stay here with Marek's stinking feet?'

'Actually, Marek, that's a good idea,' Katie said, serious now and full of relief at the idea that things might not have to change as much as she thought. 'Your sister could have a room to herself next door, with ladies to look after her. It might be nicer for her.'

Marek began to look pleased. 'You know, Piotr – you have some brain in your head for once. What did you tell them?'

'I said I ask you.'

'Weren't they a bit disappointed,' Katie asked, 'not having you instead?'

'Well, yes, of course,' Piotr shrugged, 'but I tell them about Agnieska, little bit, and they ... You know, really, they are very kindly ladies. I told them we come to visit and they looked pleased as.... How you say it?'

'Punch?' Katie suggested.

XI

EM

Fifty-Five

December 1948

'Eh, bab – don't forget your tokens!'

Em turned as her mother-in-law called from the front door. In the past she would have found Edna's help interfering, but she had learned to be more accepting as time went by. She had to admit that Norm's parents had been very good to them.

'Oh, ta!' She loosed Robbie's hand a minute and took the little bag of red-and-green tokens to pay their bus fare. 'I'll forget my own head one day. See you later.'

'Tara . . .' Edna even waved her hankie at Robbie.

'Come on, Robbie – let's get going.'

The bus tokens were included in the treatment. Someone at the school had decided that Robbie was looking peaky, and he suffered from catarrh. Every day that week she was expected to trek across to Erdington with him on the bus for sunray treatment, though no one had told them exactly what the point of it all was, other than that it would be good for him.

'I don't like it,' Robbie protested. 'Them goggles smell horrible and rubbery.'

'Never mind,' Em said, hurrying him to the bus stop. She could have lived without all this carry-on as well. It meant her having to offer to work late in the shop.

'I suppose they know best. And you just make sure you don't let those goggles slip off – that light's bad for your eyes. It can blind you.'

Robbie sat in his seat on the bus, harrumphing. Em smiled to herself at his stormy expression. She knew her little ruffian of a son was none too keen on stripping down to his undies, either, and sitting on the circular wooden planking with other children, goggles on, soaking in the bright light.

'Feel like a right pansy,' he muttered.

'Oh, Robbie!'

'Don't laugh! T'ain't funny!' He folded his arms crossly and stared out of the window as if the end of the world had come. '*You* don't have to do it, do yer?'

No, she thought, but I have to cart myself all the way over here with you. Then another thought came. If he's the only child I'm ever going to have, I ought to make the most of every moment with him. Softening, she reached to stroke his hair.

'Mom!' Outrage. 'Gerroff! Stop being soppy!'

The treatment, in the Slade Road clinic, being over, they travelled back and Em went to work. Later, as she went to Cynthia's to pick Robbie up, she walked along in the freezing, foggy evening, longing for a cup of tea. It was a nice thought that Robbie was at her mom's. She liked getting there, finding him in that house. Where would Mom be without him? She felt as if by providing Cynthia with a grandson, she had kept her happy and busy. Even her father's death had not knocked Cynthia for six, as Em had feared.

Ever since Bob had died, Em felt she had the weight of the world resting on her shoulders. There was her own grief for him, quiet man though he had been. She missed him sitting there by the fire, always with a cigarette; his smiles when he saw her, his occasional jokes, his reminiscences about the war: *D'you remember the night Ashted Wharf went up . . . ?* Now there were only Mom and Joyce and Violet living there, and Joyce, now twenty-one, had been going steady with Larry and was planning to get married the next year. Em had always felt responsible for the household, but all the more so now, with her dad gone. Cynthia had wept and wept when Bob first died, and Em knew she missed him terribly. Dot had been dropping in more than usual, from Duddesdon, but she had her own troubles. Her husband Lou was none too well, either.

Sometimes Em felt overwhelmed by her worries. It was bad enough being shoehorned in with Norm's mom and dad, and with she and Norm struggling for any sort of private life. And as well as mourning her dad, she was now mourning the fact that it seemed certain she and Norm were going to have any more children. They had talked about it off and on, but after a while there didn't seem to be anything more to say. If she ever mentioned it now, Norm got scratchy with her and said things like, 'Well, what d'you want me to do about it – eh?' She knew he was angry and blamed himself, and in her heart of hearts she blamed him too. And there was Robbie, headstrong and hardly ever her little boy any more. All that was enough – but having to worry about Mom and the others just added to her burden. She knew she frowned more than she used to, and saw little lines appearing on her forehead and around her mouth.

'Hello, bab,' Cynthia greeted her, huddled up in a thick grey cardie. 'Kettle's on. You look famished.'

'I am.' She headed straight for the range to warm up. 'My feet're like blocks of ice. There's a darned great hole in this one – look.' She took off her left shoe and held it up. The piece of card she had slipped in to cover the hole was sodden. 'Umm, something smells nice. You doing a stew?'

'After a fashion,' Cynthia said. She had never had a very high opinion of her own cooking.

Violet was sitting at the table with Robbie, doing something with him, their heads bowed over a piece of paper. She had at last got round to getting some specs, and was peering through their pink plastic frames now. The first time she put them on, she'd said it was like a miracle – she'd had no idea that there was so much to see! She looked up and smiled. 'Say hello to your mom,' she said, nudging Robbie.

''Llo, Mom.' He didn't even look up. Violet made a wry face, and Em tried not to mind.

'Joyce not back yet?'

'No – she'll be along,' Cynthia said, handing her a cup of tea. 'Here, get this down you, and come and sit down – I've got something to tell you.'

Em saw that she was looking quite cheerful.

'Mom's got a job,' Vi said.

'Oi, I was going to tell her!' Cynthia said indignantly.

Em felt herself freeze, just as she had been starting to thaw out. A job – Mom! How was that possible?

'What d'you mean?' she said stupidly.

'You know – a job. For money,' Violet said, as if Em was a halfwit.

'All right, you. Just 'cos you're going to night school.'

Violet was a bright girl, and ambitious. 'I'm not working on the factory floor all my life,' she had said.

484

'I want to get on – at least have a job in an office. So she had taken herself off to the Commercial School in the evenings.

'It's only cleaning,' Cynthia said. 'At The Woodman.'

'Where's that?'

'Over in Cattells Grove.'

Em found herself full of a mounting panic. 'But – I mean, *why*?' She found she couldn't cope with the idea. In all her years, Mom had never had a job outside the house!

'Well, I wanted to get out a bit. And for the money – you know, the usual reasons, and I heard the landlord was looking for someone . . .'

'But you can't!' Em snapped. She found herself close to tears. Mom not here, in the house the way she always was – it was unthinkable! 'I mean, what about all our arrangements? What about Robbie? If you're not here . . .'

'I've told you, love,' Cynthia said, taken aback by her fury. 'It's only mornings. I'll be back to pick up Robbie as usual – wouldn't miss it for the world.'

'What's up with you?' Violet said peering at her. 'What the hell's wrong with Mom getting a little job?'

'I . . . nothing,' Em said, swallowing down her emotion. Of course she was being silly. But why did she feel so betrayed? And as if her father was being betrayed, too. Things were just changing too fast.

'I can't just sit here grieving,' Cynthia said. 'It's no good – I need to get out and do something . . .'

There was a bang of the front door and in came Joyce, wrapped up to the pink tip of her nose in a big brown scarf. She looked full of life, her honey-coloured hair tied up, and the picture of health.

'What's going on?' She pulled at the scarf.

'Em doesn't want Mom to go out to work,' Violet said.

Joyce turned from going to hang her coat up, a frown on her face. 'What's it got to do with you?'

'Well...' Em was shrinking inside. 'Nothing, I s'pose, it was just—'

'No, that's it – nothing.' Joyce went over to pour herself tea. 'Why shouldn't our mom go and get herself a little job, if it makes her feel better? It's not up to you to keep coming round here, bossing us all around, you know. You live somewhere else now – and even if you didn't, you're not in charge here, you know!'

'Oi, that's enough,' Cynthia said.

Em was stung to the core by these words. She and Joyce always squabbled more than she did with Violet, but this time the words hit home. She *had* felt as if she was in charge of them all, especially now, with Dad gone. Just like when she was little, the way she had had to take over, as if none of them could manage themselves. The habit had formed in her without her realizing.

'It's all right,' Cynthia said gently, seeing that she was upset. She touched Em's arm for a second. 'Don't you worry – everything'll be all right.'

Em gave a grudging smile. She felt silly, weepy, but more reassured now. 'Yeah, I s'pect it will.'

They changed the subject, talking about their days. Violet's had been boring, she said. Joyce was happier with factory work – she liked the company, the banter. And Larry was never too far away.

'Eh,' Cynthia said to Em, 'didn't you say you was meeting up with that O'Neill girl? Dot said she'd seen you both.'

'Sunday, she said. That was something I wanted to ask you, Mom. She's coming over from Handsworth way, with her little boy. Could we come here? It'd just be better than Edna's.'

'Course you can,' Cynthia said. 'It'll be company for Robbie ...'

'Is that that Katie O'Neill?' Joyce said, trying to recall the facts. 'Didn't you tell me – isn't she the stuck-up little bitch who told you to get lost when ... ?'

Em nodded. 'Yes, it is her. But she's different now. Seems ever so nice.'

'I should hope she flipping well is different,' Joyce said.

'It was a long time ago,' Em went on. Though she, too, could not quite forget the hurt of it, the way Katie had rejected her all those years ago. 'I'm quite looking forward to seeing her.'

She realized, as she made her way home, that Katie's visit was beginning to loom large in her mind. Katie had always had a glow around her at school, at least so far as Em was concerned. She knew she had to try and grow out of the picture that she had of Katie. After all, they weren't children any more, picking best friends in the playground.

'I mustn't be silly about it,' she told herself. 'We'll probably just have a quick catch-up and then never see each other again. And I don't s'pose she really wants to know the likes of me anyway.'

But Katie had seemed so pleased to see her this time, and Em knew that really she hoped for more than that – she wanted Katie's friendship.

Fifty-Six

By the time Em opened the door to Katie that Sunday afternoon, she was in such a state of nerves that her hands were trembling.

On the step stood Katie, looking as smart and neat as ever in a navy coat and hat and, beside her, her beautiful boy, his deep-blue eyes peeping out from under dark curling lashes and a red knitted hat.

'Hello,' Em said, flustered. 'Come on in – it's freezing out there. Come and get warm by the fire, the pair of you.'

'Hello,' Katie said, ushering her son in with her. 'It's all right – this lady is an old friend of mine, Mrs . . . ?'

Em laughed. 'Mrs Stapleton. But you can't call me that, for goodness' sake!' She wanted to say: *Call me Auntie Em*, but it seemed too eager. 'Hello again, Michael. Oh, isn't he beautiful, Katie! I'll call Robbie – he's upstairs.'

As she did so, Cynthia came and greeted Katie. Em, calling up to Robbie, was praying inwardly: *Please let them be all right; don't let Robbie do anything wrong.* She was worried that her son might be too boisterous for the younger one, or even take a dislike to him.

Robbie came thumping down the stairs and stopped on the bottom step, taking in the sight of Michael. Katie had just pulled off the hat to reveal his head of black curly hair. Robbie's was shorter, lighter.

'Robbie,' she said. 'This is the friend I told you about: Michael. How about we find the pair of you something to do, eh?'

'Football,' Robbie said emphatically.

'But . . .' Em was about to protest, but Michael was already heading towards Robbie, seemingly fascinated by the sight of him. He stood staring up at him, wide-eyed, and Robbie, a step higher than Michael and already taller by two years, looked down and, seeing an eager follower whom he could command and teach, became instantly well disposed.

'Don't s'pose he's much good. But I'll try and show him,' he said in a weary voice, which made Katie laugh. Watching her, Em saw that something in her had changed. She seemed more relaxed than she had ever been.

'Well, it's stopped raining outside,' Cynthia said. 'They can go out in the yard, if you don't mind them getting grubby. There's just about enough room for them to kick a ball around.'

'I remember it,' Katie said, looking round her. She sounded quite emotional. 'Goodness, yes, I remember this house . . .'

Michael, hat on again, followed Robbie outside.

'I'll go and have a look – see they're all right,' Cynthia said. 'You girls go and get some tea.'

In the back room, while Em made tea and they were suddenly silent, Katie still kept looking round.

'It seems so long,' she said. 'And yet you've been here all this time!'

'Well, I don't live here any more of course,' Em said. 'Only I thought it'd be better if we met here. Sit down – would you like a piece of cake? We made a sponge.'

And then, as Em had dreamed so many times, there

they were, sitting at the table, drinking tea together. She looked shyly at Katie, wondering where they were going to begin.

'I had a lot on my plate when I saw you in town that time,' Katie said. 'You know, just after the war.' The memory had obviously been troubling her. 'I had a new job, was trying to find somewhere to live, and Michael was small – I didn't seem to have room in my thoughts for much else. I was sorry afterwards – wished we'd arranged to meet or something . . .'

'Well,' Em made a face, 'I suppose I was on my way to a hanging, as well.'

'Oh yes – goodness, so you were!'

Cynthia popped back in to say the boys were getting along fine. 'Robbie's very much in charge,' she said. 'But Michael seems quite happy.'

'It's good for him,' Katie said. Em watched her as she spoke to Cynthia, with a sense of wonder that she was here, and thinking how nice she looked, how pretty.

'Don't you worry – just pop out every now and then. I'm going to go and see Dot,' Cynthia said. 'Leave you two to it. Joyce and Vi are out, so you won't be disturbed.'

'Before you go,' Katie said, half getting up.

'What is it, love?' Cynthia came over with her coat.

'Well . . .' Katie sank to her chair again, blushing. Em saw that her hands had a tremor too. 'I know it might seem a bit silly, after all this time. But I want to clear the air. When we were living down the road, my mother didn't behave very nicely to some people . . .'

'That wasn't your fault,' Cynthia said. 'You were only a babby!'

Katie seemed very moved by this. Her eyes filled with tears and for a moment she struggled to speak. 'It's nice of you to say that,' she said. 'But all the same . . . I wanted to say I'm sorry – to both of you. When you were poorly, Mrs Brown, my mother wasn't very kind about it, and she made me feel that I shouldn't see Em and play with her. And I went along with her, and I know it was wrong of me. Truly wrong and nasty.' Katie wiped her eyes. 'I was horrible to you, Em, and I just went off and left you when you needed a friend. And I was so busy being snooty towards Molly Fox that I couldn't even see that . . . well, in her way, she was better than me, wasn't she?'

Em swallowed. This she couldn't deny. 'Molly was a good friend then,' she said.

'Well, I've always regretted that I wasn't.' Katie spoke looking down at the tabletop. 'And that I didn't argue with my mother. She was so . . . so forceful, and so worried all the time about my uncle – I think that was what it was, partly . . .' She looked up at them again.

'Your uncle suffered in his mind, didn't he?' Cynthia asked.

Katie stared at her and suddenly burst out laughing. 'It's so funny, isn't it? All these things people think they're hiding, trying to keep a secret – and everyone knows all along! Why can't we all just tell the truth!'

'Well, yes . . . I s'pose you're right,' Em said. 'But people can be so unkind.'

'Oh, they certainly can,' Katie said. 'I do want you to know how sorry I am for being so nasty myself.'

Cynthia walked round and patted Katie's shoulder. 'So far as I'm concerned, it's all past history and we'll put it behind us, love. Now – don't forget to give those lads some cake. I'll see you later.'

*

When she'd gone, they sat quietly for a minute before Em said, 'I still can't believe you're here.'

'It's ever so nice to see you,' Katie said, and again Em was struck by the change in her, the cold, closed manner all gone. 'I've missed you, you know.'

'Me too.' Now it was Em's turn to have tears in her eyes. 'Funny, isn't it – we were only babbies, but we got on so well. And now, knowing you've got a little lad as well – it'd seem such a waste, never seeing them together. Hang on, I'll go and have a look at them . . .'

From the back door she saw that the two boys were happy in the yard. Robbie was instructing Michael quite pompously in the arts of football. Em smiled and went back in.

'They're happy as Larry,' she said. 'Now then, will you tell me about your life – what's happened to you?'

Katie talked then, for a long time, about how things had been at home with her mother and uncle. Em watched her as she talked, sometimes looking at Em, sometimes away at the window. Em was fascinated, seeing the way her mouth moved as she talked, her fingers – she remembered her hands, her wide nails – the slant of her shoulders. It seemed so strange that Katie should seem so closely familiar after all this time.

'Michael's father has never once seen him,' she went on. Her voice was dispassionate. 'I won't say who he is – it doesn't really matter now. When we met, I think I was just amazed that anyone would be interested in me, like that. I hadn't a clue about men, and I didn't have a very high opinion of myself. He seemed very keen, and I just thought that because he said he was keen on me, that I must be on him. We weren't suited at all really. If we'd married, I think I'd have been very unhappy.'

She looked across and saw the sadness in Em's eyes.

'That's terrible,' Em said. For all the days of humdrum life, working, bringing up Robbie, Em knew she had loved Norm, that underneath it all she still did. 'How did you manage? I mean, when he was born?'

'I went to a friend – her family were very kind. And then I went back to work. You know, shorthand and typing.'

'That's what our Vi wants to do,' Em said, smiling.

'It's not a bad job. There's plenty of work.'

Em was just about to speak again when the back door opened and the boys came roaring in, pink-cheeked and excited.

'Nanna said there's cake!' Robbie cried. His eyes fastened on the Victoria sponge cake. 'Ooh – can we have some?'

They were soon tucking into slices of the dry cake and a cup of milk.

'Michael's getting a bit better at football,' Robbie reported. 'But he won't catch up with me – not yet.'

The two mothers smiled. 'Well, thank you for giving him a lesson anyway,' Katie said.

'Right, you two – go on, Robbie, find your cars and your bits and bobs. You two can settle down here now.'

'Oh!' they both cried, and Robbie said, 'Oh, Mom – we want to go out again!'

It was still light, so Em agreed.

Katie told Em about Maudie, and then about Sybil's house and finally, with a blush, she talked about Marek.

'I thought you had roses in your cheeks,' Em said. Maybe Marek was the one who had made Katie seem so different, she thought. 'Polish,' she added. 'My goodness! Does he speak English?'

'Yes,' Katie chuckled. 'Sometimes it's funny, when

493

he gets things wrong. He's ever so good with Michael. I think . . .' She frowned, as if trying to work something out. 'I don't know why we get on really.' There was something in each of them, of loss and need and a shared sense of humour. Not to mention physical attraction. 'It's just something you can't really put into words, isn't it? Just something right.'

'I s'pose it is,' Em said.

Katie looked closely at her and held out her cup for the top-up that Em was offering.

'Quite enough of my life. Tell me about you?'

'Oh, not much to tell.' Being unusually blunt after Katie's honesty, she said, 'Married. Living with his mom and dad, for better or worse. One son: can't seem to have any more.'

Tears came again, quite unexpectedly, and she ducked her head down.

'Oh dear – oh, Em, you're really upset, aren't you?' Katie's kind voice brought out all Em's bottled-up feelings.

'I know I should be grateful for having one son,' she said through her tears. 'But Norm wasn't here to see him grow up, either, and they've never been all that close. I don't want many – just one more, that Norm can get to know from the beginning. I think it would bring us closer, too. Not that it's bad. We're OK.' Now she felt she'd said too much, or at least that it had come out clumsily and given the wrong impression. She and Norm were OK – of course they were!

'Well, maybe it'll happen,' Katie said.

'Yes.' What else was there to say? 'But I'm trying to get used to the idea that it won't – not after all this time.'

'Is Molly Fox married?' Katie asked.

'Molly? Oh no. Well – not so far as I know. You never quite know with Molly. I haven't heard from her as much as during the war – we used to write quite regularly then. But now she seems to be doing jobs here and there. In holiday camps in the summer: Butlin's and that. But she doesn't come up here. I don't think she wants to tangle with that mother of hers.'

'Oh yes, I remember. She used to frighten me to death!'

'Old Iris? Yes – she gave me a few frights, I can tell you. She's still about here somewhere. Looks the same, only worse.'

'Was she...' Katie hesitated. 'Was she cruel to Molly? All I remember is how much Molly smelt: that stink always hanging round her. And that yard up that horrible slimy entry – it gave me the creeps. But I never really knew much about her.'

'Oh, Iris was cruel all right. She's vile – the only word for her. I worry about Molly; I don't know where she is or what she's doing. I just hope one day she'll write again, or turn up. She's got no family except her mother, and she doesn't want anything to do with her.'

'Well, that's something we've got in common, I suppose,' Katie said wistfully. 'I don't s'pose she thinks much of me, though.'

'No, probably not,' Em said. Then grinned. 'But it's never too late, is it?'

By the time Katie left that afternoon the two boys had become firm friends.

'It's a good thing we got on all right, isn't it?' Em said. ''Cause these two're going to make sure we meet up again, whether we like it or not!'

495

'You have a good Christmas,' Katie said as she left. 'I suppose it'll be hard – first one without your dad.'

'Yes – but we'll be all right. Mom's coping really well. She's even gone out and got a job.' Now she could even feel pleased and proud. Going out to work was much better than sinking into a depression!

Katie helped Michael back into his hat and coat and then put her own on.

'You do look nice,' Em said.

Katie smiled. She reached out and kissed Em's cheek. 'And so do you. I'm so happy to see you.'

'Me too,' Em said, which didn't seem enough to express just how glad she really was.

'Bye, Michael mate!' Robbie called after them along the street. Michael swivelled round and raised his thumb. Em saw that Robbie was doing the same.

'Oh, Robbie,' she laughed, and raised her hand as Katie turned and waved. Katie – her friend.

XII

KATIE

Fifty-Seven

December 1948

Ice-cold rain was lashing down the day Marek brought Agnieska to Handsworth.

It was the Saturday before Christmas and the whole household had been in a bit of a tizzy. Marek had been tense and excited, and Katie was nervous about Agnieska's arrival. What would she be like? And was she still really so delicate? She had an impression in her mind of an invalid who would need constant care. And she was full of tender worry for Marek. Sybil also seemed concerned that Agnieska should have a good welcome and be taken care of, as if greeting an injured bird that needed nurturing back to health.

'Goodness, what a day!' Sybil said, looking out of the back window at the bloated clouds.

Marek had gone to Birmingham to meet his sister's train. Sybil had taken deliveries of food and was cooking up a pot of vegetable soup, with Michael helping to cut up the vegetables.

Sybil threw out some stray thoughts. 'I do hope the poor girl's got a mac' and then, 'I must get the house ready for Christmas. Mr Jenkins said he'd go along and fetch a tree for me, even though he's going off to his mother's.'

'Oh, is he?' Katie said, trying to help Michael with the potatoes. 'Where does she live again?' Although she had shared a house with Geoff Jenkins all this time, she never felt she got to know him any better. Now that he was courting he was hardly about.

'Kidderminster way, I believe. That's it – pass me those. And put the kettle on, will you, there's a dear.'

Later, when the soup was bubbling away and they'd had a cup of tea, they heard the front door. Archie erupted into volleys of barking.

'You go,' Sybil said. 'You'll get there more quickly – get them in out of the wet. And for goodness' sake, grab Archie – she may not like dogs.'

Katie ran and pushed a protesting Archie into the cold front room. She opened up to find Marek outside, holding his coat over the heads of himself and his sister while he carried her case in the other hand.

'Quickly!' Katie said. 'Come in.' She had an impression of someone very thin and wiry, with large eyes, at Marek's side.

Piotr came bounding downstairs to greet them and there were hugs and a lot of excited chatter in Polish, and outraged barking from the other side of the front-room door. Katie was glad to have a few seconds to stand aside and take in the sight of this new person in all their lives. She could see that Agnieska was strikingly like Marek, with similar pronounced cheekbones and big blue eyes, with dark lashes, contrasting with her pale hair, which was tied back. Her face was very pale and she looked delicate, but her full lips were parted in a smile.

'Agnieska,' Marek guided her, a hand behind her shoulders. 'This is Katie.' He added a comment in Polish.

Agnieska came towards her with an open, enquiring expression and Katie saw a sweet smile. She liked the girl already, felt drawn to her waiflike looks. She said something that sounded like '*Chaisch . . .*' Then, 'Hello . . .' And held out her hand. When Katie took it, it felt bony, but there was a wiry strength to her, even though she looked younger than her twenty years.

'Hello,' Katie said, shyly. 'Nice to meet you.'

'Nice to meet you,' Agnieska said back, then put her hand over her mouth and gave a little laugh at herself, which Katie found infectious. Then she saw Michael. 'Your boy?' she asked Katie, who nodded. 'Ah – hello!'

'And this is Miss Routh,' Marek went on. Sybil had come limping through from the back, and the greetings were repeated.

'Welcome to Birmingham,' Sybil said. 'We hope you will be comfortable here. Has your brother explained that your room is next door?'

Agnieska, at a loss, looked to Marek and he translated.

'Oh!' She lit up. 'Yes – thank you!'

'Maybe,' Marek said, 'we go round there now, to meet them.'

'Oh, have a cup of tea first,' Sybil said, turning towards the kitchen again. 'You must both be frozen, and there's no hurry, is there? Now do tell me: does she mind dogs?'

'Dog?' Agnieska wrinkled her nose.

'Ah,' Sybil said. 'Well, not to worry. Once Archie's been introduced, he'll just ignore you.'

The Arbuckles were delighted to have Agnieska in their house. Marek said she had a nice little room looking out over the garden, with a cheerful pair of butter-yellow curtains. Agnieska found the mother and daughter a bit confusing at first, because she couldn't understand a word they were saying. They tried talking louder to compensate, but it didn't help. Marek and Piotr went round quite frequently that week to translate, which made the Arbuckles even happier.

'I was asking her, DOES SHE LIKE EGGS?' Edna enquired at full volume.

'Do you like eggs?' Marek asked her in Polish.

'Yes,' Agnieska replied. 'But why is she shouting? Have I done something wrong?'

'I don't know. I don't think so. Just answer the question.'

'Yes – I like eggs. You know I do.'

'WHAT ABOUT BACON?'

'Yes – this I like too.'

'ONLY WE WEREN'T SURE IF SHE WAS JEWISH?'

'Why does she think I'm Jewish? Yes, I like these things – but please tell her she does not need to shout...'

And so it went on. It was going to take time for everyone to get used to each other, and for Agnieska's English to develop.

'She's very thin,' they said to Marek, frowning in concern. 'She'll need feeding up.'

'Yes, but she has to eat small, small meals,' he explained. 'Her health is better, but there is still a little problem with digestion...'

Or, as Sybil pointed out, to the Arbuckles, best not overdo the suet puddings.

'Oh dear,' they said. 'Oh dear – we must be very careful.'

And careful they were. They treated Agnieska as if she was a delicate china doll, cooking little meals, checking on her health.

'They are very kind,' she reported, when she was round at Sybil's.

'Yes,' Sybil agreed, 'I believe they are, bless their hearts.'

After work on Christmas Eve, Mr Jenkins said his farewells and set off for his mother's for the weekend. The rest of the household, with Agnieska, decorated the tree, which had been waiting out in the garden. Sybil had a box of pretty glass baubles and they made some bows with ribbon, and Katie and Agnieska made some paper chains with Michael and hung them across the dining room. Katie found Agnieska lively company, and she was obviously loving being back in a real home. She had been properly introduced to Archie, who was now satisfied and snoozing by the fire.

Marek and Piotr were joking around in one corner, teasing Sybil and hanging things on the tree, while Katie and Agnieska sat at the table. There was leg-pulling in both Polish and English.

'What did he say?' Katie asked, amused, as Marek shot a satirical remark across to his sister in Polish.

'He say . . .' Agnieska stopped to think.

'Not too much glue, Michael!' Katie intervened.

'. . . is good my hair is . . .' She indicated its length.

'Long? Grown?'

'Grown – yes. Before, is very . . . um . . .'

'Short?'

'Yes – short.'

'She looked like a boy when I last see – er, saw her –

before England,' Marek teased. Seeing Katie's puzzled expression, he said, 'In the Uzbek camp they shaved her head: she was sick, with typhus.'

'Oh, my goodness,' Sybil said. She was directing operations from a chair near the Christmas tree. 'You poor girl. That sounds terrible.'

'Is bad,' Piotr agreed. 'I had also. Bad fever, markings – rash on body, bad head – bad everything. We catch from lice.'

'Yes, so my hair – all gone,' Agnieska agreed. 'His hair too.'

Marek chuckled.

'That's not funny!' Katie scolded him.

'Is OK,' Agnieska laughed, shaking her fist at him. 'Later I kill him.'

Christmas was one of the many times Katie had to be grateful to Sybil, for the way she let people into her house to share her life. It seemed to be her instinctive nature to do so; perhaps, Katie thought, because she had been one of a large and quite loving – if eccentric – family.

On Christmas Eve, Katie and all the Poles went to Midnight Mass, leaving Michael asleep with Sybil.

'I can't be doing with going off at night any more,' Sybil said. 'I'll go to the service on Christmas morning.'

Katie stood beside Marek in the packed church and listened to the Mass, full of happiness. How much joy she had in her life suddenly! She wondered if her father was at Mass tonight, whether he was thinking of her. Every so often Marek looked round at her and smiled, reaching to squeeze her hand. She was moved by the tender, wounded look on his face and ached for them all, for their family, wondering what memories of past

Christmases the Mass was bringing back to them. She saw Agnieska, the other side of Marek, wipe tears from her eyes. The night was a clear, cold one, and they moved out into its starriness after the Mass and embraced, wishing each other a Happy Christmas, and walked home, arm in arm, four abreast.

Originally the plan was for Agnieska to be wrested from the grasp of the Arbuckles for Christmas dinner, until Sybil suggested inviting them round as well and pooling resources. The Arbuckles were delighted and promised to bring a magnificent Christmas pudding they had made months ago, having saved their rations for the purpose. Everyone mucked in with the preparations. Sybil got the joint in before her church service, and all morning and well into the afternoon the delicious smell of beef slowly roasting seeped into all the nooks and crannies of the house, soon to be joined by the smell of roasting potatoes after she returned, and was soon warbling 'It came upon a midnight clear' and 'O come, all ye faithful!' in the kitchen, quite tunefully.

Katie and Agnieska had prepared the other vegetables and now laid the table for the eight of them. She was touched by the way Agnieska seemed to have fastened onto her immediately as a big sister. As they laid the knives and forks, she kept wondering about Marek's and Agnieska's sister. Hadn't he said they had another sister? And what about the rest of the family? It didn't seem right to pry. Instead, she said, 'What was it like in the camp – in Gloucestershire, I mean?'

Agnieska was putting the cutlery down very precisely. She looked up. 'The camp? Oh – is OK. We have many things ... er, Polish things – dancing and, er, priest, and we are working, learning English ... I live in umm, *beczka* – Marek what is ... ?'

'Hut,' Marek said. He was at the piano, with Michael on his lap, teaching him to play. 'Nissen hut – like army.'

'Oh yes, I see, 'Katie said. 'I don't suppose they were very comfortable.'

'Oh no,' she said. 'But OK. We have live like this long time now . . .'

'Right,' Sybil called from the kitchen. 'Someone go and tell the Arbuckles it's dinner time, will you?'

The meal was delicious. All the women wore their best frocks, Susan Arbuckle's being a spectacular pink silky creation, very tight across the bust.

'Very nice,' Piotr said when he saw her, and Susan's cheeks flamed with pleasure. Sybil produced a bottle of red wine, which Agnieska declined and Susan said, 'Oh dear, no – I'd better not . . .' So the rest of them enjoyed it.

As they tucked into their first course, Marek raised his glass and said, 'A toast, to Miss Routh.'

They all toasted with enthusiasm. Sybil sat back, pushing a strand of hair from her eyes, flushed in the face from her efforts in the kitchen.

'Well, thank you,' she said, raising her own glass. 'And may I drink to all of you. This is a very happy household and, without you all, I expect I should be a crabby old lady. So – good health to you all!'

They all clapped and cheered and joined in the toast. Michael, very excited, carried on clapping and Agnieska laughed.

'Eat up,' Katie whispered. Marek, on the other side of her, squeezed her knee for a moment and she looked round and smiled.

It was a very jolly meal. Susan had much to say on the subject of Percy, her beloved. Edna Arbuckle told them that her mother had been in the theatre.

'Not one of the Gaiety Girls?' Sybil asked.

'Ooh no,' Edna said, 'they were rather high-up sort of girls, you know, young ladies. No, she was just an ordinary actress. More of a chorus girl. I do just remember her – she handed me over to an aunt to be brought up – in Erdington. She wanted to carry on working, you see. I suppose I was rather an inconvenience to her. And then she died – killed in a road accident.'

'Oh dear, how sad!' Sybil said.

Katie listened. It didn't sound as if Edna had had much of a mother, either. She put her arm round Michael for a moment and kissed him. If there was one thing she was determined to do with her life, it was to do better for him.

When the pudding was brought in, after hours of steaming, another cheer went up.

'Magnificent!' Sybil said. 'We shan't be able to move after all this!'

'You know,' Piotr said suddenly, as all of them except Agnieska were eating big slabs of the pudding. 'The first Christmas time we spent in Russia . . .'

Everyone was listening immediately. The Christmas season seemed to bring out all sorts of memories.

'We were taken first to Sverdlovsk – big town in middle of country, with steel works. The Russians wanted my father – they came for us soon after the war started. They were arming against the Germans, of course. My father, he lived for ten years in America and he learned about making steel.' Katie listened, fascinated. She had never heard any of this before. 'The Russians took him to work and they took us. They did not treat us too bad in this place – they want his work. All the young ones, we were taken to a barracks – a kind of orphanage – me, my brother and sister and my mother worked there in the kitchen. I was in school. At Christmas time they put up two pictures, one each side of the room: one of Jesus Christ and one of Papa Stalin. They say to children, "Which one you want to pray to? You can go to either one." But the children soon learn – if they choose to go to Papa Stalin, he has a box of sweets – sweets falling into your hand. But Jesus? He has no sweets. You go to Jesus, you come away with hands empty. So' – Piotr raised his glass – 'this is religion-teaching in Russia!'

They all laughed. 'Goodness,' Sybil said. 'And did you stay in this place for a long time?'

Piotr shook his head. Without emotion, as if all feeling had been sucked from him, he went on, 'My father did not come home one day. No one told us anything. Then they put the rest of us on the transports – we went across Urals Mountains, to Siberia, for work camp. It took us eight weeks.'

'Work?' Katie asked. The whole thing was unimaginable.

'Digging railway – my sister, digging, at age thirteen. In snow.'

'Oh dear – that doesn't sound very nice,' Susan said.

Then there was a silence around the table that grew, in which no one wanted to ask about his little sister.

'Now . . .' Piotr said, changing the tone. 'Enough of Russia. Let us drink to this young man here. To little Michael!'

And gladly they all joined in.

*

The evening passed happily round the fire, talking, drinking and eating Christmas cake. Everyone took it in turns to play with Michael. Katie had given him half a dozen Dinky cars, which he found endless fun in roaring around the floor with. Marek played the piano and after a while called to Agnieska and Piotr to dance, so they got up and showed the others some Polish dance steps. Katie was struck by the seriousness with which they danced. She was sure if it had been her she would have collapsed into giggles. Edna and Susan clapped their hands to the music, loving it all, and when Katie's eyes met Sybil's – she had passed round a bottle of port and was still nursing her thimbleful– Sybil gave her a wink. Her lips were turned up, and Katie could see she was relishing it all. Katie watched Marek as he played the jaunty dance tune on the piano. She longed to go and kiss the back of his neck. She was so enjoying this evening too, but at the same time how she longed to be alone with him, so that they could look deep into each other's eyes and talk and talk.

Fifty-Eight

By ten o'clock everyone was flagging. Katie had carried an overtired Michael up to bed, and now the Arbuckles said they would be off. Agnieska immediately said she would go too.

'You don't have to,' Edna said.

'No – we don't want to break it up!' said Susan. 'You stay with your brother, if you want to.'

'I like to go to sleep,' Agnieska told them, and she did indeed look exhausted. 'Goodnight – and thank you so much!'

Katie was touched by the fact that Agnieska leaned down and kissed her cheek after hugging her brother and Piotr.

'Oh – goodnight. I hope you sleep well,' Katie said. 'And happy Christmas!' She was already very fond of Agnieska.

'Time for me to hit the hay as well, I think,' Sybil said, after all the thank-yous and departures. 'You can stay down here, if you like – put another log on the fire. But I'm all in.' Sybil was sagging. For the first time, almost, Katie took in that she was quite elderly. Even with her rheumatism she seemed to get so much done normally.

'Thank you for a lovely day, 'Katie said, kissing her cheek. 'This is the nicest Christmas I've ever had.'

'Oh . . .' Sybil brushed off the thanks. 'Well, I'm glad.

Pleasure. Right – goodnight all. Happy Christmas to you again.'

'Thank you, Miss Routh – Happy Christmas!' Marek and Piotr called to her. 'Thank you!'

It went quiet suddenly, as if all the energy had gone. Marek reached for a log and threw it into the flames, where it crackled, sparks whirling up the chimney.

Piotr sat back and stretched, arms above his head, giving a huge yawn. 'I go to bed. I'm sleeping already.'

Katie and Marek both tried not to show that they were pleased he was going, and wished him goodnight. As the door closed behind him, they looked at each other and smiled.

'Well . . .' Marek said. They could hear Piotr's foot-steps going upstairs.

'It's been a lovely day. I feel so nice and warm and well fed.'

'Oh yes.' Marek shook his head. 'It is just wonder-ful.' He looked up as the door closed upstairs, then held his arm out to Katie. 'Come here . . .' He was in the nice big, comfortable chair by the fire.

'Let me put the light out,' she said. 'It'll be cosy.'

Marek pulled her onto his lap and they snuggled up comfortably, Katie's head resting on his shoulder, his arms close round her. She loved the way he held her very tight, as if she was utterly precious to him. She reached up and kissed his cheek, and he looked down at her.

'You are so lovely,' he said. 'You are gift from God.'

'Oh, I don't know about that!' she laughed. She stroked her palm across his cheek, bristly and lean, loving the feel of him, his heartbeat a gentle rhythm against her ribs. He reached down and they kissed, and she caressed the back of his neck.

'I've been dying to kiss you all afternoon,' she said, and Marek laughed.

'Yes – I have the same feeling.'

'Agnieska seems well – she's settling in.'

'Yes, it's good. She is OK. She feels better.'

'It must be so nice, having someone from your family with you now.'

Marek smiled. 'Umm – it's good.'

'Marek?' she said after a moment. 'Will you tell me? At least some of it? I keep hearing little bits – what you said about your sister's hair, and what Piotr told us today. I don't know anything; I don't even know where those places are, or what happened. Or about your family, and I haven't known whether I should ask or not. I do want to know – about you, my darling. About all of it. And we shouldn't keep secrets from one another.'

Marek breathed in, then out, very hard. 'I know – I should speak about it. But it is easier now we are here, in England, not to think about it. To push it away. I just tell you because it is right that you know me. And I think if I do not talk, it will rot inside me.'

She could feel, by the way he was breathing more deeply, that this was already a struggle. She nodded, waiting, settling her head on his shoulder, one hand on his chest.

'Just start off,' she encouraged him. 'And see how you get on.'

'Well, from the beginning of things . . .' He paused. 'My town, our family town, is not very large – a lot of farmers live there. Maybe you call it a village. It doesn't matter. It is outside the city of Lwow, to the west. My father was a teacher in the school – of chemistry. My mother also had been a teacher, before she married

– of history. But then she was at home with the family. She likes to write stories – stories of the past.

Katie turned to look at him. 'What were their names?'

'Names – oh, Tomas, my father. Tomas Wozniak. And my mother, Genowefa Wozniak.' His voice caught with emotion, saying their names, and he waited a few moments before going on. The names sank into her too. She wanted to ask so many things: What did they look like? Who do you take after – whose blue eyes are those? But she didn't want to keep interrupting.

'In the family we were five children, living. One boy they lost, he died before I was born. The eldest was Pawel – he was four years my senior. Then me, Marek. After that, my sister Ewa, two years younger, then Agnieska and finally Dorota – she was just eight years when the war began.'

Katie felt a chill come over her, listening to him. She knew he had had a big family, but hearing their names, they began to come alive. But until now, no mention of them. Where were they – what had happened? She sat very still, not wanting to distract him, holding one of his hands.

'When the Germans came, first of all, for a week or so, there were non-stop tanks and lorries passing through, along the main road from the west. We could see it from our house. One day, some of them stopped and came to us. They said, "Your house is quite big – we like to stay here." They speak in Polish language, quite polite. Of course we had to let them. My mother said never to take sweets from them – they might be poisoned ... But of course we did! They were not poisoned, luckily. They shot some people in the village – they had a list. I remember hearing shots sometime.

'Soon after, the Russians ratted on us. The Germans pulled back, and for weeks there were more tanks passing, and lorries and horses and carts, from the east this time. They were so poor, so shabby-looking, those Red Army soldiers – conscripts. They were eating raw potatoes. They took our house – with gun, not polite this time. They took over the village, taking everything, relieving themselves wherever they wanted . . . Horrible. Soon they took my father – not the soldiers in the house, but others who came. They were transporting the prominent people: teachers, intellectuals, doctors. To where, we did not know. We never saw him again.'

Katie felt a chill pass through her at this bald statement.

'One morning in February – it was five a.m., dark, snow up to the waist – they came for us. I was . . . well, my father was not there of course, so I was the man of the house, if you like . . .'

'But – what about your brother? You said you had an elder brother?'

'Pawel, yes. But he was in the army. Polish army – we call it the Home Army. So he wasn't there. We heard after a long time – almost by chance, when everyone is asking for news – that he was killed in western Poland, fighting the Germans, around about that time, I think.

'God!' she murmured. It was all too much for her to find any words.

'That morning, the girls were screaming, and Russian soldier in long coat – his gun was pointing at my mother's head. My sister, Ewa, shouted something and he hit her round the face with the back of his hand – his glove. *Slap!* She fell to the floor. They told us: Take what you can carry, take food, and put on the cart. We went to the railway station and eventually everyone – a big crowd of people – was put in the train. It was a train for animals – you know, cattle. We were many people in one truck: a hole in the middle of the floor for, well, for you to do your business. When someone wanted to go, people turned their backs, maybe held up a coat. It took six weeks, at least. It was winter; very cold. At night we all slept close together, family in a group. If you rested your head on the side of the carriage, your hair would freeze to it. A lot of people had to have their heads cut free, so there was hair left on the walls ... People were sick. One lady had a baby in our truck. Can you imagine? When it was born there was no sound, no cry. The guards ...' He hesitated. 'They take it and throw it out into the snow.'

Katie gasped, a hand going to her mouth.

'All the dead, it was like this ... Not much food, not much water ... So, we are taken to the north, to a place in Russia near Archangelsk, to a camp for logging.'

'Logging?'

'Of course. They need wood for everything: for railway, for building – all these barracks, huts for their slave labour, for one thing – everything they make, they have the whole of the *taiga* forests. I was sent with the men. We cut the trees. The women and children gather branches, and my mother had some cooking work. I see them at night. Again, little food. Soup is just cabbage water. People are getting very sick – some have chicken blindness, I think they call it *beri-beri*. Some of the men, when the sun started to go down, we had to guide them back to the huts because they went blind; they are stumbling, falling.

'We all survived that together, by God's grace. Then came the amnesty. *Amnesty ...*' He repeated the word with bitter contempt. 'As if we were criminals. The Germans had attacked Russia – you remember, in 1941? So suddenly their great friendship is off, and Russia is comrades with Poland again. So, they decide we can go. Can you imagine?'

He stopped and drew in a big breath, letting it out slowly.

'Oh, it is a long story. It took us some time to get out – I was almost going alone, I was young and impatient – me and some other boys and girls. But my mother said: No, you wait, we stay together. We have to get rail permit to go south. In the end we left the camp. For days we walk, my sister Ewa was very sick, pain in head, fever. After days we come to railway. There were many of us on the train. No one knows anything, except we are told there will be a new Polish army. We make a long journey south. Trains, barges, trucks, walking. Even donkey and camel.' Kate felt his chest move in laughter for a moment.

'It was chaos, Russia – the Russians didn't know what they were doing. Finally they hand us all over to the British, when we got south, in Uzbekistan. Here we are told that for sure there will be a Polish Army Corps gathered out of those freed from the camps. Our General, Anders, they let him out of Lubyanka prison in Moscow and he came to command us. I was old enough – eighteen by this time. I decided to join. But for some time everyone would be travelling together: the army and also women and children, everyone. We went to Tashkent where there was a camp. This is very bad time – there was no food, almost, eating worms from the ground. And you know what else we could eat sometimes? Turtles – big ones, we boiled them – and storks. They make their nests high up, but there were no high buildings, so they nested in the trees. We would go and lift them by the neck. But this is not often, of course. We were hungry and many people sick, thin like insects, dying. I was worried about my mother. After all the camp, the journeys, all she had suffered, her health was very bad; she was weak. We did not know where was my father – she had to do everything alone. And Agnieska got very sick – typhus, as we told you.'

'And you – did you get sick?'

'Oh yes, like everyone – dysentery. Some typhus. But I was strong. And by the time we were moving on to Iran, I was in a separate place – with the army. My baby sister, Dorota, she got a bad fever and she died on the way. Agnieska and Ewa, they sat and held her, their dead sister, while our mother went to try and find a way to bury her. But how could she? She had no tool, no . . .'

'Shovel?'

'Yes, shovel – she had nothing. So they had to put her in a grave with others – many others together.' He continued quickly. 'Somehow, along the way, Ewa became separated from the others. I think because she was so sick. Agnieska says she cannot remember the time – she had a fever also. So Agnieska is left with my mother, and they all cross the Caspian Sea to Iran, to be put in a camp on the beach. The journey is very difficult: the heat is terrible. When they reach the place – it is Pahlavi, the name, I think – my mother is so weak, so sick. Many are sick, and their bones sticking out. After three days she opened her eyes for the last time. I think her heart is broken as well as her strength.'

'So poor Agnieska was left all on her own?'

'Yes. No one else of my family. There was no sight of Ewa. But others looked after her. After some time everyone was sent out to other camps – she was first in India some years, then East Africa: Uganda. She speaks Swahili language, you know! Then from there they come here.'

'And what about Ewa?'

'We don't know. Still we are trying to find out. But I do not have a big hope.'

Katie was struggling to take all this in. 'And you: where were you, Marek?'

'They took us first to Palestine for training. The Jewish boys thought their dreams had come true. They didn't want to leave, and they stayed to fight there. Then we went to Italy, all the way up to Monte Cassino. We get our hands on the Germans! Along the way I met Piotr and together we go on. Then – here. Here I am.'

'Oh, Marek . . .' She looked into his face. She felt powerfully tender towards him, but what he had told her was so terrible, so immense. She didn't know how he could bear the grief of it all. All she could do was hold him, kissing his face.

After a long silence she said, 'All your family. You've lost so much.'

'It was the same for everybody,' he said. By his detached way of talking she understood that he could not go into the emotions – it would be too much. 'Talk to any of the Poles – it is the same.'

'Piotr?'

'Yes. All dead. In Siberia.'

Katie made a sound of distress.

Marek gently took her hand. 'We have to make a new life.'

'Can you really not go back to Poland?'

'We had one friend – he was determined to go back.

He said he would write and tell us when it was safe. We never heard another word from him. The Russians own my country now.' His voice was very bitter. 'Soviets. Reds. They are in charge – no one says no to Papa Stalin, it seems. Not the British, the Americans: no one. Poland has been smashed apart. You know, they have moved the borders west – by about a hundred and fifty miles? So, my home is now in Ukraine – no home for us any more. We are all . . .' He made a scattering motion with his free hand.

He looked into her eyes. She could just see the dying flames reflected in his.

'You have to understand – my country has had many different borders before this war. Many wars before, fighting, people occupying this land and that. And so many hatreds: Ukrainians hate Poles as they were given their land; Lithuanians in the north hate us, as we took Wilno; some people hating Jews for reasons of wealth and religion, some Jews hating us . . . We are a quarrelsome country – but now, it has been a funeral pyre. And we are occupied by Russia . . .'

He stopped, gave a heavy sigh. 'Some people here – Poles, I mean – can't accept. One day they will go back, they say. Poland will be free. But I don't know. Everything is broken. All I can do is go forward, not thinking of the past too much. We are here. We have to make a home somehow.

They were both silent. The fire shifted.

'Katie?' Gently he stroked back her hair, leaving his big, warm hand on her head. She heard anxiety in his voice and turned to him.

'Thank you.' She turned her head and kissed the delicate skin of his wrist. 'Thank you for telling me.'

'Dear Katinka . . .' he lowered his hand and his eyes

searched hers. 'You are like home to me, and a new life. Will you stay with me and we make a life together? Will you be my wife?'

She moved nearer, until their faces were very close, in the darkness. Their noses were almost touching.

'You are my home too,' she said. There was nothing – no one – she wanted but this. 'Yes, my darling Marek – I will.'

XIII

MOLLY

Fifty-Nine

February 1949

'There's a letter for you, Miss Fox.'

As soon as Molly got through the front door, blowing on her frozen hands, her landlady Mrs Hodgkins came sliding out of her room on the ground floor. Her husband was a sick man and she always moved with an air of trying not to wake somebody. She was holding out a white postcard.

'I thought I'd better take it in for safekeeping,' she said.

'Oh – thank you.' Molly took it and went up the bare staircase to her room.

Safekeeping my eye, she thought. Does she really think someone's going to come in and steal my post? She was just being nosy as usual, poor old thing. She's not got much to liven her life up. But then – Molly laughed at herself – neither have I, come to think of it! Despite the perishing cold, she was feeling quite cheerful.

Her digs were on the first floor of a house in Camden Town. Above her lived a shy, mousy-haired, but sweet-natured typist called Sarah. Below were Mrs Hodgkins and the suffering Bert. Molly had heard him groaning once or twice. Mrs H was nosy and a bit miserable, but she wasn't a bad cook, the rent was reasonable, at eighteen shillings, and the house bare, but clean.

The room was very cold and, without taking off her coat, Molly filled the kettle, set it on the single ring heater. She badly needed a cuppa and a smoke after that freezing wait for the bus and the miserable crawl home! She sat on the bed, lit a cigarette and looked at the card, across which, in blue-black ink, was strung Phoebe Morrison's unmistakable bold, square hand.

'Molly . . .' it began. (It had taken the two of them a long time to get used to each other's first names. Molly struggled with 'Phoebe', and she was sure her former Subaltern had to think twice to prevent herself barking 'Fox!' at her.)

> Molly – can you meet me on Saturday morning – usual place, 10.30? I've news for you.
> Phoebe.

Molly laid the card down with a sense of mild curiosity and went to make herself a much-needed cup of tea. Mug in both hands, sipping the hot liquid, she thought: Well, I wonder what the Gorg's got to say?

The relationship of commander and subordinate had never vanished entirely from their friendship, but since Molly had been living in London more permanently she had seen Phoebe Morrison quite regularly and they had become more relaxed with one another. They almost never went to each other's lodgings – Phoebe in any case lived some way away in Highbury. And she was rather awkward company. So they met to do something: usually to go to the pictures and for a drink afterwards to chat about the film, while Molly stuck to lemonade and Phoebe smoked like a chimneystack. That worked well. Though the two of them had never had a very close or confiding conversation, Molly really looked forward to their outings. It felt like something sure and stable in her life, and she could tell that Phoebe, in her stiff, repressed way, valued it too. She certainly went to pains to keep in touch.

After another summer of the holiday camps, Molly had decided to try and get a grip on things. She was getting sick of her life of shifting work and of brief, pointless affairs with men who just happened to be around.

'I just don't know what to do,' she had confided to Ruth during their conversation on the beach when Ruth had encouraged her to make more of herself. 'I don't know how to go about things.'

'Well,' Ruth had said, considering the matter, 'why don't you move to somewhere where you can go to night school? If you've got a job – any job'll do really – you can make a start like that. And it could lead to something better.'

'But what?' Molly had asked gloomily. She had truly felt in those days that nothing she did would ever lead to anything better.

'Well . . .' Ruth was beginning to sound just a bit exasperated. 'The thing is, you can't always tell where something might lead. But one thing's for sure: if you *don't* do anything, it can't lead anywhere much, can it?'

Molly couldn't argue with this logic.

'What are the things you're best at – I mean, when you were at school?'

'I suppose . . . Sums. I always got along all right with those. And the Gorgon did tell me once that I'd come

525

near the top in the tests we did when we joined up.' Molly blushed with pleasure, recounting this.

'*Did* you?' Ruth turned to her in pleased surprise. 'You've never told me that before!'

'Yes – she said I'd not done much less well than you and Win.' Molly was rather enjoying this.

'Well, I'm blowed – that's marvellous, Molly! All the more reason for you to *get on and do something*, instead of just drifting.'

When the last summer season ended Molly had returned to London, on a wave of confidence and determination. She found herself the digs with Mrs Hodgkins and a job in the Cottage Tea Rooms on the Strand. She swallowed her pride and went to see Phoebe Morrison, who helped her find a place where she could do evening classes, and she decided to sign up for shorthand and typing one evening, and a class to improve her arithmetic on another.

'That'll keep me busy Tuesdays and Thursdays,' she said. 'And I expect there'll be homework.' She found she was very nervous. Would she be able to keep up with it? Was she about to make a gigantic fool of herself? But she was also excited: this was a new beginning. Surely she could find some of her old army confidence and make it work? Having the support of some of her old friends helped, too. Ruth wrote and said she was delighted to hear what Molly was up to, and Phoebe Morrison, ever practical, was a great help. They also met up with Win, from time to time.

'I'm so pleased!' Win beamed, when Molly told of her plans. And Molly could see she meant it. In the old days she would have felt spoken down to, and foolish. Now she could just accept that Win was really glad for her.

To her surprise, the classes were more than just a means to an end. She loved them. Her mind, ravenously hungry for something to do after all the menial work she had taken on, soaked up lessons and information at high speed. She was very quick at Pitman. It took her time to get used to the typing – a mechanical matter, needing practice – and to get back into arithmetic. But she was so excited, so determined! She took her books home and pored over them. She drew herself a diagram of the typewriter keys and practised in her room at night. Her teachers were very pleased with her and she lapped up any crumb of praise or attention. Most of the others in the class were pleasant as well, though one or two seemed to resent her eagerness and muttered a bit behind her back. Molly didn't give two hoots. She was taking off – she was going to fly! Who cared what that miserable lot thought – just because she was better at it than them! And the longer she stayed, growing more confident, the more her sense of humour came out and she was able to make the class laugh sometimes. She loved the classes more and more.

'I suppose I'm getting too big for my boots,' she wrote to Ruth. 'But I'm enjoying it ever so much. Thanks for keeping on at me!'

Ruth, who was in the final year of her degree, was having to work very hard, and Molly did not see much of her, but she wrote a note now and then, always encouraging her.

'Glad to hear it – keep it up!' was her reply this time.

What with one thing and another, life was beginning to feel a good deal better. For the first time in months she wrote to Em and told her where she was and what she was doing, and had an enthusiastic reply almost by return of post. Having ATS friends she could hook up

527

with in London felt very good. On one occasion when they met Win, Molly had also told them that she'd been out to visit Honor – one of the other girls in their basic training group.

'Her husband's a very nice fellow,' Win said. 'I suppose you'd call him a gentleman farmer. And now they've got their girls: twins! Not identical, Honor said, but very alike all the same – called Lucy and Miranda. They're lovely. And you should see Honor – she's looking rather plumper and sort of creamy! She seems very happy.'

'She's full of surprises, that one,' Molly said. 'I never thought she'd make it through basic training, did you?'

'No,' Win agreed. 'But then we all thought the same about you – for completely different reasons!'

'Ah well,' Molly blushed. 'Yes – let's just forget about all that, shall we?'

The others laughed affectionately and Molly felt a glow of happiness.

The girl upstairs, Sarah, wasn't bad company either, and sometimes they sat and had a chat together, usually up in Sarah's attic, with the fire on, so that Mrs Hodgkins didn't complain about the noise. And Molly didn't mind her work. It was in a nice part of London and, so far as she was concerned, it was a means to an end. What end she didn't know – she just hoped there would be one and, as time passed, she became more sure there would.

Saturday was very cold and foggy, and Molly set out through the shrouded streets to meet Phoebe Morrison at their usual cafe. In the fog the blackened buildings, many of them bomb-damaged, loomed ghostly around her. Buses appeared suddenly out of the gloom. It was so cold it had been a struggle to get out of bed, stepping out onto the cold lino and quickly shoving coppers into the metre to get the gas fire on.

'I've had enough of this winter,' Molly murmured to herself, through her scarf. It was even colder and danker down in the Tube. Everyone looked pale and exhausted, and Molly supposed she must look worn-out as well. She could have done without having to go out today.

By the time she met Phoebe in the steamy atmosphere of the little greasy spoon where they liked to meet, Phoebe was already stubbing out her first cigarette.

'Molly.' She waved from a round table at the back. Molly couldn't remember now why they had chosen this place. It was quite easy for them both to reach and, in its scruffy way, quite cosy with its stained tables and rickety chairs. It was hardly worth trying to put sugar in your tea, as there was scarcely ever any to be had, and it was a challenge even to find a teaspoon to do it with.

'I got you a cup while I was at it,' Phoebe said, indicating the white cup in front of Molly, full of sludgy-looking tea.

'Thanks,' Molly said. Phoebe was still bundled up in her green coat and Molly kept hers on too.

'Had a good week?' Phoebe tapped another cigarette out of the packet and put it in her mouth to light, leaning her head back slightly. Then she straightened her head and briskly breathed out a lungful of smoke.

'Yes, not bad,' Molly said. She was hugging herself. 'Blooming freezing, though, isn't it? I can't seem to get warm.'

'Try and relax. It helps.'

There was a silence, so Molly said. 'How's your week been?'

'Oh – the usual. We've been pretty pushed actually.' Molly knew that Phoebe worked in the government department dealing with roads and transport, though she had no real idea what she did there and Phoebe showed no enthusiasm for it.

Molly sipped her tea, wondering just why Phoebe had asked her to come. She didn't seem to have anything to say, and yet, somewhere in the woman's manner, she could sense something: a kind of excitement.

'So,' Phoebe said. 'Have you heard?'

'No. Heard what?'

'About the army. Recruiting women again. Of course, a few ATS have been hanging on, scattered about the place. But now it's serious – they've just got royal approval. They're calling it the Women's Royal Army Corps.'

Phoebe sat back with a what-d'you-think-of-*that*? look on her face.

Molly stared at her over her cup. Her mind was spinning. It had been over, for them – for all the women. Go back home, get on with another sort of life: we don't need you now. We only need the men. That had been the message. But now . . .

'D'you mean . . . ? There's really going to be another army?'

'There is indeed. I've had a good think and I'm already pretty set on joining up again. I know it'll be different – after all, there's no war on. It'll take adjusting to, in its way. But I don't find much joy in civilian life, to tell you the truth. Forces life is more my thing. And what about you, Fox?'

That Phoebe Morrison had already switched back into army parlance didn't escape Molly.

'Me?' she felt giddy. 'They wouldn't want me – would they?'

Phoebe Morrison leaned forward and said sincerely, 'My dear girl, whyever not?'

XIV

EM

Sixty

April 1949

'Is that you, Em?' Cynthia called as the front door banged shut.

'Yep – only me,' Em said, shedding her wet coat. Talk about April showers.

'Hello, love!' She heard Dot's voice as well. She and Mom were obviously having one of their chinwags.

Cynthia and Dot were in chatting position at the table with the teacups, and Cynthia was already pouring a cup for Em. Dot, their old neighbour, smiled up at her.

'All right, bab? You're looking well.'

'I'm all right – you OK, Dot? What about Lou: is he better?'

'Oh, we're not so bad. His Majesty has to take it a bit careful – they say his heart's weak, but there's no stopping that one, when he gets going.' Dot spoke with fond exasperation. 'I do worry – but what can you do?

Dot's Italian husband, Lou Alberello, was a big-hearted, vigorous man, a life-and-soul-of-the-party type. It was hard to imagine him ever quietening or slowing down. 'Norm all right?' Dot asked.

'Oh, he's all right, yes,' Em said. 'Where's Robbie?'

'Young Jonny's round,' Cynthia said. Jonny was one of Robbie's school pals. 'They're out the back. You sit

down for a bit. Have a Rich Tea? Oh, I forgot . . .'
Cynthia got up and took an envelope from the shelf.
'This came for you. Must be from Molly.'

'Oh, good!' Em took it, smiling at the address. Molly
knew Em was living with Norm's mom and dad, but
she never remembered to address letters anywhere but
Kenilworth Street.

'How's she getting on?' Dot asked, before Em had
even got the envelope open.

'Oh!' Em exclaimed. 'Oh my goodness!'

> WRAC Training Centre,
> Guildford,
> Surrey.
> 10th April 1949

Dear Em,

Well, surprise, surprise! I've joined up again!

I've been at this training centre for a week now
and am loving every minute. D'you remember the
Gorgon I talked to you about, who I trained under
in the ATS? She told me they were forming a proper
women's army again, and she and I have both joined
up. She's gone to the officers' training centre at
Hindhead.

There are a couple of us who've rejoined after
being in the ATS before, and they've talked to us
about retraining and how we'd do it. I decided I
wanted to start right from the beginning. I know
I'm here for the duration, and I want to do it all
properly this time. I want to make a real go of this,
Em. They're working us hard. We've already done
some aptitude tests, and I reckon I did all right. I ant
a decent trade – something that's not cooking. I've
had quite enough of that! It's all going to be

different from in the war, I know that. We've even got a different cap badge, for a start – some of them made a right fuss about that, and it's a funny thing, but it does feel strange. But never mind, all I know is, I'm in the right place. The army feels like home to me – I can't see myself as the marrying type.

When I get some leave, I'll try and come and see you. I hope everyone's OK and you are all getting on all right. Fancy Joycie being married – and Sid with three kids! Makes me feel very long in the tooth!

Give my regards to your mom and everyone else, and a kiss for Robbie, if he still lets anyone kiss him!

Love from,
Molly

'Oh, Mom . . .' Em, with tears in her eyes, handed Cynthia the letter. 'Read that – oh, good for Molly. When I think of all the different things she's done and all those places she's been – and I've never even moved from here! Makes me feel a proper stick-in-the-mud!'

'Never you mind, bab,' Dot said. 'Not everyone's meant to be a rolling stone like Molly. You're here, making a home for your lad, and you may not get any thanks for it, but that's what matters – and don't you forget it.'

'Thanks, Dot – I s'pose you're right,' Em said, smiling. She leaned over and touched Dot's hand. 'I know you being around has always made all the difference to everything – hasn't it, Mom?'

'Oh, it certainly has that,' Cynthia said.

Em drained her cup. 'Anyroad, I'd better not dawdle. I need to get Robbie home for his tea.'

XV

KATIE

Sixty-One

May 1949

Katie had already been certain of how much she loved Marek, but from Christmas night – when they had sat up talking almost all night, holding each other, kissing by the dying fire – she knew she was even more deeply, tenderly immersed in her feelings for him. She had never felt so completely at home with another person, or experienced so much longing for them. Life without him was unimaginable. Even being apart from him for a few hours made her yearn for his presence, for the sight of his face and their endless talking and laughter.

When, in the New Year, they told Sybil that they were intending to marry, she was as pleased as if she was a mother to each of them. And in some ways it felt as if she was.

'I couldn't be more delighted,' she said, smiling up at them. She was sitting by the fire in the dining room and they stood rather bashfully before her, close, so that the backs of their hands were touching. 'You make a lovely couple, and I'm sure you'll make a good go of it.'

Katie and Marek looked at each other, beaming with the miraculous sense of their love and happiness.

'Though it is quite quick,' she cautioned.

Katie, though rapturously in love, had thought about

it carefully. More soberly now, she said, 'We're very sure. And Marek has lost such a lot. I don't have anyone much, either. We both want family ... I suppose we feel there's no point in delaying.'

Sybil nodded. 'I see.' And they could see also that she did.

'The thing I'd feel less delighted about,' Sybil went on, 'is the prospect of losing you both. Have you thought where you might live? There's nothing much going, you know.'

Once again they looked at each other, their smiles fading a little.

'We have thought ...' Marek said.

'... But we don't really know, until we look.'

Sybil regarded them in silence for a moment. 'Well, why not stay here?'

'Could we?' Katie said. It hadn't occurred to her that they would be able to. Again she looked at Marek. 'That'd be ideal, wouldn't it?' They would only have had to go and find lodgings in a house elsewhere and start again.

'I can't see why not, at least for the time being,' Sybil said. 'I'm sure we could arrange things – that is, if it would suit you, of course. It seems foolish to uproot yourselves, especially as your sister is next door now, Marek.'

Though she was trying to sound detached, as usual, Katie was touched to see an urgency in Sybil's expression. She wanted them to stay: it mattered to her. Glancing at Marek and seeing agreement in his eyes, Katie said, 'Sybil, that's so kind of you. I'm sure we'd love to stay here. We've been very happy here, and Michael likes it – and we can always help you with the garden and everything. I'll cook ...' As she said it, her spirits soared even higher. They would work out which was to be their private room in the house, but it was so lovely here, and she would have found it a terrible wrench leaving Sybil.

'You are very good to us, Miss Routh,' Marek said, with a little bow. 'We are very grateful.'

'Oh, not at all!' Sybil pulled herself up from her chair and stood before them. Katie felt like embracing her, but didn't quite dare to. 'Your sister knows?' she asked Marek.

'Yes. We told her yesterday. She is glad.'

Sybil nodded. 'And when is the happy day to be?'

'We thought in the spring,' Katie said. 'May the fifteenth. It'll only be very quiet – at St Francis's. As long as the priest can marry us that day. I'll make my own dress and everything.'

Sybil smiled at her eagerness and, stepping forward, kissed each of them on the cheek. It was so unexpected that Katie found tears in her eyes.

'I hope you'll both be very happy,' Sybil said. 'I'm very glad that you've found one another.'

It was a busy, exciting time. As well as the arrangements to be made, they were both working hard and making plans. Agnieska, who for the moment was working in a shop, had decided to apply to train as a nurse, and Marek sometimes talked about training too, in psychiatric nursing.

'One day I shall do this,' he said. 'But for the moment I carry on earning my living – and I can be with you.'

'What would you have done if the war had not happened?' Katie asked both of them. Agnieska said she might have been a teacher, like her parents. But now she felt that nursing was something that was important to her. Marek thought he might have been a farmer.

'But now everything is different' was all he said.

Katie could see how much these choices were the result of what they had experienced, how much of the suffering of others they had witnessed, how it had changed them. They were both people of compassion, who wanted to offer the rest of their lives to help.

Over those months, once the brother and sister could see they had a safe, loving listener in Katie, the two of them talked more and more. Experiences came pouring out that they could talk about to no one else. Katie began to appreciate the enormity of what had happened to Poland: the war, the invasions of the Germans from the west and Russians from the east, the gross brutality of both, had been like an explosion that scattered a country and its people into smithereens. Soldiers and others had fled west so that the Polish government itself was in exile in London, many of its forces scattered across Europe. Through Marek and his family, she took in the scale of the Russian deportations east into slave labour, the deaths upon deaths in the Siberian snows or in central Russia. The Jewish population had been almost wiped out in Nazi death camps. And now, thanks to the border agreed by Churchill, Stalin and Roosevelt at the Yalta and Potsdam Conferences in 1945, the district surrounding Lvov, where the Wozniak family had lived, was no longer Poland, but Soviet Ukraine. And the government of Poland was no longer Polish – it was under the command of Soviet Russia. To return now would mean almost certain death.

Katie began to feel haunted by it herself. She knew Marek had terrible nightmares from time to time. She thought of his mother, his sister, of the corpses left in piles in the snow. Knowing that she was soon to carry a Polish name by marrying Marek, she felt passionately that she wanted to understand, to be a part of these people who had travelled so far, so terrifyingly and with such suffering and loss. She felt as if her world had expanded, and she had a fierce pride in knowing them, in living with and loving and going to Mass with them. The Church was a vital link with Poland. They learned that the church in Duddesdon, St Michael's, which had for years been in the Italian quarter, was attracting more and more Poles and sometimes they made their way there for Mass on Sundays. Katie and Michael would go too.

And there were lighter aspects of her Polish education. Agnieska taught her how to cook various dishes, like *pierogi*, little flour-and-water patties with a filling of potatoes or cabbage or meat.

'These are delicious!' Sybil enthused when they proudly brought out their first plateful, which Piotr, Marek and the others fell on with wolfish enthusiasm. 'So tasty with such simple ingredients – good rationing food.'

'You like?' Agnieska was delighted. 'You eat – I make more!'

'They're marvellous,' Sybil said, and Katie agreed. She and Sybil had joked that they needed to double the garden's beetroot crop, as the Poles liked them so much.

The memories were not all sad. Marek told them one night that on the ship, the SS *Atlantis*, that had brought him and Piotr from Naples, no fewer than eight babies were born on the voyage.

'It was like a – what do you call a birth hospital?'

'Maternity hospital,' Sybil said, chuckling.

'Yes. A lot of babies! Very good!'

Agnieska had spent almost five years in a Displaced Persons camp in India, south of Bombay, before a brief time in a beautiful camp in Uganda, which she said she enjoyed more. She gradually told them stories about it, which Katie knew Marek had never heard before, either. Sometimes round the meal table she would tell him something in Polish and he would repeat for the rest of them in English.

'She says,' he related one evening, 'that when India gained its independence in forty-seven, there were great celebrations, and for a few says everything in Bombay was free: restaurants, taxis.' Agnieska was laughing. 'They went to the city and had a marvellous time, living it up – you can say this, living it up?'

'Yes,' Katie said. 'You certainly can.'

'You've certainly seen a lot of the world, between you,' Sybil said.

'I've got something to tell you, lovey,' Katie said to Michael, soon after she and Marek had made their decision. They were in their room and she had sat down on the bed and pulled him onto her lap.

Michael said, 'What?' absent-mindedly.

'Are you listening?'

'Yes.' He turned his head and his blue eyes looked into hers. She was startled again by how beautiful he was, and she was full of love for him.

'The thing is, you like Marek, don't you?'

He nodded.

'Well, Marek and I are – well, we love each other and we have decided to get married.' He was staring steadily at her. 'Which means that we'll live together – I mean, we're going to stay here with Sybil . . . And . . .'

'Will he be my daddy?'

'He'll sort of be . . . He'll be like a daddy to you, a bit like he is now, that's all.'

'Oh,' Michael said. 'That's all right. Can I go and play now?' He was wriggling to get down. Katie felt a bit wounded. She had expected a more emotional response, perhaps even opposition.

'Are you pleased?' she asked, as he slithered from her lap.

'Yes!' he called, in a happy voice. 'I'm going to play trains with Piotr now. He promised!'

Katie's life was very full, besides her intense involvement with her future husband and his family, with what they had experienced and where they came from. She and Em tried to make sure they met every month, at either one of their houses, although Handsworth started to win over, as Robbie loved Sybil's house and the park so much. Gradually they rebuilt a friendship on mutual respect, and the memories and sense of humour they still had in common, as well as the friendship growing between their boys.

And every few weeks she met her father. She did not ask what excuse he made to be absent from home on a Saturday morning, sitting drinking coffee in Lewis's in Birmingham. She knew he had led a life based on untruth, and it was something she had to accept. It was an untruth that seemed set to continue.

'I can't tell them,' he said bluntly, the last time they met. They had been over and over whether his new

547

family would be able to cope with learning of her existence. His two children thought that he and their mother were married. It would be a shock beyond what he thought they could take on.

'We'll have to give it some time,' he said.

'What difference will that make?' she asked brutally. 'It'll be a shock for them whenever you tell them. Giving them time to come to terms with something they don't know about doesn't make any sense.'

'Maybe it's me that needs time,' he admitted. 'It could be very rough.'

Katie began to believe that he would never tell them. Her own feelings were mixed. She was at once angry and resentful at feeling, through no fault of her own, like a dirty secret that had to be kept locked away. There had been enough secrets festering, warping and destroying. She wanted to rip through the pretence and lies. She was also curious – his children were her half-sister and brother. What were they like: might they get along? But she was also relieved. Supposing he told them and it spoiled everything. Why upset a family that seemed united, so far as she could tell? She had a new family now – and she had a father, if only in snatches. It was more than she'd ever hoped for. And it was good.

'I'm getting married,' she told him.

Michael's face lit up in genuine pleasure. 'Are you now? Who's the lucky fella – the Polish chap you were telling me about?'

'Yes, his name's Marek Wozniak.' She felt such pride in saying his name! 'Can I bring him to meet you?'

She saw the hesitation, just for a second, the habit of secrecy and checking, before he said, 'Yes, of course. That's a fine idea.'

'And . . .' She found herself blushing, feeling like a

child. *Daddy, please, please will you...?* 'Will you come to our wedding?'

He looked back solemnly at her. 'What about your mother, Katie?'

She frowned. 'What about her?'

'In the end she was the one who brought you up all those years – for all her faults. Should you not let her know? I mean ...' His kindly face crinkled into a smile. 'Wild horses wouldn't be able to stop me coming, if that's what you'd like – but shouldn't you ask her first?'

Sixty-Two

Amid what was a time of busyness, of the careful buying of satin and lace for a wedding dress, Katie decided to give her mother one last chance. She was one of the lucky ones – she had a mother alive somewhere, so far as she knew. Perhaps she should try to rise above the past and take any steps she could to heal things. Without telling anyone else she was doing it, she posted a card to Enid Thomas, telling Enid her address, that she was getting married and that she thought Vera ought to know. Writing the card brought back a lot of bitter emotions and she half hoped there would be no reply. And, as the days passed, she decided there wasn't going to be one.

Then, one day, it came. After work she came home to find a brief letter, in Enid's painstaking looped hand. Enid had written:

> I've tried to find out where you mother is. I'm not
> well myself, so can't go far. She moved away
> months ago and no one can tell me anything. Truth
> to tell, we'd lost touch. She had got to be such a
> hard, bitter woman and kept herself to herself,
> didn't want anybody. Sorry that's all I know.
>
> I hope you'll be very happy, Katie. Come and see
> me sometime and let me meet him.
>   Regards,
>   Enid

Katie stared at the words, bitter for a moment, and sad, but knowing that she was also relieved. When Marek came home she showed it to him. He studied the flimsy sheet of paper, then silently came and put his arms around her.

'It's all right, I've got all I need,' she said. And held him tight.

There were also arrangements to be made in the house for after they were married. This turned out to be simple: Marek would move into the attic, and Sybil suggested that Katie make a curtain to divide off Michael's end of the room, for the sake of a little privacy. There was the usual daily round of work and looking after Michael, and there were those close, private loving times.

As the spring came they would take walks in the park, sometimes with Michael, or later, once he was asleep. It was bliss walking round amid the greening trees, even if they did still have to wrap up warm. They would hold hands, stopping often to kiss in the seclusion of the trees, and talk endlessly, planning their future.

'We don't get much time on our own, do we?' Katie said one mild evening as they were out strolling around. They had stopped to embrace, near the old church that looked over the park. Sometimes she felt guilty that Michael dominated her time so much. She knew how hungry Marek was to be with her alone.

'It's all right.' He held her close and she felt his breath on her hair. 'It is how it is with family. And soon . . .' He leaned back to look into her eyes. 'Soon we shall have our own family, yes?'

'Yes, my love.' She reached up and caressed his cheek. She longed to give him everything, to make him happy and settled in his new country.

How he longed for family, and for her! They had talked often about their moral view of things, how their physical relations should wait until after they were married. In reality it was not so simple. Living so close to each other, both so in love and full of longing for each other, it became impossible to resist.

The first time he had come to her room, very late. She woke to the sound of him whispering her name.

'Marek?' Heart pounding with excitement, she sat up, pleased to know he was close at any time. 'Is everything all right?'

He felt his way to sit on the side of her bed. 'Yes.' There was a silence. 'I need to be with you. Can I come into your bed?'

They had lain many times on top of the sheets, twined together, kissing. Now she pulled the covers back and felt his long, lean frame climb in beside her and his lips seeking out hers. Quietly, intensely, they loved each other and slept pressed together, his belly at her back. When the dawn came she turned to find him watching her, smiling when he saw she was awake. She leaned up on her arm and looked down at him, the light reaching in at the edge of the curtain picking out the angles in his face. How she loved that face! She always wanted to touch his cheek, feeling the sharp angle of his cheekbone. She stroked back his hair.

'You're very beautiful,' he whispered.

'So are you.' She smiled joyfully, then lay and held him. 'I love you so much. I can't really believe it.'

He rested his hand on her belly. 'Soon you will be my wife,' he said. 'My dear wife, Katie.' He said it with

552

such happiness in his voice that she almost wanted to weep.

'I must go soon to my own room,' he said, 'or little Michael will be awake.'

He kissed her and sat up.

'Marek . . .'

'Yes?'

'If we keep doing this, I might have a baby.'

'Yes.' He smiled. 'Yes, I think so. That is good!'

And so it had not been the last time that he had slipped into her bed. Both of them longed for the time when he could stop creeping about and claim the room as their own, as husband and wife.

Appropriately, the news came just after Easter. They had journeyed through the days of the Easter *Triduum*, the darkness of death being gradually overcome by light, bringing a time of flowers and holiday.

Katie had spent as much time as she could on her dress and, having got in from work that evening, was down at the back of the house where the light was best, hand-sewing lace onto the bodice. She had made tea for Sybil and the two of them were sitting together. Marek had just got in from work, come and kissed her and run upstairs to change.

Then there came a thunderous, crazed banging of the front-door knocker and screaming, high-pitched and incomprehensible. Archie leapt to his feet barking crazily. Sybil almost spilled her tea.

'What on earth?' she exclaimed.

Katie was on her feet. 'It's Agnieska – I'm sure it is.'

Marek had heard and was running downstairs again, still pulling on a shirt, as Katie tore along to open the door. Agnieska almost fell in through it. She was in more of a state than anyone Katie had ever seen, her hair half down, eyes wild, tears on her cheeks. But Katie couldn't work out what any of it was about, as Agnieska cannonballed past her, straight at Marek, shrieking in Polish, seeming barely able to get the words out. She had a piece of paper in her hand. She banged it on his chest, she slapped it with her hand, she yelled out a stream of words, then shoved it into his hand and burst into convulsive weeping, hands over her face.

Katie focused on Marek's face, the growing look of wonder mixed with disbelief, the tension as he read. He clutched the paper to him and said something in Polish. Then he became aware of Katie and Sybil, standing in helpless bewilderment at each end of the hall.

'God be praised!' he cried. 'Look . . .' He held out the paper, hardly able to speak, either. 'It is from the Red Cross. It is our sister Ewa – she is in New Zealand!'

He and Agnieska hugged each other, both weeping, and Katie found tears running down her own cheeks and saw that Sybil was very moved as well. Agnieska sobbed, repeating some words over and over again, and it took some time before anyone was able to calm down. Katie went and put her arms round both of them and kissed them.

'I'm so happy for you,' she said. She understood now how easily this might not have happened, how equally likely it had been that Ewa was dead.

'It says she is getting married,' Marek said wiping his cheeks. He seemed stunned.

'How marvellous,' Sybil said gently. 'You and she both.'

*

The morning of the wedding dawned as hazily bright and promising as any bride could hope for.

Katie arrived at the church in her pretty, lacy dress and veil to find her father waiting outside, looking very spruce and, she saw, rather dashing. She realized she was very nervous, and she could see that he was too.

'Is everyone here?' she asked.

'I think so,' he reassured her. 'They're waiting for you. Are you ready, my dear?'

She looked up at him. 'Thank you for coming.'

'I wouldn't have missed giving my little girl to her husband now, would I?' He looked at her emotionally. 'Bless you, Katie. Marek's a fine man. Don't take your mother and I as your married pattern – I mean, as if you would! But it can be so much better, believe me.'

'I know,' she said with a heartfelt smile. 'Thanks.

'Shall we go in?'

Katie gathered herself, then nodded. She walked into the shadowy, incense-perfumed church and began her walk along the aisle, under the gaze of those she loved best. Em was smiling at her, with Norm and Robbie at her side; Sybil, in a very wide-brimmed straw hat, Piotr and his Italian girlfriend Maria; Agnieska and the Arbuckles, who both beamed at her; and Maudie and John, who had Michael with them, in his little suit, gazing in wonder at his mother.

She walked towards the altar, ready to be wrapped in the words that would bind her and her husband together. Among those words would be her chosen psalm: *'But thy loving-kindness and mercy shall follow me all the days of my life . . .'* Each step drew her nearer to the end of the aisle, towards her future, where, tall and elegant in his suit, his eyes fixed on her alone, Marek was waiting.

1953

'When's Robbie coming, Mom?

'Oh, Michael,' Katie said, 'if you've asked me once, you've asked me a hundred times already!' She was busy in the kitchen with Sybil, piling sandwiches onto trays. 'I told you – everyone'll be here soon.'

'There'll be extra dogs as well,' Sybil remarked.

'Will there?' Katie looked up, a dark curl of hair hanging over her forehead.

'Well, Joan Lester is inseparable form that Highland Terrier of hers – and Mrs Rogers never goes anywhere without her dog: you know, big black Labrador.'

'Dogs!' Michael went off laughing happily. 'Auntie Agnieska doesn't like dogs!'

'Well, your job will be to keep them away from her. And make sure Archie doesn't lose his temper with them!' Katie called after him. Archie, rather an elderly dog now, was sometimes short of patience. 'Go and see if Marek's all right with the others, will you?'

They were having their own Coronation tea. The big event had been on Tuesday – for which, like so many other householders, Sybil had taken the step of investing in a first-ever television set.

'It'll be nice for the children,' she said, but Katie

could see that Sybil was going to enjoy television as well.

They all crowded round for the eleven o'clock service in Westminster Abbey. How exciting it had been to see the young Queen in all her finery! And there had been a little party in the street, but the weather was poor. Sybil had already decided she'd like a get-together, and she and Katie agreed that the following Saturday would be a good opportunity.

'We'll just make it tea,' Sybil said. 'There'll be quite a few children, and we can fill everyone up with jelly and cake!'

When the food was ready, Katie went to the back door. Everything was ready: the tables arranged optimistically out there, the cloths pinned at the corners, and all the chairs they could find, plus some borrowed from the Arbuckles. Further down she could see Marek, bent over, holding the hand of their little daughter, Dorothy, who was nearly eighteen months old. Nearby her half-brother Michael, now nine, and her brother Tomas, four, were both clinging to a rope tied from the branch of the tree and trying to swing on it at once.

'Marek!' she called, going out towards him. He turned, cupping a hand round his ear.

'I'm just going up to get changed – they'll all be here soon. I'll take Do-do and clean her up too. I suppose she's been trying to keep up with those two!'

'It's hard to stop her,' Marek laughed. 'When she wants to do something, she is like a tank!'

Katie laughed, reached up and kissed him, happy to see the contentment in his face. Marek was a complicated man, and sometimes subject to dark moods. She recognized that these could be especially bad on high days and holidays – Christmas and Easter, when he seemed often perversely gloomy. But in the main she had watched him blossom in their love for one another, in the gradual building of a family. And he had helped her blossom, too.

'Come on, Dorota,' she said. 'Time to put on your pretty dress.'

'No-o-o-o!' Dorothy, a wonderfully healthy-looking child with dark, curly hair like Michael and brown eyes, clung to Marek's hand, unimpressed at being dragged away.

Katie had to pick her up, and she wriggled, screaming in her arms, all the way to the house.

'Tomas!' Katie called to him. 'I want to change your shirt.'

Tomas pretended he had heard nothing at all and carried on playing. Of their children, he was the one who closely resembled Marek, a pale, slender boy with a wide, face with strong cheekbones and big blue eyes.

'I'll be back for you,' Katie muttered.

Upstairs she sorted Dorothy out and, once she'd calmed down, the little girl was keen to watch her mother change into her own dress. Katie put on a new sundress she had made, in pink-and-white candy stripes with a full, flowy skirt. She peered in the little mirror trying to see the full effect, and combed her hair. Dorothy made pleased-sounding noises.

'Come on, you scallywag, let's go down. Perhaps I shan't bother changing Tomas – he'll only be filthy again within five minutes.'

Sybil's house was still home, but was not to be for much longer. The housing shortage was very acute and Katie and Marek had had their name down on a council waiting list since before Dorothy was born, but were still – like Em and Norm – stuck in the same lodgings. Not that it was a great hardship. Sybil had been very good to them. They knew that wherever they lived now, she would always be part of the family. They had gradually taken over the upper floors of the house. Katie and Marek had their room in the attic, with Dorothy in there still in her cot, and Michael and Tomas were in Marek and Piotr's old room. Sybil had come to an arrangement with them over the rent, and they both helped out in the house and garden. Marek was still working at the factory and was doing well. One day, he hoped to follow his dream of nursing. One day, he said, he would make the break.

A succession of other single lodgers came and went in the smaller room at the back, and by and large the arrangement worked well. Sometimes, Katie thought, Sybil must get sick of having a young family about, and sometimes she and Marek had longed for their own place, where they wouldn't have to take anyone else into consideration. But they knew that Sybil was like a mother to both of them, and a grandmother to the Wozniak children. Now, just days ago, they had been allocated a brand-new council house, out on an estate called Tile Cross, and they knew it was going to be wrench to leave Handsworth.

At the mellow mid-afternoon everyone started to arrive. The house and street were still decked out with colourful bunting, rippling in the breeze, from the celebrations earlier in the week and, seeing that it was not showing signs of raining, they started laying out the food. Katie was arranging plates of neat sandwiches on the table when Marek crept up behind her and caught her by the waist.

'Ooh!' she squealed. 'You made me nearly jump out of my skin!' She laughed as his hands were tickling her.

'You look very beautiful,' he murmured in her ear. 'This dress brings out your curves.'

'And you're very naughty, she said. 'You're supposed to be keeping an eye on the children, not thinking about my curves.'

He was about to kiss her again when they heard voices and stepped back as Sybil appeared, leading two of her church friends into the garden, with dogs. The Wozniak children all headed straight for the dogs, excited.

'His name's Major,' Katie heard one of the ladies saying. 'He won't hurt you – he's very placid.'

'And this is Wally,' the other lady said, trying to keep tabs on a frisky Highland Terrier that was already, to the children's delight, zooming round the garden. 'I called him after my late husband . . .' Archie stood watching this behaviour with disdain.

'I'll make the tea,' Katie said, greeting the ladies and going into the house.

She was excited. It was going to be a lovely afternoon. Soon, as the tea was ready, the Arbuckles appeared from next door, Edna and Susan, with her hulking husband Percy and a large toddler named David. Soon afterwards, Agnieska arrived. She was no longer living with them, as she was in the nurses' home at Dudley Road Hospital and was looking well, and a little more rounded these days. Her pale hair was long and pinned back prettily, and she was holding a bunch of pinks that she had brought for Sybil.

'Hello!' She embraced Katie as she let them in. 'Oh – it is quiet inside here! Where are the children?'

'In the garden. Sybil's friends are here – dogs everywhere, so the kids are full of it.'

'*Dogs?*' Agnieska made a face. She had tolerated Archie, but was not an enthusiast.

'I told the children they had to keep them away from you – it's their job. But don't worry, they won't hurt you.'

'Your friend is coming?' Agnieska followed Katie into the kitchen. 'With baby?'

Katie smiled. Agnieska liked babies as much as she disliked dogs. 'Em – yes. We'll get to see her at last.'

'Her other son is quite old,' Agnieska remarked.

'Yes, he's eleven. It's a big gap. It seems to be a bit of a miracle. I can't wait to see them both – Em only had her ten days ago! Oh, and she's bringing someone else . . . Someone we were at school with.'

'How nice!'

'Yes, but I haven't seen her in years. She's up visiting, so Em asked if she could come along.'

'It will make a nice party,' Agnieska said.

More of Sybil's friends arrived, and then Piotr with his Italian wife Maria, and their two little daughters, one also a babe-in-arms. He and Marek embraced, slapping each other on the back, and soon the garden was full of chat and laughter, and children roaring, and Wally's excited yapping as the Wozniak boys chased him around and away from Agnieska.

They all sat and drank tea and began on the sandwiches, sitting around the tables under the trees. Katie wondered where Em had got to, and hoped she was feeling all right. It would be hard work for them all getting over here. Every so often she went into the house and listened to see if anyone was knocking. She wasn't sure how she felt about Molly Fox coming, yet at the same time she was curious.

It was Michael, who had been looking out for them, who at last yelled, 'They're here!' He was excited about seeing Robbie.

Katie dashed through the house and opened the door to see Em, cradling a baby in a white blanket and beaming at her, with Norm behind her. Michael seized Robbie and they dashed off to the back.

'Hello!' Katie cried. 'Oh, you've made it at last! Oh, Em – isn't she just lovely?' The baby's waxy little face lay surrounded by soft folds of blanket, her pale-mauve eyelids gently twitching as she slept.

'Meet little Christine,' Em said proudly. 'Christine Elizabeth, after the Queen.'

'Oh, lovely, and she's so perfect – how heavy was she?'

'Just under seven pounds,' Em said happily, 'and she's feeding ever so well.'

'Oh, sorry – hello, Norm,' Katie greeted him. 'Mustn't forget the proud dad!'

'All right, are you?' Norm said in his rather timid way. She could tell he was shy and hoped the chaotic atmosphere out in the garden might put him more at ease. 'Nice to see you.'

'Come on in ... all of you.' Katie had then become fully aware of the two people standing behind. One was a slightly built woman, with dark-brown hair cut shoulder-length and worn in a straight, plain style, and with slightly prominent teeth. Far more striking was the other, tall and magnificently built, with thick blonde hair piled on her head and wearing a peacock-blue dress that hugged her curves. Her build and way of standing seemed vaguely familiar, as did her face, but she could still hardly believe this was Molly.

'You must be . . .' She looked from one to the other of them.

'You remember Molly!' Em called from in the hall.

'I do,' Katie said, trying to get over the shock of how magnificent Molly looked. 'But it's been a long time. I'm Katie.'

'I know – I can remember you. You were the one who'd never speak to me if you could possibly help it,' Molly said. But there was happy mischief in her eyes and she gave a big, generous laugh.

'I'm sure I was horrible,' Katie admitted.

'You were – not that I blame you, really. Anyway, it was all a long time ago, as you say. P'raps we can have another go at it now we're grown-up!'

Katie smiled, liking Molly's easy, confident manner. 'Well, I hope so too – it's nice to see you, Molly.'

'This is my pal Ruth,' Molly said, indicating the slender young woman beside her. 'We were in the ATS together, and she's put up with me ever since. Ruth's one of these clever so-and-sos – she's at Cambridge doing science.'

'Oh, shush, Molly, stop it,' Ruth said, blushing. She smiled and shook Katie's hand. 'Nice to meet you. I hope you don't mind my coming – it's just that we were both visiting this weekend.'

'Of course not,' Katie said. 'The more, the merrier. Let's go out to the back and I'll make you all some tea.'

It was a lovely, lazy afternoon of conversations and meeting new people, and children free to romp around everyone, with the adults intervening or joining in when necessary. They all sat round eating and drinking in the warm breeze. Em disappeared inside to feed the baby and, as the sun sank lower, Sybil's friends and their dogs began to drift away, first calling out their thanks and goodbyes.

When everyone had been well fed, Katie was free to sit and talk. She liked Ruth, who told her that now she had finished her science degree at Cambridge, she had stayed on to do research.

'Does that mean you got a First, my dear?' Sybil asked across the table. 'One of my brothers went to Cambridge, but he came out with a disgracefully poor degree in the end. Went abroad instead and had all sorts of adventures.'

'How exciting,' Ruth said.

'Oh, indeed it is – well, it's exciting the *first* time you hear about it anyway,' Sybil added wickedly. 'He lives in Australia now. But you . . . ?'

'Yes, I did get a First. I think research is my thing.'

Seeing that Ruth and Sybil were getting along well, Katie went to sit with her two old classmates at one end of the table in the shadow of the trees, so that they could all catch up.

Their eyes kept being drawn to the baby, who spent most of her time asleep in Em's arms.

'I still can't believe she's really here,' Em said, smiling down at her. 'All that time I was in such a state wondering what was wrong. In the end I gave up thinking about it, and decided we were lucky to have Robbie – and then out of the blue, bingo! And here she is. I mean, it would've been nicer if they were closer in age, but I'm not complaining – I'm just so happy to have her!'

Katie was overjoyed for her too. Over these years

when they had met as often as they could manage, and had rebuilt their friendship, her own children had arrived with no trouble, first Tomas, then Dorothy, while poor Em was having no luck.

'Maybe we'll have more chance of getting a house of our own now, like you!' she joked. 'How many kids d'you have to have to get a council house?'

'I don't know if that's the only reason!' Katie laughed. 'But you must ask them to send you out where we're going: we could be neighbours again. I mean, it's all new – very rough at the moment, but there's room to make gardens and things. Oh, you must come over there – the kids could go to school together.'

'Ooh, I'd love that,' Em said wistfully. 'I'll ask – fingers crossed. We just need more room now. I couldn't put Molly up or anything. She's staying at Mom's.'

'Is your mom still determined to stay put?'

'Oh yes – Mom won't leave, except in her box, she says. She's put down for one of the flats they're building. You can hardly recognize Nechells now, with all they're doing, changing the roads and knocking things down left, right and centre. It's one big building site. I don't think it'll be the same place by the time they've finished.'

'D'you think they'll knock down the school?' Molly asked. 'It'd be a shame to see old Cromwell Street gone.'

'Heaven knows,' Em said. 'It's still there at the moment, but they're letting the bulldozers loose on anything round there. Let's hope not. The kids've got to go to school somewhere.'

'And you're back in the army?' Katie said to Molly.

Molly smiled. 'Yes, I'm in Signals. Look – d'you want to see our uniform?'

From her bag she produced a photograph of herself, sprucely dressed in her green WRAC uniform, her handsome face solemn, with a slight frown, as if she was listening to instructions.

'You look magnificent,' Katie said. She felt a growing respect for Molly, for what she had become. 'It looks an interesting life.'

'Oh, it is,' Molly said. 'It's the life for me, anyway.' She was bubbling over with it all.

Marek came up then and stood behind Katie, gently interrupting by putting his hand on her shoulder. She looked up at him. He nodded at the others. 'Sybil says it is getting a bit cold. We can go in and sit inside.'

Katie reached up and took his hand. 'All right, love,' she said.

Marek squeezed her hand. 'I'll fetch the children.'

The three women walked slowly up the garden, Em still cradling Christine. Molly turned to Katie.

'You'll have to tell me about yourself properly, Katie.'

Startled, Katie looked round at her. She saw that Molly was genuinely interested, and in her kind, honest face she saw someone she very much wanted to get to know.

'Yes,' she said. 'You too. I'd like that.'

Sybil was at the back door as the three of them slowly walked inside from the garden, which was now all in shadow.

'Ah,' she said fondly. 'Here's the class from Cromwell Street School!' As they laughed she said. 'Go along, girls – leave the men to it for a bit. You can go into the room at the back: you'll be warmer.'

'Thank you, Sybil,' Katie said. 'It's been a lovely afternoon.'

'And thank you, too – it's been marvellous,' Sybil agreed.

Katie led her friends inside to sit together in the mellow light of late afternoon, to continue a conversation that she hoped would last, now, for the rest of their lives.